FINNEGAN'S AWAKE

Edited by Mary-Theresa Hussey

Print ISBN 978-1-945419-71-3

Ebook ISNB 978-1-945419-72-0

LCCN 2020930176

FINNEGAN'S AWAKE

TRILBY BLACK

FAWKES PRESS

To the good guy with all the cool survival kits.

FOREWORD

The author and publisher would like to remind readers that the opinions expressed by the characters in this book are not necessarily the opinions of the author and publisher, but they are the opinions of many people in America today.

PART I

AGENT

1

I shouldn't have opened the door for the pizza delivery guy. Not without the chain.

Situations like this, when the pizza delivery guys actually turn out to be armed kidnappers, are exactly why there are three deadlocks and a chain on the door.

Truth is, my mind was on other things when the doorbell went. I'd just spent the afternoon doing what I do best: hunting down the enemies of America from my basement. It had been an unusually productive day. As soon as I packaged my report and delivered it to Dad, one more murdering bastard was going straight to waterboarding hell. But I was also hungry. Like most people I guess, I screw up when I'm hungry.

Instead of handing over the pizza, the delivery guy dropped it on the floor and backed me up against the wall, the muzzle of a handgun hooking up under the soft part of my jaw and lifting it. He was a big guy too. Olive skin, with black hair cut neat.

He said, "I'm after a guy called Finnegan. That you?"

Oh god. *Finnegan.* The name of my online gaming avatar. Dammit. Here I'd just been hunting the mujahideen online, and all that time they'd been using the same tactics to hunt down me.

The muzzle of the gun made it hard to talk. I lifted up on my toes to ease the pressure. Over his head, I saw the chain for the door hanging loose and unused and felt sharp grief—it's always the simplest mistakes that change things forever. But you have to choke that stuff down and remember the first rule of training: never show the enemy that you are weak.

"I'm not a guy," I said. I did my best to make it a sneer.

He looked down at my black t-shirt and ASAT camo shorts. "Coulda fooled me."

I dress for utility, not fashion. It's my training.

He tipped his head to the side, jabbed the gun harder. "How about I take you instead, leave a note, and see if this Finnegan guy comes looking for us?"

I almost laughed. But then I thought about the job left half-finished downstairs. I thought about the local man I'd met online gaming days ago and then carefully cultivated with oblique hints about my disaffection with capitalism and the West until this morning, when he'd finally whispered the game-changer to me: "Finnegan, my brother. I can kill the kufar in numbers that will take your breath away."

Kufar is an insult people like him use for unbelievers like you and me. I knew enough to suspect he really did have a plan and the means to carry it out. If I did nothing to stop him, people would die. No way could I let his men take me prisoner. I had a job to do.

I lifted my hands in mock defeat.

"Okay, okay. I'll come. Just one thing." I looked over his shoulder at the forgotten pizza. The lid had popped open, and the melted cheese—the cheese that smelled really good—was slipping off the crust and onto the floor. Getting floor germs on it, for Christ's sake. "Can we take the pizza with us?"

He said, "Pizza? Seriously?" He turned his head to look at it. It was the second I needed.

"Yeah, the pizza," I said through gritted teeth. "I haven't eaten all day." I stomped on his instep, lifted my leg and raked the rough edge of my boot treads down his shin. His teeth clenched with the pain of it. You might think this was a pretty reckless thing to do with a gun stuck in my jaw, but not really, because at the same time I enclosed his weapon hand in both of mine, dug my fingers into the soft nerves between the bones, and popped his fingers loose like bending legs apart on a crab. The gun fell to the floor, and I dug my fingers deeper. He doubled over, his brain shorting out from the pain, unable to reboot into flight mode. But I was too pissed off about the floor cheese to let up on the finger nerves.

"Maybe you should let her have the pizza," a new voice said.

There was a click by my temple. I held still. A warm draft from the door open to the late afternoon heat brushed stray hairs across my forehead. I swiveled my eyes to the right to see a new figure outlined in the light from the door, holding a gun to my head.

"You can have the pizza, little ninja girl, but you need to let go of Roman first."

The voice was light in tone, but the smooth metal of a gun barrel aimed straight at my frontal lobes was real enough. Even if I took the chance of batting it away, that would free Roman to do his worst. So, I let go. Roman stumbled, his high-tech and no doubt extremely filthy running shoe splatted straight into the center of the pizza, rendering the rest of it inedible. He cursed.

"Looks like you finally met your match, Roman." The voice behind the gun was amused. "Lucky I was here to save your sorry ass."

Roman wiped tomato sauce and mozzarella on my beige carpet and glared at me.

I returned his glare, sick to my stomach. Five years alone in this house, planning for moments like this, training for this very contingency, and I'd damn well let my guard down and screwed it up. It only remained to be seen how long I could last before they broke me and all was lost. I had no doubt that very soon, they would try.

> I can kill the kufar in numbers that
> will take your breath away.

His name was Tabernackl and mine was Finnegan. He was an orc and I was a blood elf. At least, those were the avatars we had chosen for the game.

He and I had met under a cyan sky—the forest spreading around us in fractals, the tree branches hanging heavy with snow. The game scene occasionally broke into pixelated blocks when the bandwidth dipped.

But this often happens when you use an anonymizing redirector like TOR.

It had taken weeks to get to this point. I took a deep breath and hit "o" on the keyboard to open a private chat channel between us.

    [Finnegan]: Tell me more, brother.

    [Tabernackl]: I speak of the State Fair,
    Finnegan. Do you know it? The Texas
    State Fair.

    [Finnegan]: Vaguely, esteemed brother. I
    have only recently left my caves for
    America.

I chewed my lip. I'd been playing the part of a recent immigrant to these shores, but had I laid it on too thick just now?

Tabernakl's musclular orc chest gently rose and fell with the regularity of a subroutine. His fixed green grimace told me nothing.

I imagined the human behind him—the real Tabernakl—in some cheap Dallas apartment, bags of fertilizer and bottles of fuel oil piled high in the kitchen. He would be sitting on the living room rug, or maybe a mattress on his bedroom floor, picking out letters on the keyboard with two fingers, not an online gamer per se. Just another mujahideen keen to avoid keywords like "waging Jihad" and "weapons of mass destruction" in his Gmail inbox.

> [Tabernackl]: Then let me explain. There is a place called the midway where the kufar gamble. They throw a foam ball into a milkcan or pluck a plastic duck from a tub of water. If they win, they get a cheap prize.

Did they? I consider myself to have a wide range of experiences—more than most people my age. Not many people have assessed the Hoover Dam for terrorist vulnerabilities, for instance, or hopped a freight train to Des Moines. But as for things like a trip to Disneyland or even just riding the roller coaster at Six Flags, my parents hadn't seen the need. Nor, until this point, had I. Did people really play those games like they did on TV?

> The large stuffed animal prizes are popular. They are carried about all evening. Into the crowd. I suggest we have our own manufactured and hidden among them.

Tabernakl had come up with a good plan. One of the hardest parts of a planning chemical attack is figuring out how to spread the poison evenly throughout a large crowd. But as far as dispersal went, this was both cruel and cheap: his victims would do it for him. Perhaps some of them would even make it onto public transport. Others might take the prizes all the way home. And kids were the primary target. This guy was bad news.

I glanced at my secondary screen, where a plain gray window was open, the status bar at 65%. I needed more time for my new analysis program to pin him down—Tabernakl never stayed online for long. But I'd just bring up something haram. Seriously. These guys are always tying themselves in knots over what exactly is haram.

```
[Finnegan]:     Brother,     it    sounds
interesting,  but  I  am  troubled.  We
should  not  besmirch  an  operation  of
Allah with figural representation.
```

Tabernakl was silent for a moment, and then the words began appearing again.

```
[Tabernackl]: I am not suggesting a pig
or a dog. I plan to use a dolphin. We
can make a series of them covered with
patriotic symbols of the evil empire and
a pink one for girls.
```

On the left...68%...82%...89%...come on, hunt the bastard down.

```
[Finnegan]: But why a dolphin, exactly?

[Tabernackl]: The blowhole, brother.

[Finnegan]: Blowhole?
```

...92%...93%...

```
[Tabernackl]:   Yes.   The   sarin   will   be
delivered   as   an   aerosol   out   the
blowhole.
```

I sucked in my breath, sharp. Sarin is nasty stuff. Just ask the Japanese, all the victims of Aum Shinrikyo. It first stops the lungs from moving, and then resides in the clothes of the dying to poison those who come to help. It hit me then—this was not an intellectual exercise or a game—this was real. My fingers went tingling and numb all at once and I had to squint hard at the keyboard to make sure not a single keystroke slipped.

```
[Finnegan]:   I   see   the   inspiration   given
to   you   by   Allah   is   genius.
```

I was proud of that line. I found it on a religious forum.

```
[Tabernackl]:   Thanks   brother   Finnegan.
Shall   I   price   them   up   with   my   Chinese
suppliers?
```

```
[Finnegan]:   How   long   does   that   take?
```

```
[Tabernackl]:   I   can   get   a   quote   this
afternoon.   I   can   have   them   in   my   hands
for   the   weekend   after   next.
```

In ten days. Not long at all.
…99%…100%.
Done. He could call up all the Chinese he wanted—his ass was grass now. My new Russian bots had burrowed through his proxies and matched his IP address to a GPS location, plus or minus an apartment or two.

I didn't say this. Instead, I told him I would pass his truly excellent plans on to my emir back in Pakistan and be in touch soon. Then I logged off and left it. This new Russian analysis software was pretty damn good, if a bit heavy on the computation. It would be like—well, like shooting fish in a barrel.

"Hey," I said to the only other living creature in my basement, the namesake of my blood elf avatar. "That was a good job. We should do this more often, you and I."

In his bowl in the corner, the original Finnegan swam sideways, his little mouth gasping pathetic fish breaths, his once beautiful fins rotted away to stubs. It was heart-breaking to watch. I'd turned off all his webcams and put medicine in the bowl as soon as I'd noticed, but there was no denying it now, he was near the end.

"Hey little guy," I said more quietly, "I'm gonna put you out of your misery soon. I just had to finish this one thing."

He gasped, oblivious. Even with healthy fish, you can't expect much.

But then the doorbell had rung. The pizza I'd ordered, along with an unexpected extra side of armed kidnappers. I hadn't eaten for many hours, though. Days maybe. Sometimes I forget to keep track. I wrote Tabernakl's coordinates on a sticky note and headed up the stairs.

The rest, you know.

2

My name is Rain Wooten, and until about five years ago, I had no idea my life was unusual in any way. My dad and I are a part of a long-standing secret program within the FBI, informally known as the True Patriots, and our motto is that we do what has to be done. He was recruited to this life before I was born, so my involvement has lasted as long as I can remember.

Dad and I complement each other perfectly: he does the old-school fieldwork, and I back him up with computer intel. What this means in practice is that for five years, ever since Mom left, I've lived alone in this house in the suburbs west of Fort Worth. I limit my contact with the outside world: no more school or weekend trips to the mall for me. When Dad can break his cover, he comes by to bring food, check on me, and obtain the next mission.

I know America might seem pretty safe. After all, most people shuttle between their air-conditioned offices and homes for decades without ever hitting an improvised explosive device or being kidnapped in the middle of the night. But to keep the American dream alive and running smoothly—beer and steaks in the grocery stores and fireworks in the park on the Fourth of July—a lot of stuff has to go on under the hood. And go on it must, because terrorist threats are all around us. I should know, I've stopped plenty of attacks in my day. Rooting out bastards like Tabernakl is all just a part of the service we provide.

Being rooted out *by* bastards like Tabernakl and his ilk was not. They put cuffs on me—the plastic zip-tie kind. I was smart enough to clench my hands when they went on so that the cuffs were a bit loose when I relaxed. I was also smart enough not to struggle. Those cuffs just get tighter, you know, if you struggle. It's why so many terrorists use them when they kidnap people.

After quickly making sure there was no one in the house except for me, they put me in the car, in the back seat, like a child. The other guy—Roman called him Peter—even buckled me in. I guess he didn't want to lose me in a car accident before he had a chance to torture me. He got in the driver's seat and turned around to look at me. Young-ish, I guessed, about twenty or so. He was Caucasian, but that meant nothing. Islamist extremists convert all kinds of people. Remember the Shoe Bomber? His name was Richard Reid.

"You okay back there?" he said.

"Like apart from the fact I'm being kidnapped?" I answered. "Go to hell."

He just turned around and started the car. Asshole.

We drove through the quiet streets lined with wooden frame houses, permeable to at least fifteen chemical and biological weapons known to terrorists worldwide. The irony of this neighborhood is that even though it's a nice place, if you let off a bomb around here, you wouldn't be able to tell the difference just from looking. No one goes outside here, and who can blame them? No one wants to go outside in Texas in the summer, including me, although I hardly go out anyway except to complete mission tasks. It was October now, but even so, it was pretty darn warm in the car, even with the air conditioning on full blast.

We pulled out and turned left onto Granbury. Roman said, "What are you doing? Dmitri said..."

"I know what Dmitri said," Peter answered. "Look, she's just a kid. Maybe we can get what we need without having to involve Dmitri."

Dmitri? Again, unusual. I must be dealing with a Chechen faction of Islamists or something. I wriggled around and pulled on the door handle with my bound hands. It didn't open. Damn child locks.

Peter saw it. His eyes met mine in the rear-view mirror. I ground my teeth and looked out the window instead.

We pulled into a self-storage place. You know, where you can rent those little garages. This particular self-store had seen better days. The parking lot was riddled with potholes and vegetation had grown right up to the chain-link fence. A lot of the garages were completely abandoned, the doors taken off to discourage homeless people. On some, the roofs had totally fallen in and bushes were growing inside. My captors pulled the car right around to the back, where a row of garages still looked to be in suspiciously good repair. Peter came around and opened the door for me.

One of the rules about being kidnapped is you should never make it easy for your captors to put you in a worse situation than you are already in, and those garages looked pretty bad to me. I had undone my seatbelt when we pulled into the lot and as soon as Peter opened the door, I made a break for it, pushing past him and running for Granbury.

It is harder than you might think to run with bound hands. Newton's first law and all that. Also the fear of falling flat on your face on broken concrete, it makes you instinctively slow down. I should have trained for it, I see that now, but experience makes us wiser. I got wiser all the way to the front gate when Roman caught up to me and grabbed the sleeve of my t-shirt.

"Let me go!" I shrieked. We both fell to our knees and I kicked and struggled, forgetting about the cuffs. Just feet away from our little drama, cars sped down Granbury at forty miles an hour. I screamed again as I kicked...desperate for once for an ordinary citizen to see my distress and help. But no, they just drove past. Too fast to see me. Too fast to stop.

My captors subdued me eventually. Roman had to sit on my feet while Peter held his gun to the base of my skull. I was so washed out from all the drama, and not having eaten for two days, and my wrists were hurting so bad from the thin plastic cutting tightly into my skin that in the end I agreed to walk back quietly. They led me back to a garage and Roman turned on the overhead light while Peter duct taped my trembling body to a gritty plastic chair.

Roman saw it and sneered. "Duct tape? That's not going to hold her."

Peter looked up at him and shrugged. "We're out of wire ties, unless you know where there's more." He sat back on his heels and observed his handiwork. He had blond hair, cut neatly. One of his ears stuck out more than the other. The light from the door shone through it, like a pink seashell. He stood, leaving the roll of tape on the floor.

Roman didn't look convinced.

"What kind of pizza was it?" Peter asked me.

"Are you messing with me?" I lifted my head to look at him.

He raised his eyebrows, like it was up to me to decide.

All the struggle, fighting, and threats of the past hour had drained me. So. I fell for it: that small kindness of offered sustenance.

"It was three-cheese."

"Roman, maybe we should get the kid another pizza," he said over his shoulder. "It's just around the corner."

"Pizza? You serious?" Roman said.

"Yeah, we could get pepperoni too. You want pepperoni on it?"

"No thanks," I mumbled. "Pepperoni has nitrites in it."

Peter looked at me blankly.

"Nitrites are carcinogenic," I explained.

"Jesus Christ, another pizza?" Roman said. He shook his head. "Hell. I guess I could get another pizza." He left.

Peter sat there looking at me. I sat there looking back at him —wondering how the hell I had gotten into this situation—how exactly how they'd caught me.

Internet anonymity is one of those tricky things. The whole purpose of the Internet is to get little packets of information to where they're supposed to go. There are all sorts of ways to mess with the addresses in the packet headers so it's not clear where they're really meant to end up, but at the end of the day, there has to be a way to sort them out so the machines at the ends of the cables can actually get them there. I usually stick to the Dark Web, which is a shadow network that lies like filaments of spider silk over the real Internet infrastructure. Each packet runs round and round in a tortuous tangle on these filaments, the next legs of the journey hidden under encrypted layers to obscure its path. That should have protected me, dammit.

"How did you do it?" I asked him.

He shrugged. "Not my department."

I probably wasn't going to get more than that, especially since I was the one duct-taped to the chair and not him. I felt sick and swallowed hard.

He sighed. "Look, just between you and me, this doesn't have to be hard. We could even have you home with a fresh pizza in no time. Just give us Finnegan."

Yeah, it would have been easy if I'd had someone named Finnegan to hand over to him, if the person that they were looking for hadn't actually been me.

He pulled up another plastic chair and sat in it backward, his forearms resting on its top. "You got a name?"

A sudden wave of hunger made me too dizzy to think through the implications of answering. When I'd said I hadn't eaten in two days, I meant it. Dad had been gone an unusually long time on this current operation. My system maintenance was behind schedule. Despite being on half-rations for two weeks, I'd finally run out of freeze-dried lentil soup and cans of tuna fish. All that was left in the house was thirteen cans of bacon. In a pinch, I'll eat Spam. I'll even eat Vienna sausages. But canned bacon is a whole new low.

"Rain," I told him. "Like the stuff that falls from the sky."

"Okay, Rain. Shouldn't you be in school? How old are you, anyway?"

This is an easier question to ask than to answer. The events of my life make Dark Web messages look like advertising on a highway billboard. My age has always been a variable—a parameter altered to suit the current operation and obscure my identities from past operations. Unfortunately, it's been altered so many times, even my father can no longer definitively say which of my various ages is correct.

"I'm nineteen, thanks for asking." It was an upper estimate, but not entirely out of the realm of possibility. "I'm small for my age."

Peter looked at me for a moment, lips pressed together. I looked back

"I know Roman came in way too heavy," he said at last. "He likes to screw things up like that. It got you scared...you lashed out...we did what we had to do. Fair enough. But while he's gone..." He sighed again and shifted on the seat. "Look, the way it sounded when Dmitri sent us out here, it didn't sound like we were supposed to hurt this Finnegan guy—at least not too much. Sounded more like we had a business proposition."

It all clicked into place suddenly. My new Russian bot program...it must have had a backdoor. I'm pretty good at my job, but a lot of that is finding the right tools. Clearly, I'd found the wrong one this time.

"So, Finnegan is your brother, right?" Peter asked. "Boyfriend, maybe?"

I squinted at him. "Tell me what you want with him."

Peter shook his head. "Sorry, that information is for Finnegan."

"Well, I don't have a boyfriend. Definitely not one named Finnegan."

"Maybe he's your dad."

There was flat out no way I would give them Dad to save myself. And I know Dad would agree. If he were ever taken, with all that knowledge inside his head, it would be a dark day for America.

But something in my face made Peter smile. "Don't you think your dad wants to know where you are, right now?"

In reality, that was one thing that wouldn't concern Dad for a while. Which was too bad. At that moment, I would have given anything for him to burst through the door with a semi-automatic and lay waste to this damn bastard.

Roman soon came back, a piece of pizza already in his hand. The smell of it made my mouth water again. Increased suggestibility, dammit. A typical interrogation tactic. I'd have to work hard to fight it.

"I thought you said you were good at this kind of thing." Roman put the box on the floor.

Peter shrugged. "Have some patience. We haven't really started."

"Screw that." Roman set his half-eaten slice in the box and stood up. Something in his face made me want to scoot my chair away, but I could only manage little rocking jerks. He came over and I got a good look at his round, soft, sneering face, at the tattooed words in some weird Gothic font on his neck.

Then he slapped me—hard—knocking my skull back, filling my head with gray stars. Grinding the chair legs an inch across the gritty floor.

Roman raised his hand again. He was smiling. Shit, shit, shit. He'd hit me before. But then, I could fight back. The entire lower half of my body cramped, and I clenched hard to maintain my dignity. I struggled within the duct tape but couldn't get the leverage to rip it open.

From his seat near the pizza, Peter sighed. "Enough, Roman. Let's go back to building rapport."

Roman sneered over his shoulder. "Patience, Peter. I haven't started."

He hit me again, hard enough to tip me and the chair over and onto the floor with a smack. My shoulder ground into the concrete, taking most of my weight. My brain was scrunched between bookends of pain, between the blow of my temple on the floor and my ear where he'd hit me. The top soft part of it was hurting with that unbearable and totally unnecessary pain you get when you stub your toe. It felt like he'd split the cartilage.

I sensed Roman kneel on the ground in front of me, his breath right in my face.

"I'm after a guy called Finnegan, bitch."

I considered my options. We could go on like this indefinitely, and while these idiots might learn nothing from me, I'd learn nothing from them either. I had to figure out how to get away, and I had to do it soon. The pain slowly faded. I opened my eyes.

"Fine. You got him," I said. "It's me. It's my online name."

3

"You're Finnegan? Really?" He smiled. "I guess we'll find out the truth soon enough."

Next thing I knew, he was tipping me upright again, cutting the duct tape with a knife from his pocket.

"I told you, Peter. We should have taken her straight to Dmitri. Keep the gun on her, okay?"

Peter nodded silently. I had a feeling I'd squandered that tiny nugget of kindness. What I couldn't figure out was why he'd offered in the first place.

"What kind of a stupid-ass name is Finnegan anyway?" Roman tore the last bit of tape from the chair and jerked me up. "You don't look Irish to me."

"It's the name of my fish," I said. Poor little guy. He was probably still suffering on my desk even now.

"Yeah, well that is stupid-ass." Roman glanced at Peter as he pushed me toward the door. "Hell. If I'd left the interrogation up to you, I bet you would've ended up bringing that fish back to Dmitri instead of her."

I didn't answer. Finnegan was a special fish, but not for reasons that I cared to share.

Dmitri lived in one of those mid-century bungalow houses,

you know the kind. Hundreds of them are dotted around Fort Worth. Flat and long, blond brick, and tiny high windows with bars. Inside, plate glass sliding doors opened onto an enclosed patio like an ancient Roman villa. It was decorated in a sterile style, like an afterthought.

There were a lot of guys, some in tracksuits and gold chains, others in black suits with white shirts hanging around, having coffee in the kitchen, standing watch by the doors, smelling faintly of serious aftershave. Overall, they were the weirdest group of Chechen Islamists I'd ever seen. To a man, they were white, bare chins and scalps showing through neat stubble. Truth is, I had no experience of actual Chechen Islamists other than what I'd learned online. But something seemed off.

The underlying threat of violence kept me from making a break for it. Forget those movies where the bad guys attack in choreographed twos and threes. If they fought anything like Roman and Peter, it would be a straight up dogpile. And even that would only happen if I could get loose from Peter's modified walking duct tape straitjacket. At least he had let me have some pizza before taping me up again.

Dmitri sat on a nice taupe couch and looked at me in silence for a moment.

"Roman, Peter, you pathetic *gopniki*," Dmitri said. "Who is this girl, and where the hell is my fish?"

"Fish?" The blood drained from Peter's face. He glanced at Roman, who just stood there with his mouth open.

Well, good for them. About time someone scared the crap out of those two assholes.

"I told Kazantsev to give you name, give you address, how hard can it be? He sent you email, right?"

Roman finally managed to sputter out some words. "Kind of hard to read all that on my phone. Kind of...small...with all those little letters and shit..."

"Small? Cut the bullshit." Dmitri raised his eyebrows. "Maybe you have problem with Kazantsev?"

Roman and Peter enthusiastically shook their heads.

"So, if he told you to *sosí moy khuy...*"

Roman cut in, "Course we'd do it. We're team players."

"She said her online name was Finnegan," Peter added. "Anyone would have gotten confused."

Dmitri sneered. "Anyone who can't translate 'suck my dick' from the Russian, you mean."

Dmitri had one of those round, jowly old-man faces, the type that made it impossible to imagine what he would have looked like when he was young. But it wouldn't have been a kind face, even then. He threw up his hands. "You second-generation English-speaking idiots. How many times have I warned you about using Google Translate? Now, what the hell am I supposed to do with her?"

I tried to get my head around it. He didn't want me. He wanted Finnegan. The other Finnegan. The fish.

"You're not Chechen Islamists bent on jihad," I said, "are you?"

There was a moment of silence in the room. The tips of my ears went all hot.

"Those throat-slitting black-assed goat fuckers?" Dmitri said. "Hell no, I'm in import-export. Diamonds, vodka, that sort of thing. Classy shit, yeah? Who the hell are you?"

I pulled my shoulders back and looked him in the eye. "Finnegan is my fish."

HERE'S the truth of the matter. While I occasionally get to hunt down guys like Tabernakl online, my other main contribution to the True Patriots is on the money side. The True Patriots are the most secret section of the FBI, so secret that total deniability is their *modus operandi*. It's essential for the deep-cover operations they run. Remember the whole Iran Contra thing? My dad and his colleagues learned their lesson long ago. The True Patriots don't appear on any budgets, especially ones that Congress gets to see. Hiding the money trail is essential when you've got to do the dirty work that has to be done.

In the old days, the True Patriots used to do things for quick cash like getting people to provide funds to smuggle money and treasures out from behind the Iron Curtain. Nothing too much, just a bit here and there, but Nigerian princes could have been schooled by my dad. The people never got the cut they were promised, but they did fund the fight against communism, so there's that.

By the time Dad and Mom were together, the Berlin Wall had fallen, and they had to branch out a bit: sell fake diplomas, offer people fake jobs, or promise contest winnings they would never get. Nothing too much though, and all for a good cause. Now that Mom is gone, I've taken over that side completely to free up Dad to do his work.

These days, it's much easier because I use the Internet for my projects and added my own flourish. I've catfished jerks with my fake Thai child-bride profiles. I've sold sugar pills on the Silk Road to would-be date rapists. I also used to be big into arbitrage: screen-scraping mafia-owned gambling sites and cheating the bastards out of money when they got the odds wrong. It is exactly as much fun as you think it is.

Finnegan the Psychic Fish is not quite as morally justified, but as far as sophistication, he is my *magnum opus*, and the biggest earner of them all. He's a Siamese fighting fish (or *Betta splendens* if you prefer), and his bowl is set in front of three television monitors that continuously play sports channels. You can see a live webcam of him twenty-four hours a day, and if you subscribe to my email list, you can watch his first three predictions for yourself for free.

Sports gambling is a risky business, but Finnegan and I don't take any risks at all. This is because the video predictions sent to your inbox don't match the video predictions sent to someone else's inbox. In fact, I send out all possible combinations of predictions, in proportions carefully calibrated to match the current odds. Some people will get incorrect predictions, but others will get predictions that are uncannily accurate. For a few random people, Finnegan has never gotten a winner wrong, ever (no matter how long the odds), and these are the loyal and lucrative subscribers that I collect over time. Eventually, he gets it wrong for almost everybody, but thanks to the vast reach of the Internet and a continual stream of sports matches all over the world, new suckers replace the old on a steady, rolling basis.

So that's who Finnegan is, if you were wondering. I mean, that's who Finnegan was. Sadly, his feed had gone dead ever since his eyes clouded over and he started swimming sideways yesterday morning. If Dmitri wanted Finnegan, he was going to have to hurry.

DMITRI SMILED. "YOUR FISH," he said. "Seriously?"

"What's so weird about me owning a fish?" I asked.

He waved one hand in the air, dismissing me. "A random fish? Nothing weird. But Finnegan, he's special. His predictions are magic."

Dmitri wasn't a terrorist, I realized. Not even close. He was one of my loyal and lucrative subscribers—one of the guys I'd been scamming.

"Finnegan's feed went off yesterday," he continued. "Very bad timing. There's a game tonight, and I need him now."

I scam a lot of thugs, but it was just my luck to scam a thug living nearby with enough resources and connections to track me down in real life. I suppose, given the sheer number of my victims, it had to happen sooner or later.

"Look, I hate to disappoint you, but he's not really psychic," I said. "It's all a scam."

There was a moment of silence, and then Dmitri pounded the

coffee table, once, hard. Everyone in the room jumped, including me.

"Are you saying I'm stupid? He predicted the last seven games. Seven! I saw him do it. I know the odds of that. It's one to 2...8—" He counted it up on his fingers. "—128 that he could get that right. That's impossible."

"It's very *unlikely*," I said, doing my own calculations, "but 0.8% is nowhere near—" I looked around the very, very quiet room. Peter was even more ghostly pale, and while anything that made Peter uncomfortable was good in my book, I suddenly flashed on what he had said to Roman: "She's just a kid." This is an annoying statement that has dogged me all my life and is probably no longer even true. But coming from a kidnapper, it's actually a weirdly kind thing to say. I realized that his discomfort was not just there for my pleasure. It was telling me that I was playing this thing totally wrong. Dammit. Lack of field experience, getting the better of me again.

"Okay," I said. "Take me back. I'll turn on his webcams again." I shut my eyes and tried not to think about what I would find in the bowl on my desk. I could just level with Dmitri and tell him Finnegan was dying, but if he was so convinced that Finnegan was truly psychic, I didn't think he'd react well to the news. As it says on Finnegan's website, if predicting football winners could be done with any old fish in a bowl, everyone would be doing it.

But if I could just get back to my own basement, maybe I could stick on some archived footage. Then, once Dmitri was satisfied that Finnegan was back online, I could get on with the mission to stop Tabernakl.

"No. I've been thinking about that fish for a while. I want exclusive predictions." Dmitri leaned forward. "I don't want video out there for just anyone, screwing up the odds for me."

Oh. Crap. But I saw what he meant. Like everything else for sale, odds are a market driven by demand. If Finnegan were famous and could really predict the winner, everyone would bet on that team, and the odds would drop like a stone. But of course, in reality, no matter how famous Finnegan gets, he chooses Team A as well as Team B, so the odds aren't actually screwed up at all. I couldn't say that to Dmitri though, not without getting myself into worse trouble.

If I had to shut down the website for good, that money stream would be gone, and Dad would be pretty pissed off. He never liked budget cuts.

But the bigger problem was that even if Finnegan had managed to survive, he never actually "predicts" anything. If I brought Finnegan to Dmitri, if he predicted the wrong winner for the game and Dmitri held me responsible—

No. I couldn't think like that right now. Tabernakl and his friends were still out there, still planning to manufacture killer soft-toy dolphins and get them into the hands of kids. I had other stuff to do, and it was high time I got away from these guys and back to doing it, whatever the cost.

"I will get him," I said. "Just keep in mind, he's a fragile fish. Moving him might upset his psychic powers."

Dmitri turned to Peter and Roman. "Take her back to get her fish, you pair of wood-for-brains whoresons. I want that exact fish. Don't pawn me off with anything else. And make sure she takes care of it. I don't want anything to upset his psychic powers."

I was being hustled out the door, wishing I'd kept my mouth shut, when he called out his final instruction.

"Get back before kick-off tonight. You hear me? Well before kick-off."

4

We pulled up to the house just as Roman's phone chirruped. He took it out and swiped at the screen.

"Hey, Peter, think you can handle her alone?"

Peter looked at me, a taped-up package neatly buckled up in the back seat. "Are you going to be good now?"

"Yes," I said.

The light just caught the short hairs above his sideburns, turning them gold. He said, "Then I reckon I can."

Our house was like every other house on the block: snow-white cement driveway, a border of red rock mulch around the edge of the yard, blinds drawn against the light. But that was the goal, to be exactly the same as its neighbors, at least on the outside. Peter marched me up to the front door and inspected the key lock buttons.

"Combination?"

"Untape me, and I'll key it in."

"Not a chance, honey."

"I'm not telling you the key code."

"Come on...work with me here." He raised one eyebrow. "You can always change it after I'm gone, can't you?"

I gritted my teeth. "Decimal places ten through fourteen of pi."

Peter looked at the lock. Then he looked back at me. "Which would be?"

Honestly. "Five-eight-nine-seven."

He punched them in and tried the door. It was still locked fast.

"You have to unlock the lock underneath too," I told him, "with the key."

"Where's the damn key then?"

"I seem to have forgotten it," I said, "what with all the being snatched out of the house at gunpoint and everything."

"Shit." Peter grabbed me by the arm and marched me around the side. "Tell me you left the back door open."

I stumbled on the rock mulch. "I always deadbolt every entrance twice, especially when I'm home."

"Windows?"

"Even if we broke the glass, which would set off the alarm, the frames are locked shut."

"Pet door?"

"No pets. Not with legs."

He tugged open the gate in the high privacy fence and pulled me through.

"Holy freaking Jesus on a stick," he said. "What is that?"

He could only be referring to one thing in the backyard. A low, squat shed, the walls made of 24 inches of cement. I know how thick the walls are because I helped Dad build it when we moved in. I never go in it, though. It will be a desperate day when I do.

"That's our bomb shelter," I said.

He tilted his head at me. "You have a bomb shelter in your backyard?"

Surprised, I asked if he had one. He didn't.

I looked at him for a moment. "So what are you going to do if terrorists set off a dirty bomb?"

"I'd throw the dog in the car and drive out of the city." He shrugged. "Never really thought about it."

Well, that was obvious. Anyone who thinks about it for even a millisecond will realize that's a crappy plan—you can never tell about wind direction, can you? Typical thinking though, and why my work is so important.

He pulled me around the house, experimentally tugging at the sliding glass door, testing the windows, which, as I'd already told him, were all locked. Eventually, we circled around to the front door.

Peter knelt to inspect the lock. He dug his fingernail in the crack between the door frame and the door. "Guess I'll have to see if Roman brought any lock-picking tools along." He turned to go back. "Unless..." He toed the edge of the Hessian doormat, the one that says "Welcome!" Dad must have meant it ironically. Something glinted, and he bent down. "Got it. Extra key."

The blood ran from my face, and I backed up.

"What?" He frowned at me as he put the key in the lock.

It was a trap. It had to be. Dad would never just leave things out like that, *never*. It had to be placed there for the unwary, possibly even as a Loyalty Test meant for me. I started to back off the porch, not wanting to get caught in whatever nasty surprise was about to be sprung, but Peter reached back and grabbed a tool loop on my military surplus shorts, holding me still as he quickly turned the key in the lock and pushed open the door. It opened.

"Want me to go first? In case of traps?" He laughed at me as he let go of my shorts and I staggered back.

Peter stopped just inside the entranceway and looked around the living room. There wasn't much to see, I guess, just two folding camp chairs. A few vintage issues of *2600* were scattered over the floor. No pictures on the wall. Mom was the only one who ever bothered with those, and she did not come with us to Texas. I don't spend much time in this room anyway, what with the stuff in the basement taking up all of the hours in my day. I could see in his face that the living room didn't come up to his mafia henchman standards.

"Where's your stuff?" he asked. "You guys just move in or something?"

"Not really," I said. I was still trying to get my head around the existence of the key. We'd made it through the door. But that meant nothing. Maybe it was even deliberate on Dad's part, because if you need to dispose of an intruder, maybe it's better to do it further inside, where the neighbors won't see. How exactly to do that wasn't yet clear. There was the weapons cache upstairs, but they were all disassembled and packed away in boxes for safety.

My pizza, the one with Roman's footprint in the middle of it, lay cold and congealed on the front hall floor. Wasted, just like my whole day had been wasted by this ridiculous charade. On my desktop PC downstairs were the coordinates of a man who wanted to poison hundreds of innocent Americans. I had to get that information to Dad ASAP, whatever the cost. To do that, I'd have to deal with Peter. But even before that, I'd have to deal with the duct tape wrapped around my torso.

"Where's the fish?" Peter asked me.

"In the basement," I told him. "Through the kitchen." I led the way to the kitchen, but just a few feet in, I stopped. "Hey, you think I could get a drink?"

"A what?" He frowned at me, nonplussed.

"A drink of water," I said. "It's hot out there." I wiggled my trapped arms. "I can't do it myself."

He sighed with irritation, but opened cabinets until he found the glasses. The kitchen wasn't coming up to his standards either. Not because it was dirty, by any means. It was clean. But a clean kitchen that gets used every day has a smell, the smell of garlic and olive oil infused deep in the cracks of a cutting board, of that morning's coffee grounds in the trash can, of pots of basil and wheatgrass growing on the windowsill. Not this kitchen. It smelled of chlorinated city water, of hungry cockroaches, of empty tuna fish cans. He pulled out a glass.

While he'd been looking for glasses, I'd backed up against the corner of the kitchen counter. Underneath, I'd taped a razor blade there just for emergencies. It wasn't going well, though. The blade was not coming free. The tape had rotted and was coming off in little flakes. I needed more time.

"Can you get another one? That one's dirty."

Peter held it up to the light. Like all my glasses, there was a fine ring around the middle. "It's nothing. Just the dishwasher."

As he went to fill the glass up, the blade behind my back finally came free from the counter. I turned it in my hands and started in on the duct tape. But it was really awkward, not being able to move my wrists freely or see what I was doing. The blade slipped, I felt a sharp pain in the palm of my hand. I stifled a gasp.

"You okay?" he said, looking at me sharply.

"Just get me another glass, please?"

The blade and my fingers were getting slippery with blood, but I wasn't going to give up. Duct tape is very strong and extremely sticky, but, like everyone knows, all you have to do is make one tiny nick in the side and the whole thing rips apart.

"Dammit...I've had just about enough..."

"Come on, it's been a long day."

Peter thumped the glass on the counter and re-opened the cabinet. He pulled out another glass, looked at the ring, and thumped that one down on the counter too. "You know, you really are the most annoying person I've ever met."

The blade caught the edge of the tape. I felt the tiny rip and the ease of pressure. I took a deep belly breath, marshaled my chi, and with a scream, I ripped my taped arms apart, like unzipping a zipper. I lunged at him with the blade out.

He grabbed my wrist, stopping the blade inches from his cheek and went for a belly punch with his other hand. But my training came through at last. I blocked with the ulna in my forearm and followed up with a push to his shoulder. He grabbed my other arm and started to pull me toward him. The idea was there, get me off balance, but the blood made my wrist slippery. I pulled free, but before I could run, he lunged, pinning my blade arm. His momentum pushed the two of us back, right through the door to the basement. We tumbled down the stairs.

I ended up with my head on the basement floor, feet several steps above, completely pinned by Peter's mass. The blade was long gone, knocked away. He lay there for a moment, then started yelling in my face.

"You bitch! Why do you keep on doing this? All we had to do was get the fish! Just! One! Fish!"

I must have hit my skull on the way down. Everything seemed to be half speed. I turned my head to the side and looked, where my desk was, where Finnegan's bowl sat. I couldn't help it—I let out a tiny, pathetic noise. Finnegan was floating sideways. Still. Gone.

Peter's gaze followed mine, and he saw Finnegan. He stopped shouting and his shoulders sagged. Carefully, awkwardly, he disentangled the two of us. I sat on the bottom landing, exhausted, my back against the wall, knees bent, and wiped Peter's spittle from my face with my shirt. Peter sat down next to me.

"You're bleeding," he said.

"It's nothing," I said. I wiped the blood on my jeans. "Doesn't even hurt."

"You could have just told me he was dead."

"And then what, let Dmitri kill me or whatever he was going to do? He said, 'that exact fish.'"

"Dmitri is an idiot but I'm not. Your fish isn't psychic. How could he be? Fish have a long-term memory of like, ten seconds."

"That's not true. How do salmon spawn fifteen years later in the same river they were hatched in?"

"Dunno. Smell, probably."

"You still have to remember a smell."

"But he's not psychic."

"No."

Peter took a breath. "Okay, here's what we do. First, we get you bandaged up. Where did Finnegan come from?"

"The pet store in the mall."

"Then that's where we're going."

I looked up at the desk, at my sleeping computer screen, less than five feet away, and the secrets it held. I could even see the yellow corner of the sticky note on the edge of the monitor.

"Could you maybe give me five minutes? I need to get some stuff off my desk. There's a message I have to send."

"Hell no. What kind of dumb-ass shit-head do you take me for?"

My head throbbed, and so did my ear. I put my hand up to feel where Roman had hit it.

"What if I told you it was the only way to stop terrorists from using poisoned dolphins to kill thousands of children?"

"I would say you're a pretty shitty liar." He grabbed my arm and pulled me to my feet. "Come on, let's go."

"Jesus, what took you two so long?" Roman said when we got back in the car. He saw the traces of blood that I could not completely sponge out of my jeans and laughed. "Damn, did you pop her cherry or something? That's disgusting. She's like what, fifteen?"

"You're disgusting," Peter told him, half laughing. But then Peter's blue eyes glanced over the back seat at me and he wasn't smiling at all.

He put a box containing Finnegan's bowl and various fish care items in the trunk and came back around to the front. "Look, we got to stop off at the mall."

"Hell. The mall?"

"She's almost out of fish food. Come on. We don't want Dmitri mad because we dropped the ball on this one."

I looked down at my lap where Finnegan floated in his little plastic baggie water coffin. *Rest in peace, little betta. I know you would have saved me if you could.*

PETER and I left Roman in the car, still on his phone, and went in the mall through Dillard's. On the left, faceless models displayed filmy chintz dresses, just like the ones my mom used to wear. Funny to think she was finally in fashion after twenty years— through no effort of her own.

Her name was Saffron Wooten. Not to be outdone by her own mother in the weird name department, she reportedly put down Rainbow Isis Wooten on my birth certificate. Don't ever call me Rainbow, by the way. It's Rain.

My earliest memory is of sitting in her lap, draping her silky brown hair around my head, and pretending it was my own. I remember smelling the thick sweet cloud of patchouli that followed her everywhere and peering through the warm curtain of mom-ness at the living room, strewn with about a hundred egg cartons and black fishnets...for some reason I've long ago forgotten.

Saffron met Hal Wooten, that's my dad, at a talk about UFOs in New Mexico. She was there because she truly believed in UFOs, but she also believed in a lot of stuff, like crystals, copper bracelets, Carlos Castaneda, ear candling, that sort of thing. UFOs don't exist, of course. But they can quite often be a cover-up for top-secret operations. Dad was there to see what these people knew, or thought they knew. He was looking for sightings that might be cover-ups, either for the activities of his own people that he knew about or, more seriously, enemy activity that he didn't know about.

The thing was, he did find enemy agents, the ones we call the

Others, right at the conference, and they were very close to Mom, though she didn't know it. It was pretty dramatic from the very start; he and Mom had to go on the run right then and there. Abandon the old life and start fresh in a new town with new identities and all that. I don't know how many times my dad has had to do it in total, but it's happened four times since I've been alive. We call it "Get Out Of Dodge," or GOOD for short. The last time we pulled a GOOD was after Mom was gone —about five years ago now—and Texas is where we ended up.

"You like that flower dress?" Peter asked. He had a gentle grin on his face. With his face relaxed, since he wasn't around Roman and Dmitri, I could see how fine and even the bone structure was beneath.

"I don't do flower dresses," I said.

"Every girl does flower dresses."

I looked back towards the mannequins. Behind them ambled a mall security guard, hands behind his back. I have always been taught to avoid any level of law enforcement as a priority. Although we are technically on the same team, officers on the ground without our classified knowledge can understandably take our actions the wrong way. In fact, staying under the radar of the local police takes up a lot of my time. It's the cost we pay for our elite status.

I couldn't ask for help directly, but I could use the guard as a distraction, make a break for it, and somehow find my way home. I just had to figure out how to catch his attention.

I started blinking, three short blinks, three long blinks, and then three short again. SOS—in Morse code—the universal distress signal. The guard glanced over at me and I blinked even harder.

"Hey," he said, coming over, "y'all got something in your eye, miss?"

Before I could answer, Peter gripped my shoulder and was right in my face.

"Oh, yeah, looks like you do," Peter said to me.

"Better get it out before it scratches her cornea," the guard said. "Restrooms are that way, sir."

"Thanks." Peter was leading me away. As soon as we rounded the corner to junior sportswear, he shoved me up against the dressing room wall. "You little shit, we had a deal. I should take you back to Dmitri without a fish...see how you like that."

"I'm going to scream in a minute and that guard will come back here and it will all be over." Anger was making me reckless. I could feel the scream rising in my chest, a wild pressure building hot and fast.

"Think before you do that," he said. "Think about the implications. You think Dmitri will ever leave you alone if you do that? Your life in Fort Worth will be unbearable."

I didn't need Fort Worth. I didn't need Texas. I'd just GOOD and start over—not even go back to the house—just run.

Except...I did need to go back to the house. Tabernakl's coordinates were sitting on a note stuck to the screen in the basement. I couldn't just walk away without one more visit. And I had no money on me, no ID, no means of transport to take me the seven miles back to the house. All Dmitri had to do was send some henchman to park outside my house and wait for me to walk down the street three hours later.

I let my breath out, slow and measured.

A fiftyish sales clerk walked over, her face curious. "Everything all right here?"

Peter whipped out a wrinkled tissue and began to jab at my face. "Yes, ma'am. She's just got an eyelash in her eye."

I turned my head from side to side, trying to avoid getting Peter's nose germs in my vision system. The sales clerk looked on sympathetically. "We might have some eyewash in the employee first aid kit..."

"I think we've got it." Peter's face was so close to mine, I could feel his exhaled breath on the skin of my face. "Haven't we?"

"Yes, okay," I said. "You can stop poking me with that thing. Now please."

The sales lady was already distracted by other shoppers. Peter didn't let go of me.

"We both need to get that fish to Dmitri before kick-off. Today." He punctuated "today" with a little push to my shoulder. "The sooner you stop trying to escape, the sooner we can get this over with."

"Dmitri only wants the fish," I said. "Why can't you just let me walk out of here, and bring the fish back to him yourself?"

Peter shook his head. "He wants his special fish trainer to come back with the fish. If I leave with you and come back with just a fish, I'll end up peeling potatoes in the kitchen with the one hand Dmitri doesn't cut off. You know how hard it is for a local to get in with these guys, the top guys? I can't mess this one up. We need to make it look good."

"We? Why should I care?"

He looked out at the racks of clothing surrounding us. I could see his jaw working as he ground his teeth.

"Because I care, and I'm your best hope of getting out of this situation now."

"If you're trying to get me out of this situation, you're doing a pretty shitty job of it."

"Yeah, well I'd kinda like to get myself out of it as well."

He marched us past the perfume counters. A maze of glittering glass and chrome and promises, with a thousand ways to turn and leave.

"Ever considered a career change? Going back to school, becoming a truck driver?"

We exited Dillards and entered the mall. The smell of stale popcorn and hairdressing chemicals was thick.

"Think of it as a chance to redeem yourself," I said.

His grip tightened. I gasped.

"You scam people on the Internet for a living," he said. "Don't lecture me about redemption."

Well, that money might be scammed, but it kept America safe.

"My conscience is clear," I told him.

"Well so is mine," he snapped.

We walked down the mall. Families ambled past us, their eyes flicking away when we got close. Only a black-haired toddler in a ratty pink ballet tutu met my gaze, watching us pass as she rocked backward and forward on a kindergarten-sized low-rider motorcycle, polishing the plastic seat to a shine with her diaper.

In contrast, the eyes of the wrinkled old man in Mundo De Mascotas did not flick away. They stared. To be fair, we were holding up a dead Siamese fighting fish in a baggie, trying to match Finnegan's colors. The depressed specimens in their plastic hummus containers of blue-tinted water all looked mostly black. When we finally brought Finnegan II to the counter, the owner looked down at the corpse of Finnegan I. "You want me to throw that out for you?"

"Yes, please," Peter said, taking the baggie from me and holding it out.

The man's grandson shifted the albino python around his neck, and politely took the dead fish into the back of the store. So that was the end of Finnegan I. It was a bit sad, but I guess I'm too old to be holding fish funerals anymore.

On the way out, Peter suddenly stopped and looked at me. "There really wasn't any food in your kitchen, was there?"

"There was bacon," I told him, "but not bacon you'd want to eat."

"Where were your mom and dad? They at work or something?"

"What makes you think that's not my own house?"

He just looked at me.

"There is no mom," I said. "And yes, Dad is at work."

"Does he know what you do on the Internet?"

I looked at him but didn't answer.

"I don't mean to pry. I'm just trying to understand the situation."

"Well it's none of your business, you freaking *bratva* kidnapper."

"Just cause I'm a mafia kidnapper, it doesn't mean I can't be curious." He stopped in the middle of the mall and, crossed his arms over his chest. "I mean, hell, your dad can afford that big house but no furniture and no food? And if your fish scam really works, how come you don't buy anything for yourself?"

A child's scream echoed around us. To our left, multi-story play equipment towered up like the innards of some giant robot, children climbing over it like tiny parasites. I looked at Finnegan II, sanguine in his plastic baggie. In fact, I had recently bought something for myself: a pizza. And look how that had turned out.

"Hey," Peter said, putting his fingers lightly on my shoulder, "it will be over by tonight. We'll take the fish to Dmitri, then I'll take you home."

After all the trouble he had caused me, I damn well hoped so. But this time I said nothing. I just wiped at my nose and nodded.

Peter pointed over my shoulder at one of the many stores in this mall that sold quinceañera dresses. "Tell me, are those dresses more your style than the flower ones?"

I turned and looked at the hemispheres of ice-cream colored tulle draped over circular hoops. It was so ridiculous, me in a dress like that, I couldn't even get mad at him. Actually, I laughed.

"Wouldn't match my boots," I told him. "not with the steel toes and all."

He smiled for the second time. For a guy with one sticking-out ear, he had really even, white teeth. And a nice smile. I looked back down at Finnegan II and did not lift my eyes up until we got to the parking lot. Peter might be just a dumb guy who had no idea what was going on, but I did.

It's called Stockholm syndrome, where kidnapped people

start to care for the people who have kidnapped them. When some asshole has momentarily stopped being quite such an asshole, it can seem like they're a hell of a lot nicer than they actually are. Less than three hours ago, this man had held a gun to my head. Two hours ago, he'd thrown me down the stairs and called me a bitch. No amount of light banter could make up for that. I wasn't going to...*no, I wouldn't let myself*...forget that.

Anyway, if Dad ever found out I made a friend, he'd make me do a Loyalty Test. And more than anything else, I never wanted to do another of those.

LOYALTY TESTS CAN COME at any time. The beginning of a Loyalty Test is not necessarily announced. How to successfully pass a Loyalty Test is never mentioned. If you are truly, deeply loyal to your core, it will be obvious what to do. That's a part of the test.

If you get invited to a birthday party, even if your mom says you can go, decline. It is a Loyalty Test. Normal people aren't friendly to folks like us, they just ignore us. All others are paid agents of the enemy.

If your father leaves you in a car while he completes an operation inside a bowling alley in Kansas City, do not ever leave the car. It is a Loyalty Test. If you get thirsty, roll down the window and get a handful of snow. If you get hungry, just wait. If you have to pee, look for a paper cup and use that. If you have to poop, for *fuck's* sake, just wait.

And if you see your mother's face on a missing person's poster at a convenience store in Philadelphia, do not, I repeat, do not draw attention to it. If Mom's family knew what she was really doing and truly loved her, they would be happy. They would not want her to come home like the poster says. Those are fakes. They're Loyalty Tests.

These are just examples, and they aren't even that hard, just stuff you'd normally give to a kid. My mom's Loyalty Tests were harder, and she always struggled to pass them. Eventually, the day came when she failed, and I've been alone ever since.

5

"Hey, Finnegan. Hey, little fish." Dmitri leaned in close to Finnegan II's bowl on the coffee table and made kissing faces. Finnegan II would have sprung into action had another Siamese fighting fish appeared on the scene, but he was bored by the antics of a primate on the other side of his fishbowl glass.

The mafia boss sat back on his couch and snapped his fingers a few times.

"Hey, look over here, you dumb-ass fish."

But Finnegan II remained unmoved.

"Hell. I've seen junkyard dogs with more charisma than that thing," Dmitri said to the henchman beside him.

"He's probably a little traumatized," I said. "What with his bowl being moved and all."

Roman sneered. "Hey, stick your finger in the water, Boss, and chase him around with it."

"No, you'll contaminate the water...his fins will rot," I warned. From the bowl, Finnegan II flicked his obscenely long tail. Dmitri wasn't far off when he called him a dumb-ass fish. Having been bred for hundreds of years for his beautiful fins, he was now so burdened by them he would never survive in the wild. Finnegan II's life tasks had been selectively reduced to eating the food that dropped from above, looking decorative in his bowl, and earning Dmitri millions of dollars.

Dmitri looked at me. "Show me his thing."

"Um..." Crap. I sat down on the ottoman near the coffee table. Finnegan's "thing" was pretty simple. You placed two items that represented the teams in his field of view, and whichever one he swam to would be the winner of the next game. Except, of course, I always videoed him swimming to both teams and posted the video accordingly.

"The game's less than two hours away." Dmitri cocked his head to the side and gave me a smile more teeth than lips. "Go on, make him do his thing."

"Like now?"

"Yeah, now."

Shit.

"It's all in the box, isn't it?" Peter asked from behind me.

I got up and walked over to the kitchen table that held all of Finnegan's stuff. Peter followed and watched me root through the beer can jackets and little pencil sharpeners shaped like football helmets.

"Help me out here," I whispered to him, "I don't even know who's playing."

"Cleveland Browns and Buffalo Bills," he whispered back.

I found a bobble-head of a blue buffalo and handed it to him. "Who's the favorite to win?"

"Damn, girl. How can you run a gambling website and not know basic stuff like this?"

I uncovered a Browns keychain bottle opener and snatched it up.

"It's not a gambling website, it's a scam website. Get the difference?"

"It's the Buffalo Bills, three to one. The Browns have had a terrible season so far. Can you make him swim to that buffalo thing without Dmitri suspecting?"

"Probably not."

We returned to the coffee table and set up the items in Finnegan's line of view. The fish viewed the memorabilia with even less interest than he'd regarded the mafia boss. The seconds stretched into more seconds. Possibly even a minute.

"There," I said. "He flicked his fin."

"Which way?" Dmitri asked.

"The Buffalo Bills. Definitely towards Buffalo Bills."

"Hang on," Roman said. "I didn't see a flick."

"Sometimes the fish is subtle," I said. "There was a flick."

A tall black-haired guy behind Dmitri gave a derisive snort. "That wasn't even subtle. It was equivocal."

Dmitri's gaze flicked to his henchman and back to me. "We don't want equivocal. There will be a lot of my money riding on this."

"Look," I said, "I'm the one who's interpreted his last seven predictions. Correctly. He flicked towards Buffalo Bills."

"Well, okay, if that's..."

Who knows what happened next? Maybe Finnegan II thought he saw a glint of light that looked like a bit of falling food, or he decided to exercise more for the health of his little two-chambered heart. Or perhaps he'd channeled a spirit from the grave...the spirit of Finnegan I who was upset about being flushed down the toilet in Mundo Des Mascotas instead of being properly laid to rest in a tissue box next to the bomb shelter.

He swam toward the Browns bottle opener—straight for it—until he bumped his nares against the glass and stayed there, his little decorative fins waving about, clearly choosing the team least likely to win tonight.

"Well, that's one fish who knows his own mind. Peter, get that bookie Eisenhower on the phone," Dmitri said. "And someone turn on the TV. Let's see if that pre-game show is on yet."

Despite running a sports website, I don't know much about sports. This isn't as stupid a strategy as it sounds, though. There are plenty of smart folks who think about sports pretty hard all of the time, and, like anyone who's spent any time getting good at programming, I've learned the hard way that you shouldn't reinvent the wheel.

That is why, when the Buffalo Bills' quarterback flipped over in a freak tackle, injured his ankle, and was carried off the field on a stretcher, I sat still, my bottom barely gripping the edge of the couch cushion, as the *bratva* shouted and waved their beer cans and goldfish crackers around me. I had no emotional context for such an event, so I couldn't get a visceral handle on the enormity of it. I did know the odds had changed a little in favor of the Browns, although I tried not to hope too much.

But when the Browns managed a 44-yard interception, causing them to defeat the Buffalo Bills 37 to 24, and Dmitri landed a friendly slap on my shoulder, I did sigh with relief. Fractions can seem pretty small, but there's a heck of a difference between unlikely and impossible. Every once in a while, that difference pays off.

"Fish Girl," Dmitri said, "your fish is magic. Pure magic. I would not have bet on the Browns without him."

"I'm glad it worked out," I said, and I meant it. "So, can I go now?"

"Hang on," he said. "That fish is not special because *he's* special. He's special because of you."

I couldn't think of an answer to that.

"Think of the possibilities," he went on. "Not just football. Basketball, boxing, soccer...you and me and a couple of trained-up fish could make a lot of money."

"Yeah," I said. "We do all of that. I'll come back tomorrow, and we can—"

"No," he said. "I think I don't take risks. I think you stay here as a guest."

"When my dad finds out about this, you're going to be sorry."

Dmitri turned his cold eyes on me. Crap. I hadn't meant to say that.

Dmitri didn't laugh, but he humphed like I was funny. He said, "If your dad can make me sorry, he's a special man indeed."

6

I pulled on the two metal handcuffs that fastened me to the bedframe, one arm on each side.

"I thought Dmitri said I was a guest," I said to Roman.

He shrugged. "This is how he treats guests. You think you can get out of that?"

"Give me time," I said.

That was the wrong thing to say, because then Roman shackled my feet.

He stood back to inspect his handiwork. I resisted the urge to test my bonds again and give him the satisfaction.

"Where's that weird-ass twit gone?" he asked the guy standing behind him. I guessed he meant Peter.

The guy behind him looked at me funny. "Had some personal stuff to take care of, apparently. Dmitri gave him a few hours off."

Roman's soft, china-red mouth twisted up in a nasty fake cheese-orange smile. He'd eaten a whole bag of Cheese Puffs during the game. But before the hamster in his brain could get the wheel up to speed, Dmitri's voice drifted down the hall, like an irritated father.

"Hey, Roman...Roman! Bring the car around, we're going to

go pay Eisenhower a visit." And then quieter but still audible: "This is going to be great."

"Stay here," Roman told me, one hand on the doorknob.

"Sure," I said.

They walked out and shut the door behind them. I settled in. The last few hours had exposed some lacunas in my training regimen, but when it comes to waiting, bound and locked in a darkened room, (thanks, Mom, thanks, Dad) I am an old hand.

Hours later, a yellow stripe of light appeared at the door, and my eyes flipped open like a shot. I hadn't been asleep, more like a deep alpha state, transcending the persistent itch behind my knee that I could not reach. It was Roman...I could smell the artificial cheese flavor from across the room. There was a sweet undertone of alcohol. He was drunk.

"You awake?" he shut the door, cutting off the light again.

"Yes." It was still night. The light well at the basement window was dark.

"How 'bout I take some of those shackles off?"

"Yes," I said. "That would be really great. There's this itch behind my knee that I can't quite reach—"

I could sense him moving closer. "I just need a little trade. Nothing much."

I heard two sounds then. Innocuous in daily life: in this context, terrifying. The jingle of a belt buckle, and the quick scratch of a short zipper.

But I had to get out of these shackles. I had to get back to my basement and to my dad, whatever the cost.

"Fine," I said.

"If you're nice to me now, I'll go easier with the rest of it. You might even like it."

The smell of old urine, then, mixed with some sort of unwashed underwear smell right in my face. Smooth, mushroom-shaped flesh tried to force its way past my lips.

A sudden wave of panic broke over my head and realized I

had vastly underestimated the price he wanted me to pay. Time to improvise.

I bit.

He felt it and jerked back, but not before I did some damage. I tasted iron, and he lurched away and stood there, hunched, panting, and cupping his crotch in his hands while I sputtered and spat.

"You broke the skin, you little..." He let go, then pulled his gun from his waistband and raised the barrel to my face. I tossed my head to the side—some base animal instinct to avoid the final shot—even though it was useless. Oh, stop it, I told myself. Engage your higher reasoning.

"Think before you shoot," I snapped. "Dmitri will be pretty pissed if you kill me."

The barrel of the gun shook close to my eye, and then with a frustrated snort, Roman aimed it up at the ceiling and brought the butt of the gun down hard on my temple. My head recoiled off the mattress and gray snow pushed in the edges of my vision. I struggled to see through the small clear window in the middle.

The room flooded again with yellow light from the hall. I squinted at the silhouette there.

"Hey, what are you doing here?" Roman said. "Shut the door."

"What are *you* doing here?" I recognized Peter's voice. "Thought you said getting off with her was disgusting."

Roman laughed. "Turns out I'm a disgusting guy."

"Leave her," Peter said. "Get out of here."

Roman whirled around to face him. "Or what, you pussy-faced little shit?" He took a step forward and pushed Peter in the chest. "You get out of here. Before I run to Dmitri and tell him all about you."

"Tell him what?"

"That you're a cop."

It happened so fast, I heard it rather than saw it. The sound of neck cartilage popping, like someone's dodgy knee. A heavy weight slammed down on my chest—I tried to scoot out from under it—but my chains snapped taut and I was trapped. I watched the oxygen drain from Roman's stunned face like a time-lapse sunset. Watch his eyes watch me—and then blink slow and...watch nothing.

"Goddammit," Peter said. "That is going to generate a shit-load of paperwork."

He dragged the weight from me and I could sense him rifling Roman's pockets. A tinkle of keys and he was releasing my arms.

"You okay?" Peter asked, leaning in and looking at my face. "What's that on your head?" He brushed my hair away with his fingers, and at the feel of his touch, my whole body recoiled. I scooted away until the shackles at my feet snapped taut.

"Come back, Rain, there's a bit of blood on your face."

"Not mine." I wiped my mouth with the back of my hand before he could get to it.

Peter grunted, looked down at Roman's body, and nudged him over. Roman's neck rolled loosely, nauseatingly, as he flopped onto his back and his wounded crotch was exposed.

"I'll be damned. That's my girl." Peter glanced at me with respect.

I started to shake.

"Jesus, Rain, I'm so sorry." Peter bent and released my feet. "I'm sick that you had to go through this. I never thought it would go this far."

I couldn't get my teeth to unclench enough to tell him to go to hell.

He stood, opened the door, and peeked out. Then he shut it and came back to me. "I would have gotten you out earlier, but we're down to the short strokes of a big operation. We're talking three years and several million dollars big, you understand?"

I tried to shake my head no, but it might have just come out as shaking.

"I finally got it organized. Though I never should have left you." He put his hand over his mouth, then took it away, his jaw set hard. "Well, what's done is done. I'm going to get you out of here without blowing my cover. In a few minutes, my buddies are going to fake a drive-by shooting out front. With any luck, Dmitri's men should all head that way. There'll be a car waiting out back to take you to safety. Okay? Understand? Come on, stand up for me now."

He grabbed my arm, near the armpit and tried to lift me. The part of me that understood he was trying to help me—that wanted to please him so that he would help me more—tried to stand. But whatever chemical my muscles needed to work had been all used up fighting Roman. My legs folded like a marionette. We sat on the bed. He took my jaw in his hand again and this time I was just too wrung out to fight.

"Where's that teenage ninja girl who's always trying to kill me? I need her back now."

"Who are you?" I asked. It was still hard to focus. I lifted a hand and smeared the blood on my temple, my own blood this time.

"Roman was right. I'm with the FBI."

It hit me like a bucket of water in the face. "You're with Dad! Dad found me!"

"Wait a sec there...what's this about your dad?"

But then a giant hand squeezed my ribs. I struggled for breath. "Oh, God, it's all a Loyalty Test! Did I pass? Do you know if I passed?"

Peter shook his head. "Wait...are you saying that your dad is an FBI agent?"

I nodded.

"Shit." Peter stood and slammed his hand into the wall. "Shit. No one ever tells me anything around here."

He paused a moment, as if thinking fast, and then quickly unzipped his hoodie. I watched as he took off a black vest and put it around me, leading my arms though as if I were a toddler. It lay heavy on my chest like guilt. He put the hoodie over the vest.

"When your dad finds out I could have let you go in the mall...when he finds out I left you alone with Roman..." Peter winced. "Okay, Rain, tell me straight. How high is your dad's pay grade?"

I spread my fingers across my chest, feeling the soft jersey of the hoodie slipping over the stiff Kevlar underneath. Trust no one, my dad had always taught me. Even within the FBI, there were rival factions, most of whom were enemies of the True Patriots. But Peter had to be for real. He had to be.

"He works the big jobs, international terrorism. Chemical attacks on major cities, that kind of thing."

Peter pressed his lips together. "My shit is cooked, isn't it?"

"Pretty much," I said.

Peter rubbed his jaw with his hand. He pulled a tiny wire from behind his ear. "Hey," he said into it, "screw the integrity of the operation. Whatever it takes to get the girl out, we do it, okay?"

A pause, as he listened to the answer.

"Yeah, I mean it, whatever it takes," he said. "You'll have to trust me." He tucked the wire away and pulled me up. "Can you walk now?"

"Yes, sir," I said. I stood.

"That's my girl." A popping noise came from the front of the house, then far away shouts and thumps. He went to the door and peered through again. "Come on quickly, Rain. This shit's about to get real."

THE FIRST TIME it got real with me, I had to leave my toys behind. Leave the apartment and the girl I played with across the hall and everything in my tiny four-year-old world. I don't remember any of the toys now, but I remember that's why Mom let me put a quarter in the toy machine at the front of a restaurant. Let me put a quarter in and turn the handle and get a little surprise in a plastic egg-like thing.

It turned out to be a cube of clear plastic with a black fly embedded in it. Mom explained in the car that it was supposed to be an ice cube, a joke ice cube. "You put it in someone's glass with real ice cubes and they get surprised by the fly."

I sat in the back in my car seat and touched my tongue to the ice cube, pretending it was really ice, wet and cold. It was better than listening to the drama in front. At four, I couldn't understand the words, but I could hear the anger that went on and on, mile after mile, day after day. My spit made the plastic wet, but it was never cold. And it tasted funny, of bitter chemicals. Even then, I knew if I put it in a real drink, I'd know it was fake just by the taste alone.

THERE WAS a moment when my heart stopped, when two guys shouldering heavy artillery pushed past in the dim hall. But they didn't stop us; they were headed for the front of the house.

"Hey, Peter." One guy paused just before he went up the steps. "Dmitri is looking for you and Roman."

Peter said, "Where is he?"

"Last I saw he was heading for the back of the house. Keeping his high-value ass well out of trouble."

"Damn," Peter said to me. "I thought for sure he'd pull a Putin and lead the charge from the front."

"Is there another way out?" I asked.

He thought for a moment. "Let's try the garage."

Neither he nor I paused to consider that the guy in the hall might have been wrong. So, when we burst into the garage, we were pretty unprepared for the bright lights, the men milling around, and Dmitri's explosive voice.

"Peter," he bellowed, "good, you've already got Fish Girl. Where's Roman?"

"Uh...somewhere behind me." Peter gave me a wild glance.

"No time to wait," Dmitri continued. "In the SUV, all of you. I want the fish in my lap, Fish Girl next to me, and Peter will drive." One of his men handed him Finnegan's bowl, and he climbed carefully into the rear of the nearest SUV. His voice rose to a shout. "The rest of you follow."

What do you do when a Russian mafia boss tells you to get in his SUV? If there was one thing my training had taught me, it was how to deal with unforeseen contingencies. Peter's slight shake of his head had told me all I needed to know, that our best bet for escape was to go along. So, I slipped in next to Dmitri, and Peter got behind the wheel.

"What's the plan, boss?" He met Dmitri's gaze in the rear-view mirror.

"Those damn meth dealers are always drive-by shooting at me. I always shoot back, two, three times through window, then it's over." Dmitri leaned forward. "Not this time. We're going to follow those bastards, blow their asses sky-high, and then lay low in the Presidio ranch for a month. Cross the border if we have to."

"Do you really need me for all that?" I asked him, panic rising in my chest despite my resolve. The weekend after next, Tabernakl had said. He'd have everything ready to go by then. I had to get home. I had to—very, very soon—warn Dad.

He turned his ice-blue eyes to me. "The Cowboys play the Broncos on Sunday. I want you with us."

By us, he meant himself and Finnegan. I glanced at the bowl. At least Finnegan was taking it all in his stride. But Finnegan's world consisted of a featureless sphere, six inches in diameter. I bit my lip. Maybe if Dmitri gave me Internet access...

"They'll be a few blocks away by now. Someone will have called the cops," Peter said. "Maybe we should just head straight for Presidio?"

"No, goddammit." Dmitri's fist slammed down on the back of the front seat. "This time, I fight back."

A black-suited man opened the door and pushed me over to the middle. "No room in the other vehicle," he explained, cocking his pistol. "Hey, Peter."

Peter said, "Hey, Victor."

I met Peter's gaze in the rear-view mirror and the message was clear. *Don't do anything rash.*

"Belt up, little Fish Girl." Dmitri reached over my shoulder and clicked me in. He covered the top of the fishbowl with his hand and leaned forward again. "Now, go."

The door rumbled up and the two Russian mafia SUVs shot with a squeal onto the quiet suburban street. It was the dead of night, which was good, really, because Peter was blasting through the four-way stop signs without even touching the brake pedal. No other cars, except...down a side street...red brake lights...

"There they are. Back up, turn left!"

Peter gave a faint groan. I wondered if he was friends with the federal agents in the drive-by shooting car. But there was no way to ask him. Dmitri grinned and thumped the side of the SUV. Victor lowered his window and racked his gun. Behind us, the other Russian SUV was making the turn. Those guys had been packing some pretty big military shit. I hoped they made sure we were out of the line of fire before they shot at anything.

The red lights on the vehicle ahead went dim. Someone had taken their foot off the brake.

"Damn," Dmitri said. "Can you get a line on them, Victor?"

Victor took aim. But before he could let off a shot, sirens rent the quiet night. Blue and red lights lit up the manicured oak trees around us. Yellow lights in upstairs windows flicked on.

"Shit!" Dmitri slammed the seat again, then quickly steadied Finnegan. "How many of them are there?"

Victor shifted. He stuck his arm out the window, squinted into the darkness and let off three rounds. The sound of the blasts made my ears ring. "At least five."

We ran a light and swerved out of the suburbs onto a bigger

road. The businesses lining the street were lit, but everyone was home asleep. Almost everyone. Peter put his foot down and we shot ahead past six guys in a rusting pickup, but not before three more police cars peeled onto the road behind us.

"I can't get a good shot like this," Victor complained. He unbuckled his seatbelt and turned around, bracing his spine against the front driver seat.

Red traffic lights swung above the road ahead, just behind a highway overpass. Peter turned onto the access ramp, pushing me into the expensive cloth of Dmitri's sleeve. The feel of his warm flesh beneath churned my stomach.

The whole area was under construction. Peter struggled to keep his speed in the narrow lane marked by orange and white striped barrels; if we went off the road, we would immediately be mired in dirt and machines.

"There were way too many cops, way too fast," Dmitri said. "This had to be a setup."

Victor gave him a hard glance. "Agreed."

I bit my lip. In the front seat, Peter was silent. We passed bright work-lights on the left and humming diggers ponderously re-arranging the earth, and then the SUV shot onto the highway.

"Hey, where the hell did you say Roman was again?" Dmitri asked Peter.

Peter glanced in the mirror at me. "He was right behind us."

"Yeah," I said. "He was right behind us."

"Goddammit, Peter, don't bullshit me here! I'm not stupid."

We passed two cop cars that were hanging out with some bulldozers on the median. They fired up their lights and tried to cut us off. Peter swerved to the right and squeezed the SUV through the gap, but the other Russian SUV, the one that was supposed to be covering us, squealed to a stop. At our speed, the tableau was far behind us in a flash. But I could see that the other police cars would struggle to make it around the stopped vehicles. Precious seconds lost to them, gained for us. We were almost alone on the highway.

"I wouldn't bullshit you, Dmitri. I don't know what happened to him."

"Out with it," Dmitri said. "Your loyalty is to me, no one else."

"Dmitri, look—"

"Shit," Victor interrupted from the back seat. "You think he's a snitch."

"Exactly," Dmitri said. "A snitch."

Despite this accusation, Peter held the wheel steady, somehow. Maybe it was simple—he was going way too fast. Out on the highway, green exit signs had been erected, but were still covered with packing paper. The lines of orange barrels started up again. What were they going to do, anyway, blow his brains out at ninety miles per hour?

Victor shifted. "But Roman...a snitch? No way."

Peter shot a glance at him. "You mean Roman?" he asked in a small voice.

"Think about it. The cops show up...and the guy nowhere to be found," Dmitri said.

"Q.E.D.," I said. I used my helpful voice.

Victor screwed up his face at me. "What?"

I said, "*Quod erat demonstrandum*. It's Latin for..."

Peter was looking at me in the mirror again. I could see his silent plea. I pressed my lips together.

But Dmitri was nodding. "I have suspected we had an infiltrator for a while. Now, I know."

Ahead of us, a huge unfinished intersection loomed, two major highways joining in a tangle of overpasses and underpasses: at least they would in a year or two. Now they looked like the science fiction ruins of some advanced civilization.

"Maybe it's for the best," Dmitri went on. "Now that I know Roman was the snitch, we can move forward."

Lines of pylons rose into the sky, and bridges ended abruptly in thin air. Peter's hands were white on the wheel.

"Peter, I want you to take his place. When we get out of this, you're going to go through all my records, find out exactly what the bastard was up to."

Up ahead, two semis were passing a third, blocking the inner two lanes. Peter pulled into the slow lane and undertook them.

"Sure thing, boss." I could just imagine that shit-eating grin.

"We still have to shake these guys," Victor pointed out. He looked a bit peevish at Peter's promotion.

"It's a matter of damage control." Dmitri leaned back, his hands gently cupping the sides of Finnegan's bowl. "But even if we don't shake these cops, we still have plenty of capital for negotiations."

I didn't like the way Dmitri was looking at me.

"What do you mean by capital for negotiations?" I asked him.

"I mean fingers," he said. "Yours. Someone must want you back. We'll send them straight to the police, let them figure out who." He grinned. "One or two in an envelope does the trick every time."

I balled my hands into fists and shoved them between my legs. "I thought you said I was a guest."

"The nature of a guest is fluid," he answered. "Now you are capital."

Goddammit. I had been telling Dad for ages that I wanted to go on a real operation, that I was ready to do what it took to fight crime and keep America safe, but a girl had to have limits.

I shot my hand out, grabbed the rim of Finnegan's bowl, and overturned it.

Dmitri let out a shout as the water slopped onto the seat and the floor. Finnegan landed on my knee and flapped a few times before flopping into the floor to sacrifice his little life for me.

"Get that fish back!" Dmitri shouted.

Victor, next to me, tried to obey, lowering his legs, then lifting them in a panic as he realized he might squish Finnegan. Dmitri slapped my knees aside and bent as low as his old-man's belly would allow to locate Finnegan on the floor before it was too late.

I looked up and saw that we were not in the lane for South Texas, but the exit-only lane for Abilene. The exit-only lane—closed because of the construction. Worse, Peter was looking at us, not the road.

"Peter, look out!" I yelled at him.

He swerved too late, and the SUV headed right for a bridge pylon. We plowed into the crash barrels at speed, exploding them all before coming to rest. It took perhaps five seconds for my physical mass to decelerate, but some unspecified amount of time for my biological systems to catch up—to realize we had crashed—to lift my head and open my eyes.

We were stopped just half a foot from the concrete. Sand from the crash barrels coated the inside of the car. Cool dregs of fish-bowl water were pooling around my buttocks. In the front, Peter's airbag had deployed, and he flapped about, trying to work his way free. Victor was twisted at an awkward angle. There was blood at his temple, and he wasn't moving. On the other side of me, Dmitri was slowly rubbing his eyes.

I pulled the gun from Victor's limp hand. The handle was still warm. I checked the safety and pointed it at Dmitri's temple.

"Don't move," I told him, "because I'm really pissed off right now. Especially about the finger thing."

Dmitri's reddened eyes rolled up. The slack skin of his cheeks started to jiggle with rage. "Peter?" he yelled. "Peter, you there?"

"Yes, boss?" The airbag finally deflated, and Peter turned around to face us.

"Disarm her. Now."

Peter saw me and the gun and his lips compressed into a thin line. He glanced at Dmitri, then at me. In his face I could see the last several years of his undercover career—all that kissing Dmitri's ass and enduring Roman's insults—finally paying off as he got access to Dmitri's inner circle now that Roman was out of the picture. His whole undercover operation was about to end—whether he wanted it to or not—because of me.

"I just promoted you, Peter," Dmitri said. "I expect a certain level of responsiveness."

To hell with all that. I hadn't asked to be kidnapped. And I really was upset about the finger thing. I was upset about all of it.

"Peter," I said, "don't forget who my dad is. Your shit is cooking."

It took him a moment more to decide which course of action would ruin his career more. Then a sigh, Peter pulled out his gun and aimed it at Dmitri's skull.

"Dmitri Andropov, I'm placing you under arrest."

7

When Agent Peter Angelopolos came onto the ward, the eyes of the nurses followed his trajectory. Even the jaded senior nurses glanced up, then down at their clipboards, then up again, covertly. In his clean white polo shirt and slacks, with a freshly shaven face, he looked like a professional sportsman on his way to a press conference, not the twitchy aspirational thug I first met.

The guard at my door aimed a playful fist at his shoulder. He dodged it and landed an air punch just short of the man's jaw. The guard laughed and everyone in the room indulgently chuckled. This, apparently, was the real Peter. It gave me an ache in my chest. When my dad walked through his office, it must have been the same. I would have liked to see that, especially given the persecution that was our daily lot.

Peter walked to my hospital bed. "How's my ninja girl?"

I set aside the book I'd been leafing through, *Principles of Cognitive Psychology*, and raised one eyebrow. "I study kung fu, not ninjitsu."

"I know. I'm just messing with ya." He gave me a chummy slap on the shoulder. I gripped the sheets as a sudden wave of nausea broke over me.

"Hey." From the bedside chair, my caseworker, Carol Anne Cheung stood. She put a hand on Peter's shoulder. "Go lightly with her, okay? She's fairly traumatized."

Carol Anne had shiny black hair in neat braids that reached her shoulders. After the car crash and Dmitri's arrest, I'd expected to be cleared by the hospital quickly. I hadn't expected it to take the rest of the night, and I hadn't expected Carol Anne to show up in the morning either. Truth was, I didn't quite know what to make of her. Carol Anne smelled like a cocktail of expensive grooming products: hand cream, hair serum, shoe polish, and perfume. Each of her nails was a shiny, flawless ellipsoid of dark polish flecked with gold. She asked a lot of questions about a lot of things, about my living situation, my family, even my feelings. Complicated questions—ones that required a lot of mental energy to answer.

"There's no right answer," she told me at one point.

It was meant to be reassuring, but of course, there *was* a right answer. There is *always* a right answer: it's the one that gets caseworkers and authorities off your back so that the mission can continue. This has always been true my whole life, but now, with Tabernakl planning his attack on the State Fair, it was truer than ever.

Eventually, she stopped asking questions, but it didn't feel like it was because my answers satisfied her. It felt like I'd been diagnosed. Still, she'd shown me the textbook in her bag and there was some interesting stuff in it. We weren't playing for the same team, but I found myself respecting her, nevertheless.

"I'm fine," I told Peter, shaking the black fog from the edges of my vision and swallowing the bile rising in my throat. "The medication makes me woozy."

Carol Anne's nostrils flared, just the tiniest bit. "She's a bit banged up."

"Two concussions under observation," I told him. I grinned, like it was a joke. "Stitches on my wrist, bruises to the face, bruises consistent with a serious fall, various scrapes and scratches—" I indicated the drip hanging at the side of the bed. "—and chronic under-nutrition, apparently."

I met Peter's eyes. Our relationship had not, by conventional measures, gotten off to a good start, what with me trying to kill him three times (okay, maybe four) and blowing his cover during a high-speed chase out on the highway. His behavior hadn't been that laudable either. He'd stood by while I was tortured by Roman, thrown me down the steps, and refused to let me escape in Dillard's. However, you had to consider the big picture. He had arranged a drive-by shooting just for me and killed Roman at a critical point.

I needed someone, badly, to get me out of here, and he was the most likely candidate. These people surrounding me might be patching up my cuts and bruises, but I was in even more danger now than when I was being pistol-whipped by Roman. They might be FBI, but they weren't Dad's FBI, and that put me in grave danger.

As anyone who watches action movies will know, renegade factions at odds with each other happens all the time in the FBI. Of course, simplifications have to be made in Hollywood for the sake of pace and drama, but the infighting—that bit is pretty straight up. There are others who don't have their priorities straight, who would rather see a fellow agent go to jail and America fall to her enemies than, for instance, fudge the budget a bit here and there. Given the sad state of our nation, it will come as no surprise that these others outnumbered the True Patriots by quite a lot. In fact, I have never met another member of the True Patriots besides myself and my father, although Dad assures me that once I start doing more fieldwork, that will change.

I guess all this sounds counter-intuitive, but in a moment of weakness in that dark basement room, I'd blurted out the secret of my father, and all this trouble was the result. So, there you go. Somehow, I'd have to get away yet again. Carol Anne seemed genuinely nice, but she had fixed ideas about what was best for

me. Peter, on the other hand, seemed like a man I could talk to—
if I played my cards right.

"I came by to say thanks for supporting me at the suspension
hearing this morning," Peter said.

I should probably mention that they hadn't suspended him.

"Sorry for wrecking the car," I said, "and your operation."

"It's okay." He rubbed his neck and smiled. "Actually, that
stuff was kind of cool."

Part of me suspected he might be buttering me up—but I
didn't really mind being Peter's bagel. The nurses peered
through the observation window at us. I gave them a cheeky
smile.

"I brought you this too." He tossed a pink kid's lunch box on
the sheets. "I thought you might like something healthy. No
nitrites."

"Wow." I unzipped it. "Baby carrots and organic hummus,
that's really great."

Carol Anne flipped the lunch box lid up with a wine-red nail
and sniffed. "Little bunnies? How classy," she said.

Peter shrugged. "My daughter left it behind when she and
her mom..."

He trailed off. Carol Anne raised an artificially arched
eyebrow even more.

"Shit, Carol Anne," he said, "what's your problem? What
kind of person doesn't like cute bunnies?"

The raw garlic in the hummus made the back of my throat
burn. I was actually pretty touched that he'd thought of me. "So,
what's the situation?" I asked.

He sat at the foot of the bed. "We're trying to salvage what
we can. Dmitri's cocaine and assault rifle deal is off, of course.
But the good news is, we have you now." He rested his hand on
my shin where it made a ridge under the sheets. "A real live
Dmitri kidnap victim, and we're going to nail his ass to the
wall."

I could feel the heat of his palm through the thin sheets. A swell of nausea pushed at my chest. "What happened to the other people he kidnapped?"

Peter shrugged. "Wouldn't we all like to know?"

Not a thought I wanted to dwell on. "Did you find my dad?"

"They're still making inquiries, Rain. You were right. Whatever operation he's on, it's pretty classified."

Dammit. I'd hoped for a different answer, but it made sense. "Listen," I said, "can I talk to you, in private?"

Carol Anne looked at the sheets, where Peter's hand still rested. "Is it really necessary?"

"Please?" I asked her.

She looked at me and then at Peter for a moment. Heavy gold glinted at her neck and ears. Peter tilted his head at her.

She sighed. "All right, Rain. Give me my book back and I'll read it on the other side of the room, out of earshot."

I gave her the textbook, and she went to sit in a visitor chair by the window.

"She has a big test next week. I was helping her review stressor characteristics," I told Peter. "Listen, I need a favor."

"Anything, Rain, you know that."

"The doctor said I could be released this afternoon. Could you drive me home?"

He gave me a half smile. It revealed his very white teeth. "What's the rush? Hanging out in bed all day, nurses waiting on you hand and foot? Man, I'd live it up while I could."

"I have to get home. I have stuff to do."

"What stuff?"

"I don't care to elaborate."

"Miscellaneous stuff, huh?" He looked at me for a moment. "Hey, Carol Anne," he called over his shoulder, "what were your guys' plans for Rain here? You got a crisis placement for her?"

"Victims Services found her a bed, over at New Transitions," she called back. "Lucky to get it, everywhere else is full."

"It's a residential treatment facility, a mental hospital," I told him. "I'd rather be at home. I'm not a mental patient."

Carol Anne sighed and came over to my bed.

"You're not fine," she said. "You were kidnapped, tortured, and sexually assaulted yesterday. Even one of those is pretty heavy stuff. I don't want to scare you, Rain, but there are going to be repercussions that you will have to deal with."

I bit my lip. From her perspective, it made sense. She looked at me there in the hospital bed and saw a bruised young female, a textbook victim like the ones she'd just been reviewing for her evening class. All during our long morning chat, I had told her nothing about my history, nothing about the hardships and many Loyalty Tests I had been trained to endure since birth.

I wanted to tell her that any day a bomb doesn't go off is a pretty good one for me. A day when only the bad guys die is even better. But of course, I could say none of that.

"That's not quite true," I said, "it was only attempted sexual assault, and the bastard who did it is dead now. The rest of it, the kidnapping, it's over, right? We're good."

"I admire your resilience." She tilted her head at me. "I can see it's protecting you. But if that protection starts to crack—" She sighed. "—when that protection starts to crack, I don't want you to be alone."

For an instant, I felt this crazy dizzy thing, like when you look over the edge of a mountain road and want to leap over the crash barrier and fall forever, even though your brain knows you'd hit the ground all too soon.

"Plus," Carol Anne said, gently, "you're a minor. The state has a duty of care here."

I swallowed, hard. "I'm nineteen."

Carol Anne and Peter glanced at each other.

"Honey," Carol Anne said, "the doctors and I both agree you don't look a day over fifteen. Unless you can prove it..."

"All my ID is back at the house." In fact, all three sets of ID were back at the house—the ones that said I was fifteen, seventeen, and nineteen. I put my head in my hands. This was getting complicated.

"You know," Peter said, "shrinks aren't such a bad thing. They even make us go talk to them. Occasionally."

Carol Anne looked sharply at Peter like she suspected some sarcasm but couldn't prove it. But then her phone bleeped and she pulled it out. "I have to take this," she said to us. "Excuse me."

I watched her stop outside the door, and I forced the dizzy feeling down. Emotions are luxuries only civilians can afford. This was my mess, and I'd have to clean it up myself.

"Peter, listen to me," I said, "you look like a guy who can think for himself."

"What's that supposed to mean?" he asked.

"I mean you follow company policy like a guideline, not a law. Like with me, you had to think out of the box a couple of times, right?"

"Circumstances justified it," he said, a little defensively. He took one of the carrot sticks he had brought me and bit one end. "But making judgment calls on the ground is one thing. I don't break the law on a regular basis."

"Even if it meant saving thousands of lives, saving maybe half a city?"

He stopped chewing the carrot. "Now what would make a girl like you say a thing like that?"

"Here's the thing," I said, "I help my dad out, on the Internet. I hunt terrorists, ones planning large-scale attacks with poison gas and stuff."

"Bullshit," he said. "That's a job for experts."

"You think I'm not an expert?" I looked him directly in the eye. The last twenty-four hours had knocked me out of my comfort zone. Dealing face to face with people was not something I was used to. But terrorist attacks? Here, I knew what I was talking about. "How about the sarin threat, Peter?"

"Okay," he said, "what about the sarin threat?"

"Breathe sarin in, and your nose runs a bit. Soon your chest gets tight. Acetylcholine contracts your muscles, but the sarin stops it from degrading. Your muscles can't relax. You drop to the floor...vomiting, pissing, and shitting. But what kills you is the spasming. You can't relax enough to breathe. Anyone who comes to help you is poisoned by the residual gas in your clothes."

"Rain, I'm not arguing with you there...but..."

But I was just getting started. "Or how about botulinum toxin? Everywhere these days. I bet Carol Anne's face is pumped full of it. But if it gets deeper into your system...say you buy contaminated food, like this hummus, or baby food. Seven toxins start their work. Eyelids droop, muscles go flaccid. Soon the child can't even manage a breath and suffocates, unable to even whisper goodbye. Is that what you want to happen? Is that how you want your daughter to die?"

He shifted on the bed. His face was white. He said, "If you have information about an imminent attack, here or anywhere, you'd better tell me right now."

I looked at the sheets. As Dad had drilled me endlessly, I should only give specific information to the True Patriots. But the circumstances were out of my control, and the State Fair attack could be big. Should I risk betraying the True Patriots' operation? Did I trust Peter?

"Just take me home. I can handle it from there."

The color slowly crept into Peter's face. He shook his head a little.

"Thousands of lives at risk. But taking you home is all I have to do to stop it? Bullshit." Peter folded his arms across his chest. "Remind me. What exactly is it you do for your dad?"

I looked around the room. The nurses were still glancing through the window, but they couldn't hear. Carol Anne appeared to be absorbed in her phone call. I'd have to take the risk, sooner or later. Still, I kept my voice quiet.

"I monitor chat forums, data-mine Internet transactions. If I'm not there, watching, all the time, there might be another biological weapons attack. I might not have time to warn anyone."

"Hold on, what do you mean, another biological attack?"

"Christ," I said. "Do you even work for the FBI? There have been so many. New Orleans, Mount Rushmore, the State Capitols Chlorine Attack...I mean, Christ! If we hadn't stopped them, who knows what would have happened?"

Peter stared at me, mouth open. "State capitols? I've never heard of any of these. Not these specific ones, anyway."

"They must have been above your clearance level."

He let out a soft snort. "Come on. Stuff gets leaked."

"Not by us," I said. "Remember the anthrax letters?"

"Yeah, just after 9/11."

"Twenty-two people got sick. Five died. Two hundred and eighty million people were terrified for their lives." I stabbed a finger into the bed sheets. "Never again. We let that happen, on a regular basis, and the terrorists win. The bastards win, Peter. Secrecy is a part of the way we fight back."

He was still shaking his head. I didn't have him convinced. Not yet.

"Rain," he said. "This is just too weird. Why do you do Finnegan's blog then? Why the betting scams?"

The dizzy feeling was back, that desire—and fear—of making the leap into the unknown, but this time, I leaned forward and made the leap—towards Peter—towards trusting him. "My dad's operations depend on it. Financially. You get what I mean?"

"Not really. FBI operations are funded by taxpayer revenue."

I lowered my voice even more. "Not the ones where deniability is paramount."

He put his hand on his forehead like it hurt. "You're serious."

"You know it's been done before," I said. "There's precedent. Iran-Contra was just the tip of the iceberg."

He chewed his lip and wouldn't look at me. Crap. But I had seen this before with the few people Dad recruited to our cause.

"You're in denial," I told him. "It's a normal reaction. But before you do anything, just ask yourself, are you absolutely sure you know everything the FBI is up to? Are you absolutely sure there's no way I could be telling the truth?"

"I'm ninety-nine percent goddamn sure."

"But are you a hundred percent goddamn sure?" I asked. "Can you really ignore me if you're even one-thousandth of a percent goddamn unsure?"

Peter rubbed his temples. "Wait a moment. Let me think."

Beyond the door, Carol Anne was pacing. Whatever conversation she was having, she wasn't happy about it.

"Thing is," Peter said, "Carol Anne here won't budge an inch unless you tell her everything you just told me." He glanced at her just beyond the door. "She's not going to go for me taking you out of here alone. It will look too weird."

I screwed up my face. "Thing is, the enemy could be anywhere. I'm already taking a chance with you. I can't trust anyone else."

"There's something else you're not taking into account," he said. "Dmitri Andropov."

All the hair on my neck stood up. "What do you mean?"

"Dmitri's been operating in Fort Worth for about fifteen years now. You know how he does it? No matter how good a case we get against him, sooner or later, witnesses retract their testimony." Peter said. "Some of them completely disappear. That's why we're so glad to have you."

"Okay sure," I said, "but—"

Peter leaned in. "No 'buts.' He knows where you live."

Crap. If this could get any worse, I didn't know how. All I wanted was to get away from Carol Anne's concerns, get my report to Dad, and then go to sleep for about forty-eight hours. It was bad enough when I'd been Dmitri's captive. Being a witness for the FBI could turn into a worse nightmare.

"I'll barricade myself in. It's a secure house."

"Secure? No offense," he said, "but there was a key under the front doormat, one you didn't even know about."

I didn't know what to say to that. I couldn't really account for it myself. But he was right. With a shudder, I thought of the bomb shelter in the backyard. I could barricade myself in there, but sooner or later, I'd have to come out again, and who knew what would be on the other side of that door when I did?

"Look," Peter said. "Go to this New Transitions place tonight. I'll come by tomorrow, take you to your house, and you can show me what you have. How does that sound?"

I closed my eyes, exhausted. I had ten...no, nine days. Would another eight hours make a difference?

"Is that it?" Carol Anne's voice rose high enough to reach through the door. "I've already been here an hour after my shift was supposed to end waiting for you guys to—"

"Okay," I said. "One night."

He patted my leg through the sheets again. But higher up this time, on the thigh. "Sure. Tomorrow. You and me, we sort this crap out, okay?"

Carol Anne hung up the phone and came back in through the door, her eyes flashing. "There's been an incident at New Transitions. The facility's been locked down."

Peter asked, "What happened?"

She shrugged. "All I know is they're not admitting anyone else until everybody's down off the roof, including the goat."

I didn't know what to say. Just a moment before, going home was what I wanted. Now that Peter had put me in the picture, I wasn't so sure.

"Is it gonna be another Sunrise Hotel job then?" Peter asked.

"Not if I can help it," she said. "I meant what I said about her needing support, and a hotel room isn't enough." She turned to her phone again. "Let me see what I can do. I haven't opened an official case file yet, so we still have some options. I have a friend who might be able to help."

8

Carol Anne Cheung pulled to a stop in front of a 1950s ranch house with a cactus in the front yard, the kind that has no spines on its flat green paddles. We walked up the front step past the miniature plastic streetlight and stood on the porch, replete with flimsy porch swing and decorative quilt. A woman introduced as Desiree opened the door. Gray wiry hair cut straight across the ends formed a pyramid around her scrubbed face. Heavy silver earrings dangled on either side of her face.

"Rain," she said, "come in! We are so glad to have you with us!"

Inside, everything was shabby eclectic—clutter chic. To our right, the dining room was dominated by a golden wood table and buffet filled-to-bursting with faceless angel statues, china dogs and cats with abnormally large heads, and stuffed teddy bears in unnatural colors.

Carol Anne sat at the table and pulled out a thick sheaf of forms.

"Gosh," Desiree said, "I'd forgotten how many forms there are."

Carol Anne shot her a sympathetic smile. "More every year."

She held them in the air, looking for an empty place among piles of books and magazines.

Desiree started shifting piles away from Carol Anne. "Oh, hang on a sec...there's just a little bit of...gosh...a little spillage there." She looked around for a napkin or towel among the clutter, but then just took the corner of her dress and mopped the table. "Didn't have time to clean up after you called."

"It's no problem," Carol Anne said, setting the papers on the clean spot. "We all get a little behind sometimes."

I squinted at the table, covered with dried rings and little crumbs. I saw that one of the chairs had a cardboard box on its seat, overflowing with letters, newspapers, some sort of paper maché sculpture, and paper plates with yellow feathers stuck to them. There was a strange smell in the house, of grain, meat, and old cat litter. Garlic maybe, mixed with lemons. And something faint, underneath. Patchouli, perhaps.

Desiree turned to me, her earrings swinging. "While we're doing this, would you like to meet the crew?"

I didn't particularly, but even I understood that was the wrong thing to say. She led me into the hall.

"To the right, sweetie, just in there."

I stepped into a living room equipped with a sagging tomato-orange couch and a mismatched coffee-colored love seat. Bird-cages, an obese cat, and spider plants crowded the picture window. Sunbeams streamed through and glimmered on dust motes in the air. In one of the cages, a tiny brown owl with a wing taped to its side stared back. The other was empty. At one end of the red couch, a little blonde girl perched, watching TV. She clutched a calico cat that was phlegmatically resigned to its captivity. On the other end, a boy in black lounged, absorbed in his phone.

He put aside the phone and looked at me. "So," he said, "you must be Rain. The emergency foster kid." Blue-black dyed hair flopped over black glasses and an eyebrow pierced three times.

He was anywhere between thirteen and sixteen, still on the first part of his puberty journey.

"I am," I said.

"What's your story?"

"What do you mean, my story?" I aimed for a bentwood rocker crammed in the corner behind a crate-style coffee table and nearly tripped over a basset hound. With a long-suffering sigh, the dog pulled itself to its feet and waddled out of the way. A similar hound observed me from under the coffee table and let out a bored fart.

"Everything brought to this house has a story," the boy explained. He shifted on the seat, and through the dog fart, I caught the faint whiff of roadkill. Skunk, maybe. "Take Pretty the Owl over there, for instance. Accidentally shot in the wing by some yokel, she'll never fend for herself in the wild again. Now she's with us, scoffing pet store mice and hocking up bone and fur pellets." The owl stared back at him and did not blink. "And over here, we have Reagan. Abandoned in the camping section of Walmart by her meth-head parents on her seventh birthday. For the past nine months, she's had nightmares about a monster at her window. Now she refuses to speak to anyone." From her corner of the couch, wide-eyed Reagan let go of the cat long enough to give me a tiny wave. She leaned forward and pushed a plate of cookies on the coffee table towards me.

I looked down at supermarket cookies. Little patties of high-fructose corn syrup and partially-hydrogenated vegetable oil. But what the heck. I took four.

"And you just missed the exchange student from Turk-menistan," the boy said. "She spent all her money bribing offi-cials to get out of the country and had nothing left to pay for dorm rooms on campus."

"Okay," I said, "I'll tell you. I'm the daughter of a top FBI agent. Yesterday I was kidnapped by the Russian mafia who were after my psychic fish. Fortunately, I was rescued by another FBI agent while the mob was distracted by a staged drive-by shooting. Unfortunately, I'm now a witness, and I don't have any money or a car, so I'm stuck hiding out here for a while."

The boy leaned forward and took a cookie. He chewed it thoughtfully for a moment.

"You know...as one pathological liar to another, I'd recommend you ax the bit about the psychic fish. Too bizarre. Takes me right out of the story."

Reagan picked up a notebook and pencil and began to write furiously.

I thought about it. "You're right. The fish isn't really psychic. So what's your story?"

"Me?"

"You were brought into the house, like the rest of us, right?"

"Actually, I come with the house, I'm Leif, Desiree's son."

"What's with the tortured rebel look?"

"What can I say?" He shrugged. "I'm no good at following rules, but I have a deep and sensitive soul."

I looked around the room. "What's supposed to be in that cage over there? The empty one...next to the owl?"

That got Leif out of his seat. "Shit, has that freaking macaw gotten out again?" But as we all crowded around the cage and peered into the deep tray at the bottom, it was clear the macaw hadn't gotten far. Nor would he, ever again. Reagan stifled a sob.

Leif poked his hand into the cage and nudged the little, clenched feet sticking up in the air. He sighed. "Reagan, go tell Mom we need another shoebox."

Leif explained the situation to me as he, Reagan, and I formed a little procession out the back. Because his mom could never turn away anything in distress, be it human, plant, or animal, all the animals in the house also had something wrong with them, some injury, disease, advanced age, or sometimes all three. It meant that pets were dying all the time.

"This is the fourth one in three months." He held up the shoebox with a blue feather poking out one corner. "Do me a favor and grab the shovel, will ya? It's next to the back door."

I found it, and we walked to the end of the yard, where a little line of stick crosses poked up out of the rock mulch. Leif began to dig. "The sad thing is, it's no good for Reagan. Look at her." I turned and saw her picking dandelions and wiping her eyes on the scruff of the cat. "Thank goodness that cat of hers is too young to kick the bucket."

I went over to where Reagan was inadvertently weeding the yard.

"Hey," I said. "You okay?"

She nodded, then fished in her pocket for the paper she'd been writing on and gave it to me. I looked at the note she shoved in my hand. It said: *Whats your sycik fishes name?*

"Finnegan."

Her eyebrows shot up and she indicated the note. I traded the flowers for the note while she scribbled on the back with a pencil hung around her neck: *Why?*

"Because he has lots of fins."

When she shifted her cat and gave me a shy smile, I found myself smiling back.

"What's your cat's name?"

Good Kitty.

That night, we shared a room. I sat with her while she drew me pictures of the monster that had made her mute, a dark scribble with sharp, curved claws. She pointed at the window until it was clear that the monster always tried to come in there. I stood and inspected the frame.

"Reagan, no wonder you're scared. This window is completely insecure, even for civilians."

She gave her cat a little squeeze. It squeaked like a dog's chew toy.

"I can't sleep with it like this either," I said, biting my lip. After all my dealings with the Russians, how could Carol Anne allow this? It just went to show how naive even experienced professionals could be, and why secret organizations like my dad's were so necessary.

The best way to secure a window was by installing bars across it, but clearly this was beyond our capabilities. There was a special clear film I could use that made the glass difficult to break, but Desiree wouldn't have any, nor would she get me any this late in the evening. No point in asking.

"We'll just have to secure it another way," I told Reagan, running my finger along the aluminum channels. "Do you have any pencils or things like that?"

We jammed pencils and crayons in the channels so even if the window was unlocked, the panel of the window couldn't be slid back. It wouldn't stop a Russian from breaking the glass, but at least they wouldn't sneak in without waking us. I stepped back to survey the work. But then Reagan reached up and gave the window a good yank, scattering the pencils and opening it wide.

I frowned. "We need a strong single length." It didn't look like anything in the room was suitable. Just child's toys of plastic and wood. I spied the candy-pink lamp at her bedside and picked it up. "These things sometimes have threaded steel dowel in the middle," I told her, then paused, looking at the cord. "Pull all the pencils out, Reagan. I have an idea."

We pulled the metal screens out and lined the channels with miscellaneous plastic ephemera: a single Barbie ballet shoe, a Polly Pocket sun hat, and several acrylic craft gems that speckled the carpet. Then we replaced the screens and I cut the cord from the lamp, stripping the wire with my teeth and working one length of the shiny bare copper into each of the screens.

"Stand back," I told Reagan and inserted the plug in the socket.

No fuses blew. The lights did not dim. Kid's toys might be mechanically inferior, but they make excellent insulators.

"Here's how it works," I said. "Right now, it's an open circuit, no current flowing. But if someone were to touch one or both of those screens, they'd complete the circuit with their bodies and get a nasty shock."

Reagan looked at me wide-eyed and silent.

"It's only 110 volts," I reassured her. "Not enough to kill a Russian or a monster, but it will give them a surprise. Give me time to knock them on the head with my kung fu while you bite them."

Her nose wrinkled up.

"On the ankle. Where did you think I meant?"

She didn't wake me once during the night. The next morning, her blonde hair spread out on the pillow like silk, Good Kitty purring contentedly at her feet.

HERE IS the type of Loyalty Test my mom had to pass. I was ten, I think. We lived in Illinois. Dad had an important operation coming up, and he needed support. Mom promised everything she could, but here's the thing: he had just found out about her 401K, the retirement fund she'd gotten when she was an administrator at a college for five years before she'd met and married Dad.

"Does it have to be that?" she'd pleaded. She'd lose half of it in penalties. There wasn't much in there for retirement anyway. She hadn't worked since she'd joined up with my dad.

"Haven't worked?" He'd been furious. "What do you call this? You are working, on an operation of vital importance for the safety of millions of Americans. Your crappy little job filing student reports at some shitty little college was nothing compared to this."

"It was a top state university," she'd said in a tiny voice.

I know all of this because they went over it again and again, day after day.

But it wasn't the thought of retirement that scared her. The FBI would refund the money as soon as the threat was over, like they always promised. Really, she was scared to go to the bank and turn in the paperwork. She thought it might leave a trail the terrorists could follow.

I mean, Christ, just to go to the grocery store, it took me and her an hour to get the wigs and the sunglasses right. Her nerves couldn't handle the stress more than once a week. If we ran out of milk, that was it for a few days because Dad refused to do her jobs for her.

"Wake up, you lazy cow. This is your life. Whatever it takes, you have to adapt."

When we came home from the store one day without any butter, running flat out because a poodle had licked my leg, Dad slapped his two hands hard on the kitchen table, piled us in the car and drove us to downtown Chicago. He let us off outside the Stardust Hotel.

"If you can't hack it in the suburbs, you can just wait here until I'm back from my next operation," he told her.

"How long will you be gone?"

"You know I can't say."

"Can you at least give me some money?"

"You have enough money," he'd sneered.

She'd gripped her purse and looked back at him, shaking her head in little no motions.

"Then adapt," he'd said, and drove off.

In fact, the Stardust was cheap enough for Mom to pay for about a week with the grocery money she had in her purse, and we found the food banks, full of plenty of vegan and whole-grain food donated by well-meaning liberals. But as the end of the week approached—and passed—and there was still no Dad, she started to worry. I wanted to leave. I wanted to go to one of the homeless shelters that had fliers posted up on the wall at the food bank. It was horrible staying in that room all day, with its scratched piece of stainless steel for a bathroom mirror and the dinner plate-sized hole in the ceiling plaster. I'd never been allowed near other children much, but at least I'd had a home-schooling program of mixed traditional academics and FBI agent training. But now, all my homeschooling just stopped. Mom just sat and stared at the wall without moving, for hours. Only fresh wet tracks appeared, silently, on her cheeks, every once in a while. But she refused to go.

"What will your daddy think if he comes back and we're not here?" she'd said.

"We could leave him a note," I told her.

Too risky, she'd said. Too risky leaving a note out where the enemy could find it, too risky going to a shelter where the enemy could be hidden among the homeless. We had to stay as we were told.

Then one day the greasy guy from the front desk knocked on the door and started yelling at Mom, his black comb-over flapping every time he jabbed the air with a finger. He stopped when she started crying—went and got two cans of Coke for us from the vending machine and started over again in a kinder voice while I sat on the bed and drank the most amazing drink I had ever tasted in my whole carob-drinking, sprouted-wheat, grated-carrot life.

It was my first moment of awakening—the realization that my Mom had not told me about everything in the world. I mean, I'd sort of guessed there were bad things like genocide that she glossed over occasionally, but I had never in the depths of my little, innocent heart, suspected she was keeping me from wonderful things like cans of soda as well. I knew then I would have to take my education into my own hands.

Whatever his solution was, she refused. She showed him out and leaned against the shut door with her shoulders tight, like she was afraid he'd try to come back. But then she went to the mirror and peered into it.

"Adapt," she'd said.

She brushed the straggly little hairs escaping from her ponytail. Then she took the entire ponytail out. Did I mention my mom had the best hair ever? Nut brown and wavy and long. I watched, sitting crosslegged on the bed, sipping the sparkling forbidden nectar.

"Adapt," she'd said again. Like an order. Like an insult.

Then she called the desk guy on the hotel phone and kicked me out onto the stairwell. If I thought the room was boring, the seven flights of stairs of the Stardust Hotel had it beat by miles. I mean, you can only recreate Galileo's Leaning Tower of Pisa experiment down the hole in the middle for so long before you've pretty much got the gravity thing worked out. It was too dangerous to test for repeatability anyway, not after I hit the heroin addict on the shoulder with a spit wad.

The stairwell was hot, airless and crap. I got to know it well over the next week—the guy at the front desk had a couple of buddies. But after a couple of days of increasingly brave exploration, way down at the bottom, shoved back in that dirty triangle space, I discovered a treasure. A purse, stolen and then abandoned by someone after they'd stripped it of money. Inside the purse was the wallet with a few things of no use for drug procurement. A frequent flier mileage card, a photo of two boys at the zoo, and a library card. So I went exploring.

The library was a big warm building where the air was perfumed with paper and ink and knowledge. I quickly plowed through the junior non-fiction section and regularly used up my allotted time on the free-access computers. I started in on the adult non-fiction, on the aisle at the low end of the Dewey decimals. Around the middle, I encountered *Gödel, Escher, Bach*; *A Mathematician's Apology*; and *The Elements of Mathematics*. Then onto *Flatland*, Mandelbrot, algebra, game theory. And on, and on, and on.

The books led me to a place like a crystal matrix, clearer than glass. Like a single note more beautiful than sound. I stopped biting my nails and picking holes in my skin. When I was there, of course. In my books, in my library, in my mind. My second revelation.

It was almost Thanksgiving, when I came back to the Stardust Hotel, a note in the pocket of my food-bank coat scrunched forward to avoid the hole where stuff slipped into the lining. I'd found a book on alphabets of the world and written a note for Mom.

It said: "I Love You," transliterated into Greek, Egyptian hieroglyphs, Cyrillic, and Deseret.

But I stopped at the door to our room. It was open. I saw Mom standing there, and Dad, too.

"Dad?" My joy at seeing him at last was tempered by the fact that I only had one note. I couldn't give it to Mom without Dad getting his feelings hurt.

"Out," he said. "I'm talking to your mom."

"Mom?"

"Go. I'll call you when we're done." Her voice was pleading as the door slammed shut.

But she didn't. I worked my way through six of Isaac Asimov's non-fiction essays on the stairwell before going back to find the door open, Mom already in her sunglasses and wig, packing our Goodwill clothes in a plastic grocery bag. She was favoring one foot, and every once in a while she had to wipe her nose. She tried to hide the tissues, but I saw a flash of blood.

"Are you okay?" I knew my note would be too pathetic to cheer her now. I tried to give her a hug, but she waved me back. It made me more frantic. "What's wrong, Mom? Tell me."

She took a shaking breath. "It's nothing really. I just..." She stopped for a moment. "Turns out I didn't understand what 'adapt' was supposed to mean. I got it...a little bit wrong."

This frightened me. That I might get it wrong too. "What does it mean?"

Behind her, the bathroom door opened. It was my dad. The toilet behind him was in the last whine of a flush. He was drying his hands on the yellowed hotel towel.

He said, "It means she's cashing in her 401K."

And that was my third revelation. I mean, I loved my mom, I really did. But everything bad that happened to her? It was her own fault.

9

I sat at the table, my bottom comfortably supported by a thickly padded ergonomic plastic pod. Whiteboards ringed the room, the layered faded texts of poorly-erased notes hinting at a rich archaeology of past meetings. Under my seat, I discovered by touch a selection of plastic levers that promised even further seating customization, but I resisted the urge to experiment. This was my first time in a real meeting room. Where real meetings happened, like with people with real jobs. One had to maintain a certain gravitas.

Especially here in the lion's den—the regional den of lion dens—the FBI Dallas Field Office, Number One Justice Way.

Carol Anne had called early in the morning after my night at Desiree's. "Come to the offices," she'd said over the phone, "the FBI just wants to have a chat before your dad gets here. No pressure. I'll be with you the whole time. You can end the conversation at any point."

The news that Dad was coming to get me was an immense relief. I could complete my mission at last, and I knew he'd be happy with my work. Even better, he'd know how to handle Dmitri Andropov—he'd have some scheme that was better than hiding me away waiting for some unspecified court date. In fact,

I was so happy that when Carol Anne picked me up from Desiree's, it wasn't until we were speeding down the highway that I remembered the plans I'd made with Peter.

"I was hoping to see Peter," I told her. "Will he be there?"

"Yes," Carol Anne had assured me.

But he wasn't. And although the meeting room was pretty neat, the meeting itself wasn't that great. They kept on asking stuff I couldn't answer, not without getting the True Patriots into trouble. I did my best to obfuscate. Carol Anne slowly lost her patience. Agent Hannah Lipman had been intensely doodling on her clipboard for the past twenty minutes, and Agent Joe Lopez was flat out confused.

I couldn't figure out why Peter hadn't shown up. Maybe he figured he didn't need to take me home if Dad was going to show up, which was fair enough. Dad could take me home and I could give him Tabernakl's geocoordinates directly.

Meanwhile, Agents Lipman and Lopez of the FBI had taken me through a whole shopping list of completely irrelevant trivia: why I wasn't at high school or college or work, why there was no food in my house, why my dad thought it was okay to leave me alone for so long. Then we got around to why Dmitri had kidnapped me.

"He mistook me for a computer hacker who'd scammed him," I said.

"Peter seemed to think Dmitri got that bit right," Joe said.

"Of course, I pretended I was a hacker," I said, "I was really scared of both of them."

Thing was, I was getting pretty scared right then. If I didn't end this soon, it was all going to come out. I was scamming suckers out of their money for the greater good of the nation, but I sure couldn't count on Agents Lipman and Lopez to understand that. And I couldn't tell them about the terrorist-hunting unless it was okay with Dad. Otherwise, who knew what other secret operations I might mess up? As the lies piled up, it was getting hard to keep track. I had a feeling they knew that.

"What was the last school you say you went to again? And is there something wrong with your knee?"

I looked down at my left knee, jiggling up and down on its own.

"Okay," I said, putting both hands on my thigh and pressing down, "I'd like to end the conversation now."

"Excuse me?" Joe flicked his head to the right like he hadn't heard. His voice had an edge I didn't like. "What makes you think you're the one who gets to end this conversation?"

I looked over at Carol Anne, who did not meet my eyes.

"I want my dad," I told him. "I'm not saying anything else until Dad gets here. When is he getting here?"

Hannah slapped down her pen. "There could be a small problem with that."

"Problem with what?" I asked. From the way they looked, it suddenly crossed my mind that he might be dead.

Carol Anne shook her head. "I had it wrong when I talked to you on the phone. We haven't found your dad yet."

I froze. That was bullshit. She'd lied. It was a typical strategy for the Others, and dammit, I'd almost fallen for it.

Joe said, "But we found something. Do you remember giving us that DNA sample?"

I did. It placed me forensically at Dmitri's house so that the FBI could nail the bastard.

"The thing is, we did some searches. The government keeps a database of FBI agent DNA. It's so that we can identify bodies in case an operation goes wrong."

"Okay," I said.

"No one who works for the FBI was related to you," Hannah told me. "Any idea how that could be?"

"That's just because his clearance is so high," I said. "It has to be."

"Clearance has nothing to do with it. We'd know if we got a hit, even if the database couldn't tell us anything else."

Joe leaned forward. "We checked with the CIA and NSA too. Nothing."

I thought about it a bit, trying to work through the possibilities. And then, all of a sudden, I understood why they looked like that. "You're saying my dad isn't my real dad. Holy shit."

Had my mom deliberately lied to him, or maybe she'd just got it wrong? Okay, not to panic. Whether we were biologically related or not, he was my "real" dad.

"Rain, stop thinking for a minute and listen to Agents Lopez and Lipman," Carol Anne said.

"I'm not lying about him. You have to believe me."

"The thing is, we also did a more general DNA search," Hannah said. "We got a hit at two unsolved murder scenes."

Tears pricked at my eyes. "Whatever he did, I'm sure he had to do it."

"No, Rain, it wasn't your father's DNA that we found. It was a relative on your maternal side. We think it was your mother's."

TWENTY-THREE BILLION LIGHT-YEARS of space stretched above my head, 500 billion stars in the Milky Way, 200 billion galaxies beyond that. But looking up at the Tennessee sky, you'd never have known it. The light pollution from nearby Nashville muddied everything except for Orion's Belt and parts of *Ursa Major*. Streaky thin clouds obscured the rest.

"Get your shoes off the dash," Mom told me. "You'll scuff it."

Reluctantly, I unfolded my leg and put my foot down. Out the window, the trees on each side of the road were the real void. A flat, featureless black that made the back of my eleven-year-old neck prickle. We were out of the city, that was for sure.

"Mom, when we get there, can I steer the car?" Sometimes she let me do it when there was no one about.

"Not this time," she said. "You're too big for that anyway."

From the trunk of the car, we heard a thump.

"Did you bring any snacks?"

"No." It was her no-arguing voice.

I looked out the window again, trying to ignore my stomach. The yellow lines on the road flicked by at a steady rate. Flick—flick—flick. Behind us, another thump.

"Can I just do it for a mile or two?"

"What?"

"Steer the car."

"No."

"Please?"

"No, Rain, I have important stuff to do. I don't want to be distracted."

Another thump. It was hard to ignore.

"I'm supposed to be in training."

"What?" Mom said.

"I'm supposed to be training how to drive a car in case of emergencies."

"I didn't even want to take you tonight!" She thumped the wheel with both hands. "Dammit, Hal!"

I kept my mouth shut.

"All right," she said, "if you keep out of the way and do as you're told, we'll see."

"Thanks, Mom."

"And get your foot off the dash."

It had slipped back up without me even noticing, I swear. I took it down again.

Behind us, another thump.

"WHAT IS IT, RAIN?" Joe Lopez asked me. "You've gone kind of quiet there. Looking a little bit pale. Anything you want to say to me?"

"Sure," I said. "I want to say this: just because my mom's DNA matches some DNA found at an old murder site, it doesn't mean she was there."

"It's a one in a several billion chance," Joe said. "That's pretty definite in my book."

"Bullshit," I said. "If you took thirteen of my DNA loci and matched all thirteen to some DNA at one murder site, that would be a one in nine billion chance. But you matched it to how many people, how many sites? You ran it through CODIS, didn't you?"

Hannah Lipman looked up. "That's right. CODIS."

CODIS was the national FBI DNA database. I'd tried to hack into it a couple of times, just out of curiosity. Dad wasn't keen on it. He said if I had DNA to match, he could have his people do it with much less risk. But I'd wanted to anyway. I wanted all of it. Not just the convicted offenders, but the arrested people, missing people, unidentified remains, going back for years and years. Imagine all the cool shit you could do with that.

"Twelve million records," I said. "That takes the odds of matching down to about, say, one in ten thousand, right?"

"About that," Hanna admitted.

"And it couldn't have been a perfect match. You wouldn't be saying it was my mother in that case. You'd be saying it was me."

Joe glanced at Hannah, then back at me.

"She's got you there, Joe," Hannah said. "Maybe she knows more about it than you do."

Joe didn't look amused by that. "*You* tell me what the odds are then," he said to her. "We can take it from there."

Hannah shrugged. "One in a thousand. Give or take."

"One in a thousand is still pretty unlikely," he told me. "Pretty goddamn unlikely."

I looked down at the pale wood grain on the table. It *was* pretty goddamn unlikely. But I wouldn't let him trap me.

"It's still a long way off from impossible. So, stop bullshitting."

"I can stop bullshitting," he said. "If that's really what you want." He came around the desk. "Tell me, you or your family ever been to Tennessee?"

THE TWO RADICAL anarchists blinked when I shone the flashlight in their faces. Their hands were bound, and they couldn't shade their eyes. I waved the light at them experimentally and they blinked. Mom had pulled off onto a dirt road and driven for ages. Now that we were in the darkness of the forest and my eyes had adjusted, it wasn't so featureless and terrifying. I was actually pretty excited. There was loads of opportunity to steer the car around here. Maybe Mom would let me do the pedals too. Then Mom opened the trunk, and I saw what was causing all the thumps. Jesus, you'd think even radical anarchists would retire once they hit about seventy-five or so, but not these guys. I guess evil runs deep.

I had to help them out. The woman couldn't stand at first. Mom wouldn't touch them. She stayed back, with the gun, while I helped the old lady stay upright. She smelled medicinal and foul, like a bathroom.

"You don't have to do this," the old man said.

"Walk," Mom ordered, "down that trail."

They looked into the darkness. She prodded them in.

"I know you're afraid of the police," the old man said. "But I'm telling you, we don't have to involve them. We have a man—"

"Hank," the woman cut in.

"Yes, Hank. Our grounds manager. Get in contact with him, and he'll sort it all out. He can sort anything out."

"Walk," my mom said in a flat voice.

"I'm not kidding. However much money you want, Hank can get it to you."

"He'll take it straight out of our accounts," the lady added.

"You think we care about money?" I asked.

"Shush," Mom told me.

"If this isn't about money, you two are even sicker than I thought," the man said.

"You're the sick people. Planning to flood the capitol building with chlorine gas? Don't you know there's a day-care in the basement?"

"Planning to...what?" The old man sure looked surprised. But he wasn't.

"Don't play innocent. We know all about your plans."

The old man shook his head. "Honey, you've been told a pack of lies."

"You've been under observation for months by super-reliable agents. Shut up and walk."

For a while, there was no sound except the crackle of leaves and twigs under our feet. Then the man twisted around to look at his wife.

"Doris," he said, "what did you mean, 'He can take it straight out of our accounts'?"

She sighed. "I mean I made Hank a signatory, Agnew. We talked about that."

"We talked about making him a signatory on the house-keeping account."

"Yes," she said. "That's right."

"You said accounts, as in plural."

"Well," she said, her voice going a bit high and trembly, "I thought he could sort out some other stuff too...he's so good at sorting out..."

"Stuff? What other stuff?"

"Well, he said he had a way of moving money around that made it look like—"

"Christ, Doris, we already have an accountant!"

"Accountants won't do the things he said he could sort out..." Her voice trailed off, and I could sense her shoulders shaking. She was putting a lot of weight on my shoulder, and her smell was suffocating. I felt trapped. Slowly, we passed under the trees, just a few thickening clouds visible between the branches. Almost all the leaves had fallen for winter now. Just one or two hanging on.

"Agnew?"

"What?" he snapped.

"It couldn't have been Hank. Whoever snatched us knew the night code for the alarm."

A pause, and then Agnew said, "He knew it."

"You gave him the night code?"

"He's the one who suggested we get one. I...damn it all to hell!...I just told him to take care of it."

"That's why she doesn't care if you offer her money, Agnew," Doris sniffed. It sounded like her nose was really running. "She's with him."

"What?"

"They've already got our money. Now she just needs to finish the job."

Agnew started to tremble. I could sense it made Mom nervous. She lifted the gun and prodded him, but the touch of the barrel on his back triggered some animal instinct that caused him to break for it. He crashed through the bushes, disappearing into the shadows and becoming nothing more than a delocalized sound of panic in the dark. Mom crashed after him, cursing. For a while. Then we heard Agnew give a sudden, despairing shout that was cut off by a splash.

The old lady flinched. "God's sake, what was that?"

"A quarry," I told her. I'd half expected it. I recognized where we were now. Dad had taken us out here picnicking a few times. The woods were full of old quarries, flooded. I'd been attacked by mosquitos and grumpy at the time, but now I understood how good an agent my dad was. Always planning ahead, always professional, always thinking, even when he was on a family picnic, "This looks like the perfect place to off someone."

Mom stopped her pursuit, then gingerly took a few steps

forward, shining the flashlight into the water. But I didn't rate his chances. His hands were bound behind his back.

"You know, you're both wrong," I told Doris. "It's not about the money. It's about fighting evil."

"You really believe what you told me." She looked away. Tears were pouring down her cheeks and mucous coated the old-lady mustache on her upper lip. She wiggled her face like it tickled, but it was stuck fast. She could not wipe away this indignity with her hands bound. "Oh Agnew," she muttered, "what a pair of fools we were."

The bushes crackled. Mom was coming back. The woman looked at me with urgency. "All right," she said. "How about if I admit it. I admit everything. Agnew and I planned to blow up the capitol. We're communists...red as they come."

"Anarchists," I corrected her.

"Yes, anarchists. Whatever. It's all true. But here's the thing, if you take me back, I'll sing like a bird."

"Really?" I said.

"We weren't acting alone. Loads of us planned to blow stuff up. Not just in Nashville. We have plans for all fifty states. If you take me back, I'll give up the ringleaders."

"Okay, wow. I'm glad you see the error of your ways."

"Of course, honey. Look, could you maybe just loosen these? Just as a show of faith?"

I reached down and began to pick at her knots.

Mom took her by the shoulder and started to drag her away.

"Mom, wait, she has information she has to tell us."

Mom wasn't listening. She dragged the woman to the edge.

"Mom, wait, this is important!"

Somehow Doris's hands got loose, and with a banshee scream, she scratched at Mom, broke the skin, pulled out handfuls of her hair.

One shot of the gun and the scream faltered. Another shot, a push, and a splash, and the old anarchist's wail was submerged forever. Mom crashed through the undergrowth to me. She tried to give me a hug.

I pulled away. "You blew a big chance to save the kids."

"I followed instructions. Remember Chicago? Do you?" Her voice was breathless, harsh. "We follow instructions, Rain. Our job is not to question."

"But the anarchists--"

"Stop questioning me, Rainbow! You are a stupid, stupid little girl, and a bad secret agent! You have no idea how the world works!"

I felt my confidence fold in at once like a house of cards. She was right, of course. And because I'd loosened the enemy's bonds, Mom had almost been pulled into the quarry too. I felt the sobs well up in my chest.

"Mom." I ran into her arms

She held me and stroked my hair. "Shush, Rainbow, shush. Somewhere, someone else is taking care of the other bombs."

I let her hold me. "I wish you didn't have to kill them, though."

"Me neither," she said quietly. She started to tremble—slow at first, but it grew in strength until her bones were shaking helplessly with the cadence of a jackhammer. "It doesn't matter," she kept on saying. "It doesn't matter what I've just done. The important thing is that he won't hurt you now."

I'd always been unsatisfied with her reasoning. Chalked it up to another bizarre failing in my mom. Even at eleven, it was clear to me that the frail old anarchist could not have done me any harm.

"You've gone really quiet now," Joe Lopez said. "Super quiet. Anything you want to share with us?"

I should never have let them take my DNA. I saw that now. But that was only the beginning: I should never have trusted

Carol Anne, I should never have walked into the FBI building, I should never have answered even a single question. Every time I forget my training, I regret it. I knew that. I knew that, and yet I still had done it.

"I want my dad," I said. "I'm not saying anything more until he gets here."

"What if he doesn't show up?" Joe asked me. "What if we can't find him?"

All the hair on the back of my neck stood straight up. Of course. A trap. Of all my mistakes, the stupidest was that I'd believed they could contact my dad. Or that he would let them.

"We've looked pretty thoroughly, and no agent has stepped up to claim you as his daughter."

"I'm not lying," I said.

"You don't sound so sure," he countered. "Maybe it was like this. You must have been scared in Dmitri's basement. You wanted Peter to get you out, so maybe you made up that bit about your dad to light a fire under his ass—"

"That is so not true," I said. "You've got that totally wrong."

"Then go ahead. Prove me wrong."

I bit my lip. I had so much evidence. My whole entire life, for instance. But I couldn't tell him any of it. Not a single word, no matter the cost.

Joe threw his hands up in the air and walked away from me.

Hannah picked up her clipboard again. "Thing is, Rain, the murder forensics wasn't our only DNA hit. The DNA matched to a missing person. A woman called Saffron Dunn."

That was when I knew, without doubt, that I was not just among the ignorant. I was among the enemy. There were people behind this little chat that had it in for Dad, going back years. I scanned the room again with a new eye. Was there a hidden camera in that clock face, maybe? A microphone in Hannah's clipboard? Suddenly, it was hard to breathe. My fingers, resting on the tabletop, began trembling.

"I would like to leave now," I said.

"She was missing for sixteen years..."

"Carol Anne, you said I could leave when I wanted to."

"...and her body was found five years ago."

I closed my eyes. This was what people did not understand. Terrorists are not academic what-ifs. They are real. Very, very real. They are the ones who killed Saffron Dunn. Saffron, who was my mother.

Here's the other thing: if I did not get home soon, more mothers would die.

"Come on!" Joe pounded the table. "Saffron Dunn's family has been waiting twenty-one years for answers!"

The pounding had made me jump. I didn't feel so well anymore.

"You could answer them," he said, more quietly but no more kindly. "You could do this for your mom's family, if only you'd stop lying to us."

"Take me back home," I said to Carol Anne. "My real home. Please."

Carol Anne sighed. "Maybe you should ease up, Joe."

I could feel the air shift in the room.

"Hey," Peter's voice rang out behind me, "Why the glum faces? The party can start, now I'm here."

Beside me, Carol Anne closed her eyes and let out an exasperated huff. Joe paused mid-breath and tried for an avuncular expression, but you could tell he'd rather have laid into the guy with his fists. Suddenly, I saw a way through.

I turned around. "Hey, Peter."

"Hey yourself," he said.

"Do you think maybe you could take me home?"

He held out a hand. The way he held it out, like a white knight or something, made me smile. I took it and swung to a stand.

"We are not through here—" Joe asserted himself, but it was too late. Peter and I were already out the door.

10

The door shut behind us. Peter and I walked down the corridor, past a large open-plan office full of cubicles. I could feel eyes on us, like those of prairie dogs, about to dip into their dark communal tunnels.

"Thanks for getting me out of there," I said to him. I hoped I sounded normal. I could smell his clean scent, the summed vector of washed cotton, shaving foam, shampoo for men. I wondered what he'd been doing after leaving the hospital last night. I guessed he'd done whatever FBI agents did when heroics were not immediately required. What would that be? My knowledge of men in their twenties began and ended with what I had gleaned from the TV, and like a fast-paced, super-saturated commercial break, options flashed through my mind: Peter lounging in front of a widescreen TV in sock feet, eating chips and guacamole while scratching his golden retriever behind the ears. Maybe throwing balls in the backyard with his kids while his wife cooked dinner, although his comment in the hospital about his daughter leaving behind the lunchbox seemed somehow final. Maybe he was playing pool in some downtown bar where the men all had cleft chins and wore plaid shirts. Or rising up out of a hot tub just as a busty blonde placed an ice-cold beer in his hand...well, perhaps that was a bit unlikely on a weeknight. I tried to imagine him sitting on the toilet or popping a zit in the mirror. It wouldn't compute. He was just too good-looking.

"It's not a problem," he said.

"You know about the DNA stuff?" I asked him, rubbing my hand. It still tingled where he had touched it. The rest of me felt weak and shaky from the tension in the meeting room, but I tried not to let it show.

"Yeah. They told me about the DNA." He looked sideways at me without breaking stride, the tip of his tongue pressed against his top teeth. "Is it messing with ya?"

"A bit," I said.

"Want to tell me about it?"

"Tell you what?"

"It's just kind of weird, isn't it? Those two CODIS hits? Any idea how it could have happened? I mean, it wasn't really chance, was it?"

How long had he been listening at the door? I felt a swift flash of rage, but just as quickly it burnt away. They had probably told him earlier. Anyway, he was getting me out of here, wasn't he? I leaned in close to him and kept my voice low. "The hell it was chance. It was planted, for sure. These are old enemies, Peter, enemies of my dad, enemies of the nation. They are everywhere, and I won't be safe if they...if those guys...if they..." Suddenly, my throat wouldn't work and I couldn't finish my sentence.

"Hey." He stopped in front of the water cooler, took my arm, wiggled it a bit. "I've seen you face down hard bastards without flinching. Men that would make pussy-boys like Joe crap a golden goose. Remember Roman?"

I looked at the carpet and nodded.

"However loud those assholes barked back there, they aren't anything to be afraid of. You got that?"

"I got it," I told the carpet. My cheeks burned. Some bad-ass field agent I was turning out to be.

"Good," he said. He patted my shoulder. "Let's get you to that foster home then, ASAP."

Oh no. No, no, no. Not more delay. I had to get home.

"You have to believe me about the sarin, Peter. You have to," I said. "Please, just take me back to the house."

He stood there for a moment. Then he sighed. "Okay," he said. "If you're not too tired."

———

"THIS ISN'T GOING to be easy," Peter warned me as we made the last turn onto my block. "Things have been moving quickly."

"What's that supposed to mean?" But I soon saw for myself. Official-looking vehicles parked along the street. Yellow tape marked off the boundaries of the yard, and people in suits wandered around.

I plastered my fingertips to the window glass. This spectacle had brought out something I'd never before seen in suburbia. Neighbors, dozens of them, standing on the rock mulch, looking out from their porches. They stood around, these people I'd never seen, the men in polo-shirts and relaxed-cut jeans, the women in soft yoga pants, chatting to each other and rubber-necking my house—my anonymous house, my nothing house, which was now the center of attention.

I saw more people with tripods, fuzzy microphones, and snapped my head around to look at the vehicles again. Yes, trucks with transmitting equipment, parked behind some sort of barrier. Oh no.

"I trusted you," I turned to Peter, furious. "I freaking trusted you."

"You can still trust me," he said. "But as of this morning, this turned into a murder investigation. Saffron Dunn's murder, in fact. There are protocols."

I shook my head. Protocols! These people had no sense of priority. Saffron was dead. Nothing could bring her back. But I still had a job I had to do.

"How the hell am I going to get Tabernakl's coordinates now?"

"Tabernakl? Who the hell is that?"

"The freaking mastermind behind the sarin attack!" I blurted. "I've been hunting him down for months. Five days ago, I finally locate him, I go upstairs to get my pizza, and you freaking kidnap me...and won't let me go home...for three freaking days!"

Peter's mouth fell open. "That's what this is all about? You found a terrorist? You know where he lives?" He whacked the steering wheel. "Why the hell didn't you just tell me?"

"I did." I almost sobbed. "Don't you remember in the basement? I did. I told you about the poison dolphins and I begged you to let me send that message to my dad. I begged you."

"Dammit," he said. He pulled to the side of the road and sat in the car, breathing heavily. "Okay. You did, but you could have been a bit clearer later on. Like in the hospital and shit."

"I didn't think I could trust you." I jabbed a finger at the scene outside the house. "I was right."

I couldn't bear to look at his face. I turned back to the house, its secrets laid open. I couldn't figure out what to do next.

"Look, come in with me," he said. "Let's just see what the situation is, go from there, okay?"

We got out of the car and walked up to the front step. I could feel the wake of our passage generating ripples in the crowd and felt naked. Peter shut the front door behind us before the backsplash of attention hit.

People were in the house. Things had been labeled, and plastic had been laid down. Someone was on their hands and knees, photographing the pizza. I looked around wildly.

An agent in a paper suit was coming for us, removing his blue rubber gloves with a snap. He looked at me warily, but he already knew who I was. Peter had phoned ahead to say we were coming.

"Hey Fred," Peter said to him. "Thanks for taking the time to show us around."

A flash of movement at the basement stairs caught my eye.

"Peter, is anyone down there, down in my office?"

Fred looked at me. "We're everywhere."

It was the worst violation yet. My nostrils grew peppery. I took a quick breath.

"It will be okay. Those guys are trained to be careful," Peter assured me. He turned to Fred. "Would it be okay if we had a quick look down there?"

He shrugged. "There's nothing left. The CART guys took an image of the disk, tagged it up, and took it away an hour ago."

"Everything?" I squeaked. "Like all the little bits of paper and stuff?"

"Yeah, they don't screw around with that shit. Bits of paper, rubber bands, tissues with boogers on it, they bagged it all."

For a moment, I really couldn't breathe. There was a buzzing in my ears. Fred and Peter were saying things, but I couldn't really hear them. I took a few steps forward and looked into the kitchen. The counters were covered with evidence bags. Fred told the truth. They really had bagged everything.

I felt Peter's hand on the small of my back. I realized he was talking to me.

"Fred tells me he has something he wants you to see."

I looked from one agent to the other. The conflict between them had suddenly cleared away, like an afternoon thunderstorm. A new tendril of anxiety brushed up the back of my spine.

Fred led us to the garage. For a moment, I didn't see it. Then I did. They'd opened up the gray metal box that housed the alarm system. Except...I went in closer. I'm not a hardware girl per se, but the problem was obvious.

"Where is the alarm system?" I asked. The box was empty. Not entirely, mind you. Fred swung the front panel back with the tip of a screwdriver so I could get a better look. LED lights had been taped to the back of the panel so that they would glow, so that it would look like a real alarm. But the complex electronics that Dad and I had chosen out of the catalog for him to install, well, they weren't there.

"It's a typical system, in its way," an agent nearby said to Peter. "A lot of people just buy the chassis. The appearance of a kick-ass alarm system is nearly as effective as an actual one, and a hell of a lot cheaper."

"But not something you'd do if you were really scared of a specific threat, is it?" Peter asked.

"This won't stop professionals, no."

I reached up to get a closer look at the missing wiring, but the Fred pushed my hand back with the cold shank of the screwdriver. "Don't contaminate it."

"My prints are already on it," I said. "The outside at least."

"Let's keep it that way."

I dropped my hand. Dad had removed it, or never installed it. But why?

"You want her to see the other stuff?" Fred said to Peter.

My stomach clenched. What other stuff?

They took me upstairs, all of us stepping carefully around the evidence bags laid out in a line on the hallway floor. They led me to the empty bedroom, where they'd pulled the contents of the closet out onto the bed. Dozens of gun cases snapped open. But no guns. Rocks nestled in the sparkly black foam padding where hard metal should have laid. Ammo boxes were scattered around, pebbles spilling out.

"What did you do with the guns?" My voice was high, shrill.

But Fred informed me they hadn't taken anything out. It was all like that, a closet of heavy boxes that turned out to be full of rocks. Before he could stop me, I pushed my way into the closet, pulled one of the heavy Saur cases off the top shelf, thunked it on the bed, and opened it up. More rocks. Just like the ones under the casual weekend footwear of the crowd outside.

"This is our weapons cache. We were storing the weapons," I said, confused. "One of my jobs...I thought one of my jobs was protecting it, that was why I had to stay here all the time." I dumped the rocks on the bed and tore at the foam padding. But there was nothing underneath except swirls of glue.

"This is weird," Peter said, peering into the closet. "Like a set of props for a film."

"So, who was the audience?" But Fred was looking at me. "Any ideas?"

"Stop the bullshit," I said. "Where did you put the guns?"

"Nowhere," Fred said. "There were no guns."

I shook my head. "What did you do with the guns?"

"Rain," Peter said urgently, "if this is all a setup, how did that key get under the mat? Remember the key?"

I slammed the Saur case shut. I saw how they'd played me. First, the insinuations about my dad's DNA and my missing mom. Then, Peter softened me up with a tour of my house, ripped apart to make it look like a fake. The others were clever. But did they really think I'd believe my dad had lied to me for all these years?

I had to escape. I had to think of a plan, and fast.

"The bomb shelter," I said, "is that a fake too? Did you just walk in and find an empty shell?"

"No," Fred said. "That bit's real enough, at least the door is. We haven't gotten in yet."

So, that bit was real enough. All of a sudden, I felt an icy calm come over me.

"I know the combination," I said. "How about I open it?"

Peter's brows furrowed. "Good idea."

Fred nodded. "Let's get her down there."

They took me down. I tried hard not to let them see me shaking. In the kitchen, I stepped sideways on my foot and made myself fall. Peter and Fred both leaned down to help me up, but the razor blade I'd used to cut my duct tape and attack Peter was nowhere to be found either. If only I'd thought to tape like twenty razor blades under the counter edges. Maybe the blade was an evidence bag on the counter. I put my hand on the edge of the counter as if steadying myself and had a good look at the bags.

And I saw it. The sticky note. In a bag with a bunch of used tissue, just like Fred had said.

"You okay?" Peter said. "You need to sit down or something?"

I looked at the coordinates. I looked at them hard and memorized them. Just like my training had taught me.

"I'm fine." I straightened up. "Sorry about that."

I have to admit that I hardly ever went in the backyard, not after the shelter was built. Bomb shelters, if they are to be useful, must be regularly inspected. You have to set traps for vermin, out of date supplies must be replaced, and so on. But Dad usually did it when he came home. He'd tell me he was going down there, that it would take a few hours, and I just let him go without me. But everything would be there. Food and water and iodine tablets...and Internet access, of course. I could last down there a long, long time.

The combination lock was just as I remembered it. I touched my fingers to the metal buttons, warm in the autumn sun.

"Could I get a little room here?" I asked Fred and Peter. "You're crowding me, it makes it hard to remember."

They stood back a little.

"Thanks," I said. But of course, I knew the combination by heart. The tenth through thirteenth digits of e. I punched it in fast and heard a little click and before anyone could stop me pulled the door open wide. Fred shouted and made a grab at my shoulder. Then a rank smell burst from the black innards of the bomb shelter, so vile and strong it was like a slap in the face. Peter retched and Fred let go of my shoulder to cover his mouth.

Smell or no smell, I dove into the entrance stairway and slammed the door behind me, cutting myself off from the sun and air.

PART II

VICTIM

11

I stood there in the foul gloom, sniffing cautiously, trying to identify the stink. It was the smell of rotten meat. Like a possum had gotten in the composting toilet and become trapped. My eyes had not yet adjusted from the bright sun outside, but I took a step down into the shelter.

Through the metal door behind me, I could hear a rhythmic banging. The FBI were using some sort of tool to break in. They sounded desperate. If this was all a plot to make me give up my dad, it was a pretty elaborate one. I would probably have a while before they made it through the door, though. We'd built that door to last. It might give way to a jackhammer, but I assumed that, if these FBI were as bureaucracy-ridden as my Dad had led me to believe, that would take a few hours to arrange.

My foot twisted for real and I fell, bumping my hip on the wall.

I bent down. Something had been left on the steps, several somethings. At first, I thought it was the dead possum and reeled back, but I screwed my eyes shut until I saw stars. Then I opened them and looked again. It turned out to be a pile of blankets, some books, and an empty water bottle.

Anything on the steps is always a tripping hazard, but in a

critical path, it can be lethal. Dammit, I shouldn't have let Dad take care of the bomb shelter by himself. He wasn't always that tidy. I knew that. I should have come down and made sure little details like this were properly taken care of. I stepped over the clutter and continued down the stairs.

At the bottom, I hit the light switch and discovered it wasn't just the stairs that had been left a mess. The entire bomb shelter was reduced to total chaos. Clothes, unwashed dishes, and packets of food were scattered everywhere. The first aid kit lay open on the table, its insides spilled onto the surface. The antibiotics bottle was open and empty. A pool of vomit congealed on the blankets on the lower bunk.

And in deep shadows a human shape, covered by blankets. I froze, but the shape did not move. It was so still, it might even have been just a human-looking pile of blankets. But the tip of a definitely human nose just caught the dim light.

Picking up a coffee mug (it was the heaviest thing in arm's reach) I crept closer, but I needn't have bothered. She was long past caring about me. Nothing alive could smell that bad.

Even in death, she clutched the blankets to her chest. Her skin was a deep brown, receding into black in the shadows of the blanket. I couldn't see her body, but a bare foot poked out, the bones of her feet high ridges under the skin. Her hair was braided into uneven rows that had grown out and morphed into dreads. I could see where she had fastened the braids with the plastic tabs that keep bread bags closed.

I backed up, covering my face with my shirt, all the hairs on my neck standing straight up. She'd come down here, eaten all my food, swallowed all my medicine, and then crawled into bed to die. What had killed her?

I shook my head to clear it. There was no denying that something had made her very sick, and it might still be down here. Maybe I had already breathed it in. Maybe my only hope was to run back up the stairs, surrender to Fred and Peter, and hope they would take me to a hospital first. But then...the bastards would come down here with their forensic team, and I would never know the truth.

I took an experimental breath through my t-shirt. Foul, but no congestion blocked my lungs. I held out my hands. Understandably tense, but not cramping or twitching. Not a nerve agent, then.

The vomit was old and dry. It was a risk, but if I didn't touch it...or her...

A quiet humming caught my attention. I picked my way through the detritus to the back of the room, to the multi-monitor computer Dad and I had left down here. Eerie, how the electronics went on about its business while the rest of the room decayed. The desk was a bit dusty, but I could see no fluids or anything on the keyboard. What the hell. I hit the mouse with my hand and the screen came to life.

The desktop wallpaper was a photo. I recognized the scene with something like a thump in my gut. The fawn-brown dead grass, that denim-blue sky, the Rocky Mountains beneath it with one massive peak rising to the south. It was Colorado Springs, the last place we had all lived together, Mom, Dad, and me, before Mom was killed, and Dad and I went on the run that last time.

My knees suddenly felt quite shaky and I sat down in the chair. I turned my attention to the windows that littered the desktop. Some plotted signals in real time. Others scrolled text, each with a hashtag title: #CFBLIVE, #HelmetSticker, #FridayFocus. The scrolling text was made up of tweets, in real time, about football. Strange.

A small black window in a corner looked like a command shell. I hit the up arrow to retrieve the last command.

>> Set debug_level = 2

Sweet. I deleted the "2," replaced it with "3," hit enter, and watched the screen light up in color. Text messages began to scroll.

So, it took me maybe an hour to figure out what was going

on. At the end of it, I knew what she had been doing while living in my bomb shelter.

I also knew how she'd died.

SHE WAS A COMPUTER PROGRAMMER. The stuff on the screen was all her work.

Now, to understand how freaking cool and bad ass this girl was, you have to understand how hard it is to predict odds. Go on, try plotting the odds that the Buffalo Bills will win at the Super Bowl this year. You'll get a jagged signal, highs and lows made up of tiny highs and tiny lows made up of *even tinier* highs and lows. That bit where the quarterback flipped over while Dmitri and I watched it live on TV? A big drop. But there are little blips too, like maybe this guy writes a positive blog post about his replacement. Maybe someone else is injured on the opposing team.

Odds form what's called a stochastic time series. You see it around a lot. Like an EEG signal on a sick person, or the waveform of audio, or, most famously, the stock market. Buy low, sell high—it's what investors want to do. (For professional gamblers it's the same: place a lay when the odds are low and a back when the odds are high.) But here's the thing about the term stochastic: it's a precise way of saying the shit that makes it go up and down can sort of be figured out, but there's this random element that totally fucks it up.

It made me blink. If she could predict that random stochastic element on the sports betting sites, she would be like a Finnegan, but not a pretend one, a real one. It was a step I'd always been too scared to take. But if she could, she could make a hell of a lot of money. I stared hard at the screen.

YOU SEE, here's the thing. She made a hell of a lot of money.

No one can predict the future, not even Finnegan. But in fact, she didn't need to get in there before the future happened. She just needed to get in before the sports odds changed. Given the neurological processes of humans and average type and click speeds, I reckoned her bots only needed milliseconds.

She wasn't the first person to figure that out. Her bots competed with other bots who monitored the odds and placed their bets accordingly. The key was this: she didn't monitor the odds, not for prediction anyway. She didn't model sports statistics, either. Like I've known for a long time, and she clearly knew as well, odds don't change based on the actual probability that team A or B will win. It's a market. Odds change based on who the punters *think* will win.

In the end, it was so obvious it made me want to scream. The data was there, like a gift. Every sports fan in the world has an opinion, and there's a hell of a lot of them who will tell you all about it in chunks of 140 characters. She mined the Twitter feed, looking for key phrases, and estimated what everyone was thinking in real time. Then, she predicted the future bets, like a real Finnegan, and that was how she made her money.

I turned back to look at the still figure on the bed. But why? Why come down here to this windowless concrete room and write programs to make money like this...like me?

As to how she died, I was able to reconstruct it from her web search history. A week ago, she'd started googling what to do about fevers and abdominal pain. Six days ago, the general queries stopped and focused on appendicitis instead, like what to do if you can't get to a hospital, if you're in an undeveloped country or hiking in the backwoods. Surprisingly, you can treat the condition with antibiotics, and often it even works. We had the antibiotics—What bomb shelter would be complete without a comprehensive medical kit?—and they must have worked because the searches stopped. For a few days. Then they started up again, but with new query words. "Peritonitis," "septic shock," and "how long does it take to die?"

And yet, she'd never once tried to save herself. I saw the evidence of the final few messages she'd started to write. They were to Dad...the ones she'd been too ill to deliver (I only ever communicated with Dad by paper messages left in specific drop off points; I assumed her situation would be similar). They all mentioned the previous messages for help she'd sent, how she was too afraid to go to the hospital without him. She, like me, had been taught to stay away from the authorities, to always go through Dad and his friends. But Dad had never answered, and she'd simply crawled into bed, trusting to the very end that he would come.

There was no way he wouldn't have known. If he hadn't been able to pick up the messages himself for some reason, someone else in the True Patriots should have done it. The only explanation was that the True Patriots couldn't risk her being found—they couldn't risk her story being uncovered.

Rage built, slow and steady, in my chest. For fuck's sake, I would give my life for the True Patriots, of course I would, but not like this girl's death, not if it was completely meaningless and avoidable.

What now then? Did I open the door at the top of the steps and let the FBI in then? Did I reveal it all, just to spite Dad and the True Patriots and to hell with fighting the terrorists? Would Peter ever take me seriously about the sarin attack again, if I did?

I shook my head. I had to deal with the sarin attack first. The rest could wait. I started up Google Earth and typed in Tabernakl's geocoordinates, the ones I'd memorized from the evidence bag upstairs.

There was a bit of lag in the system. I looked down at the desk, and saw a piece of paper crumpled, half behind the monitor. A final note? Something for her parents? I grabbed it and spread it on the desk. It said:

Animals beloved in the eyes of Allah: camel, cat, deer, donkey (but meat is haram)

Dirty animals—do not use: pig, dog, snake

Dolphin should be okay.

I read that last line again. *Dolphin should be okay.*

I looked at the screen. Google Earth displayed a picture of my house from above. My house. I could see the bomb shelter in the backyard. I looked up at the coordinates I'd entered, but they were correct. The terrorist I'd hunted down was in my own backyard the whole time.

There was no Tabernakl sitting in some cheap Dallas apartment, bags of fertilizer and bottles of fuel oil piled high in the kitchen. No mujahideen sitting on the living room rug, or maybe a mattress on the bedroom floor, picking out letters on the keyboard with two fingers. Tabernakl lay dead on the bed behind me. Tabernakl was this girl, writing out notes to herself to make her seem like an Islamist online gamer as she tried to find other terrorists online to hand into the True Patriots.

We'd both set out to find real terrorists online, and we'd damn well recruited each other instead.

My hands shook and the mouse slipped, and I had to try twice to start it up. The game. Yeah, it was there like I knew it would be. Already installed on her computer: username and password pre-entered. And, oh hell. There he was, that stupid orc character, holding his useless mace and sword, just freaking standing there, Tabernakl. Chest rising and falling, rising and falling, rising and—

"Fuck!" I banged my fist on the desk.

I almost logged off. But then, text began to scroll across the screen.

"Angrendir whispers: we shall strike them from every fingertip."

I stared at the chat window on the screen. Angrendir. Yes, Tabernakl had mentioned someone called Angrendir, and in the panic of the last four days, I'd completely forgotten.

Angrendir was still typing. "Its me, tabernakl. Where've u been we were worried me and my cuz..."

I started to type back. "Who the fuc..."

I paused. To Angrendir, whoever he was, I would look like Tabernakl the orc. I'd been an agent of the True Patriots this whole time, and now I knew Tabernakl had been an agent of the True Patriots as well, but neither of us knew who the hell Angrendir really was.

For all I knew, he really was sitting in some cheap Dallas apartment, picking out letters on the keyboard. Maybe he already had the dolphins piled high around him. Maybe he'd been the one to suggest the sarin. Maybe he had some ready to go.

I backspaced and started again.

"Sorry, I was pretty sick there for a while. I'm better now."

I stared at the screen, hardly daring to breathe.

"No prob. Did that Finnegan brother say he'd pay for the dolphins — how long till they get here?"

I bit my lip. But I had to answer with something.

"One week tops."

Angrendir typed quickly. "You remember stormshadow I told you bout him. He can get us in. He can get the dolphins in place no prob he says inshallah."

I glanced at the desktop, frustrated. This computer did not have my tracking app installed. I was going into this blind.

"Maybe they'll come sooner. How can I get them to you?"

"Whats wrong with the original plan?"

"The thing is—"

The silence in the room was suddenly shattered as a water bottle clattered off of the bunk and onto the floor. I froze mid-sentence. No way could that noise have been me. Slowly, I spun the chair around. The girl's arm extended from the blanket, and her eyes were open. Her chapped lips parted. I knew she meant to cry for help.

All I would have had to do was touch her and I would have felt her skin still burning hot. Stupid, selfish me, I had been too disgusted by her smell, too afraid of catching her disease, even after I knew I didn't need to be.

I looked back at the screen. Angrendir was typing something. But this girl, she was in the last stages of septicemia for sure. She might only have hours left.

I typed, "I have to go."

I didn't wait for an answer. I logged off and stood up. "Hold on. I'm going for help," I told the girl. She didn't respond, just stared across the room with eyes as dead as glass as I hurried past.

I climbed the stairs, threw back the bolts on the door, and pushed it open, right into the face of an FBI agent. Startled, he fell on his ass, a chisel flying to the side.

The bright sunlight blinded me. I ran into it.

"Someone, please," I said, "call an ambulance."

I sensed people around me. Someone took my arm and I heard Peter's voice in my ear, "Are you okay, Rain? Are you hurt?"

"It's not for me. *She* needs an ambulance."

"Who? Who's down there?"

"Tabernakl," I said.

"Tabernakl, the terrorist?"

There was a clicking noise as someone in the crowd racked their gun. I opened my mouth to speak but couldn't say the words for a moment. But I had to, before a bad situation got worse.

"No. She's just another missing girl," I said at last. "Like my mom was. Like me."

12

When humans looked up at the sky and imagined their place in the universe, they used to get pissed off about the planets. Almost everything rose in the east and set in the west, circling round in the heavens nice and predictably, all except the planets. The planets mostly went round with the stars, tracing a path through them that advanced a little every night. But then Jupiter or Saturn or one of the others would start going backward, tracing a path like a little pretzel in the sky. Astronomers couldn't figure out why, and it pissed them off.

They named them after gods. Later, when there was only one God allowed, they created elaborate mini-sub-orbital retrograde machines to explain it. But it was never quite right. The models were always extremely complicated and a bit arbitrary.

Then this guy Copernicus says: Wait, I can explain it all— simple, clean and neat. All you have to do is admit that the Earth orbits the sun.

"YOU REALLY DON'T THINK my dad is an FBI agent, do you?"

When nearly dead missing girls are found, there's a lot of

stuff that goes on, and it takes a lot of people to do it. I couldn't really take it in. I just sat in the back of one of the extra ambulances with a big bottle of sports drink someone brought me (full of yellow #5, but I needed the fluid and sugar) and watched the paramedics and other official folks milling around. Peter sat with me, maybe to support me, maybe to make sure I didn't run off. Maybe a bit of both. I'd had some time to consider my model of the cosmos, sitting in that ambulance, and Peter had let me do it, answering my questions gently and with more thoughtfulness than I expected. Yet another face of this guy, who was more complex than I'd first thought.

"We know he isn't, Rain. We know it for a fact."

"I don't understand."

"Look," Peter said, "we take FBI impersonation pretty seriously. We've known about Hal Wooten for decades, and we've been looking for him that whole time."

"Until now."

"Finding you is the closest we've ever been."

Of course. They still didn't know where he was, nor did I. It was the way he'd always operated. I'd felt inconvenienced by it plenty of times, but I'd never really questioned why it was that way until now.

I opened my hand. The bandage over my razor cut was getting grubby at the edges. I picked at the bits of dirt adhering to the sticky edge.

"Tell me what you know."

He looked out at the ring of vehicles parked on my lawn and people marching past in white suits carrying equipment cases and coils of extension cords. "When we kidnapped you, it kinda threw me. Dmitri was up to his usual screwed-up shit and Roman and I screwed it up even more and that's why we ended up with you, that all made sense. But you were just a kid, for God's sake. And not just a kid, but also the freaking weirdest kid I'd ever met."

"Weird?" I asked, confused.

"Yeah, weird. You fought like a goddamn Navy SEAL but talked like a nut case conspiracy theorist. You lived in this nice big house, but the inside of it was like a medieval monastery. There had to be a damn good reason for it, I knew, but I couldn't put my finger on it. Then the DNA you gave us broke the case."

"It sounds pretty random," I said. "You rescue this girl from the Russian mafia, and it turns out she's a hot lead on a case that's been cold for years."

"Yeah, but often a case breaks that way," Peter said. "Just random things—simple things. We got the Oklahoma bomber because a state trooper stopped him driving without a license plate. It was just good luck he was still sitting in the local jail by the time anyone realized who the hell he was." He turned to me. "It was always gonna be something like that with you. Nothing less than a gun to your head was ever going to drag you out of that basement otherwise, was it? Look at Tabernakl. She could have walked out at any time, but she chose to die instead."

Thanks to my picking, the edge of the bandage started to curl up. I closed my hand to stop it getting worse.

"You say you've known about him for decades. How?"

"Over the seventeen years Saffron Dunn was missing, she often sent letters to her family. They passed the letters on to us. We knew your dad had brainwashed her and how. She was still careful with her location. Too careful. We never found her."

I pressed my lips together. She had certainly kept that quiet, even from me. Dad would have been furious if he'd known. But maybe that made sense, in a way. I probably would have told him if I'd known.

"She shouldn't have contacted them at all," I told him. "She wasn't always the sharpest tool in the toolbox."

"That's what you think?" Peter sounded surprised. "I don't know. I do know your dad was good at what he did. I think maybe a lot of smart people fell for it. Maybe even smart people in particular fell for it."

I frowned. "These letters my mom sent. Can I read them?"

He was silent a moment. "At some point, sure. They're not an easy read. Hal...he wasn't always kind to your mom." He looked at me. "I have a question for you now."

"Okay," I said.

"Why are you even talking to me about this now? What changed your mind?"

I sighed. "I haven't said I've changed my mind. I am only considering another explanation for events."

Peter frowned. "You're considering it pretty seriously though."

"The balance of probability has shifted," I agreed. I started picking at the bandage again. "It was the key under the doormat."

Peter laughed. "All of this crap going on around you, and it was that key that changed your mind?"

I nodded. "The existence of Tabernakl proves nothing. Maybe my dad really is a con man and set us on each other to make up a terrorist threat that wouldn't exist otherwise, but maybe we really do work for a secret organization, and we accidentally did it all on our own. I don't know, and she can't tell us. Probably she doesn't know any more than me."

"Okay," Peter said. "I guess that kinda makes sense."

I pointed at the scene in front of us. "Even now, all of this could be an elaborate conspiracy on your part to turn me into an enemy of the True Patriots. But the existence of the key doesn't fit. You had no idea who I was then."

"That would be a pretty elaborate conspiracy," Peter said. "To be honest, we're a government agency. We don't have the budget for that."

I nodded. "I sure know how that is."

But did I? With a little stab of pain in my heart, I realized it was quite possible that I had never actually dealt with the real FBI. Not even a super-secret faction of renegade FBI agents. So I didn't know how it was. Not at all.

"Do you guys at least know how old I really am?"

He shook his head. "Nope. Somewhere between fifteen and nineteen is all."

I sat back in the shade of the ambulance, irrationally irritated that he didn't know. I needed to find the center the shifting sands of my world somehow.

"Do you know why he did it?"

Peter looked over at me. "Only he knows for sure, but it looks like it was for the money," he said. "Unless you know something different."

It kind of made sense. The endless stream of True Patriot big budget operations, absolutely critical ones that had to be funded to save the nation, and the equally endless stream of budget cuts that threatened our security—all of them had needed money. Lots of it. A constant supply. But not everything we'd gone through was about the money.

"Sometimes Dad came up with some crazy shit," I told him. I paused. Old habits like fear and distrust die hard. But I took a breath and forced myself to go on with this new thing—this trusting thing—because I suspected it might lead me to the truth. "Once, Mom and I had to live at the airport to stop some Al Qaeda guy in disguise from getting in the country. We ate out of trash cans and slept on benches for three weeks. I don't think we earned any money then."

Peter glanced sideways at me. "Did you find the guy?"

I shrugged. "Dad told us we'd know him by the black miniature parrots, but we never figured out exactly what he meant by that."

Peter nodded. "Hunger, exhaustion, terror, they're all brainwashing tactics. That's the setup he had for you in this house and—" He jerked his head at the entrance to the bomb shelter. "—and her down there."

The memories of that time came back to me, strong and fast: how the hot sun had soured the crusts of the sandwiches we'd found in the trash cans, the arms on the bench seats in the lounges, put there to stop anyone from sleeping comfortably, and the white and bloodshot rims of my mother's eyes when airport security ambled past. It was that horrible moment when you know you are about to break into sobs and there is no way to stop.

Peter put his arm around my shoulder and I wept into his shirt.

"Hey," he said at last, "there's something you should know."

I started to pull away so that I could look up at him but froze when I realized a thick string of mucus connected my nose to the red and white cotton weave of his shirt. I pressed my face back into his chest, my nose bumping against the warm solidness of his body beneath the thin fabric.

"What?" I said to his armpit.

He must have felt the dampness. He fished in his pocket and extracted a wrinkled tissue.

"I never betrayed you, not like you thought."

I took the tissue. I was past caring about his nose germs now. I used it to mop up my nose and his shirt. "I know that now. You were doing your job."

"Part of that job is helping you."

I shook my head. "I've done some bad things. When they find out...I'm going to be in trouble."

"You were his victim too," Peter said. "You were duped just like the rest of them."

I felt the sobs rising in my chest again. "I'm such an idiot. Everything I did was a waste of time. Everything. Finnegan, Tabernakl, the whole online gaming thing—"

But then my breath caught. Shit. Angrendir.

I hadn't finished my conversation with Angrendir down in the shelter, whoever the hell he and his buddy Stormshadow really were. Probably more of Hal's victims, just like me and Tabernackl.

Probably, but not necessarily.

I thought about it a minute. Then I sat up. The tissue was a sodden mass, so I wiped the last drips from my nose on my shirt and asked Peter if he would take me back to Desiree's house.

I know—with the new trusting experiment I was running—I should have said something to Peter then as he walked me back to the car. But I figured the FBI would already have the logs from Tabernakl's computer, so I wasn't actually hiding anything at all. What I was thinking was that maybe I could find out a bit more in the meantime. I couldn't salvage much from this wreck of my life, but I still had my training and my specialist knowledge. That was my anchor in this new world—the things no one could take from me. And maybe I could be of some use to the real FBI for once. Maybe I could find Angrendir and this Stormshadow person for them. And maybe…just maybe…they'd lead me to—

"You okay there?" Peter asked me.

I realized I was standing beside the car. The door to the passenger side was open, but I was just standing there, not getting in.

"Yeah." I shook myself. "Yeah, I'm fine."

We got in the car and drove off. Peter was saying something, but I just mumbled things back. I wasn't paying attention. I was thinking about how I didn't need to read Mom's letters to find out all the answers to my screwed up life. All I had to do was find Hal Wooten and ask him some carefully crafted questions. Then I'd find out for sure what was the truth.

I'd have to find him first though, before the FBI did.

But maybe—if I used all my skills—maybe I could do that too.

13

Shortly after we'd moved to Texas, my dad had taken me out to dinner. Even back then, I only left the house when necessary, and only for as little time as possible. Going out was unusual for us, but we were on a highly critical operation, or so Dad had said, and this was the heart of it.

It was an older cafe, an IHOP, built on the side of a highway and right on the migration path of the grackles. Hundreds of the black crow-like birds were outlined against the deepening indigo of the evening sky on tree branches, power lines, and highway signage. They roosted on the IHOP sign itself and lined the apex of the IHOP-brand blue roof. The pavement around the cafe was spotted white with grackle poop.

We were there because the True Patriots had recently uncovered a Taliban plan against the new Lithuanian troops in Afghanistan. "It's already a delicate situation," he explained in the parking lot. "NATO and the USA don't want to risk Lithuania pulling out altogether."

I cradled the package in my lap. I said, "You can count on me, Dad. Just tell me what I have to do."

"There's the target. In the corner booth. You see her?"

Through the large, plate glass windows, I could. She was reading a menu. It was hard to make out details.

"That," Dad told me, "is the cultural attaché to the Lithuanian Embassy, Vilna Chodkiewicz. She's come all the way from Washington just for us. You remember the plan, right? You remember the cover story?"

"Yeah," I said. "She's your new wife, and I'm your daughter from a previous marriage, and this is a meeting so that we can get to know each other to see if I should come live with you."

"Exactly," he said, "and why are we doing it this way?"

He'd drilled me on the story plenty of times. I answered without hesitation. "Because the Others won't be watching her so closely if they think this a personal matter. They especially won't be watching me."

"Good girl." He opened the car door. "Let's go. And don't forget, those soldiers in Afghanistan deserve to know the danger they are in. We can't let them down."

"Yes, Dad," I said. On the way to the door, I let out a little giggle. "But it is a little ironic, isn't it? Me pretending to be your daughter when I really am your daughter?"

He turned to me without a hint of a smile. "It's the old double bluff, Rain. The sharpest tool in the secret-agent toolbox."

Inside, we walked straight to the booth in the corner. Vilna Chodkiewicz stood up and enclosed me in an enthusiastic fruit-and-coconut scented hug.

"Isobel," she said, "I'm so excited to meet you at last."

"Uh..." I looked over her shoulder at Dad, who wagged his hand in a get-on-with-it gesture. "It's good to meet you too," I said. "Dad told me a lot about you."

"That's so sweet." She released me. She took Dad's elbow and dragged him down into the booth next to her.

I perched on the other side and tried not to glare as she picked at something on his jacket sleeve. I had to remember it was all an act. I just had to put up with her pawing him for half an hour or so and it would be over.

The waitress came. "Y'all ready to order?"

Dad picked up a menu. "Could I get some coffee for now? We'll be ready in a minute."

Reluctantly, she left us to it.

Vilna was about Dad's age, her face heavily made up to match the heavy plastic beads nestling above her freckled bosom. I'd expected someone with a different aesthetic. You know, more cultural. Like maybe a black dress, severe bun, and avant-garde spectacles. But I had to admit, the disguise was effective. She sure looked like an ordinary middle-aged Texan woman, the kind you see in the grocery stores all the time.

"I must compliment you on your accent," I said. "It sounds very natural."

She glanced over at Dad. "Well, it is natural."

"Anyone for chicken and waffles?" Dad asked.

I got the hint. I looked for the waitress. She was going down another row of booths, topping up coffees. There were people in the booth behind us, and across the aisle. Any one of them could be an enemy agent. On the other hand, no one was looking directly at us, and there was no time like the present. I held out the package under the table.

"Take it," I said to Vilna.

"Take what?"

I extended it further and it bumped her knee. She jumped.

"Hurry, before the waitress sees."

She reached under the table, lifted it out of my hands, and brought the brown paper parcel up to examine it.

"Careful, the waitress might see," I reminded her.

She frowned before setting it on the bench next to her. "I can save it for later, I guess."

I almost said something, but Dad raised an eyebrow at me. "Remember what we talked about in the car?"

The reminder was timely. I tried for a light, friendly expression.

The waitress came over with coffee for Dad and fresh bottles of pancake syrup for the table. She took our order and left again.

Vilna took a deep breath. "Your father and I have been talking. I know you have, well—" She tipped her head to the side. "—different needs. Your dad told me all about it."

I frowned. That seemed a little off. Sure, we had a cover story to maintain, but there was no need for a foreign government agent to know I was halfway through MIT's online computer science courses. But as we were midway through an operation, I'd just have to wing it.

"I know I'm kind of unusual for a girl," I admitted. Dad looked slightly unsatisfied with this answer. I decided to ad lib a bit. "I guess I can even seem a little weird, sometimes."

"Oh honey," Dad said. He turned to Vilna. "It's been hard on her. She needs a lot of support to overcome her demons."

Vilna's golden-brown eyes were intense. "I was so sorry to hear about your mom."

It was one of those things. Kind words about my mother's death, sure. But from the Lithuanian cultural attaché who was sitting just a little too close to my dad, they made my blood run cold.

"Hey guys, can we just stick to the basics?" I said. "There's no need to improvise that much."

"Improvise?"

"She means she'd like to stick to the plan," Dad said. "The bit where we plan her future. Right, *Isobel*?"

"Well, Daddy, I did what I planned to do." I jerked my chin at the package on the seat. "Maybe we should just go."

Dad frowned. "We don't want to leave right away. It might —" He leaned forward. "—give the wrong impression."

"Yes, please don't leave, Isobel," Vilna said. "I'm sorry if I offended you. We just wanted to explore all the options. It seems crazy to spend all that money on your care when we have this big old house—"

"Back up there a moment," I said, "What do you mean, crazy to spend money on my care?"

She closed her eyes and winced. "Okay, I apologize again. Bad choice of words."

"Bad choice? Which word was bad?"

Dad held out a placating hand. "Relax, Isobel we don't want a scene."

"Look—" I leaned forward and lowered my voice. The waitress was passing, burdened with plates for another table. I didn't like the way she kept glancing at me out of the corner of her eye. "—you have your package. All the evidence to save the soldiers is in there. Maybe we can call it a—"

"You're talking about this?" She plopped the package on the table. "What's supposed to be in here?"

"Put that away," I whispered, angry. "*They* could be looking."

I risked a glance at the waitress. Yes, she was serving food to another table. But she was looking over at us. So were the people she was serving.

"Jesus," I said, shielding my face with my hand. "I thought you were a professional."

"Right." She picked at the tape on the brown paper. "Let's get to the bottom of this, shall we?"

"Do you have any idea what you're risking?" I turned to Dad. "Stop her, Dad."

"Isobel," he said, "I think we need to calm down here. I think we need to remember who we are."

I gritted my teeth. "Maybe we should remember what's at stake here."

His lips compressed into a thin line. "Oh, there's plenty at stake," he said.

Vilna had the paper open. She pulled out a long rubbery thing. Through the thin membrane, a chunky substance could be seen. She dropped it on the table.

"Oh my God," she said, "is that really a condom filled with shit?"

"Isobel," Dad said, like he was angry at me.

Vilna flicked it away from her coffee cup with a blood-red artificial nail. It flopped over, reluctantly.

She rubbed her nail furiously on a napkin. "What is going on in your head, girl?"

I realized both of them were looking at me.

"I don't know how that got in there," I said. "Clearly, one of our agents has betrayed us."

"They give teenage girls condoms?" Vilna turned to Dad. "So they can fill them with shit? What kind of sick, godless people run that place?"

"Listen," I said, "our agents risk their lives to keep America safe. Sure, hiccups happen, but I expect a little more respect. It wasn't that long ago you joined NATO."

"Don't make it worse for yourself," Dad hissed at me.

"The enemies are closer than you believe," I told him. "The entire mission could be in peril."

"My God," Vilna breathed. "It's exactly like you warned me, Henry."

"Isobel," Dad said, "look around. No one is paying any attention to us."

I looked. It was true that the waitress had disappeared back to the kitchen. The people in the booth also seemed to be fully occupied with their food. I frowned. But then another thought occurred to me. I raised a finger to my lips and eyed the caddy of condiments on the table, the fresh one the waitress had brought over, even though the other had not been completely empty of syrups. I began to disassemble it, examining each bottle for listening devices. Vilna took another deep breath to say something more but froze as the package on the table suddenly moved. It wasn't empty after all.

All of us stared as a diamond-shaped green head emerged from the crumpled paper. A forked tongue sampled the cafe air.

"NOW folks, who had the baked potato soup here?"

The waitress loomed above us, soup in hand. Two more plates were balanced on her arm.

The snake, sensing a massive heat source heading in his direction, made a break for Vilna. Vilna screamed and leaped up onto the booth seat, overturning the soup onto the waitress, who also screamed, threw chicken and waffles into the air, and beat at her chest to get the steaming liquid off.

The people in the neighboring booth joined in the screaming.

Dad leaped up, and before I knew it, he had me by the arm and was dragging me for the door.

"I'm taking her back," he shouted to Vilna. "We'll continue this conversation later, okay, sugar?"

"Back where?" I shouted at him, struggling in his grip.

"Don't bother," she screamed. "You take that nutcase back where she belongs."

We got to the car just as someone set off the fire alarm. The entire flock of grackles burst into the air, beating their wings in terror. IHOP customers poured out the door. We legged it for the car.

I had to try two or three times to get the passenger seat belt buckle in the slot. My heart beat fast and strong where the shoulder strap pressed against my chest. Dad was having trouble too. He couldn't quite get the key in the ignition. When it finally slotted in, he put his hands on the wheel and took a few deep breaths. His face contorted weirdly, like he was struggling to keep some emotion in check.

"Sorry, Dad," I said.

"No, Rain, you delivered," he said. "You were my masterstroke."

The cloud of birds swirled around us and the crowd outside the IHOP was still growing. He wiped the sweat from his forehead and started the car.

"I think maybe I need some debriefing here," I told him. His praise about delivering the package warmed me, but I was still confused. "Did you tell Vilna that I came from a mental hospital?"

"It's the best way to throw them off," he explained. "If they think you're nuts, they won't look into it further."

We had to drive around the parking lot to get to the exit. At last, my Dad was talking sense again. But I couldn't shake the image of Vilna's hate-filled eyes. They made me feel unclean, like the crap in that condom.

"But why were those items in that package?"

His lip lifted in a sneer. "I thought it would be obvious, especially to you. The snake contained the microchip."

"Why would anyone put a microchip in a snake?"

"Exactly," he said. "The perfect hiding spot."

"But the...thing." I couldn't bring myself to say "condom."

"Rain," he said, "that woman in there was an impostor, one of the Others." He shook his head. "She was so good, she even fooled me. But all of our packages contain feces in one form or another, and only our true contacts know to expect it."

"Like a shibboleth."

He looked over at me. "What?"

I sighed. "So you've never seen that woman before?"

"Never," he said. "And I never will again."

"Good thing the snake got away." I thought about it a moment. "It did get away, didn't it?"

He briefly took one hand off of the steering wheel to reach in his pocket and hand me a retractable pen. "Click it, three times, quickly."

I did.

"That's my girl. You just exploded the snake and destroyed the chip. Now let's get out of here before she calls for backup."

I dropped the pen, horrified, but it was too late. I could only hope that the snake's death had been quick.

As we circled past the front door to get to the exit, the impostor Vilna burst out of it. She stood there next to the newspaper machines. People milled around her, but she just looked at us.

I wasn't sure what Dad's plan had been, or how I'd fitted into it as his masterstroke. At least, if the FBI was right, Dad's retractable pen probably did jack all and a lucky snake might have gotten away with it.

At the time, I'd glared out the window back at her, furious that her treachery had resulted in the death of an innocent reptile. I must have looked exactly like the raving lunatic Dad had made me out to be.

But that look she'd given us? Even at that distance, I could see the confusion and hurt on her face. My mom had looked like that a lot of the time. Most of the time, even.

So many questions...and only one man could answer them.

14

"About time you showed up. Come in quickly, and shut the door," Leif said. "Don't let the monkey get out."

Irritated by his tone and exhausted by the day's events, I left the door ajar behind me. "I don't have time for this now," I told him. "I need to borrow your laptop."

"Why would I let *you* touch my laptop?"

To find Angrendir, I needed to get online. I considered my options. If I told him everything, it could take hours. And why would I even do that? I barely knew the kid, and certainly didn't trust him. He'd need careful handling if I was going to get access to his laptop. "Someone told me there's an imminent terrorist threat on US soil. I need to investigate."

He tried to shunt around me to slam the door. "Who told you that?"

I blocked his way. "Today I found a missing girl hiding in the bomb shelter in my backyard. Hunting terrorists before she got ill. Thing is, she found something. It might be something real."

"Seriously? She just happened to be hiding in your backyard? Don't you think that's kind of unlikely?"

"Not really," I said. "My dad was the one who secretly employed her. He's such an extremely super-bad-ass secret agent, not even the government knows about him." I clenched my fists. "It was for our own safety."

Leif spread his palms out in a mockery of supplication. "How many times have I said, Rain? You gotta ease up on the lies there. Pick one or two, pad them out with some realistic detail and—"

"Oh, just screw you, Leif. The security of the entire nation is at risk."

I made to push past him, but this time he blocked my way.

"No, Rain, screw you. In this house, we have real problems, like a psychotic monkey on the loose."

I said what I should have said when I first opened the door. "What monkey?"

With a terrified hissing screech, a calico-colored streak of fur shot past our feet and out the front door. From the kitchen, a long, sustained crash...it sounded like an iceberg of china had broken loose into a linoleum sea. Then a grunting noise, somewhat like an angry pig.

Leif raised an eyebrow. "That one."

To be fair, I realized the monkey was a pretty serious problem after Leif explained it to me. A woman had rung a local university lab yesterday, looking to unload her pet capuchin—maybe they could use it for experiments, and she didn't give two hoots if it ended up dead. The lab occasionally got these requests and always refused them, but the receptionist was a friend of Desiree's and got the woman's number. Early that afternoon, they had stopped by with the thing in a cat carrier and returned to work, not for a moment thinking that the monkey might be able to undo latches secure for animals without opposable thumbs. Not guessing either that it would be smart enough to wait until they'd left the house.

"I came home to find Good Kitty trapped under the butcher's block," Leif told me. He glanced at the door. "Now, thanks to you, Good Kitty is in even more shit. You know she's not allowed outside."

"Leave off, Leif. If what you say is true, Good Kitty is way safer out there," I said. "Tell me you called animal control."

He shook his head. "If they come and see this...look, I don't want to risk anyone taking Reagan away."

"What do you mean?" I asked.

"Look at all this." He indicated the piles of animal cages, plants, books, dishes, empty food wrappers, and other miscellaneous objects covering every horizontal surface of the living room with his arm. "If anyone except for Carol Anne comes out here and sees the parrot crap on the windows and the dog vomit on the carpet, they're not going to be too happy with Mom. They'll say the house isn't fit for human habitation. They'll take Reagan away and who knows where she'll end up? You know how many foster carers are pedos? Do you have any idea?"

"It can't be that many. They must check for pedos." I looked around for his backpack. Maybe I could get the phone out and call them myself, but I didn't see it in the living room or dining room.

He glared at me, arms crossed on his chest. I sighed.

"Okay, Leif, fine. Just tell me the situation."

"Have a look for yourself."

I peered into Desiree's country-style kitchen. I'd already had my suspicions about its fitness as a food-preparation area. Toaster crumbs drifted behind the cracked vintage sugar bowl, gray muck grouted the baseboards, and greasy fuzz coated the screen at the window, but now there was monkey crap smeared across the walls and cabinet doors as well. The acrid, feral stench of it made me wince.

The monkey squatted in the sink. It turned its head to look at me in that jerky, twitchy monkey way, its lips swinging slackly. It was covered with bald patches and open sores. When it bared its mouth at me, I saw the reason for the slackness...all its teeth had been pulled.

I ducked my head back out, just as the monkey let loose with a projectile that nearly hit my head. It slapped to the ground behind me like a beanbag, and I bent to pick it up. A peanut butter sandwich, in a baggie. The corners had clearly been gummed.

"Leftovers from my lunch," Leif said.

"Your backpack?"

Leif nodded. "In there, with my laptop...and phone."

"Any guns in the house?"

"Are you kidding? We're Democrats."

"All right." I motioned him closer. "It's not perfect, but I think I have a plan."

Leif held a blanket and hid behind the kitchen doorway while I entered and tried to scare the damn thing in his direction. The primate hopped across the kitchen, too small and fast for me. I resorted to throwing shards of dinner plates in its direction, thinking I could herd it towards Leif. But that was an even dumber idea, as it picked them up and tossed them straight back at me with excellent aim. I threw up my arms to shield my face.

"Leif," I called, "are all your neighbors Democrats?"

"If I knock on doors asking to borrow guns," he shouted back, "I'm gonna get shot!"

The capuchin crouched on top of the fridge. It snarled, reached up and deftly unscrewed a halogen light bulb out of its socket. Before it could take aim, I turned the sink on full and aimed the sink sprayer at it. That worked, at least it would have, had Leif been less bleeding-heart liberal and more aggressive with the blanket. As it was, the monkey gummed his forearm and shot into the living room.

The two of us ran in there, Leif clutching his arm and moaning.

"Stop being a baby." I looked around. "Where is it?"

A furry arm emerged from behind the TV and turned it on. I guess in its little monkey brain, it thought it was distracting us.

"Oh hell. Now we definitely can't use the sink sprayer," I said. "Stay here. Make sure it doesn't go anywhere."

Leif moaned. I went back into the kitchen.

The capuchin had done his damage, but I found all the pieces of Leif's old style phone, eventually. I wiped the crap off of the keys, slipped the battery back in, popped the folding cover on, and thank goodness, even with the cracked screen, it powered up. I went back to the living room. "Hey Leif," I said, "does your mom have a phone book, or do you reckon I should just dial 911?"

But Leif did not look at me. He had let go of his arm, which was blooming an impressive, monkey jaw-shaped purple. He was looking at the TV.

On the screen, Tabernakl was being carried on a stretcher down our driveway. The image was from across the street; it was hard to tell how close she was to death's door. Underneath, a caption scrolled by: "Missing girl, found alive after five years in a Fort Worth bomb shelter."

"Crap," he said. "All along, you were telling the truth."

Seeing her there on the TV broke my heart all over again.

Please stay alive, I thought. *Please, please don't die on me. I called for help as soon as I knew.*

Leif turned to me, stricken. "Tell it to me straight, Rain, when are the terrorists going to strike?"

15

E ven after the animal control guy got there, it took a lot of running around and crashing into houseplants before one of us cornered the monkey on the buffet and got a clear shot with a tranquilizing gun. The feral primate plucked out the dart, but too late. Faceless angel statues and pastel-colored teddy bears toppled to the floor like tiny fallen souls as the monkey staggered and sank to its haunches.

"That your monkey?" the animal control guy asked.

"Hell no," I said. I explained the situation, as far as I knew it.

"Doesn't surprise me. Those things are worse than Rottweilers," he said. "One second they're eating grapes from your hand, the next they're clawing out your jugular."

The monkey fell on its side, blinking, as the sedative took hold.

The animal control guy reached up, his hands safe in thick leather gloves, took the limp monkey off the shelf and laid him on the table. It sprawled there like an abandoned child's toy. "Can't fix a monkey, not even if you cut off its tail and pull out all of its teeth," he said. "Poor little guy, made for the jungle and he doesn't even know it."

Leif hovered at the door, his face white.

"Look," the guy said to him on his way out. "I know your mom. I know she helps us out with homeless animals a lot, so I'm not going to report the mess in here this time. Get her to clean it up, though, okay? Don't just nod at me. Really do it, okay?"

So that was resolved, but here's the thing, the crappy thing I wish I didn't have to report. I didn't help Leif clean up. I just walked to the room I shared with Reagan and closed the door. I lay down on the bed. When Leif knocked on the door later, said through the cheap veneer that his laptop was drying out and though it was a bit sticky and stank like monkey piss, it would work for hunting terrorists, I didn't answer.

When he said never mind, we could go over to his friend Izzard's house and borrow his super-bad-ass gaming PC with high-speed broadband and shit, I turned my face to the wall and pulled the pillow over my head. I knew I couldn't go to the door, not even to tell Leif to fuck off. I guess I was tired, but every time I closed my eyes, I saw that desktop wallpaper of Colorado Springs in the bomb shelter. Every half a minute or so, my chest would spasm with grief and I would grimace with the effort of not screaming. All lost. All gone now.

Colorado Springs was the last place I was ever happy. I had liked how the Rocky Mountains sat in the West, like a picture postcard but with a fresh wind effect. How the sun set over them like in an illustrated Bible for children.

Dad was away a lot of the time then, on operations for the FBI, he told us. His lack of attention allowed my mom to blossom.

She got a prescription for anti-depressants, found a self-help group for agoraphobics, dyed her hair nut-brown again and even got a part-time job as a Walmart cashier. She didn't tell him, of course. Out of character for him, he either didn't know or didn't confront her about it.

Then, despite the clear and present danger, she sent me on to middle school. It was the beginning of the end. Elementary had been bad enough, and with my practice SAT scores, I could get into the state colleges (though not, I admit, my goal of Caltech or MIT) but she said that I still needed to learn to socialize with my peers. Learning to socialize, as in learning to feel like shit about my clothes and hair and sitting by myself at lunch. I tried to explain, but no matter whom I talked to, they all seemed to think *I* was the one who wasn't making an effort.

I started doing poorly in math. Right after I sat at the back of the class and divided an angle into perfect thirds, right after Mr. Torres told the entire class that trisecting an angle in Euclidean geometry was impossible. I mean, honestly, Euclid never said you couldn't fold the paper. After that, I just couldn't see the point in trying.

But no matter how crap the day was going to be, there was always that moment when I opened the apartment door and saw the sunrise turning the tip of Pike's Peak pink. Felt as if I could walk up there, or at least send my soul up there, and in a way, just by looking at it, I kind of did.

And then one day after school, my mom had come into the kitchen with two Walmart backpacks with the tags still on and—with no explanation—handed me one. Said to me, "Pack now, and get in the car."

WHEN WE GOT in the car and started off, though, it wasn't Colorado Springs. It was that dark, lonely road in Tennessee again. I half-lucidly realized that my exhausted brain had sent me to sleep without the normal shut-down routines. My memories had drifted seamlessly into a dreamscape.

That could be the only explanation, because it was not Mom but Tabernakl in the seat next to me. Not the orc from the online game. The girl behind the orc.

"Are the sides of the road parallel?" she asked me. Her eyes were clear and black. Her lips were smooth and whole again.

"Yes," I told her.

"No," she said. "Parallel lines never meet. But look at that."

She pointed through the windshield where the sides of the road grew closer and closer until they finally met at the horizon.

"That's different," I said. "If you actually went to that point, you'd see the sides are just as far apart as they are here."

"But we can't go to that point. It's at infinity."

"Well, if you went halfway then. Or even just a bit down the road, like we're doing now. The road isn't getting any thinner, is it?"

"It is." She smiled. "Look behind us."

I did. The road behind us got thinner and thinner until it met at the horizon.

"That's just the perspective, the way the light hits our eyes. Angles and stuff. It's complicated."

She shook her head and pointed out the window. "Use your eyes, girl. It's wrong."

"No. There's a difference between complicated and wrong."

From the trunk of the car, a noise. But not a thump like before —this was a rattling, twanging, desperate noise. It made the hairs on the back of my neck stand up. I looked back, and then front again at the road. Which one of us was driving, anyway?

Not Tabernakl. She sat with her long, thin hands folded across her lap. "Something is at the window."

"It's okay, Mom locked the anarchists in the trunk," I told her. "They can't hurt you."

"Something is at the window."

"We can sort this out. After we kill the anarchists, we'll drive to the library and find a book on optics," I said. But it was hard to think clearly. The twanging sound was getting louder.

"We need to reassess our axioms, Rain."

"We could try non-Euclidean geometry, but most libraries don't—"

"Now," she cried, "the monster is at the window now!"

I forced my eyelids to open. Reagan was kneeling next to the bed, shaking me. "Rain, wake up! The monster is at the window."

"You're speaking," I said. I thought she was. My brain startup routines weren't engaging either, and sleep lay heavy on my head like a wet blanket. Tennessee mixing with Texas, Tabernakl morphing with Reagan. I felt motion sick. I sat up, swaying slightly. "Reagan, it's just nightmares. You were having a nightmare."

She turned her terrified face to the window. "Listen." Her voice cracked.

From behind the closed curtains, a drawn out, scratching twang-twang.

Shit. The Russians had found me. They were taking off the screen in preparation for cutting through the window.

Reagan grabbed my arm. "Please help." Her words were a half-sob. "Good Kitty never came back. She's still out there."

"Sweetie, the Russians won't hurt Good Kitty." Seeing her panic was heartrending, but I also needed her quiet so I could think what to do about the Russians. "Why isn't the electric wire shocking them?"

"Desiree found it. She made me unplug it."

Shit again. I crawled onto the floor and worked my way over to the outlet. It was too dark to see, but I could feel the outlet was empty. The twanging got louder, as if the mafia henchmen had sensed my movement. I scrabbled with my palms on the carpet until I found the plug and inserted it.

The whole window assembly shook violently, and sparks flew from behind the curtain. A terrible, inhuman noise tore through the night.

And then that charred barbecue smell drifted in. The smell of love, snuffed out.

I could hear doors opening in the rest of the house. Desiree burst into the room.

"Reagan? Rain? What is going on here?"

Only now was I fully awake and just realizing that I might have made a terrible mistake.

As if she had never broken her silence, Reagan pointed at the window. Before we could stop her, Desiree strode over and swept the curtains back. The scene was clear in the muddy orange glow of the street lamps outside.

Electricity...it makes muscles spasm. They contract, involuntarily and remain clenched for the duration of the current. A human, on receiving a shock, will nine times out of ten involuntarily jerk away, breaking the circuit and saving themselves. One time out of ten, they will clutch whatever is electrocuting them—helplessly grasp, with all their strength—the very thing that is killing them. So it was with Good Kitty. Reagan's clawed monster had put her hooks deep in the weave of the screen, and the current held her trapped there while her calico fur sizzled and her little heart fried.

I jerked the plug out as quickly as I could and Good Kitty leaped off the screen, running into the night, her only crime—the thing that unwittingly turned her into a monster—being the desperate need to return to the one she loved.

16

I put my forehead against the cool glass and looked out the window. In a car for real this time, not in a dream. I looked out at the weeds by the side of the road and the trees with their empty branches flashing past, and the moon behind, appearing motionless in the sky. It wasn't motionless. The illusion was for some reason dependent on the inverse of the distance. It had to do with the derivative of polar coordinates, or would it be better to use trigonometric functions in rectangular space? I'd figured it out once before. I breathed on the glass, drew some blunt angles in the condensation. Better than paying attention to Carol Anne Cheung in the driver's seat beside me. But the details slipped away like roadside through the window. Drips of water ran through my diagram like tears.

She smelled like cosmetics and women's magazines. She glimmered with mineral dust on her cheekbones. Even the cloth of her dress had an opalescent luster. And every once in a while her nostrils would flare and her burgundy red lips would wrinkle into a tight line.

Apparently, they'd been having a party to celebrate finding Tabernakl. They'd identified who she was. A girl called Alicia Bagatelle, who had disappeared from Colorado Springs five years ago. Apparently Carol Anne, one of the few still sober, had been lumbered with retrieving me from the scene of my crime.

"They still haven't found Good Kitty," she informed me, "Thanks to your actions tonight, Reagan may never speak again."

"I'm not some out-of-control crazy cat torturer," I said. It was what Desiree had screamed at me, several times before Carol Anne had come to get me, and it still hurt. "I was just trying to secure that window—to make Reagan and me feel safe."

"You were safe." Carol Anne glanced my way. "No one but Peter and I knew where you were."

It hadn't exactly felt that way, but now I wondered if I could have done something different. In my mind's eye, I saw that little line of crosses in the back garden, marking the row of decomposing corpses in shoe boxes beneath. Desiree took all sorts of animals into her house, no matter how damaged or broken they were. But now that I had screwed up big time, she would no longer have me there.

I hadn't even said goodbye to little Reagan. All I had was a note Leif had thrust into my hand as I was frog-marched out the door, folded seven times and shoved into the front of my pocket.

"Forget it," I said. I wiped the window clean with my hand and looked at the moon, motionless as ever.

I felt her eyes on me. "I'm sorry. What I said was harsh. Are you feeling okay, Rain?"

Assume the motion of the car is dy, and the distance to the object is r. Looking out the window, it was all passing on the right. But cosine diagrams have the point of rotation on the left. The effort of reflecting in my mind confused me. Did it mean the angle became negative?

"It's kind of been a long day," I said. "What with finding out you think my dad is a fraud and the missing girl in the backyard. Not to mention monkeys and cats."

"Well," she said, "we can certainly agree that it's been traumatic. You want to tell me what's going on?"

I continued to look out the window. If only I could remember what the derivative of sine was. Was it the trig function that was the negative of itself, or the one that turned into the other one? So much light pollution in the city. You couldn't even see Orion's Belt.

"Never mind," Carol Anne said. "You can tell me when you feel ready."

The question bubbled up out of my mouth before I knew it. "Is there anything in that textbook of yours about girls like me?"

"Not remotely." Carol Anne rubbed her temples. "As far as I know, there's never been anyone quite like you."

"Oh," I said.

"There were those women rescued after years of captivity in an attic," she said. "One of them had a kid. But that's not really you and your mom though, is it? Your father never locked the door."

"No," I said. "We kept it locked ourselves."

"Maybe you're more like someone rescued from a cult." She frowned. "A very small cult, I guess."

"Maybe," I said. Was patriotism like my religion? But if my country was not what I thought it was, if there were no angels and devils as I thought of them, then what did I do next?

She looked over at me. "I can tell you what I think, if it's any help." When I nodded, she went on. "You're going to have a long road to recovery. Flashbacks, depression, difficulty forming attachments to people—"

"Really?" I asked her. I remembered Reagan's golden hair, spread out on the pillow as she slept quietly that first night I was there. That little bit of peace I had given her—now gone forever. "I'm not sure, but I don't think I want to be attached. I mean, I feel this big hole where there should be an attachment."

"I know it must hurt, but if it does, that's a good sign," Carol Anne said.

"No, it's a bad sign," I told her. "Everything I get attached to ends up dead." I turned back to the window. "Or hurt worse than before."

"It won't be like this forever, Rain," she told me. "This will end. If you want, I could contact Saffron's family, the Dunns."

I blinked. Of course. Peter had said she'd sent them letters. You always think of your mom as a mom. Not a daughter or a sister, but she had been both—before she met my dad. "They probably hate me, Carol Anne."

"There are no guarantees in life, but they've already lost a daughter. They might find it a comfort to discover that she gave them a granddaughter."

I shifted in my seat. The thought of meeting them aroused nothing but dread and shame.

"Think about it," she said. "Meanwhile, let's get you to that hotel."

I thought about it. But this is what I thought: that anyone that ever got attached to me had better damn well carry a gun.

17

Buzzzzz.

I rolled off the bed, snatched up the bedspread, and barreled into the bathroom. I locked the door and threw myself flat into the tub, pulling the bedspread over me.

Buzzzzz.

They'd caught up with me at last. I hoped it didn't hurt too much, getting blown apart. Hopefully, my nervous system would shred away with flesh before it got the chance to inform me of total system failure.

Buzzzzz. Buzzzz.

I folded the bedspread away from my face. Whoever was trying to blow me up sure was one incompetent son-of-a-bitch.

I crept back into the empty hotel room, bedspread wrapped around me as a makeshift bomb disposal suit. I located the sound of the buzz. As I feared, it was in my bag, the stuff I'd had at Desiree's. But I was awake now, my paranoid instincts tempered by logic. I crept to the window and pulled aside the curtain. Yes, there was the FBI agent sitting on a chair outside my door, still alive, cigarette in her hand. This was my new reality.

I let the curtain fall and went to my bag, clenched my teeth, and opened it, wincing at the faint smell of monkey feces. That stuff had been scattered all over the house, but, dammit, I'd been really careful not to pack any. Or so I'd thought. I could see a faint luminescence rising up through the folds of my clothes. I reached in, rooted around, and felt a plastic case. An old-style phone with little buttons. Ah. The source of the monkey shit smell.

I pulled it out. Through the spider-web cracks, the screen read: IZZY.

I hit "Accept call" and put it to my ear.

"Hello?"

"Rain?"

"Leif?"

"Thank God, it's you. I didn't know if they'd let you have a phone in jail, so I slipped mine in your bag when you weren't looking. I'm borrowing Izzard's phone."

"I'm not in jail. I'm in a hotel."

"Wow, it sure looked to me like they were gonna take you straight to juvie."

"I don't think they can arrest you for accidentally almost killing a cat."

"Damn, you're probably right." A pause. "Man, it would have been so messed up to say I knew someone on the inside."

"If it makes you feel any better, there's an agent on guard outside the door and I don't think she'd be happy if I left."

"FBI?"

"Yes."

"For real?"

"Yes."

"Fuckin'—messed—up. Hey Izzy, she's got a real FBI agent guarding her."

I listened to the resulting mumbling. It sounded like they were high-fiving each other, or whatever normal kids did to show approval among their peers.

"So," I said, "are we done here?"

"Can I put you on speaker phone? Izzy wants to know what kind of heat the agent is packing."

"Fuck off, Leif." I almost hung up, but then I looked over to the bedside table, where I had emptied my pockets. At the paper shoved in my hand in the midst of the chaos the night before. Folded seven times, now half popped open like an origami of guilt. It said *Dont fele bad Rane I know you did your best.*

"How's Reagan doing?"

There was a pause. "They took her away, just like I thought they would."

"It's not your fault, Leif, it's mine."

"Dude, we all should have known better. None of us ever twigged that the monster stopped visiting once we kept Good Kitty inside all the time. If only that freaking cat had tried one of our windows even once..."

I didn't answer. Blaming everyone or no one, it wouldn't bring Reagan back.

His voice dropped to a whisper. "I'm gonna go nuts home alone with Mom."

I was about to tell him that I didn't really care when his voice rose again.

"So, listen, about the imminent terrorist attack you kind of mentioned yesterday..."

"Oh God, that?" I leaned back on the bed. What had I been thinking? I had no resources. My computer setup, with all its configurations and settings, was now dismantled in some forensics lab. I had no weapons, no transport, and no money. Possibly, I even had no training. No real training, that is. Just half-assed stuff that I thought was real and ended up frying beloved pets in the night.

"Yeah? Well, me and Izzy, we want to help."

"What?"

"We want to help and shit. Go kick some terrorist ass."

"Yeah," came a muffled voice from the background, "Your days are numbered, evil terrorist bitches!"

"Seriously?" I shut my eyes. "Jesus. You don't even know the first thing about it."

"We are *totally* ready to learn."

"Look guys, I don't even know what hotel I'm in."

"What kind of an anti-terrorist agent doesn't know what hotel they're in?"

They had a point. I looked back at the bedside table. A laminated card rested there, explaining hotel services and advertising local businesses. I picked it up. "Welcome to the Sunrise Motel!!! Conveniently located on Highway 183" it said at the top. And underneath, in a green starburst: "Free Wi-Fi in all rooms!!!"

"Never mind, I got it."

Free Wi-Fi. I had nothing now, it was true. But if I just had some equipment, it sure would help with the hunting down Angrendir and StormShadow. I tested the idea of it, like prodding a sore tooth with my tongue. Maybe I would fail, probably I would fail—but yeah, I still wanted to do it. I still needed to try. "Hey, can you get me a laptop?"

More mumbling. "Yeah, we probably can."

"Can you get it to me here," I asked, "in the hotel?"

"Christ, girl, you don't ask for much. Neither one of us can drive."

I wanted the laptop, but I didn't want to explain to Leif why. It was complicated, and if he knew the whole truth, he might not be as excited about helping. I thought about it a moment. Then I said, "Despite what video games may have led you to believe, saving the world from terrorists takes a bit of effort."

He sighed like he was exasperated, but I could tell he was excited underneath. "Fine. Give us a couple of hours, okay? We'll get one."

A FEW HOURS LATER, there was a knock at the door. The door cracked open, banging the chain taut. The smell of pizza hit me like the memory of Roman's fist.

"Rain?" It was Peter's voice. "Feel like company?"

"Peter?" I asked, sitting up on the bed. "What the hell are you doing here?"

"Were you expecting someone else?"

The agent outside let him past, Agent Jenny Sala-something, the third or fourth agent to take a shift waiting outside my door. Peter gave her a chummy slap on the shoulder, told her to get some lunch at the chicken place across the road, and closed the door behind her.

"Not totally by the book," he said to me, "but Jenny's cool. She's a friend."

I tried not to let him see how happy I was he'd showed up. "You heard what happened?"

He walked over to the hotel desk-table thing and set down a bag and pizza box. I got a good look at the earnest squareness of his jaw and the rough golden stubble that covered it before he turned to me. "How do you do it, girl? How do you always manage to get yourself in so much damn trouble?"

Suddenly, I didn't have to fake my irritation after all. "I managed fine until you kidnapped me four days ago," I said. "You brought pizza then too."

He winced.

Oh, what the hell. Now that I thought about it, I was pretty hungry. And pizza is pizza. If I only ate food with happy memories, I'd never eat again. I went to the table and lifted the lid.

"It's uncured pepperoni." There wasn't an extra chair, so he sat on the edge of the bed. He grinned at me. "No nitrites."

That was surprisingly thoughtful of him. I sat at the table and occupied myself with stuffing as many pepperoni-cheese calories down my throat as fast as I could.

"Any news?" I asked around a mouthful of pizza. "Have you found out anything more about my dad?"

"Actually, we were wondering if you had any ideas." He paused. "Now that we're on the same team."

I squinted at him. The jocular grin was still there, but his eyes had slightly narrowed. I was starting to learn the many personas of Peter Angelopolos (assuming that was even his real name), and this was the working face, the one he wore when he wanted information. It was true, we weren't enemies anymore. But on the same team? I wouldn't have gone quite that far. In fact, until I found my dad and got the answers I needed about the True Patriots, we were not on the same team at all. But to find my dad, I needed to stay fast and flexible. I didn't need the FBI getting in the way. So I swallowed my pizza and shrugged.

Peter's blue eyes met mine for one heartbeat, then two, and then he said, "If you have some information as to where he is, Rain, you'd better give it to us."

I stared back at him.

"Thing is," I said, "if we're on the same team, it's got to be two-way. If you have some information, you should be giving it to me."

"I know this is early days," Peter said. "But at some point, you are going to have to start acting like a civilian."

That just pissed me off. I knew he was looking at me and seeing a girl somewhere between the ages of fifteen and nineteen, and not even a normal girl. Both he and the FBI had treated me like a child, brainwashed by my dad and stunted in every other way.

"You should know something," I said. "I was damn good at what I did."

Peter shook his head. "I'm sorry to be the one to say this, but you probably never found anything. Just the crumbs that your dad left out for you."

That hurt. I put my pizza down, suddenly uncertain and no longer very hungry.

"There is good news. Alicia is still alive."

"Has she said anything?"

"She's still critical, in a coma. The Bagatelle family is flying down to Dallas this afternoon."

"Oh," I said, disappointed.

"Look, I really came by to apologize. To tell you that I know we screwed up with you. All of us did." Peter shifted on the bed. "We had no fucking clue what was going on there. That foster home was supposed to be a stable base for you, a haven."

I picked up a crust and inspected it for any last bits of cheese to avoid looking at him. "My basement was my haven, Peter. When I went out, if I left, I'd maybe talk to one person. Maybe no one at all. You guys boxed up and carted away the only haven I've ever had."

"You're doing pretty damn good for someone who never talks to anyone."

"Don't forget, I have a lot of experience with crazy situations too."

"Damn." His voice was quiet. I looked up, and saw the jocular grin was gone. Just those blue eyes, looking at me sincerely now. "I wish there was some way we could make this easier for you."

His words made my chest all tight. I didn't trust him completely, but there were still things he and I shared that no one else did, like how it felt to tear down the highway in Dmitri's car in the middle of the night, or how it felt to kill, or how it felt to watch someone die.

"Thanks," I said.

"Look, I brought you some stuff." He hefted the grocery sack onto the table. A two-liter bottle of diet soda tore through the plastic and thunked on its side. "At least have a drink with me before Jenny comes back."

I unwrapped some glasses from the bathroom and poured the heady drink into it. Thing was, what with that weird taste that hotel bathroom glasses always have and the lukewarm temperature, it was some pretty nasty shit.

"Is there ice down the hall?" Peter asked me with a grimace.

"I think so."

"Stay here. Don't let anyone in, I'll be right back."

It wasn't even thirty seconds after he left that there was a knock on the door.

I know. He'd just told me not to open the door. But I looked through the peephole and knew who it was anyway.

Leif burst in through the door, followed by a tall, floppy-haired boy and a girl with blue hair and brown roots.

The girl said, "Was that the agent who's guarding you? Walking past us down the hall?"

"Most likely," I told her.

"Lucky you. He sure creams my twinkie."

The tall boy made a retching noise.

Leif shot me an appalled look. "Rain," he said, "let me introduce Izzard and his older sister Bailey."

"We brought you some gear," Izzard said. He had one of those cheerful springy body shapes that would be a liability if society collapsed and the survivors turned to cannibalism. "Unfortunately, we had to bring my sister too. She's the only one who can drive."

"Fuck off, Izzy." The girl plopped on the bed where Peter had been sitting and crossed her bare legs.

I took the laptop from Leif and popped the lid open to have a quick look. I was grateful that he'd come, but anxious to get him and his friends out of the room before Peter came back.

"Looks fine," I said. "Thanks."

Leif looked over my shoulder. "Sorry it's not more. All I could find was Desiree's old Windows laptop."

"It will tunnel, that's all I need." I snapped the lid shut and put it in my bag. "Thank you so much, Leif, really. You're a good kid."

He looked uncertainly at the bag. "Uh, don't you want to do something now? We're totally up for hunting some terrorists now."

Finnegan's Awake

"Yeah," Izzard chimed in, "we totally want to know how you do it and shit."

"Thing is, Leif..."

"Check it out!" Bailey's exclamation caused us all to turn in her direction. She reached in the grocery bag Peter had left on the table and extracted a...oh hell...it was a flowery dress, the one from Dillard's that the mannequin had been wearing when Peter had frog-marched me through there. "Nice," she said. "Just like mine. That will totally go with your boots."

We all looked at my steel-toed combat boots.

She stood up, spread her own flowered skirt, and then lifted one foot, encased in a black patent Doc Marten. Izzard nodded.

Leif winced. "Bailey, the thing is...we kind of need to focus on saving America right now."

"The thing is," I said, "if Peter finds out I'm doing this I'm kind of going to be in trouble. He only went to get ice."

"Right," Leif said. "You make the call. We're out of here."

But just as he said it, the door cracked open and Peter's voice came in through the widening crack: "Christ, these contract hotels. Three out of four ice machines broken."

Then the door swung fully open. Peter saw Leif and dropped into a stance, drawing his gun. The ice bucket clattered to the floor, exploding ice everywhere. Bailey let out a little squeak. Forgotten, the dress floated to the floor in lazy curls.

"WHO THE HELL ARE YOU GUYS?" Peter demanded.

"Don't shoot, they're friends," I cried.

Peter entered but didn't lower his weapon. "Not a clever move, Rain, telling your friends where you were."

Leif glanced at Izzard and then back at Peter. "Is she officially in witness protection now, or something?"

"Yeah," Izzard said, "does this mean we have to join her now that we blew her cover?"

149

"Hang on," Bailey said, "I was just giving these fuckups a ride. I had no idea."

Peter lowered his weapon. "This isn't witness security. As soon as we find somewhere else for her"—he glanced at me —"preferably without cats, she's going there. Alone."

"That's no fun," Leif said.

Peter holstered his gun. "You have any idea how much witness security costs? We don't do it for just anybody."

Leif looked at the ground, his black hair flopping over his forehead.

"I'm going to need to see some ID," Peter said.

Bailey rooted in her lime-green purse and handed him her driver's license while Leif and Izzard fished in their jeans pockets and pulled out dog-eared laminated cards.

Peter looked at them dubiously. "Middle School IDs?"

"What do you want?" Izzard countered. "I'm fifteen."

"What's that on your head?" Peter asked. "In the photo."

"Religious headgear. It's my human right to wear it."

"Looks like a sieve."

"I happen to be a follower of the Church of the Flying Spaghetti Monster. I'm a Pastafarian."

Peter gave Izzard a hard, narrow-eyed look.

"It's a bona fide religion. Look it up online."

"So where is it now?"

"What?"

"The sieve. You're not wearing anything now."

"I'm sadly lapsed in my faith."

"Really."

"It's still pretty painful. I don't like to talk about it much."

Peter handed the IDs back. "You shouldn't have come here, guys. You need to leave now."

Leif looked glad to be heading for the door. "Whatever."

Izzard turned on one foot and marched for the door. "You're the man with the gun." He gave me a stiff wave. "Nice to meet you Rain."

Bailey headed for the door too, but then she turned. "Can I have a private word with Rain?"

"No," Peter said.

"It's about tampons."

He flinched. "On second thought, I don't guess I need to know details."

She took me by one arm and pulled me to a corner. "Just wanted to say thanks for giving Leif this chance."

"What do you mean, chance?"

"Chance to pull his head out of his ass, think about something else for a change." She rolled her eyes at the three males across the room. "Between me and Izzy, we think Leif might be a bit bored and depressed."

"Jesus Christ," I said. "You think he's bored, and it's somehow my problem?" Why was she even saying this to me?

"Yeah, he needs something better to do with his time, build up his confidence. And you need help fighting terrorists, so it's kind of win-win, right?"

I looked at her. Then I sighed. "Yeah, win-win."

"Good. Remember, we're still here if you need us again. Okay? Serious. You text me. Anytime. Yay for America and shit."

She looked sincere. I wouldn't ever text a girl like that, but then I remembered that she had a car. "Okay."

She started to root in her purse. "Guess I'd better get you some tampons so that Agent Hot-n-Hunky over there doesn't get suspicious." She handed me some paper-wrapped parcels. "And don't gross out, but I have something else."

"Thanks, but I don't need—"

She pressed a small plastic cylinder in my hand. "You do. Lip gloss. It's opened, but I don't have major germs or anything. I think it's easier for girls to take on the world when we're wearing the right lip gloss."

I'd never worn lip gloss in my life. I looked down at the sparkly tube. Perhaps that was where I'd been going wrong all this time.

"Here." She took it back and before I knew it, she'd swiped some on her finger and smeared it on my lips. "Spread it." She demonstrated by rubbing her lips together.

I did, feeling the novelty of the cherry-scented gelatinous texture.

"I knew that color would be perfect on you." She smiled and squeezed my hand.

I nodded, distracted, still rubbing my lips and wondering how she could tell one way or the other. Despite my training and experience, there were still so many things—little and big—that I still didn't know about.

Some stuff I knew I didn't know. That stuff, I could handle. It was the stuff I didn't know I didn't know about that terrified me.

18

After Peter closed the door, I picked up the dress from where Bailey had tossed it.

"What were you thinking, bringing me this?" I asked. "What possible use could I have for this?"

"Christ, kiddo," Peter set his gun on the table. "It was nothing. Just something nice...I just got the idea that you didn't have many nice things."

"Of course, I don't have nice things," I told him. "Those aren't things I can have."

"Rain, it's over. Your dad's not in control anymore. You can decide what you have now. You can choose."

I looked down at my camo shorts and plain t-shirt. I tried to understand what he meant.

"Are you suggesting...what? I start wearing makeup? Dress like Bailey?"

"What's so wrong with Bailey?"

I let out a long, frustrated breath.

"Christ, Rain," he said, "you're so serious. All the time."

"Life is serious."

"It doesn't have to be," he said. "Not always. If you decide to move on, hell, I know you could do it. You might even like it."

I rubbed my lips, feeling their strange greasiness. "I wouldn't even know where to start."

He half smiled. "Go on, try on the dress. I'll pour some soda with ice this time. If there's any left in the bucket."

Fuck it. Why not? In the bathroom, I unlaced my boots and pulled my shorts and shirt off. The rayon dress slipped over my head easily enough. It floated lightly over my skin, cool and drafty. But looking in the mirror, I could see it wasn't that great. I reached into my shorts pocket and extracted the lip gloss. Put on another coat. The results were mediocre at best. I never would be a beauty, not like Bailey. I looked down at the boots that she had liked so much, but truth be told, I couldn't face all forty laceholes just then. I left them on the bathroom floor and went back out to the room.

Peter handed me a plastic cup. "You look nice."

"It doesn't look right on me," I said.

"It could. Try looking in the mirror," he said. "Do you see the problem?"

I looked. I reached up and released my hair from its ponytail. The long brown curls fell around my face, framing it. But it still wasn't quite right.

Peter came up behind me and put his hand on my shoulder. Through the thin dress, I could feel the warmth from his body behind me. It made me stupidly weak at the knees, but I ignored it. He didn't mean anything by it, I knew that.

He sighed. "Stop frowning. You have to stop frowning all the time."

I studied my face. "I'm frowning?"

"You're making it worse now."

I closed my eyes and tried on a smile, opened them again.

"Now you're grimacing like a madwoman," he said, laughing.

I hid my face in my hands. "I can't do it."

"It's okay, don't stress about it." He patted my shoulder. "Sit down, drink."

I turned to face him. "There's no point in trying to change. No one will ever want someone like me anyway."

He cupped my shoulders in his hands. "That's not true. Haven't you noticed?"

For a moment, I almost couldn't breathe.

"Noticed what?"

"That Leif is totally in love with you?"

Oh. Leif. "You're mistaken. For starters, I'm taller than him. I'm also four years older."

"Love can overcome," he said with a half-smile. But then he turned serious. "I mean, look. If I were ten years younger, I'd totally be smitten with you too."

I really felt like I might fall, but his hands steadied me. There was a warm slipperiness between my thighs and knew my body had independently decided what it wanted. But did I?

"Really?" I asked, my voice small.

"Really. And not just you in a flower dress. All of you, like you are. Frown and everything."

Thing was, boys like Leif, even taller and older versions who might be able to catch a monkey, they would never be enough for me. I needed someone who understood what I had gone through. Understood because he had been right there with me. It could only ever be Peter.

"So what does ten years have to do with anything?" I asked.

He suddenly became very still. Like a deer caught in head-lights. But he didn't loosen his grip on me.

"If I was Bailey, okay, fine," I said. "She couldn't find her way out of a paper bag if you cut three holes in it. But I have been through more things...I have *done* more things...than most girls will do in their entire lifetime. A lot of that was with you. It sort of makes my age irrelevant, don't you think?"

"Don't say things like that," he said, shutting his eyes. "You're also a part of this case and I have a duty of care."

The air hung heavy between us.

"You said I could decide what to have now. You said I could choose."

"I guess I did, but..."

All of a sudden, I knew his body had made its own decision about what it wanted whether his mind had accepted it or not. I went up on my toes and touched my lips to his.

You can try out stuff on your pillow, even run your fingers across your body late at night, but there's nothing like the real thing. He didn't push me away, so I threw my arms around his neck and pressed my body against his. Soon it wasn't just about soft lips and scratchy stubble and the complexity of tendons in his neck under my lips. His hands were on my hipbones, tipping my pelvis up and onto his. The urgent force of it kind of shocked me. I mean, it would have been hard to break away if I'd wanted to. But here's the thing, I didn't want to.

He lifted his head away from our kiss and gently touched his lips to my forehead. "Dammit, kiddo, I'm going to let you go now and then I'm going to leave. This is not going to work."

Instead of pulling away, I laced my fingers into the short hairs at the back of his neck.

"Of course it can work," I said. "Even if we can't always be together physically, there are other things we can do. I can always help you."

He gave me a quizzical look. "Help? What do you mean by help?"

I leaned my head against his chest, could feel the miracle of his heartbeat thumping there. "Help. Like when you're working in the field."

He moved his hands from my pelvis to my shoulders, pushed me away so that I had to meet his eyes. "You mean like you helped your dad?"

I looked back, confused. "Yes?"

He tossed me away from him. I landed on the bed and scrambled upright as fast as I could, not understanding this sudden turn of events.

"Dammit." He backed away from me, wiping his mouth with his hand, as if my spit was bleach that had slowly eaten through his skin and now burned into his flesh. "Goddammit."

"Peter?"

He went to the window and peered through the blinds. Then he turned to me, his next words spit out through gritted teeth. "Fucking hell, Rain. How could you think..."

"Wait...please, Peter...what did I do wrong?"

"How could you *ever* think I could be like...like your dad..."

"I don't think that way, I don't." I was on my knees on the bed, shaking, everything shaking. My next words came out as a pleading sob. "If you don't want me to think that way, *I won't.*"

"I don't want you to do *anything* I say," he said. "I don't even want you to *want* to do it. It's disgusting."

"You think I'm disgusting?"

In a flash, he'd left the window and shoved his face in mine. His forehead was so close, I could have leaned forward and bumped it with my own.

"No, Rain," he said. "You're not the disgusting one...*I am.*"

"Then what am I?"

There was nothing in his face but dead cruel pity.

"Damaged."

I don't remember my feet touching the ground nor my hand grabbing my bag. I do remember my other hand on the door-knob. And Peter's arms around my waist, holding me back.

"Rain, stop! I didn't mean...I just meant you don't know what you're doing!"

Well, I knew what I was doing all right. I thrust a precision elbow back and felt the crunch of nose cartilage. He let go and I flew outside. I bowled straight into Agent Jenny Something-or-other and sent fried chicken flying in ten directions and slammed headlong onto the ground. Her instincts kicked in and she grabbed my ankle as I tried to scramble away from her.

I hooked a bare toe in her eye. She cried out and let go and I was gone, around the front and looking at that endless landscape of orange cones and concrete slabs and dirt. Another vast Metro-plex highway under endless construction. Impossible to flee on foot. Game over. But I had nothing else to do, so, hopeless as it was, I started walking.

I was maybe halfway to the portico of the hotel when behind me, I heard Jenny's shout.

I started to run.

19

A t the front of the Sunrise Motel, I felt it more than heard it: the diesel growl of an engine tickling my thorax. I looked right and I saw it, the shuttle bus, idling under the lobby awning. I forced myself to a walk and stepped on board. A chemical-scented cool draft lifted the loose hairs on my head and raised a field of goose bumps under the thin tissue of my dress.

"Which terminal do you want?" Sunrise Motel's airport shuttle driver was a substantial Black man. He looked me up and down.

"Terminal D." It was a wild guess. I looked behind me, but neither of the agents had rounded the corner of the hotel yet.

"D is international," he said. "Are you really leaving the country with one carry-on...and no shoes?"

I looked down at my dirty bare feet. My knees were scraped from my altercation in the corridor and blood was dripping down my calf. They were still shaking.

"Please just go," I pleaded.

"You look like a nice girl. We have a few moments before I'm supposed to leave. Why don't you just sit there, and I'll call the police for you?"

"No," I said, "Please, it won't help. They already know."

"You saying the police were there?" His face went hard. "You saying they're involved?"

I didn't know what to say, so I just stood there, trying not to tremble. Behind me, the doors closed with a hydraulic swoosh.

"Ladies and gentlemen," he said into the mouthpiece to the three Asian businessmen sitting in the back of the shuttle, "hang on to your hand luggage. We are leaving for the airport slightly ahead of schedule." And then he drove straight across a dirt lot, knocked over some cones, and pulled onto the frontage road.

"Bumpy," he said to me, "but faster."

From behind the tinted glass, I could see Peter and Jenny run into the front parking lot. Peter looking around wildly, holding his nose and staggering as if he were drunk. Jenny with one reassuring hand on his shoulder. The intimacy of it made me flood white-hot with jealousy and rage.

"Hey." It was the bus driver again. "Hey, sit down while I'm moving, okay? I don't want you to fall and hurt yourself more."

"Okay," I said, and staggered to the nearest seat. "Thank you."

"Not a problem," he answered. "I know it probably didn't start out too good, but you have a blessed rest of your day."

———

PETER WAS RIGHT to be suspicious. I had not shared all of my information about Dad.

The sun set as I walked down the street somewhere in North Dallas. Back behind the industrial area, behind the semi junkyards and hubcap dealers and the places so dodgy they just walled the lot in with eight feet of plywood and let German shepherds prowl loose. Back where the pecans reached their black branches, still heavy with this year's green crop, to the oranges and golds in the sky.

What I had not told Peter was about the backup plan Dad

and I had worked out. We've always had one, the GOOD plan. When the shit hits the fan, it pays to have a place to run to that absolutely no one else knows about—a safe place to hide out in, to clear your head, to decide your next move. The rest of our life might well have been a sham, but the running away bit? That was real.

Now that the trusting experiment I'd had with Peter had come to a premature and definitive end, I was grateful for my paranoid instincts on that front. I'd find my dad on my own without them. Then, either I'd find out the FBI was right, that he was a con man and my whole life was a sham, or it would turn out that the FBI were lying sons-of-bitches, and (although I had strong reservations about how the True Patriots had treated Alicia Bagatelle) there was a good chance I'd slip back into the underground as a member of that society once again.

I kept walking; I had been for hours. Eventually, the houses started up again, a mix of tiny clapboard shacks and rambling larger homes, the biggest hulks long ago divided into apartments. Fine woodwork was patched up with chipboard, and stained glass was blacked out with aluminum foil and duct tape. Dad might have connected me with Dmitri's arrest, or he might not have. Either way, he would have for sure seen Alicia on the news, carried out of our bomb shelter on a stretcher. So, there was a good chance he'd also be headed for the Bug Out House, the BOHO, we called it.

It was risky for me to go there alone, not knowing what I'd find, but the airport was a terrible place to stay. Free Wi-Fi, sure, but the whole damn thing was under surveillance. The BOHO was self-contained. It was even off-grid. No Wi-Fi, but if Dad were there, I wouldn't need it.

Out here, people were not too bothered about curb appeal. The front yards were full of stuff, of plastic toy ride-on horses, bleached by the sun, or rusting washing machines, or car radiators, or the aluminum skeletons of yard chairs flapping shreds of rotten webbing. They put themselves out in the yard too. They didn't wait for network news vans, police search tape, and kidnapped girls to draw them outside, just a warm autumn evening. Kids chased each other in the dirt while adults sat on the porch. The legs of a face-down man protruded from an open doorway. The rest of them watched me pass.

Dad and I had driven out here when we had to. Me walking was a new thing. It wasn't a good thing.

A guy sauntered over to his chain link fence, nylon skull cap pressing on his hair. His maroon boxers puffed out the top of his shorts. When he opened his mouth to speak, gold flashed.

"Hey girl," he said to me.

I tugged down the hem of Peter's flower dress. It made me look like even more of a target. Great. Just one more way Peter Angelopolos had screwed up my life.

"You should be careful." He hooked his hands in his boxer shorts, sucked in one cheek, and looked all the way down my bare legs to my flip flops, the ones I'd bought at Terminal D. "There's lots of broken glass on the ground around here."

"Terence." From the shadows of a sagging gingerbread veranda, I saw three heavy women in Walmart neon knits. One of them slowly shook her head. A warning. To me, or Terence?

He glanced back at her, shrugged, and turned to me. "You lost?"

I shook my head.

"Ain't my business, but you don't wanna walk down that road too far."

"I know where I am, thanks," I said quickly.

"Okay. Ain't my business. Just saying..." He jerked his head back, at the women on the porch. "...here, there are people around." Then, he pointed down the street. "You go down that road, you might never come back."

I nodded and walked away. The bushes grew wilder and the houses crumbled beyond habitability. The sun dipped below the horizon and the shadows spread. I saw no one.

When I finally got to the safe house, it took a bit of courage to actually enter the yard. The weeds had grown up, and so had the bushes. Anything could be hiding in there. Snakes, meth-heads, zombie cats.

Or Hal Wooten.

I circled round the back, striking a balance between keeping to the shadows and not rustling the underbrush. Thorns scraped at the skin on my calves and my naked toes curled at the thought of spiders under the leaves. The gray wooden clapboards moldered in a loose approximation of parallel lines; the house had structural problems.

It looked empty, but it was designed to. The barred windows had been blacked out and sealed tight. I'd have to get inside first, then reassess the situation.

At the back, the porch had once been enclosed, but the screen wire had long ago popped free of its battens and curled up. We'd left the porch there for camouflage as it looked so rickety and rotten, but as I squinted into the deep black cube of space it enclosed, the space I would have to cross to get to the back door, I realized we might have made a tactical error.

Still, it's the anticipation that messes with your mind. I crossed the open ground to the back door and ascended the slanted steps.

The stink was the first warning that something was wrong, a sour note above the rotten smell of wood. Unwashed human and dirty food. I sensed things on the porch that shouldn't have been there. As my eyes adjusted, I saw a filthy nest of blankets, plastic grocery sacks filled with clothes and newspapers, two cinder blocks and a plank of wood forming a small table with food wrappers and empty cans spilling off of it.

I lunged for the door and punched in the first three numbers of the access code, but then I sensed a dark mass coming for me and had to duck before I could punch in the final digit. A thick two-by-four smashed into the door frame just at head height, scattering black splinters of rot over the back of my neck. I whirled around to see a rangy figure—too tall to be Dad—

swinging back its makeshift club for another swipe. But, the space on the porch was limited—not enough to get up much velocity—and I grabbed the wood. There was a moment when I looked into the stranger's glassy bloodshot eyes, watched the realization dawn that things were not working out quite as he'd planned. Then I twisted the club out of my attacker's hands and jabbed the end right into his soft middle.

It worked out for me better than I could have hoped. Knocked off balance, he staggered. One foot slipped off the back of the porch and he fell off sideways into the weeds and dirt. I lunged for him, but he scrambled to his feet and legged it across the yard, throwing himself over the fence and pulling pickets down as he screwed that up too and plunged headlong into the weeds on the other side. His desperate thrashing in the dark reminded me of Agnew. But there were no quarries, not around here. I let him run.

Back on the porch, I found two eyes staring, white, round, and scared. A foul lump had emerged from the tangle of blankets and was clutching one of them up to its chin, as if it would somehow protect. A gravelly voice emerged from its mouth.

"Ma'am?"

I hefted the two-by-four. "Get the hell off my porch."

He nodded. "Okay, lady. Just gimme a second to get my stuff?" But he seemed reluctant to make a start on it, like he needed my permission to rise.

I had no time for this. Not so close to my goal.

"Get the hell off now!" I leaped onto the porch and over-turned the makeshift table with a clatter. Then I started kicking bags off the porch. A few arced high and landed in the grass with little plastic pops. Others caught in bushes and retched their contents out onto the dirt. The man scurried to his feet and began to rescue his junk, his shoulders hunched, glancing at me to make sure my next kick was not coming for his head. I gritted my teeth, considered giving in to the raging sick need to knock his skull in. Hell, there was no one to see. But he clattered down the steps out of reach and rolled a grocery cart from its hiding place in the bushes. He stuffed his nasty blankets in the bottom and began to load the bags on top, muttering.

"Told us, didn't they? They told us not to come down here. Crazy people down here. Scary-shit crazy people."

I realized he meant me.

"Wait," I said. I set the wood on the porch came down to where he was. He started to back the cart away, but I put out a hand and grabbed it. "How long have you two been living on my back porch?"

He gave the cart a tug, but I held firm. "Not long, lady. No one was here and we didn't mean to hurt nothin. Not even Gabe, miss. He just gets scared and thinks he's back in Desert Storm."

"What do you mean, 'not long?' Like, a day, a week?"

"Coupla days maybe."

"Three, five? Last Wednesday? No one came to the house the whole time?"

He shrugged. "It's just been me and Gabe. But I don't know what days are which, ma'am." His voice was getting all high and trembly.

I sighed. This wasn't getting me anywhere. I picked up a bag at my feet and put it in his cart.

"There's another man who might have come down here...a man crazier than me."

The bum busied himself with moving the bag to a different corner. "We been all alone, miss...last two rains maybe?"

North Texas had been dry for a month. I watched the bum fuss over his bags like kittens in a basket.

Crap. There was no way Dad could have missed Alicia's rescue. It had been all over the media. So, if he hadn't come to our little bolt-hole, it was because he thought the safe house would be compromised; maybe he thought I'd flipped and told the FBI about it (which I hadn't) or I would be here, waiting with a hefty two-by-four in my hands looking for answers (which I was). Or maybe he just didn't care—didn't see me as an asset to the True Patriots anymore—and was willing to let me go. There was a fourth option: he could have snuck in without the homeless guys knowing, and was even now waiting, come what may.

The bum finally got things arranged to his exacting standards. He wheeled his grocery cart away across the rough ground, in the direction Gabe had fled a few minutes before. "We won't be back, miss, okay? We're cool? We're cool."

I went back onto the porch. The house might be empty, but there was no way to tell for sure from outside. I punched in the final digit. The door, the newest and firmest thing on the house, swung open silently.

I bolted it behind me and waited in the dark for half a minute. Nothing. Then I opened the door again, changed the combination on the lock (I drill myself so I can do it under pressure) and slammed it shut again. Then I shot two more bolts for good measure, testing the screws to make sure they were in the door frame nice and tight. No one would get in now, not without a Sawzall and a small stick of dynamite.

No sounds but the rustling of dry weeds against the outside walls.

Then, silently, I walked through the house, waiting a moment in each empty room. I decided the bum was telling the truth, so I went back to the kitchen and turned on the light, giving the cockroaches a few moments to marshal their forces and beat a retreat. Then I walked across the nicotine-yellow lino, set my bag down on the splintery table and sat in the folding chair. The bare kitchen bulb cast harsh shadows on the table top and the mildewy air of the kitchen pressed thick around me. The windows were blocked up tight, adding to the claustrophobic atmosphere. Yet I could still faintly smell a man's aftershave on the fabric of my dress. In the absolute stillness, I could hear my pulse beating; those helpless, involuntary contractions of the heart.

"Peter Angelopolos," I whispered, as if he were a demon to summon by name to that rank room. Something deep within me spasmed with desperate need. It made me lift my chin, eyes closed. No Peter, though. Just a raw wound of want. Just that scent at my neckline, dispersing like exhaled breath. I laid my head down on my arms. Pathetic. Damaged. And now completely alone.

20

All those birthday wishes you got on your Facebook account? Your name and your email on the profile? That's all I need to reset your online bank account password. No, really. I'm in there.

Think no one knows how you vote? Your ballot was sealed, but it's public knowledge where and if you vote. And your party affiliation, and your donations. Every time you answer the door to a political campaigner, don't be fooled by that avuncular script. They've been watching you carefully for some time.

Phone number, previous addresses. University degrees, high school attended. Businesses, bankruptcies, and approximate income. Loyalty cards. Model, make, and year of every car you've ever owned. Traffic violations, county court judgments, criminal convictions, sexual crimes.

The names of your family members, how old they are, where they live.

I don't even need to pay for that shit. Websites put that crap out there for free, hoping I'll pay for more, like for your current GPS position, maybe.

But make no mistake. It wasn't going to be that easy to find Hal Wooten. He was the kind of guy who still paid cash at the gas station, who scrupulously lied about his ZIP code at the cash register. To contact him, I never used email. In fact, once I'd written down Tabernakl's geocoordinates, my instructions had been to walk three miles down to the vacant lot behind the big craft store and insert the message through the occipital bone of a raccoon skull.

Shit. Had he ever even planned to pick up those messages? If I went out behind the big craft supply store and shook that raccoon skull, would the rolled-up messages of my last three reports rattle around inside?

We kept the house off the grid for a reason. It meant that amenities were basic. The next morning I had a cold camp shower using water from the rain barrel and a plastic contraption hanging from the head of the real shower, stepping on a grocery bag as a shower mat to keep my feet off the dark mold streaking the tiled floor. I changed into a new t-shirt and shorts from the stash of seven identical outfits stocked in the bedroom closet just last year, stuffed my feet back into heavy steel-toed boots, and cooked up a pot of rolled quinoa with dried organic milk flakes. Sat eating in the silence. Spartan though it was, it was great to be around my own stuff again.

But also weird. Weird to be alone. Weird to be offline. Weird not even to hear the hum of a fridge or an air-conditioner. Weird that the geography of my consciousness had shrunk to the borders of my skull.

Leif's phone buzzed, making me jump. Critically, I'd forgotten I had it. I dug it out of my bag.

Leif here just checking if you need help today.

Christ. I'd have to fob him off with an excuse. Then it occurred to me that this might not be the simple text it appeared to be.

Sending and receiving voice and text data is just one of the things cell phones do. That's because little phones aren't that powerful (otherwise, they wouldn't be that little), so they need to know the closest base station they can transmit their call data to. If you're on the move, that base station might change...it might even change in the middle of a call. So underneath the hood, your phone is always chirping little request messages, and the base stations are broadcasting their acknowledgment messages, and if the two of them think they might like each other, they go through a little authentication protocol. Technically, each authentication protocol is carefully designed by extremely smart people to be robust against attacks. The problem is, every time a new protocol comes along, there are still phones and networks that use the old protocols. The protocols get layered over and around and through each other by engineers at various companies who a) don't talk to each other and b) just want to get the damn job done. And when there is no protocol of protocols, things can interact in strange ways—ways that aren't robust against much at all.

I lifted my fingers from the screen. The FBI would be looking for me now, and they would have for sure gotten to him. Even if I carefully turned off all the location-based services and never made a call, this damn phone could easily betray my location and put an end to my hunt for Dad and his current victims.

Heart pounding, I snapped off the back, took out the battery and sim and dropped the eviscerated phone back in the bag. I sat at the table for a long time, trying to slow my breathing. Eventually, it did. What was done was done. All I could hope was that getting the phone's location was as fiddly and inexact as I suspected, or that the FBI was still screwing about trying to get a warrant.

I spent the morning going through the house, looking for evidence: evidence of Hal the conman or evidence of Hal the secret agent. At least one of them would be true, and I intended to find the truth.

I found our new documents right where they were supposed to be, further support for the hypothesis that Dad had not yet come by. Fake birth certificates and social security cards, all ready to go in case we needed to run. His new alias was Henry

Eagan, mine was Isobel, just as it had been back at the IHOP. I
slipped the cash and preloaded credit cards into my wallet, and,
after a moment's thought, took my new ID as well. I was
twenty now.

I found the gun locker hanging open, empty. Just a pair of
practice nunchaku hanging from a hook. Disappointing, but not
entirely unexpected. Not after the empty gun stash at our house.

For lunch, I made a pot of lentils with a can of organic diced
tomatoes. Over the past few days, my systems had been subject
to a cocktail of dangerous food additives and hormones arising
from more emotions than in all the past five years put together,
and I felt like a hollow shell of a girl that had been sandblasted
from the inside. Slowly, as I performed my maintenance rituals
and cleansed my body, I was regaining my calm.

While I was eating, a low growl emerged from the boiler
room, making me jump. But it was just the generator, topping up
the batteries. When it shut off, an echo remained. Like voices
spoken at a whisper around corners.

After lunch I started again, room by room, disciplined this
time. I looked in every drawer and under every piece of furniture. I examined every can of tomatoes top and bottom, unfolded
all the bedding, gave it a shake and folded it back again. I over-
turned the sagging couch and searched within the springs. I
pulled down the ladder and went through the attic with a flashlight, pushed my fingers into every crack of loose plaster, and
unscrewed every electric fitting.

Everywhere, Peter's ghost followed me—not really his ghost
—more of an empty space where he should have been, my mind
filling this void too. With the heat of his hand on my shoulder, or
the taste of his skin on my lips.

Or with his eyes, looking at me. With his last thought of me:
damaged.

Like that was news. So fuck him.

I found nothing. Early evening, I reheated the lentils for
dinner and sat there, staring at my bag. I had to admit it, Dad

had been thorough. I was not going to find any traces of the real Hal Wooten in this house, no matter how hard I looked. In the absence of any other clues, Angrendir was all I had left. But to contact him, I needed to get online.

Depending on Leif's phone, I might be able to use it to make my own Wi-Fi hotspot. I opened my wallet and pulled out the cards that I had found that morning. About five of them were unused sim cards. From my bag, I pulled out a USB drive, loaded up with all the emergency apps one is likely to need on a GOOD. I booted the laptop from the drive, connected the phone, and had it rooted in about sixty seconds. In another thirty, I had its device ID changed and one of the new sim cards activated. Periodically scrambling the device ID and rotating carefully through the sim cards, I should be reasonably safe, though nothing is ever guaranteed.

I went back to the home screen and looked through the apps and settings. Yep, the phone Desiree had bought for Leif was a basic model, but it had Wi-Fi capability. Thank goodness I wouldn't have to make the trek back to the highway to buy a dongle. I'd walked nearly eight miles in flip flops yesterday and the skin between my toes was raw. Plus, it would have eaten up half a day.

The laptop's DVD reader had some sort of tick in it that meant it kept on trying to read the empty tray. I pressed the tray in hard and it stopped. Then I looked in the bag and realized Leif had forgotten to give me the charger. I looked at the battery status. Not good. I grabbed the phone off the table. I only had Izzard's number, but Leif was with him, thank goodness.

"Dammit, Leif," I said when he got on the line, "you forgot the charger. Where is it?"

"Nice to hear from you too," he said. "Nice to hear you're alive and stuff."

Oh God, I had no time for this emotional stuff. I felt my careful calm slipping. But then I remembered how I'd gotten the laptop off of him in the first place.

"Don't mess me around," I told him. "This is a matter of national security."

"Oh yeah? First, you disappear off the face of the earth, and then I like texted you twenty times and you don't even bother to answer."

"Look, I had to go on the run. Back at the hotel, I was...compromised."

That changed his tone. "Shit, like terrorists infiltrating the FBI?"

"Terrorists infiltrate everywhere, Leif. But they especially like to infiltrate the FBI."

"Oh," he said, kind of quietly, and I felt the power in my lies.

"Have they contacted you?" I asked, pressing my advantage. "Have they fed you some story about how my dad was a con man and I'm some sort of brainwashed victim?"

"Well..." he said. "If you call, I am supposed to—"

"You tell them where I am," I said, "and you'll be playing right into their hands."

"No, wait," he said. "I...I found the charger for the laptop still in my bag today. I forgot to give it to you. Bailey and I can drive it out to you now."

"Okay. But we do it my way. I have to be sure this isn't a trap."

"No prob," he said. "Just tell me what I gotta do."

21

It was three a.m. The road, silver in the moonlight, wound through the empty lots of an imagined landscape and occasionally branched into a cul-de-sac of nothingness. Only the road, sewer system and a few foundations had been put in before the development was abandoned many years ago. Now, the only residents were fossils of broken ammonites and fossilized bivalves from some prehistoric sea, unearthed by diggers and left to weather away to nothing.

From the manhole cover in the middle of the road, a sound emerged. It sounded a lot like someone banging on the underside of it.

I pulled out Leif's phone and checked it. He'd been banging for ten minutes. It was probably enough.

I know what this looks like, me doing all of this just for a charger. But it wasn't paranoid delusions that made me act this way. When I'd trialed this run two years ago, Dad had made me wait for what seemed like hours. I suspected he'd gone off to get a hamburger or something and forgot. Technically, I should make Leif wait another hour or so, but I was pretty sure he was alone. I'd watched him get out of Bailey's Jeep at the river and enter the culvert. I'd then hoofed the quarter mile here to wait for him, making sure there was no one in the shadows but me. It was inconvenient for Leif, but safer for me. As soon as I had what I wanted, I'd send him back home to his comfortable life with his mom and friends and get on with my plans.

I picked up the crowbar, walked over to the cover and lifted it partway.

"Fucking hell," he said. "Let me out already!"

"Keep your voice down and your fingers out of the way." I rolled the cover off and let it thunk to the asphalt. "I had to be sure you weren't followed."

He looked up at me, face white in the moonlight. Something in his eyes was wild, vulnerable in a way I hadn't seen before. His shoulders were bony right angles, even whiter than his face, if that was possible, and very thin. Had I looked the same when Dad had let me out?

Leif handed me a black cord. "Your charger."

I took it. "Thanks."

My dad may have done a lot of bad things, but I realized the practicality of his methods. Because Leif thought he was on a secret mission, he wanted to do it. Never mind that the real purpose of the mission wasn't quite what he thought, it worked for me. It also kept him from telling the FBI anything so I could get on with my plan without them.

"So, what now?"

"What do you mean…what now?" I asked. "You go back, and Bailey picks you up. We're done here."

"That's gonna be hard. She drove off. She's probably home and back in bed by now."

"Goddammit!" After all this. I sat down on the ground. "Shit, Leif. What were you thinking?"

He was quiet a moment. "I want to help you find the terror- ists. That's all I ever wanted."

I gritted my teeth. When I'd stoked his enthusiasm to get the charger, I hadn't quite counted on it backfiring on me like this. But I couldn't leave him there. There was nothing in the area. No cars, no streetlights, and definitely no public transport. Not in the middle of the night anyway.

"Fine. You can spend the night in the safe house. I'll send you home tomorrow. But you'll have to strip first."

His eyes got big. "What?"

"I need to check your clothes for bugs."

That sobered him up. He stripped and handed me the clothes one by one, which I checked, even his socks and (not quite so thoroughly) his underwear.

Finally, he heaved himself onto the pavement and we started the walk back to the BOHO. He seemed to stumble a bit more than usual, and when I looked over, I saw he was shaking a little. The contrast between him and Peter couldn't have been greater. It was just my luck that he wanted to be with me, and Peter didn't.

"You okay?"

"That was screwed up, Rain. The culvert, the stripping off, everything. Like some sort of dystopian cyborg rebirthing experience."

"It's over. You performed well."

"Really?"

Shit. The way he was looking at me, it was like he was an eight-year-old kid.

"Yeah really."

He pulled his back straight, walked a little faster. "I guess I did. Hells yeah."

THIS IS what really happened in Colorado Springs, that day my mother gave me a Walmart backpack and told me to pack. We went out of the apartment building and actually got in the shitty car and drove down the block, the suspension rattling like a can of nails. Me asking why the whole time, what had gone wrong, where had we been compromised, when would we meet Dad?

At last, harassed beyond reason, she'd spit it out. "We're not meeting him, Rainbow. We're leaving."

And after a few moments of stunned silence, I'd argued. Because I knew she wasn't happy, had never been happy, but wasn't it better to be safe than happy? And she told me that finally after sixteen years she'd figured it out. Found a strange set of keys he left out after he went to sleep one night, walked around the darkened neighborhood clicking the unlock button until a new red car three blocks away flashed its lights. A wallet in the glove compartment with another name on the driver's license. Photos of another woman and twins in its folds. Presents in the trunk: expensive, department store dresses, American Girl dolls, a Lego Egyptian pyramid kit. Stuff for Christmas.

"I planned on getting you some boots," she'd said. "Wasn't even going to have a tree so we could afford it. Those things...they weren't meant for you."

WE GOT BACK to the safe house in the early hours. I showed him Dad's bed and crawled into my own, and we slept until about midmorning, when I rehydrated some eggs while Leif had a look around.

"Cool, numb-chucks," I heard him say from the other room. Then, "Ow."

He came in the kitchen rubbing his elbow just as I put two plates on the table.

"What's the plan for today?" he asked.

I'd thought about nothing else on the walk home last night. He had gone to a lot of trouble to get me the charger, and although he should have gotten Bailey to wait, otherwise he had followed my instructions perfectly. His enthusiasm actually kind of reminded me of my own field-work aspirations, the ones I'd had before the kidnapping.

His presence in the safe house also silenced the whispers in my head. It was odd: I had spent years alone in my basement happily without a second thought, but the past few days around people had changed something in me. Admittedly, not every experience had been particularly great, but some of them had been a lot better than being alone. It had made my new loneliness harder to bear.

Maybe I could show him a little bit of stuff before I put him on the bus back home.

I said, "I have an online character named Finnegan. I need to see if any of the terrorists have contacted him while I've been offline."

I'd have to be careful. He still thought it was simple, that we were searching for terrorists to stop an imminent threat. For me, it wasn't so simple. Finding out that Tabernakl was really Alicia Bagatelle had shaken me badly. I knew that Angrendir was a lead I couldn't ignore, but I didn't know whether it led to the biggest terrorist attack Texas had ever known or just another scared and missing girl trapped in her own delusions.

"So...you're like a spy...who has an avatar spy...in an online game world?" He sat down and took an experimental bite of the eggs. "That's cool, but what are terrorists playing online games for?"

"They aren't playing because they like it," I said. "They use game characters to hide. Everyone knows the FBI are listening online for keywords like 'killing' and 'attack.' So these guys hang out where everyone is messaging about killing and attacks."

Leif picked up a napkin and pretended to wipe his face, but I could see he'd spit the eggs into it.

"How do you tell who's real and who's fake?"

I remembered Alicia on the bomb shelter bunk, her chapped mouth opening as she tried to beg me for help.

"I've been with this group for a while," I said. "It's one man controlling the rest. One of them is for sure going to lead me to him."

"Cool," he said. "Can I watch?"

"Okay. But finish your eggs. For real. And try not to distract me, okay?"

Considering the limits of the phone's Wi-Fi, I disabled all add-ons and set the video to low quality before spawning Finnegan into the winter forest.

"Hey," Leif said over my shoulder. "Does that icon mean you have mail?"

The forest was crowded with other players, so I glanced down quickly. The messages were from Tabernakl. I lobbed one of Finnegan's spells at an Alliance minion and ran down the hill towards the valley.

"Yes."

"Don't you want to open them?"

I did not. They were from a few days ago, from the period when I'd been kidnapped by the Russians. She might be pleading for help in them.

Three goblins lurched down a slope in stop-motion lag. I sent Finnegan into the trees to avoid them. The sound of Leif mouth-breathing on my shoulder made it hard to keep my eyes on the screen.

"You can't just open mail here. Usually, there are delivery points outside an inn. I'm not near an inn."

"What a lame game. You'd think terrorists would choose *Call of Duty* instead."

I looked up Angrendir. Nothing. But then I saw someone called StormShadow was online. Angrendir had mentioned him.

"We're good anyway," I told Leif. I parked Finnegan in a quiet meadow and started typing.

We will strike them from every fingertip.

He immediately knew it was me. We opened a private channel.

```
[StormShadow]: bruv where have you been
we've been bricking over here!!!
```

```
tabernakl    sends    us    all    these
reassurances and then disappears off the
radar
```

I stared at StormShadow's words on the screen.

```
now we're trying to do this dolphin
thing without any help, by the grace of
allah its not as easy as that blvd
brother made it sound but i got a job at
the state fair, we are so stoked I can
go anywhere now without suspicion. we
gonna strike down loads of unbelieving
kufr sluts and bros next weekend but
like i said we need your help.
```

"Shit," said Leif, "he sure types fast."

And loose. Too loose, too desperate. I knew now who I was talking to, and she should have done her research better. Compared to me and Alicia, this girl was a total amateur.

```
[Finnegan]: Brother we have a bigger
problem. Tabernakl was betrayed by a man
very close to us. I need to find him.
```

```
[StormShadow]: son of a pimp what do you
mean close to us?
```

```
[Finnegan]: He's someone we all know, in
real life.
```

```
[StormShadow]:    well    it    can't    be
angrendir he's my big cuz bro. we've
been together from like when we were
kids.
```

I frowned.

"Did you know that?" Leif asked me.

"No," I said. "It's bullshit anyway. They can't know each other. She thinks she has to protect him, that's all."

"What, StormShadow is a girl?"

"Most likely," I said. "If I'm right about who controls her." StormShadow had been typing while we talked.

```
[StormShadow]: look you guys and my cuz
are the only jihadi I know
```

```
[Finnegan]: I know there is someone.
Maybe you think you have to protect him,
but I am telling you he is pure evil.
```

```
[StormShadow]: if you're implying my cuz
then you are wrong shaitan never
whispered in his heart not once
```

```
[Finnegan]: You know who I am talking
about.
```

```
[StormShadow]: as allah is the one n
great I do not
```

```
[Finnegan]: Yes, you do.
```

```
[StormShadow]: listen brother this is
war the final jihad just saying
```

A sudden chill of doubt crept down my neck. Beside me, Leif became very still.

```
[Finnegan]: What's that supposed to mean?
```

[StormShadow]: okay so tabernakl got himself compromised but we are not. its gods will we go forward.

[Finnegan]: What, you know God's will now?

[StormShadow]: jihad has purified my heart so actually i do

I frowned. Then I lost my temper.

[Finnegan]: Just cut it out with the Jihad crap. Stop trying to distract me. I know there is no attack, no sarin, nothing. Tabernakl never ordered any dolphins. It's all bullshit.

There was no answer for about thirty seconds.

[StormShadow]: looks like shaitan is in *your* heart bruv. maybe Tabernakl never ordered the dolphins. maybe i did instead.

[Finnegan]: It's all a massive bunch of bullshit, and so are you.

Beside me, Leif sucked in air between his teeth.

[StormShadow]: bro I am the real thing how dare you

```
[Finnegan]: Give it up. You spell kufar
like two different ways and you never
capitalize Allah.
```

```
[StormShadow]: so what. allah knows his
own glory and capital letters are just a
western jewish mind control plot IS THIS
BETTER?
```

"Holy shit," said Leif, "capital letters are Jewish?"
"Don't be an idiot," I told him.

```
[StormShadow]: MAYBE YOU AREN'T THE REAL
THING, BRUV. MAYBE YOU ARE A KEFFR CIA
SLAG PRETENDING TO BE A RIGHTEOUS
WARRIOR GOING TO TAKE US ALL DOWN
```

```
[Finnegan]: Listen, StormShadow, whoever
you really are, realize the truth. Hal
does not work for the FBI, he is using
you...
```

I felt Leif's hand on my shoulder.
"You can stop typing now," Leif said, pointing at the chat
window.

```
[StormShadow] has logged off.
```

"That's totally fucked now," Leif said. "Thanks to your weird
reverse psychology strategy there. What the hell were you
thinking?"
I shrugged and closed down the window to look at what was
underneath.
"Hey, would Bailey let us borrow her car?"
"Why do we need her car?"

I moved to the side so Leif could see for himself the window underneath—a small, unassuming window with a status bar at 100%.

"See those geocoordinates?" I told him. "That's where Storm-Shadow was just now."

"Damn. Since when did my mom's computer do that?"

"Since this morning when I installed all my tools," I said.

I looked over at him, face intent on the screen. Oh hell, why not take him along? Given my limited experience outside the basement compared with his wider knowledge of the world, he might even help me blend in. "Looks like we have some field-work to do."

22

We had to take the bus because Bailey wasn't answering her phone. Leif said she'd be at school. Coincidentally, that was where Google Maps said we were going—not hers, but another one on the west side of Dallas. I hadn't been in a school of any type since Mom left. The thought of it made my stomach all fluttery.

Leif and I stood across the street.

"It's big," I said. "Maybe no one will notice us."

"You look young enough to get in, but we still need uniforms," Leif told me, "black trousers and white shirts like those students are wearing. And badges."

With Dad's pre-paid credit cards, it was all doable. I outfitted us at the strip mall nearby and we were back in time for lunch. Kids were walking on and off campus, so we went straight in, but when we found the computer lab, the room was dark and empty.

I tried the door handle. "Damn."

"Seems unlikely they'd let students play online games in the lab," Leif said. "Just saying."

"Depends on how well they locked down the network." I cupped my hands against the glass and peered in at the rows of desks and screens. "And how closely the students are watched. I bet I could do it."

"Everyone is at lunch. We should be too." Leif hefted his new insulated lunch bag, one I'd bought for him with the credit cards from the Walmart across the street. "Plus, I'm hungry."

"You should have eaten more eggs this morning."

I paused at the door to the crowded lunchroom. The smell, the noise, it all was just like Colorado Springs. Leif took my arm.

"There, in the corner," he said.

At a table next to the trash cans, two boys sat alone, eating their lunch.

"They're Hispanic," I said.

"No, they're not," he said. "Come on. That's what we came for, right? Arabs."

Leif dragged me through the sea of plastic seats. I let him. We had to start somewhere.

"Hi," Leif said to the boys as we sat down. "We're new."

They looked at him. So did I.

A tall girl in a headscarf set down her tray on the last free corner, as far away from us as possible. Leif glanced at me, all smug.

"Great," she said to the boys. "Who are they?"

"Ease up, Salmi," one said to her. "There's plenty of seats."

"And shame on you."

"What?"

Salmi jerked her chin at his spoon. "Brother," she said, "the gelatin. Is it halal?"

The boy opened his mouth and let a half-masticated glob of red gelatin dribble back out.

The other boy shook his head. "You've been looking up haram on the Internet again, haven't you?"

"Don't take it out on me because I'm educating myself, Niaz."

"Don't take it out on us because you got shit about your hijab again."

"Oh yeah? You want to know what those bastards called me today?"

He rolled his eyes. "Same thing as yesterday?"

The other boy shook his head. "If you don't like what people say, just take it off."

"Yeah," Niaz said. "It's not like Mom and Dad care."

She scowled. "I wear this so that people will pay attention to the things that matter about me, like my intelligence and kindness instead of my looks."

Niaz narrowed his eyes at his sister. "You walk around in that; all people think is that you're freaking Jihad Jane."

She let out a frustrated huff but didn't answer.

He turned to me. "You want to know something ironic?"

"I...uh..."

"Our father works for Lockheed Martin. On drones. He has a higher security clearance than all the other parents at this school."

Leif leaned over and whispered in my ear. "Not yours though."

I looked up to see Salmi observing us carefully. "What was that?"

"Nothing," Leif said. He suddenly became very interested in his Walmart deli sandwich.

"No, seriously," she said. "It sounded like you implied her dad had a really high-security clearance or something."

"Jesus, Leif," I said. "Nice undercover work."

She turned to me. "So what does he do then?"

I didn't answer.

Her left nostril flared. "You going to tell him you sat with the terrorists at lunch today?"

The general noise in the cafeteria did not dim, but at our table, it was dead silent.

"That depends," I told her. "Are you terrorists?"

She speared a round of cucumber on her tray with her fork.

"You ignorant person," she said. "I am not even going to dignify that with an answer."

Probably I deserved that. I didn't think they were terrorists, just ordinary kids. We sat in silence for the rest of the meal. Leif kept on making "sorry" eyes at me that I refused to acknowledge. Instead, I looked at the minute hand on the wall clock, inching towards the hour. It would be better for us to leave with the crowd, though I had no idea where we'd go. Maybe back to the computer lab, presenting ourselves as new students. Storm-Shadow could be any one of the several thousand kids on the campus. She could even be one of the staff, a librarian or teacher. Finding her could take several days.

A group of boys at another table got up to leave. One of them pushed into Salmi's shoulder as he passed. Water from her glass sloshed. She only had time to glance wide-eyed at her brother before another one plucked the hijab off her head and threw it high in the air. It floated over the heads of students, some of whom cheered, and then fell to the tile. I glimpsed it through the legs of the crowd, ground into the floor by someone's tennis shoes.

Salmi slapped protecting hands over her glossy black hair, but there was too much of it. A tall boy pulled free a lock, running his fingers through it like a comb. The scent of orange cheese filled my nose and I looked up him—at Roman's grinning face.

To hell with that. I leaped across the table, flung his hand down with a forearm block, and thrust my shoulder square into his chest with all my energy. We barreled into the next row of tables. The surprise didn't give me an advantage for long. Roman was a big guy, and when he wrapped his arms around me and threw the two of us to the floor, I realized he knew a thing or two about fighting. Calls and shouts from the other students filled my ears. He was working me down into a bad position under him and I simply didn't have the muscle mass to resist.

I rotated my pinned hand as far as it would go and found that sweet spot on his forearm just between the two bones. He let out an agonized shout. I had him beneath me in no time, moaning. Then I looked up—at a crowd of students—all filming me on their smartphones. Where had they come from? I looked down at Roman, but he wasn't Roman. That man was dead. This was just some red-headed footballer.

Someone pulled me off of him.

"Security is coming. Get her out of here." I recognized Niaz's voice. Then I saw Leif was pulling my arm and heading toward the exit.

I sort of let it happen, and so did the crowd. Behind us, the footballer made loud, gurgly sounds. I vaguely remembered smashing his nose in with an elbow. And then we were out in the sun, running away across parking lots until we could run no more.

After that we were bending down, hands on knees, both of us trying to breathe in an alley full of dumpsters. At last Leif had enough extra oxygen to speak.

"I don't get it."

"Don't get what?"

He breathed some more. Then he said, "I don't get this mission. I don't get you."

The weird thing was, I didn't get myself. Carol Anne had warned me about flashbacks, but I hadn't quite realized what she'd meant. For a moment, my brain had really seen Roman there. Not imagined Roman, not remembered Roman. For a moment, he really had been there, ready to finish the job. How could I have gotten reality so wrong?

"ALL THOSE PRESENTS, the car, the wallet, it must all be part of a cover for his current operation." I'd told Mom. "It must be."

We pulled onto Garden of the Gods Drive. Here, it was just

an ordinary street full of strip malls and traffic lights. If we stayed on it, we'd eventually wind up in the foothills, in a park where red sandstone monoliths had been pushed up out of the ground long ago by continents colliding and weathered into strange, organic shapes. Hence the name, but Mom would turn off long before that. She was heading for I-25, the interstate. Ahead of us, I could see the tips of navy clouds peeking up over the white peaks of the Continental Divide. Colder weather coming. I looked in the back seat to make sure my coat was there.

From the driver's seat, she sighed. "I got to thinking, Rainbow, if the government can set him up with such a nice car and presents, how come they haven't paid any of my 401K plan back? I mean..." Her hands clenched the wheel. "...that, and my inheritance, and my stocks, and all the rest of the money I've scrounged up for his work over the years...is it over a hundred thousand now, two hundred? And all the sacrifices...always on the run..."

"The budget cuts," I said. "You know that. Dad says after the elections, the new administration will sort it out and they'll pay us. We can start our new life."

She held up a hand. "Rainbow, he's been saying that since before you were born."

"Yeah, but this time..."

"This time, Rainbow, I asked some questions."

"Mom, you know you have to be careful doing that."

"The time for caution has passed."

"But anyone could be part of the conspiracy. You can't trust anyone."

"I chose a private detective from the phone book, Rainbow. Someone who had no possible connections to him or us. I had him followed."

"What? How did you pay for it?" We were only allowed a little bit of housekeeping money. The rest of it had to go to funding Dad's operations. She didn't make that much at Walmart.

She ignored the question. "Want to know how he spends his time when he's away on operations?"

"Mom, this is crazy talk."

"He sells solar panels," she said. "The ones where you can get a grant from the government."

Mom had really gone off the deep end this time. I sat there, silent, planning the best approach for talking her back around to reality.

"He has a whole other family," she turned to me, one hand on the wheel. "Just an ordinary family. No anarchists, no Islamists, no heroin drug dens. They live in another state, it's why he's gone for months at a time. The wife is a fourth-grade teacher and they have two kids, twins. They just started soccer on Wednesdays."

"The detective was lying to you. He worked for the Others."

"He followed them around for three months, on and off. He took pictures, had copies of documents, all kinds of evidence. I saw it all, Rainbow. Believe me, I looked for just one thing to tell me I was wrong. But there's only one possible explanation."

We were stopped at a light. This was not good. There was some explanation, to be sure. But my mom didn't always have the intelligence needed to see the big picture. Dad had said that before. And if she did something rash, the True Patriot mission could be harmed.

"Okay," I said. "Tell me what you think that is."

"He's ill."

I felt my face screw up. "Ill?"

"Mentally ill. Paranoid schizophrenic, possibly with split personality."

The light changed, we started off. I fell against the seat.

"I've been reading about it," she continued. "It all fits, the delusions of grandeur that made him think the safety of the U.S. depended entirely on him alone. The paranoia, controlling every part of his life, every part of ours. Even the weird things he made me do, like never speaking to men who wore red ties..."

"What?"

"Just after you were born. He made me do it for three years. But you know what the detective said? He said that was straight out of a movie about a university professor who thought he was a secret government agent too."

"Dad watches movies?"

"Not with us. But don't you see? It's got all mixed up in his mind...reality, fiction...there's no difference to him."

"Mom, where are we going?"

She took a breath. "You know that new life we've been waiting for? It starts now."

"We have no money!"

"Your dad taught me one or two things about moving money around, Rainbow."

Christ, we were going to be in trouble when Dad found us.

"Mom, this is so dangerous."

She brushed her curls back from her face. Her hands were shaking. "There is no danger. There never was. Unless it was from him."

"What will Dad do when he finds out?" It came out a half-whine, half-accusation.

"I never stopped loving him, but he's ill. He doesn't know what he's doing. As soon as we're far enough away, I'll contact the authorities, let them know what's going on. We...we'll have to come clean about the old couple in Tennessee...and a few other things...but..."

"They'll take him away."

"They'll give him the help he needs, Rainbow."

"They'll lock him up. Destroy him."

"It's not about him anymore."

"When he's gone, then they'll destroy America." We'd pulled to a stop in three lanes of traffic. I threw the door open and stepped out into the sea of cars. "Mom," I said, "don't be your usual idiot self! You've been duped by the Others!"

"Don't you dare get out now," she'd screamed through the open door, "not after I've been planning this for months! I have a safe house expecting us and everything!"

The light turned green, the car behind her honked.

"How dare I?" I screamed back. "How dare you put me in such danger? Me and the rest of the country!"

I could see the desperation in her eyes, tears were threatening to spill over her cheeks, but the rest of her face was wrinkled in frustration. Lately, we'd been arguing more and more often, and I knew it enraged her that she could no longer pick me up and put me in my place. She wiped her nose with a jab of her hand, then gripped the wheel and faced the traffic.

"Fine. If that's the way you feel about it," she said through gritted teeth, "then just fuck off back to your dad."

I slammed the door and walked away.

23

"Rain," Leif said, "stop walking for a minute. I have to tell you something."

We were almost back to the BOHO, crossing the parking lot of yet another abandoned row of shops lining a potholed street. At the end of the lot, a dirt lane led into the trees, heading straight for the house. I turned, irritated. The air was sticky and hot, thick with exhaust fumes. Leif had been complaining like a baby about his feet ever since we got off the bus.

"What is it now?"

"There's a Starbucks over there by the highway. I can see the sign and I'm heading for it. I'm going to wait there until school is done, and then I'll phone Bailey for a ride."

"You're giving up?" I squinted at him. Irritating as he was, I suddenly realized I had been getting used to his company. "What about the terrorists?"

He brushed damp hair back from his forehead. "Yeah Rain, what about them? You keep on telling me they're gonna attack the Texas State Fair like it's some watermelon stand down in Waco."

"What do you mean?"

"The State Fair here in Texas is a huge deal. It has a car show, a wine show, pig races, rock stars, roller coasters, acrobats, and more every night...it's so big, they have a full-sized football stadium in the middle and play full-sized games in it while the fair goes on around the outside."

"Okay," I said. "I did not exactly know that."

"My dad used to take me every weekend it ran, every single year. If those terrorists attack, we're talking a hundred thousand, two hundred thousand dead easy. Families, kids, babies and shit."

"That's why we have to stay focused." I was hot, thirsty, and could feel a headache coming on. I did not want to have this conversation. I wanted to get back to the BOHO, get some water, and sit in the dark.

"Sure, but what about StormShadow ordering the dolphins? What about him saying he works at the fair? If we were really gonna focus, shouldn't we tell your dad about this and let him and the FBI handle it?" He threw up his hands. "All you talked about on the bus was how to get back in that school. Why should we care about the school? That was a dead end."

"It's complicated."

"Yeah?" He stepped in close and squinted up at me.

I took a step back. "What?"

"There's still no fear in your eyes. I just told you all that shit about people dying, and you're still as cold as ice."

Dammit, he was right. Maybe I hadn't disproved it, but I didn't believe it. Not really. Not since I'd found Alicia in my bomb shelter and had a chance to re-assess everything my mother had told me on that car ride out of Colorado all those years ago. At the time I'd thought she was deluded. Now, way too late, I was starting to think different.

He started to walk away, and I grabbed his arm. If I let him go now, the FBI would get to him, and he'd tell them everything he knew. Then they'd come for me, and my hunt for Dad and his victims would be over. "This man, Hal, he's the key to it all, I know it. He's the one controlling everything. I get him, the whole conspiracy tumbles down."

"Dude," he said. "If there's one thing social media has taught me, it's to check my sources. You gotta show me some evidence."

"That's not...it's not possible."

"Thought so." He wrenched his arm from me and turned away. A little tumbleweed, its branches tangled with litter, rolled across the asphalt and hit him on the shin. He kicked it away and kept walking.

"I can't show you because if I told you everything, your life would be in danger," I called after him.

He stopped. "What?"

"You're right," I said. "My story doesn't make sense. But that's because I haven't told you everything I know." I bit my lip. I had to think of something, and fast. "This guy, Hal, is high up. Maybe one of the top two or three terrorist warlords in America. My job is to take him down before the shit hits the fan."

"Why you?" He didn't look convinced, but at least he was walking back towards me. "I mean, no offense, but you're kind of young, you're a girl, and you've screwed up everything so far."

That stung. After all, he was the one who'd told Salmi my dad was an FBI agent.

"I'm the one who knows him best." I swallowed. I really wished I'd said something else to justify my actions. But now that I had created the lie, it was too late to stop digging myself deeper. "Hal is really my dad."

"I thought your dad was a super-secret top FBI—"

"He was. They turned him."

Leif looked down at his feet. "That's fucked up."

I shoved my hands in my pockets. "Listen, Leif, you're a good kid. But you're right, you shouldn't be involved. It's too dangerous."

I turned to walk away. I felt his hand on my shoulder. It made me hate myself and him all at once.

"I'm not a kid," he said. He turned me around and took my hands in his. "Maybe that's the problem between us, you treating me like a kid."

The palms of his hands were soft in mine, the white skin rubbery and moist. All I'd wanted was a bit of company and more time without the FBI breathing down my neck, but my words were about to backfire on me yet again.

"Leif, before you say anything more—"

"Don't dismiss me because I'm younger and slightly shorter. You and I, we could be something amazing."

"Dammit, Leif, we don't have time for this."

"You had time for Peter." His voice cracked a little.

I took a deep breath and looked up at the sky, at the little white clouds that did nothing to shield us from the heat of the sun.

"Peter was a waste of time," I told him at last. "I know that now."

"Really?"

"Yeah. But so is everyone, at least until we catch my dad."

"If I trust you on this...if I help you—"

"If you help me, I have to depend on your loyalty one hundred percent. You can't question anything. It's too danger-ous. Is that clear?"

He opened his mouth to speak, but before he could say anything, something way on the other edge of the parking lot caught my eye. Two men, one tall and thin, the other hunched over a grocery cart, talking to someone in a black SUV.

"Freaking hell," I said. "Those two were supposed to clear off." I shook off Leif's hands and fumbled in my bag for my monocular.

"What, those bums?" Leif was unimpressed. "Probably just buying some drugs." He reached for my hands again. "We haven't finished talking, Rain."

"That SUV doesn't look like the kind of car a drug dealer would drive." I stepped sideways out of Leif's reach and squinted through the monocular. I started to tremble. It was hard to hold the monocular steady.

"What, you're an expert on drug dealers now?" Leif asked.

I ignored him. Every muscle in my body was tensing, preparing for the chase. I dropped the monocular onto its neck strap. "It's him. Freaking hell, it really is him."

The two homeless men watched the SUV as it pulled away. I sprinted across the lot, but it was too late. The SUV picked up speed and headed down a frontage road onto the highway access ramp.

"Shit!" But the two men were on foot. I changed course for them.

The thin one, it was good old Gabe, took off as soon as he saw me coming, but the little round one couldn't leave his cart. He rolled it desperately over potholes and clumps of weeds until I caught up with him and grabbed his filthy coat.

"What did you say to him?" I yelled. "What did he say to you?"

The bum threw up his hands to shield his face. "Don't hurt me, miss!" He backed up and tripped over a tuft of grass, landing on his bottom.

"I freaking well will hurt you," I said, stepping forward. "I'll knock out all your teeth if I have to."

"Don't," said a breathless voice behind me. "Let him go, Rain."

I turned to see Leif, coughing and clutching his stomach as he jogged over to us.

"Stay out of it, Leif," I warned him. "You don't understand."

"I won't stay out of it." He spat a mass of phlegm on the ground. "You expect me to stand by while you beat up a helpless old man? To hell with all your secrecy and your bullying. To hell with you." He bent down and extended his hand. "Y'all right there, sir? You need some help up?"

"Thank you, young man," the bum held out his arm and let Leif assist him to his feet. "What nice manners." He turned to me and gave me a hard glare. "Some people could learn from that."

I gritted my teeth. "I thought I told you two to get the hell out of this area."

"You told us to get the hell off your property, and we obliged." He shrugged. "It's a free country otherwise and I'll go where I want."

It all made sense to me now. My dad could have installed a remote webcam on the BOHO property, but that would have involved Internet presence. The Luddite son-of-a-bitch had hired homeless men to watch the place instead.

I clenched my fists. "There's only one thing at the end of this lane. You're going back to the house to spy on me."

"Funny thing about that," the bum said to me. "A man just drove by who seems to think he owns that old shack. That you was in it illegally." He pulled himself to his full height. "For your information, he told us to stay away. We're only here anyways 'cause Gabe forgot his Navy Cross. Forgot it cause you and your nice manners kicked it under a bush. Once he gets it, we'll be outta here."

"Come on, Leif, I have to see if the bastard managed to break in." I started up the lane but stopped when I realized Leif wasn't following.

Leif walked slowly towards me. "Let the poor man get his medal in peace."

"I meant my dad, you idiot," I said. "Remember? The terrorist warlord?"

He shook his head. "I'm not going anywhere with you, Rain." He lifted a finger and pointed it at me. "You are freaking insane."

I brushed his hand aside. "What is this?"

"You are a complete lunatic, a total nut case. If I gave you a roll of tin foil, you'd make yourself a hat."

"So the whole BOHO thing, that's all fake, is it? Storm-Shadow is a character I just made up?"

"I don't know exactly how this dog and pony show works, Rain. But I know one thing. Top terrorist warlords do not drive around in SUVs either." He raised his finger again. "The difference between me and you is—"

But he got no further because the massive thud of an explosion threw the three of us to the earth.

24

I didn't have to guess what had happened. It wasn't my first bomb explosion.

When Saffron Wooten drove off and left me in the middle of the road, I watched her go to the end of the block. And then—with a bright flash and a tearing boom that broke windows up and down the street—explode. Burst into shockwave and shrapnel and small...small bits of Mom all over the road.

Yeah. That bit sucked.

When they brought me back to Dad in the crowd, the skin on my face and hands was red and weeping, but I had no idea why. There was blood and matter in my hair, but it wasn't mine. My throat was raw with either smoke or screaming, it was anyone's guess. I didn't even know what he was doing there. Mom and I thought he was on an operation until next week.

I just know that he grabbed my arm hard.

"What are you doing here?" he kept on asking me. "What the hell are you doing here?"

I couldn't answer.

"She's one lucky girl," someone said. "There're two or three cars up ahead that—"

"Mind your own damn business," Dad snapped at him. He pulled me through the crowd, shouldering past the police and EMTs.

I swallowed. It hurt like hell. "Dad, I think I could use an ambulance, actually."

"Don't exaggerate. Keep on walking. Those folks, they could be with the Others."

It was true, some of the emergency response team were looking in our direction with funny expressions. But an ash-smeared woman stumbled past, cradling the stump of her severed wrist, and they lost interest in us.

He led me away, fast. I couldn't break his grip on my arm. Nor did I want to. I was scared. Around the corner he stopped, knelt, and cupped my face in his hands. Behind him the Rockies rose up. Like torn strips of paper. Flat and blue and far, far away.

"She doubted me. She left my protection and the terrorists got her," he said, low and angry. "Do you understand?"

I tried, but it was hard. I felt like my head was underwater. He shook me.

"I'm going to have to depend on you more than ever now. Do you understand?"

It hurt, but I said it: "You can always depend on me, Dad. Always."

SOMETIME LATER, impossible to tell how long, I sat up. Leif was still laying on the ground, his eyes open, blood trickling out his nose. Fucking hell. Dad had done it again.

"Are you okay?" I asked him. My head was ringing. It drowned out my words.

He shrugged and mouthed back at me, "I can't hear you."

The homeless man sat next to his cart, rubbing his head.

I stood up and stumbled onto the road.

It was filled with people, some running, some walking towards the explosion. Many had their phones out, laughing, repeating "Oh my God, oh my God." Others carried rusty fire extinguishers, faces set hard. When I got to the BOHO, a crowd had already gathered to watch the flames shooting from the windows. I stood there too, watching the fire, averting my eyes from the scattered debris in the weeds. Poor old Gabe. If only he'd listened to Dad. Instead, he'd gone back to the BOHO and triggered the bomb that was meant for me.

The laptop was gone, along with the last of my food and clothes. All I had was the bag on my back containing, among other things, my new documents, Leif's phone, and the nunchaku.

Cars drove up; more people got out to watch. A fire truck arrived, parting the crowd. A few minutes later, I could see Leif's lone white face on the other side of the fire truck. He was talking to the firemen. I should have been angry at his betrayal, but to be honest, it was a relief that he was gone. At last, I could be done with the lies.

One fireman scanned the faces on this side of the truck. I took one step backward, then another.

"Hey girl," a woman said. "Watch where you're going." She had her phone out; I'd jiggled her arm.

"Sorry," I said. When she turned towards the fire, I saw my chance—a big handbag gaping open. I plucked her keys out and pushed my way to the edge of the crowd, pressing the unlock button repeatedly. A blue Fiesta flashed its lights.

It wouldn't get me far, but it would get me far enough.

Phone number, previous addresses. University degrees, high school attended. Model, make, and year of every car you've ever owned. It's all out there on the Internet, telling me who you are. And license plate numbers, they work pretty well too.

Through the monocle, I'd seen the SUV's number plate. I'd immediately memorized it, just like dear old Mom had taught me. It was the one bit of information I'd been looking for. A few hours on a library computer, and I'd have the son-of-a-bitch doxed.

I had him now.

———————

25

"I'm so going to kill you," the girl said.

"You're not cause I'm going to kill you first," the boy answered back.

From my perch on an oak limb, I watched two kids, maybe eight or nine years old, make their reluctant way to the SUV parked in front of a large, colonial-style house. A few minutes on a public library computer and a one-dollar PayPal payment and I had the address. The name on the documents was a woman, but this was definitely the same SUV as the day before.

Neither child looked up. Nor did the woman who followed them out. And why should they? The camo pattern on my BOHO clothes obscured my silhouette, and I was quiet. I'd been in the tree since three in the morning, waiting.

"But I'm super faster at killing," the girl insisted.

The boy straightened his back. "But I already poisoned your Cheerios with ricin this morning. Feeling sick yet?"

"I'm feeling sick cause I'm looking at your face."

It wasn't what I'd expected, this little pastiche of suburban life, this family with their nice clothes and expensive school bags. The boy's was made to look like a monster with cloth teeth around the zipper. The girl's flashed sparkly LEDs when she jiggled it.

"Mom! Dakota's staring at me!"

"Stop staring at your brother, Dakota."

"Mom! Decker poisoned my cereal with ricin!"

The mother's tone was mildly irritated, like she'd heard it all before. "Dakota, next time he puts one in, just pick it out, okay? One is not going to hurt you. Got your backpack?" Thump. She shut the door and walked around the car. From my angle in the trees, I could not make out her face clearly, but I had to admit, she did not have the aspect of a paranoid brainwashed victim.

"Decker, if you put Rice Krispies in her Cheerios again, I'm throwing out the box. Are we clear? Now buckle up." Thump. She got in the driver's side.

The black SUV pulled out of the driveway, subtly gleaming iridescent blue in the pale dawn light. He must have washed the dirt off before driving it home, but I recognized a decal on the back, an image of a smiling sun. The SUV passed under me, carefully negotiated a speed bump, and disappeared down the road.

I turned my attention to the house, a white building with columns in front and black shutters. Warm buttery light spilled from the kitchen window. Maybe she'd just forgotten to turn them off.

No, a shadow moved there. Someone remained at home.

I crawled to the end of the branch and dropped onto a wooden jungle gym. A nice model, with a little tree house-thing and a slide. I skirted around a trampoline and a mosaic bird bath to the covered porch, where a pair of motorized toy ATVs, one camo, one pink, were lined up. Things not meant for me.

The sliding glass door was locked, but when I realized it did not open directly onto the kitchen, I spent a minute looking in. A pool table and a seating arrangement dominated the space. A dartboard on the wall, and a vintage Coca-Cola ad. Something that looked like a mini bar in the corner. I backed away and skirted the side of the house. The garage door was open, and yes, the door to the house unlocked. I opened the door onto a hallway.

The wood floor gleamed so brightly, he was just a silhouette at the end of the hall. A man in sock feet, shirt half tucked in, peering down the hall. The handle of a toothbrush dangled from his mouth.

"Olivia, you're back quickly. Forget your phone again?"

"Hello, Daddy."

"Rain?"

The toothbrush clattered on the floor. He took off down the hall. Well, crap. Maybe I should have tried a less confrontational approach. I followed him. The house was a tight space, and that gave me an advantage, but he knew the layout. He threw out an arm, swung to the side and barreled into a living room, ran smack into the back of a couch, rolled over it, and scrambled over the matching armchair. Two quick leaps and a smashed shin on the coffee table and I cleared the furniture just as he made it to a flagstone fireplace. It rose up to a cathedral ceiling. The second it took me to look up was long enough for him to swing a poker in my direction.

A nice way to greet your daughter. I flicked out the nunchaku across my waist, caught the poker right at the connecting rope and wrapped it tightly. A twist of my wrist and the poker went smashing into a fat pottery lamp behind me. Pretty spectacular, if I say so myself.

Dad's face was a study in fear. His eyes bugged out and his mouth was an "o" of surprise. He stood, one foot forward, as if he could surf away on that Persian rung scrunched up under his socks.

I swung the nunchaku around in a single figure of eight, simultaneously building up deadly momentum and guiding its course straight for his skull. He wheeled his feet, kicking the rug away, and headed for the dining room. The end of the nunchaku grazed against flagstone. I swung the loose end under my armpit with a snap and headed after him.

He edged his way past a twelve-seater black lacquer dining table, throwing the chairs down in my path. I jumped on the table and scooted across its slick surface instead. He disappeared into another room, this one with a widescreen TV on the wall and...fucking hell...how many could one man own?...a leather couch. He ripped a family portrait off the wall and was punching numbers into the powder-gray cabinet underneath.

And behind him, a fish tank. What a fish tank. Water plants, fluorescent light, colored gravel, a little aerator. And bettas. Three of them, each with their own glassed-in section.

Papers and boxes spilled from the safe onto the carpet as Dad shoved a clip in a handgun and pointed it at me.

"Drop the nunchakus, Rain."

"You didn't rack it, Dad," I said, stepping forward. "Don't you think you should rack the gun first?"

He looked down at the gun. I smashed the nunchaku up under his chin. His head snapped back, and he flew back onto an armchair, moaning.

I moved past him, picked up the gun, and inspected it. I turned and shoved it in his hands.

"Don't you remember how to load the chamber, Dad? Look at me! Don't you remember teaching me back when I was six?"

He lifted his head and looked stupidly at the gun I'd given him. Blood streamed down his chin.

"Don't you remember drilling me, when I was seven?"

"I think I bit my tongue," he said.

"Do it," I screamed, "show me you remember!"

He drew a wavering bead on me.

"Nice fucking try, Dad! It's not fucking loaded!"

Bam. The gunshot sent me to my knees. It was a moment before I realized there was no pain. I looked up and saw a fresh hole in the wall above the TV. Underneath, a bright blossoming of colors, the noise had caused all the bettas to display their fins like psychedelic magnolias. In front of me, Dad was looking even dumber than he had a moment ago. I decided the shot could not have come from him.

"Step away!"

A female voice. I turned to see that the woman who had left to take the two children to school a few minutes ago had now returned. She had a handgun and was standing in an efficient triangle configuration, ready to put the next bullet in my torso. The nunchaku dropped to the floor and I lifted my hands.

"Vilna?" I said. "Vilna Chodkiewicz?"

The Lithuanian cultural attaché had put on about thirty pounds, but it was her. She flinched and I knew she recognized me too, but she didn't lower the gun. "Henry, you okay?"

"Olivia, you're back quickly." Dad struggled upright. "Forget your phone again?"

"What the hell is going on here?"

He wiped his chin with the back of his hand and smiled.

"Nothing much, darling. Seems like Isobel here has forgotten to take her medication again."

PART III

CRAZY

26

Vilna lowered the gun. "We meet again, Isobel."

"What do you mean?" I turned to Dad. "What's this about medication?"

Dad slowly pulled himself to his feet, fingers exploring the bruise rising on his chin. "I think I'm going to need some ice for this."

"The kids can wait in the car a minute, Henry. Sit and I'll get it." Vilna tucked the gun in her purse. "You sit too, Isobel," she said as she headed for the kitchen.

He was so close, I could see the veins at his neck, pulsing under thin skin. I could have done it, leaped for him and squeezed them until his eyes rolled up white in his head and he rattled out his last breath. But it would probably earn me a bullet in the back. So I sat.

Dad sat across from me. It was the first time I'd gotten a good look at him without seeing the hero I thought he'd been. Short black hair, suspiciously free of gray. A dignified, intelligent forehead, somewhat ruined by the shadow of acne scars on his cheeks. Incrementally pudgier. That was really the kicker, wasn't it? He had the physique of a desk man. One who had been there for some time.

"Just for the record," he said, "it was your mom who taught you to shoot."

I crossed my arms. "So, it's Henry now, is it?"

He looked at me with tired eyes. "It's always been Henry. You know that. And please call my wife by her real name, Olivia."

Vilna-Olivia came up behind him and handed him a baggie of ice and a wet towel. She perched on a chair as he cleaned himself up. Around her pumpkin-shaped face, her hair was an unlikely flick-back of brown and blond streaks. I squinted, then realized it was a dye job—no more intended to look real than the peanut-sized gems in her bracelets or the carroty cast of her skin.

"You've gotten taller," she told me.

"Yes, you look more like your mother every day, Isobel," Dad added. "How are you, anyway?"

"I'm pretty pissed off," I said. "I figured out that you killed Mom. Plus, you almost killed Alicia and me and a homeless man is dead."

He rolled his eyes. "Jesus. Is that what you've concluded? Without even getting my side of the story?"

"How was I supposed to do that?" I stood up. "I've been trying to contact you for weeks."

Dad rubbed his temples. "How many times, Isobel? Use email or pick up the phone. I refuse to communicate by messages left in that raccoon skull."

"You shouldn't have suggested it."

"I didn't..." He let out a frustrated sigh, set the baggie of ice on an end table. "Here's how it's going to go, Isobel. First, I want you to sit down."

"Fuck off. My name is Rain."

Olivia's hand twitched toward her bag. Dad's eyes flicked to her, giving her permission.

"Sit down NOW!" he roared.

Right on cue, Olivia pulled out the gun.

I sat.

"I'm going to get your pills." He stood. "And you're going to take them."

"If I don't, she's going to shoot me?"

"Isobel, *you're* the invader here. *You're* the one who is violent and out of control. We're the ones being reasonable."

"You should know what kind of man you married," I told Olivia. "You should know the things he's done. Particularly to teenage girls."

She winced. I could probably disarm her. I just needed a chance. One, preferably, before I had to take any pills that affected my reaction times.

"I know what you're thinking," Dad said, "and you're not going to do it."

"Tell me why I should even consider cooperating with you, you murdering, FBI-impersonating son-of-a-bitch."

He leaned in close. The vessels under the skin of his nose were redder and rougher than I remembered. His breath was laced with minty toothpaste.

"Because maybe what I'm saying is true. Because you're about to murder two innocent people while their kids wait outside in the car."

"Yeah, right."

"I know what you and your mom got up to in Tennessee," he said. "So don't you come in here calling *me* a killer."

"What is this?" Olivia's voice was high.

He ignored her and placed his hand on my shoulder.

"Do you still believe that crap she told you about them being anarchists? Did it make sense then? Does it make sense now?"

"She said you made her do it."

"She always said that, Isobel. She always blamed me for her illness, just like you do now."

He lifted his hand and went to get the pills. When he handed them to me, I looked at them, two white dots nestling in his palm. They could easily be cyanide.

I threw the chair back and legged it for the door, at least, I tried to. About two feet into my flight, something bashed me to the floor. For a moment I thought I'd been shot, but then my eyes focused enough to see Dad swinging a baseball bat onto his shoulder; he must have picked it up when he was getting the pills. I felt a weight on my back and the cold jab of a gun barrel at my temple.

"Henry might be useless with a gun," Olivia said to me, "but I'm a country girl born and bred in Texas. Don't mess with me now, girl. Take the damn pills."

"You'll have to blow my brains out," I said, but not too clearly. My head had been taking a lot of knocks lately. "Think you can really kill me?"

"I'll do it. To protect my family from your crazy shit, I'll damn well do it."

And then she had me by the hair, pulling my head back. I opened my mouth reflexively in pain as Dad knelt and shoved the pills in.

I tried to spit them out, but it was too late. They dissolved almost immediately on my gums and lips. I sputtered.

"Like giving medicine to a damn cat," he said, standing up.

"Now what?" Olivia eased my head back down.

"You take the twins to school," he answered. "If the police come to the door because of the gunshot, I'll field it." He toed me in the side. "Meanwhile, Isobel here goes upstairs, nice and quiet, and we wait for her to come to her senses."

27

I awoke with a jerk, the contents of my stomach rising fast. I lurched out of bed—somehow, I'd been put in a bed—kicked away the sheets that tangled around my feet and found a bathroom with the door open and the light on. I retched, hard, and then fell against the wall, my body exhausted and my head still dizzy.

Getting up to return to bed seemed too much effort. I looked at the tiles on the wall, a pseudo-random mix of different colors. Or maybe they were random. I killed time trying to spot a pattern.

A shadow blocked the light, and I saw that Olivia had come into the bathroom.

"Oh, hi," I said.

I heard the water run. She held out a wet washcloth to me. "You got some in your hair."

"Thanks." I took it, wiped my mouth with its cool cat-tongue texture and sponged the locks of hair that had fallen out of my ponytail. Hell. If my name really was Isobel and this really was my medication, no wonder I'd stopped taking it. I staggered to my feet and rinsed my mouth with a handful of water from the sink. Olivia helped me out of the bathroom and back into bed. She sat at the foot.

"Henry had to go to work," she told me. "You were out for about four hours."

I blinked to get her image to focus. It didn't work.

"So he married you after all."

She laughed softly. "Yes, Henry and I have been married for ten years."

"That's not possible," I said. "Mom has only been dead for five years."

"Honey, your dad left your mom a long time ago," she said, "whether she accepted it or not."

I narrowed my eyes. "What do you mean?"

"I'm saying Henry divorced her a long time ago. She was the one who convinced herself he was on some long-term under-cover FBI operation. Every time he went back to visit you, she insisted it was true."

I guess I should have been upset, but I couldn't work up the outrage. Everything seemed two inches further away than normal. I leaned my head against the headboard. She rose and walked to the window. When she drew the curtains open, a fuzzy white light flooded the room, blinding me.

"Before you judge, Isobel, hear me out. Can you do that?"

I sighed. "I guess I can."

"Her illness ruined your lives for years." She turned her face to me, an indistinct blob. "Once he found you both living at the airport, eating out of trash cans. Another time he found her in a graveyard, convinced a secret agent had been buried alive by Neo-Nazis. She'd even started digging into a few graves and had you helping her. He loved you, he loved her, but who can blame him for leaving?"

I remembered the grave episode, remembered not being able to wash the grave dirt from my fingernails, and the nightmares that followed.

"So, really, he was here with you all this time, starting a new family?"

"Yes," she said.

I thought I'd hated him back when he was a killer and criminal. Somehow, him being an ordinary man should have made it a thousand times worse, but my heart felt like it was full of cotton balls.

"So he left me with her, his own child with a crazy woman? Why would he do that?"

"Isobel—" She came back to sit on the foot of the bed. "—it's complicated. Saffron was always wild, but she was like a rabid animal if Henry ever tried to take you away. She would self-harm. He thought she might kill herself." Olivia paused a long time, looking down at her hands. "Eventually she did."

It wasn't how I remembered it. But then again, I couldn't quite remember how I remembered it.

"That whole scene in the IHOP, where I was supposed to be Dad's crazy daughter, meeting you to see if maybe I should live with you..."

She nodded. "You do remember something. That's a positive sign."

I frowned. "That means I've been living in an institution this whole time?"

"Until you broke out six days ago."

I tried to remember. Honestly, I did.

"It was a big deal, they're saying you kids had been planning it for some time," she added. "Some ended up on the roof, but you got away."

Then I said, "Have you ever heard of Alicia Bagatelle?"

"The kidnapped girl who was rescued a few days ago? Yeah, I heard about that."

"Thing is, I found her locked up in a bomb shelter in our backyard. Dad put her down there."

"Isobel, think about it, does that make any sense? How could that possibly happen?"

"I swear it happened. I remember it clear as..." Then I paused. Because it *was* clear—the events were clear, anyway, but all the emotion I'd felt was gone. Like the sound turned down. Like maybe it was just something I made up inside my head or heard about. And then, the more I thought about it, the more the events of the past few days seemed just a little bit unlikely. I mean, who gets kidnapped by the Russian mafia these days? Is the Russian mafia even still a thing?

"You probably saw Alicia's rescue on the news, worked it into your fantasy." Olivia laughed a little. "If Henry really had kidnapped her, he'd have gone on the run by now. There's a nation-wide hunt to find the man who did it."

I looked at my hands, still feeling pretty ill. I considered whether I should try to vomit again.

"Are you and Dad going to send me back to that place?" I asked.

"Henry doesn't want to. And he's right. Just look at the state of you. Your forehead is all scraped up and there are bruises all on your arms. You look like you haven't eaten real food for months."

I sighed. Suddenly, I felt incredibly tired. "Please don't send me away."

"I tell you what," she said. "You take those pills, and we can give it a try for a day or two. See how it goes. To be honest, I always felt bad about how that whole meeting thing turned out. Your dad warned me—" She shrugged. "I just have a thing about snakes."

"Okay," I told her. "Thank you."

She stood. "Stay there a moment. I have something for you."

Like I was going anywhere. She left the room and came back with my bag.

"I found it outside under the oak. Henry told me to keep it from you, but...let's call it a peace offering, or a show of trust, just between us two girls."

I sat up when she handed it to me.

"Hope you don't mind, but it stank," she added. "I sprayed it with deodorizer."

I looked inside. The nunchaku had not been replaced, but I saw, nestling among the last few things I had left, the remains of Leif's phone. My nose filled with the scent of chemical flowers. For a moment I felt fully awake. But the sharp smell dissipated, and the dullness returned. I leaned against the headboard once more.

"The smell is monkey crap." I frowned. "I think it is, anyway."

"Monkey crap?" A little line appeared between her shaped eyebrows. "How weird. That's exactly what I thought it smelled like, too."

AFTER OLIVIA LEFT, I pulled out the phone and stared at it. My arm felt heavy. The phone looked heavy. It might have been ten minutes, it might have been three hours, but I chose a new sim from the ones floating around in the bottom of the bag, replaced the battery, powered it up, pressed "phonebook" and then "call."

"May his Noodly Appendage bless you!"

"Izzard?"

"Rain?"

I frowned. "What did you just say about appendages?"

"I've found my faith again. Hey, it's good to hear from you. Leif was like totally weirded out by—"

I pulled the phone away from my ear and looked at it. Izzard's voice coming from the phone sounded real enough, but was it? The display was lit up, but for some reason, I couldn't get my eyes to focus on the actual number. I'd thought I'd dialed a number from the phone's memory, but maybe I'd really dialed a random number and was leaving some incomprehensible crap on someone's voicemail. I put the phone back up to my ear. Izzard was still talking.

"Anyway, where are you? Bailey and I can come pick you up."

"Cut the bullshit, Izzard. I know the FBI is looking for me. I bet they made you say that."

"I can't totally deny it," he said. "Hey, maybe checking in with them might not be such a bad thing."

Well, I'd found Dad, so maybe it wasn't a bad thing. Except... I'd see Peter again for sure. The memory of our bodies pressed together made me shudder with longing, but the thought of seeing him again—knowing that he knew how I felt and didn't care—the reality of that was unbearable. No. There was no way I could do it.

Not to mention all the explaining I'd have to do about the explosion at the BOHO, and Gabe. Would they believe I had nothing to do with it? Maybe, eventually. But it would take a lot of effort on my part.

"If I check in with them, I won't be checking out."

"It's not that dramatic, is it? I think they're just kind of confused, you agreeing it was all a setup and then running off and kicking that footballer's ass in some high school. Man, you and Leif, you got up to some way crazy shit yesterday."

"Yeah, crazy shit. There's a thing about that." I glanced at the bedroom door—still closed. "Some events happened that...well...they caused me to question things."

"Question everything. That's what I say."

"It's possible that my mom was mentally ill, that she was the one that imagined all the terrorist stuff."

"That would be twisted," he agreed.

"They say my name is really Isobel. They say I'm not taking my medication."

"Oh, shit. So you're crazy too? A little bit of schizo-paranoid action going on there? I'll level with you, it would explain a lot. Like the whole Leif-crawling-through-the-sewer episode. And making him strip. That was weird, Rain, you have to admit."

"That was Dad's—" I stopped. No, it must have been my idea. It must have been my idea all along.

"Izzard, I need to ask you something."

"Ask me what?"

I took a breath. "Are you real?"

A moment of silence. And then a loud, sharp laugh. "Dude. No way. Bitch! You think I'm like a figment of your imagination?" He went on like that for a bit. I let him. At last, he calmed down. "You're going to have to seriously consider both sides of this."

My blood ran cold. "Am I?"

"If you're Isobel, and I'm Izzard, that is beyond weird coincidence. It totally makes me out to be your alter-ego."

"So I might have made you up. I might have made all of you up."

"No worries, man. You've been through some totally hellish shit. How about me and Bailey, we come pick you up and meet Carol Anne for a bit of lunch. You know, like in public place, keeping it safe for you—"

"Thanks for the offer, but I can't."

"Why not?"

"Cause you're not real. You're in my head."

"But I'm not actually in your head. I'm on the phone."

"I have a phone in my hand, and I think there is a voice coming out of it, but I can't be sure."

"Freaking heck, Rain. Can't you tell the difference?"

"I don't think that's how it works," I said. "If you're really crazy, you really can't tell the difference. And stop calling me Rain. My name is Isobel."

"If you're going to accuse me of being a figment of your imagination, I insist we consider whether you're a figment of my imagination."

"That's just pointless," I said. "Knowing you aren't real ahead of time kind of destroys the tension."

"That's taking it too far," he said. "Where are you calling from exactly?"

"My dad's house."

"Oh, shit, Rain. You have to get out of there. Now."

"Relax, alter-ego. It's my dad."

"Google it, Rain. Your dad is the subject of a nationwide manhunt. Your dad has been implicated in six more missing person cases. They're bringing in a backhoe to dig for bodies under the driveway at your old house."

"Not my dad, Izzard, not my driveway. That whole Alicia thing has nothing to do with us. I must have seen it on the news, got confused. Made it up."

"Fine," Izzard said. But he didn't sound like it was fine. "You go on believing that. Just tell me where you are."

"Again, pointless. At some stage, I have to choose my reality."

"Rain," he said, "could you please choose the reality where I am a total dickhead who should not have screwed with your head even for a moment and is now very much regretting it?"

"You believe the world was created by a spaghetti monster. It kind of screws up your credibility."

"That's only to annoy my mom's born-again boyfriend. Really, I'm a typical agnostic."

"You don't understand. I don't give a shit about your crappy religious beliefs. Until now, I always believed that my mom was killed by a terrorist car bomb."

There was silence for a moment. Then he said, "Listen to me carefully. If she was killed by a car bomb, then your dad was the one who set it."

"Right," I said. "Until now, that's what I believed." I closed my eyes, a wave of nausea rolling over me as I suddenly realized. "Jesus. I actually came here to kill him."

I let my hand and the phone drop to the sheets. I stared at it. That was the truth. It was why I'd lied and run from the FBI (if

I'd ever even met them). Why I'd told all those lies to Leif (if he even existed). It was behind the lies I'd told myself.

I thought Henry Eagan had killed my mom, and I'd come to kill him. An innocent man. My dad, even.

The phone kept on making noises. I brought it back up to my ear.

"I am online, Rain. I am looking at the list of the missing. I think you should know what it says."

"Mom killed herself," I told him, "and if I don't sort myself out, I could end up the same way."

"Some of these people go far back. One of them could be your mother."

"You're just upset because you're losing control of my consciousness."

"Will you shut up for a minute and listen?"

"Fuck you, alter-ego," I said. "Reality starts now."

"No, wait. Rain? Wait, don't cut me—"

I put down the phone, making sure to hang up this time. After a moment's thought, I slipped off the back, removed the battery again, and threw the whole assembly in the basket-weave trash can by the bed.

EVER SINCE I WAS LITTLE, I've had this thing in my brain that means I see and think about numbers as colors. One is black, two is yellow, and three is a bright orange-red the color of the setting sun. As the numbers get higher and more complex, they take on multiple colors based on their digits and divisibility. It comes in handy when having to memorize a string of numbers, but I've never thought about it much otherwise. I didn't even realize until a few years ago that not everyone thinks of numbers this way, that I was the weird one—with too many neural connections in my brain.

Some people believe that it is a chemical imbalance that allows particularly thick connections to grow in the frontal lobe like a rain-forest. Extra connections get made, some that are really useful, like ones that make abstract concepts easy to understand or give you an extra aptitude for math. But from there, you start to see how easy it would be to grow too many connections: connections that serve no purpose, like the ones that make "1024" diamond bright like the sun and "81" gritty like a red brick. Like the ones that made me hear wordless whispers in the silence. Or maybe connections that were flat out wrong, like the ones that made up the murders, the terrorists, and the fears. Maybe they made up Angrendir and StormShadow to fulfill my unresolved need to rescue Mom from herself. Perhaps they imagined Leif, Bailey, and Izzard to fulfill my need for friends, and created Peter to fulfill my need for love.

I had to admit, my extra connections could have done a slightly better job on the love-fulfilling front. But, sadly, mental illness isn't about happy wish-fulfillment. It's not that easy.

The hours stretched into night, and the numbers grew gray and uniform. I struggled to make it from the bed to the toilet and back again. In the pale hours of dawn, the light returned to the room, but only the light, no colors, no emotions. I buried my face in the pillow. I knew what I had to do.

I couldn't actually remember thinking all this when I quit my medication the first time, but I would have known this: the medication that dulled my mind would also kill my soul. That would have been enough reason to stop.

The next time Olivia came in with water, another pill and some saltine crackers to calm my stomach, I thanked her. She asked me if I would like a book.

I pretended to swallow the pill and said yes.

Already my stomach felt calmer, that heavy sleepiness was lifting. I felt one-inch closer to the front of my eyeballs.

I could do this.

28

As guest rooms go, it was pretty nice, I guess. Two windows with rosewood blinds looked out onto the tree-lined street and a crackled-paint dresser with a large mirror held a bowl of what appeared to be purely decorative balls. The sheets were a clean and smooth cream. Desiree's house was full of texture deposited by the activities of life, scratches on the legs of tables, grubby dark shadows around the light switches, white sheets stained cream in the middle by years of night sweat. In Olivia's house, the texture was purchased; it only imitated decay, and where it imitated poorly, like in the crackle paint, you had the feeling it was giving you the finger. Everywhere I touched, I seemed to shed bits of weed seeds, or dirt from my boot soles, or flakes of dandruff from my hair.

Once I looked up and saw the door was open. Decker and Dakota had poked their heads around the door and were looking at me silently.

"Boo," I said.

They slammed the door shut.

As my nausea receded, my eyes focused, and I explored more, I found further oddities. The drawers of the dresser mysteriously held not one but three Christmas wreaths, one red and green, one silver and blue, one gold. The corners under the bed were free of dust-bunnies. The windows were sealed shut.

A knock at the door interrupted my explorations. It was Olivia, with water, a bowl of red gelatin and a plate of saltine crackers on a little rosewood tray with legs. "For your stomach," she told me and retreated towards the door.

I thanked her and lifted the tumbler of water to drink. Heavy, with bubbles in the glass and a cobalt rim. It looked hand blown by Mexican craftsmen over a mesquite fire. But maybe it was made in China.

"How are you feeling?" she asked, stopping at the threshold.

I set down the tumbler.

"Much better, thanks."

My dad poked his head around the doorway. "Hey, Isobel," he said. "How's my girl doing?"

"She's doing well," Olivia answered. "Doesn't she look better?"

He came into the room, studying me. "Much, much better. You feel okay?"

"Yes," I told him. "Totally good."

"That's great. Isobel, if you're feeling up to it, why don't we have a little chat about things?"

I took a saltine and said. "I'd really like that."

He sat at the foot of the bed as Olivia's steps echoed down the hall. He stuck out a foot and toed the edge of the door.

It swung shut with a click.

"What the hell are you playing at?" he said.

My mouth dropped open. "Playing at?"

"My cover is so close to being blown right now. All thanks to you and your misguided vendetta." He shifted on the bed, like he wanted to lean forward and throttle me. "What's that about, anyway?"

I moved back against the headboard. "Hang on," I said. "Didn't you just tell me all this FBI stuff was in my head? That it isn't real?"

"Just like your mother. So fucking slow on the uptake. What did you expect me to say in front of Olivia?"

"So you made out I was crazy instead? That's pretty harsh, Dad."

With a jolt it all made sense. The upset stomach, the feeling of disconnection.

"You dosed me with flunitrazepam."

"Call them roofies, Rain. It's so fucking annoying when you use that jargon crap."

"If you're really an FBI agent, how come they have no record of it?"

He sneered. "Of course there's no record of me. For the things I do, deniability is paramount. You know that. It has to look like I don't exist." He stood up. "Dammit, it has to look like the money doesn't exist!"

I tried to keep my voice even. I said, "And Alicia?"

"Also an FBI agent."

I looked at him and said nothing.

"They broke her, and she turned. I had to do it."

Just yesterday, I had justified my lies to Leif by saying something similar. But then again, agents are turned all the time. It's a fact.

"So, you just put her in a bomb shelter and waited for her to die?"

"Sometimes one life must be sacrificed to save many. You know that."

This was true, all true, and it was like a shadow passing over the sun. Somehow, in my gut, I'd known. You can't just walk out of your basement and change your life in a week. It doesn't work that way. You can't just decide reality is a nightmare and fix it by pretending to wake up.

"Dad...the terrorist attack plan, it's all real? StormShadow and Angrendir, they're not your agents? You mean there's a cell, a hotspot, forming right now, right here?"

He looked at me a long moment. "What do you think?"

It was a trick question. Thinking has nothing to do with Loyalty. It never has. This, I have known all my life.

"Shit," I said, throwing my head back against the headboard. "Shit, Dad, this is serious. They're going to attack the State Fair."

He brought a knuckle to his mouth and turned from me a moment. When he turned back, his face was deadly serious. "You know what you have to do."

Loyalty Tests can come at any time. The beginning of a Loyalty Test is not necessarily announced. How to successfully pass a Loyalty Test is never mentioned. If you are truly, deeply loyal to your core, it will be obvious what to do. That's a part of the test.

"Yeah Dad, I'm ready," I said. "Come on. Let's hit the State Fair together."

His fist dropped to his side. "Hold on, you're forgetting. I still don't know what happened back at the house. I don't know exactly how you fucked it all up and blew our cover there."

"Me?" I said. "I fucked up? I couldn't exactly help it. I was kidnapped by the mafia."

His eyes narrowed. "What did you say?"

"You heard me. The Russian mafia."

"Why would you have anything to do with the Russian mafia?"

I frowned. The FBI wouldn't have made public how the arrest of Dmitri Andropov and rescue of Alicia Bagatelle were connected, but surely the True Patriots would have access to that knowledge. Then again, my dad was an important man. Maybe he'd been too busy to check in with them.

"Their boss was one of Finnegan's marks. He wanted exclusive predictions and kidnapped me at gunpoint."

"You always told me you were untraceable."

"No one is completely untraceable," I told him. "Plus Russia breeds some pretty good hackers."

Dad didn't look mollified. He had high standards. It meant we often clashed on technical matters.

"But I did pretty well," I said. "I almost escaped all by myself and I definitely got the head of the mob captured. You would be proud of me. And only two people died. Mafia guys, so it's kind of okay."

"Two people died." He sat back down on the bed. "This really happened like you say?"

"Yes," I said. "It's what started the whole thing off. I never would have led the Others to the house, not if I could have helped it."

He just sat there and looked at me. I mean, dammit, a "sorry, I see how that could have happened" would have been nice.

Instead, he said, "Maybe, maybe not."

That hurt. Maybe he wanted it to hurt; he could be like that.

"Go ask your people. If they don't tell you the same story, they're the ones fucking up," I told him. "Maybe you should question why the True Patriots haven't told you everything."

"We don't have time for all that," he said. "Not if what you say about the terrorists is true."

It was a disappointment. I wanted so much for him to know, or care, about what I'd been through, to tell me, just once, that I'd done a good job. But he was right not to. The harsh reality of the anti-terrorism fight is that we must always put our emotions second. There was not a moment to lose.

"What do you need for me to do, then?"

"We'll have to set you up somewhere else. Get you some more computers. You know what you need?"

"Of course," I said. "Easy."

"And then you'll have to make up for lost time. Get another Finnegan. We'll use one from the tank downstairs. We can't afford to miss any more games."

"Wait," I said. "How does Finnegan help?"

"An operation is all about funding," he said patiently, "You know that. You want me to go after these guys, we're going to need cars full of gas, bodies on the ground, ammo for the guns. None of that stuff is cheap."

I looked down at my hands on the sheets. The bandage over my cut was long gone, just a grubby square left on the skin where the adhesive still stuck. The cut itself was still raw and barely scabbed.

"Dad, I've been through a lot, lately. I'm not feeling that great. You think maybe you could fund this one operation without me?"

The corner of his mouth twitched. "A minute ago you wanted to go in the field. Now you're too tired?"

Put that way, it did sound childish.

"Now that Alicia's gone, you're the final revenue stream. You think solar panels are the least bit profitable? Fuck it. Look around you. All this shit is one football game away from bankruptcy."

Suddenly, it was all too much.

"Fuck you!" I shouted scrambling to my knees. I'd never questioned him before, but the way the True Patriots had treated Alicia had been terrible. I didn't want to end up the same way. "I'm done with sitting at a keyboard. Put me in the field, it's where I belong!"

"You will do as you're told! Do you want a thousand deaths on your conscience, do you?"

The door burst open and Olivia rushed into the room. She was fumbling with her purse, the one with the gun in it.

"I heard shouting," she said.

Dad stood, his face pale.

"Olivia," he said, "you did give her the medication, didn't you, the second dose?"

"Of course," she said, staring at me. "What happened?"

He strode to the head of the bed and started to root around on the nightstand. "She just started in on me. Totally out of control."

"You just admitted you were an FBI agent!" I said. "You tried to get me to go back to doing Internet scams."

He looked at me like he was confused. "We were discussing dinner...what she would like to eat for dinner. Fish, wasn't it?"

"You called me Rain!"

Olivia took a few steps in the room.

"Isobel, honey," she said, "I think there's something you ought to see."

"What?" I snapped.

She bent down, extended a careful hand towards my bag, and pulled out my wallet. "Look inside."

Dad frowned. "You gave that to her?"

"I searched it first," Olivia said.

I sighed. "I already know what's in there."

"Just open it."

I opened the wallet, pulled out the learner's permit I had picked up at the safe house.

Isobel Eagan.

"Is this what you think proves I am crazy?" I said to her. "It's not going to work, Olivia. This is a fake ID my Dad and I made up in case our cover was blown. The name is Isobel, but that's just coincidence."

Dad's lips were in a thin line. "Coincidence, Isobel? Really?"

"You planned it!" I threw the ID down on the bed. "There were IDs for you as well, in the name of Harold!"

He smiled. "Where are they, then?"

I faltered, remembering. "They were at the BOHO,"

"The what?"

"Bug-out house. It's like a safe house."

"A safe house?" Olivia asked. "You're saying we can drive to a real house somewhere and they will be there, and we can see them?"

"No, Dad blew it up with a bomb."

"Really? Well isn't that swell," she said. "The one thing that would prove your story was true, blown to smithereens." Olivia shook her head. "Just listen to yourself. How can we believe anything you say?"

"I don't know." I put my hands to my temple. It really was true, about being crazy. You really couldn't tell. I should have been watching for this. I knew the delusions would start up again, and dammit if they hadn't sucked me right in. I should have been better prepared to resist.

Dad shook a crumpled tissue he'd picked up off of the nightstand. A white pill fell out onto the crackle paint with a little tic.

"I can explain about that at least," I said quickly. "The pills make me feel really bad, Dad. I was just hoping I could handle it."

"You clearly can't," Olivia said.

Dad held his hand out to me, the pill in the middle of his palm. "Sweetie, you're going to have to trust me on this one."

There was no getting out of it, not with the two of them looking at me. I took the pill and put it in my mouth. Too late to back out now—I could already feel it dissolving. I took a swig of water.

"That's it, darling," he said. "Now let me see you swallow."

29

The world spun to the right. I opened my eyes, tried to slow it down, but it all fell past me in a blur. I looked at the corner of the door, seeking some steady point of reference, an origin upon which to hang my coordinate system. It slipped, slipped, slipped. I closed them.

When I opened my eyes again, it was dark. Moonlight through the blinds made pale stripes against the wall. I sat up. Stomach still bad, but not catastrophic. Yay for Olivia's saltines and gelatin.

I dug around in the trash can for the phone. Still there, thank God. Olivia had not emptied it. I put the pieces on the bed and tried to get them to go back together. It wasn't easy. It felt as if my fingers were little Vienna sausages, and the blurriness in my eyes was back. At last, some little plastic tab on the battery cover gave up and popped in.

Messages from Izzard and Bailey. Messages from Agent Cheung. They must have given her the number. None from the only person I wanted to hear from. But even if Peter was a man who existed only in my mind, I couldn't force him to call.

Oh, and there, at the end, one from Leif, with his new number.

So which figment of my imagination did I feel like talking to tonight?

I rang Leif.

"Hey Leif, are you sleeping?"

A sound of rustling. "It's like three-thirty in the morning. Of course, I'm sleeping."

"Sorry," I said. "I guess I'll..."

"No no no," Leif interrupted. "We can talk now." More rustling. I imagined him sitting up in bed. "What's on your mind?"

"I'm getting some mixed messages about reality. I don't know what to believe anymore."

"Izzard told us all about your last call. We're all like shitting bricks over here."

"So are you going to ask me where I am?"

"Would you tell me if I did?"

"There's a deeper issue here," I said. "The one about you being real or not. Either you are imaginary, I am crazy, my father sells solar panels, and my mother is still alive. Or you are real, I am sane, my father is an FBI agent, my mother is dead, and thousands more could die."

"There's a third possibility," Leif said. "The one where I am real, you are brainwashed, and your dad is about to bury a hatchet in your head."

"Whatever, Leif."

"How can I prove to you that I'm real, Rain?"

I bit my lip. "Actually, I have a plan."

I made him go get a coin. He grumbled—apparently it involved turning on the light.

"Got it. Now what?"

"Flip it."

"Flip it? What's that going to prove?"

"If you're for-real real, then you have access to the physical world. You should be able to use it to generate a random sequence." I'd found a broken pencil stub and a notepad in the nightstand drawer. *Brighten your day with a solar array!* was printed across the top of the page. I'd worked the wood on the stub back with my thumbnail until it stuck out in a hairy mess from the graphite. I was ready to go. "Then I'll test the second-order statistics to see if you pass."

"Ouch, Rain. Say that again in normal-people talk."

"Okay. Sorry. One flip is fifty-fifty heads or tails. But I need for you to do it lots of times."

"Then what...you test it to see if it's really even odds?"

"Something like that," I said. "If you're in my head, making it up, it won't be the same. The data will look funny."

"Oh man. Of all the crazy-ass round-a-fucking-bout ways to test for reality...how many times exactly? I have school in the morning."

I puffed out my cheeks. "Can we start with a hundred?"

A pause. "Then you tell me where you are?"

I shut my eyes. If my Dad was an FBI agent—revealing his location could compromise him to the enemy. But I needed Leif on-side.

"I will, but you promise me one thing."

"What's that?"

"Promise me you won't lie. It's vitally important you not lie about the coin flips."

"Yeah, okay, I promise. How hard can that be?"

"Okay, go."

"Heads."

I wrote it down. "Again."

"Heads," he said, and then, "Another heads. Hey, that's kind of weird. Heads again."

"No value judgments, please. Just the data."

"Sorry." A pause. "Uh, heads again. And, uh, heads after that."

"That's better. Keep it going."

"Okay, wow, heads again. And...uh...okay Rain, you are not going to want to hear this."

"I said, no value judgments. Just give me the data."

"Can I have a do-over on this one?"

"No, do-overs are not allowed. I need that one, specifically."

"Yeah, but if I tell you, it's not adding up to a fifty-fifty sequence, is it?"

"That's why we do it lots of times. It's heads isn't it?"

"It's heads."

"All right, don't panic. If it's eight heads, it's eight heads. Just give me the next one."

"I can't," he said.

"Why not? Did you drop it on the floor?"

"No..."

"Leif, just give it to me."

"But...what are the chances of nine heads in a row?"

"Exactly the same as the chances of eight heads and one tails."

"But if it were nine heads, that *would* be weirder, wouldn't it?"

"No, it would be an equally likely outcome. Just say it. Is it heads?"

"Well, I *have* to say heads now, don't I? You won't believe me if I say tails."

"Just tell me what it is. You promised."

"Okay," his voice got small. "It's heads."

"Was that so hard? Don't stop. We have ninety-one more to go."

"No problem. Uh...flipping again. Uh...okay...uh...tails."

"You said tails?"

"Yes."

"Are you lying?"

"No."

"Cause if you were lying, I would know. I would hang up this phone and never speak to you again."

"Okay, I admit it! I lied! It was heads! Ten heads in a row, dammit all to hell!"

"I can't do this if you lie to me!"

"But...I can't take the chance that you'll think I'm not real! "

I gritted my teeth. "The only way you could mess up the statistics would be to lie to me!"

"Have some pity, Rain. I'm not an idiot."

"Look, Leif, any con artist worth their salt knows it's a sure way to get caught—making up random numbers instead of using real ones. Your brain, it can't handle long strings of one thing, you want to make it look more even, so you screw it up! Freaking noob!"

"Oh. You're telling me that if I told you a bunch of improbable shit, that would have made me seem more probable?"

"If you hadn't lied, I could have measured the kurtosis. Determined if it followed the correct distribution for a binary sequence."

"Dammit, Rain, don't use kinds of those words at three a.m. You could hurt someone," he said.

The phone started to bleep.

"What is that?" I asked him.

"Nothing, you just gotta charge it soon."

That could be a problem, as, not expecting for Dad's murder to take too long, I had left the charger back at the safe house.

He said, "Wait a sec. Hold on one goddamn minute here. If I made up fake random numbers like a real person would, doesn't that prove I'm like a real person?"

"No, you stupid boy. It means I probably made it up inside my own head! What a waste of time this has been!"

"Wait," he said. "Give me another chance. You just had to explain it to me. Now that I understand, I can do it right."

"What, like, start over?"

"Yeah, Rain. Total fresh start. Please?"

"All right." I took a few breaths to calm myself. I ripped off the top sheet of paper on the notepad. The sheet underneath said: *Solar Panels: Put them where the sun does shine!*

Leif said, "I got the coin here. I'm ready to go now."

"Give me the first one."

But he said nothing. Instead, there was a bleep. It sounded final.

I took the phone from my ear. The screen was dark. The battery had, at last, run out.

WHEN WE PULLED the GOOD for Colorado Springs, we drove there from the east, across the Great Plains. It's one of those black spots on the map of the world, maybe not a big one, but when you're in the middle, it's big enough. We drove straight through the night. The headlights lit up tendrils of snow blowing across the road, the temperature sensor on the dash dropped to twenty-two, then ten, then three degrees. I pressed my face against the window glass and peered up at the sky. This far away from the cities, the stars should have been good, but the glass was too grubby to see through, and Dad would never let me roll down the window. I padded a sweater up against the window when it became too cold to bear and fell into a semi-sleep.

The cold woke me.

The car was no longer moving, and the interior was lit with a diffuse blue light. I tried to wipe a hole in the condensation on the window to see where we were, but it was frozen. I scraped it off in tiny white curls with my fingernails and peered through at a parking lot.

"You awake back there?" Mom asked me from the front seat. She was bundled up in various bits of clothing, looking pretty much like a pile of laundry.

"I'm cold," I told her.

She opened the passenger door and got in the back seat with me.

"Come here," she said, peeling back her layers and bundling me next to her. "You're shaking, you little thing."

I laid my head on her chest and listened to her heartbeat.

Cuddling with Mom wasn't something that happened very much now that I was older. That made it even more special. "How much longer?"

"Your Dad's inside, getting some food. We'll find a place to stay later this morning."

"Mom? I want to go home."

She held me a moment. "We can't, baby. There is no home. Not for people like us."

Dad being Dad, he was gone a long time. The blue light grew whiter. Then a golden-cherry beam of dawn sunlight struck the patterns of frost on the windshield. Fronds of gold and copper and diamonds glittered and spread and chased the blue shadows down the ice.

Mom gave me a hug. "Just think," she said, "everyone with a home is still asleep. They missed that."

"Yeah," I said. The tip of my nose was numb and moist, and if I sniffed too hard, the cold snot went up my nostrils with a particularly unpleasant feeling. But the rest of me was warm at last.

"I know it's the hardest on you, Rainbow," she said. "Your Dad and I, we took this path, but you never had a choice."

"I'd choose it," I said.

"Really?" She stroked my hair and a bit flopped over my face. It was getting darker, long and curly, just like hers.

I pressed my head against her chest, felt the line of her thin collarbone against my cheek.

"Of course I would, Mom. I just want to stay with you."

30

Olivia came in the next morning to see how I was doing. She had that little tray with a bowl of Rice Krispies on it and a new pill. I palmed the pill without too much effort.

My phone call with Leif was equivocal at best. Just the sort of complicated shenanigans you'd expect a crazy mind to come up with to avoid actually having to give a random sequence with the wrong kurtosis. But you fall off the horse, you just got to get back on. I couldn't spend the rest of my life upchucking into a toilet. And this time, I was prepared.

"Have you been thinking," she asked me, "about what you want to do next?"

"Do I have a choice, Olivia, or has Dad already decided to strangle me and disintegrate my remains in an acid bath?"

She let out a nervous laugh. "You don't really believe he'd do that, or you'd be trying a lot harder to get out of here."

I smiled to show her I was joking. "I guess the medication is helping me come around to reality at last." My fingers, out of sight behind my back, flicked the pill into the crack between the mattress and the headboard.

"That's good. You see, Henry and I were talking about plans

this morning, and I called up our local community college, to see when classes started."

"Okay," I said, but I frowned. Community college did not sound that great. But to be honest, I couldn't say what would be better. Now that my past was unclear, so was my future.

"It might be good to put some structure in your life. Maybe take up some activities like volleyball or French club too. Try to get some friends."

My gaze flicked to the nightstand, where I had stowed Leif's phone.

"Real friends," she went on, "not missing schoolgirls that you see on the news. Henry also wants to limit your computer time."

"If I have to, I guess I'll do it."

"In the meantime, we'll take you to your psychiatrist on Monday and try to find a better option for those drugs. Something to make you feel less sick."

I felt a flash of guilt about the pill, now lost behind the bed. "Okay, Olivia, thanks."

She sat on the side of the bed and put her hand lightly on my thigh. "I know your mom had you believing a lot of things, and I know all that just doesn't go away overnight. But try to trust me. This is a good home we've made here, and we'd like to welcome you into it."

* * *

"HERE'S THE PLAN," Dad said to me later that afternoon, "your stepmother is taking the twins round to her mother's for a few nights, so we've got some time. I'll take you to the store. You point. I buy. Then we get you set up with a computer again."

"Hold on, Dad. Olivia told me if I was going to stay, you'd be limiting my computer time."

"It won't be in the house," he said. "I signed a lease on an apartment not too far from here. You'll start up the Finnegan scams from there."

"She told me I was going to go to community college, join some student clubs and stuff. Won't that eat into my day?"

"Yeah, well, you're not coming back. I can't have her distracting you with all this integrating into the family shit. As far as she'll know, you've gone off the deep end and run away again. Come on, get your shoes on."

I sat there, absently feeling the smooth cream sheets between my fingers. I'd kind of come to like all the crackle-paint furniture and ubiquitous chenille throw-pillows.

"So just to be clear, we are back to hunting terrorists again," I said.

"We are back to all of it. Just like before."

I looked at him for a long time, nausea rising fast in my middle.

"No," I finally said. "I'm not giving in to the delusion this time."

Dad let out a laugh. "Come on. Don't waste my time."

"I'm really not, Dad. Not this time."

He looked at me. Then he came in closer, his eyes narrowed. "Tell me the name of the psychiatric hospital we kept you in."

I thought for a moment. I only knew of one, the one Carol Anne had planned to send me to. "New Transitions, I think."

"Really? How many patients are there?"

"How should I know?"

"Here's some easier questions. How many floors does it have? What color is the carpet? Do they have blinds or curtains on the windows?"

I couldn't answer.

He leaned in very close. "What's the name of your psychiatrist?"

"I don't know," I said at last.

"Yeah," he nodded. "You don't because you don't have one. You're fucking up on the Loyalty again, Rain. Questioning things. You know what happens when you fuck up the Loyalty."

"Yes," I said in a tiny voice.

"That's right," he said. He held his hands up and flicked his fingers. "Boom."

He stood.

"I'll see you downstairs in a minute. I hope I don't have to remind you how important it is that Olivia knows nothing." He shut the door behind him.

You know those moments when you're screwing it up? You know you're screwing it up, and you do it anyway.

I went around the room, gathering my few possessions. I picked up the paperback Olivia had lent me and hesitated, but my stepmother had plenty of books. I put it in my bag. In the depths of the bag, Bailey's lip gloss tube glinted softly. Or I thought it was Bailey's. Had I bought it myself? If I had, then why could I not remember it, not even a little bit?

Nah, Bailey had given it to me. I could remember her voice and her smile clear as day. I could even remember her laughter and floral perfume.

If there has been once certainty in my life, it is this: we do what has to be done. Dad had made up the story about my insanity for Olivia's sake, nothing more. The drugs were unfortunate, but necessary. This has always been true.

I took out the lip gloss and held it in my hand. Tiny particles caught the light and sparkled.

We do what has to be done, but if I went back underground, I'd have to give up contacting Leif or his friends again. It went without saying that I could never contact the others at the FBI. With a stab of grief, I knew that meant I'd never see Peter either. I knew how we'd left it, but after a few days, maybe he'd have reconsidered. If the way I felt about him was anything like the way he felt about me, he would have reconsidered. No way could something that real be one way.

Shit. I sat on the bed. Shit.

We do what has to be done. This was my life—not one I'd choose—but you can't choose your family, can you?

I laced my boots, then I paused. Then I picked up Bailey's lip gloss from where I'd dropped it on the bed.

Some things you can't choose. But some things you can.

WHEN I CAME DOWNSTAIRS, Decker and Dakota were eating Oreos and milk at the breakfast bar in the kitchen. Olivia came in from the door to the garage.

"Right, kids, did Dad pack your bags?"

They nodded. Dakota pointed to two backpacks at the foot of their stools.

"I'll load them while you finish." She came around the breakfast bar and picked them up. "We're leaving straight away."

"Olivia, wait," I said.

She paused at the door of the garage. "Yes?"

"I...I just wanted to say goodbye." My chest spasmed. "And to thank you, for being so kind."

"Of course I'm being kind." She set the bags down and came over to me. "We got off to a rocky start, but you're family, Isobel."

I shook my head. "I'm crazy family."

"That doesn't matter. Are you okay? You look upset."

"I'm fine. I just wanted you to know that I'll always remember how nice you were."

She put her hands on my shoulders. "Hey, we'll only be gone for a few days. So you and Henry can get you settled in without us three getting underfoot."

At the breakfast bar, Decker and Dakota stared at me over a nearly empty plate of cookies.

It wasn't a few days. It was forever. But I nodded. I'd said too much already, and I didn't trust myself to speak more.

Dad came down the steps, two more bags on his arms, and stopped short.

"What's this?"

Olivia drew back. "Just saying goodbye, aren't we?"

I nodded again.

She gave him a smile, like she'd just won something. Dad's eyes narrowed, but she had already turned away.

Dakota said, "Mom, can we take the iPad?"

Olivia looked from Dad to Dakota. "Where is it?"

"In my room."

"I'll get it." She shouldered past Dad and went up the steps.

He came further into the room, walked up behind the breakfast bar. He lifted his hand and stroked Dakota's light brown hair, but he was looking at me.

"What's this about goodbye?"

Dakota turned her head and looked up at him. "She said she'll always remember us. For being kind."

"Is that so? Well, how could you show her how kind you are?"

Dakota sighed and looked down at her plate, but Decker solemnly held out the last Oreo to me.

"Thanks," I said, taking it. More chemicals and empty starches. But I felt all trembly, in that way that sugar can sometimes help.

"You're a kind boy." Dad watched me eat it. Then he called over his shoulder, "You find that iPad yet, Olivia?"

She came down the steps, holding it up in her hand. "Right where Dakota said, for once."

"Better go then."

The kids obediently hopped off the breakfast bar stools and headed towards the door. I blinked. It was like everything shifted to the right half an inch. I put my hand against the wall. Dammit.

Dad gave Olivia a peck on the cheek as she passed him.

She smiled at me from the garage doorway, mouthed, "back soon," and then shut it.

Okay. It was show time. Here, I changed how it was going to

be for me now. I rubbed my lips together, feeling the slickness of Bailey's lip gloss.

"Dad," I said, "screw all this computer shit. Take me to the State Fair now. All I need is a gun. I know what their plans are, I know how they operate. I can shut them down at a fraction of the cost."

"Oh," he said. "We're back to that again? Putting you in the field? You think you're ready?"

"I'm ready." The trembly feeling was getting worse. I put my other hand against the wall.

"Because I thought, just now, you were playing pretty fast and loose with my cover again." He slammed his hand down on the counter top. "What the fuck was that all about, Rain, 'you'll always remember her kindness'?"

"I will. So what?"

He paced back and forth behind the bar, running his fingers through his hair. "So now when you disappear, she'll be suspicious, won't she? She'll think maybe you didn't want to go. Then she'll want to look for you." He stopped and turned to me. "I'll have a hard time keeping the police out of it. It's gonna take some planning."

"Here's an idea," I said, "how about I don't totally disappear? How about I pretend to go to—" I blinked to clear my blurring vision."—community college like Olivia said and go to the apartment during the day? After we deal with the State Fair thing of course."

Dad shook his head. "No way. Absolutely no way to any of that."

The world shifted another inch to the right. And then another. Shit.

"The cookie. You dosed the fucking cookie, Dad. Jesus, how much did you put in here this time?"

"You dosed yourself. The moment your Loyalty wavered."

"I just wanted to say goodbye to her..." I staggered a step

toward the garage door. Wondered if I could make it ahead of him.

Dad smiled. "Decker's a bright boy, don't you think? Ready for training." He came around the bar. "Ready to join you."

My knees gave way. I fell to the floor, sitting with my legs sprawled. Dad stood there, looking down at me.

"Or maybe," he said, "to replace you."

"I'm not imagining this," I said, blinking hard, "I'm not, am I?"

"No, this shit is for real."

He kicked me in the shin. I knew this because I watched it happen, but the drugs had numbed the feeling in my leg.

"Coming here was a stupid mistake, Rain. And now you've fucking made Olivia suspicious, you little shit!"

He kicked me in the chest. It knocked me back on the floor. I heard my head hit the tiles. Damn, that should probably hurt. A lot. I spoke to the blurs of lights on the ceiling.

"Dad, listen to me. We should bring Olivia on side. She could help."

"Not gonna happen. Not just cause you can't get your fucking shit together, Rain. Why do you think I'm with her? Because I love her?"

"What?"

"Yes, Rain, this is my deepest undercover operation yet. She's a part of the conspiracy against the True Patriots."

"That's a lie. Her record checks out fine." I struggled up onto one elbow. Whatever the drug was in the Oreo, I could focus, just not for long. "Same with everyone in her family, and all her friends for like three degrees in every direction."

"You researched her?"

"Mom did ages ago. So did I. After I got your license plate number, and just before I came here. It's called having my shit together."

"You think you know shit about anything? The others are devious. You can't trust them even if they look clean."

"Oh fuck off, Dad. I know a thing or two. After all, I found you." I fell back against the floor again. Looked up at the ceiling. Too much effort to do anything else. "There's only one other reason you'd try to keep this from her."

I felt him more than saw him, a black blur, squatting beside me.

"Yeah?"

"You're a con man after all," I told him, "and all of this is bullshit."

31

He laughed. "That's a good one. A real creative twist."

"It's the truth," I said. "I should have tried harder to kick your ass when I had the chance."

He grabbed for me, and I rolled to the side, trying to get away. It was no good, like one of those dreams made real where you try to run and can't—can't even scream in terror. He sat on my back and pulled my arms behind me like I was a pet monkey.

"Funny. I was just thinking the same thing," he said.

I could still cry. Tears ran down my cheeks, and snot coated my upper lip. With my arms pinned, I couldn't even wipe it away.

His breath tickled my ear. "You and your mom always fought like cats and dogs, but I never thought you would actually get out of her car."

When you're little, it's like holding a big beach ball, loving your mom and dad, so big you can't get your arms around it. So real, you can't conceive of the possibility that they don't have a big beach ball they're holding onto for you. That they look at you and see meat—and feel nothing.

"We were arguing about you," I said, bitter. "My Loyalty to you saved me."

"Yeah, whatever."

"I turned out to have my uses."

"Once I had Alicia, I didn't actually need you. Now that she's gone, I do. At least until I get another pet."

The snot on my upper lip cooled in the air.

"You still have Angrendir and StormShadow, right?"

"Who?"

"Angrendir and StormShadow." Maybe he didn't know their online names. "The other girls that work for you."

"There's no one else. My goddamn luck, I'm stuck with you, Rain."

I was trying to process the implications of his answer when the door to the garage flew open.

"Henry!"

I turned my head to the side and made an effort to focus. Olivia stood there.

"Jesus! Did she attack you again?"

My vertebrae popped as Dad shifted his weight on me. "Why are you here?"

Her eyes were wide. They kept flicking from me to him.

There was a moment of silence, then he said, "Jesus, Olivia. Maybe you could drive off without your phone just this once. Just for fucking once."

"Yeah, but what if I need to call you...if I have a flat..." Her voice trailed off. "I mean..."

I could feel Dad taking deep, exasperated breaths. "Well, you're here now. Get your gun and help me restrain her."

My vertebrae popped again. But Olivia shook her head.

"No," she said. "This is enough, Henry. This is the third time. What if you hadn't been able to stop her? What if I hadn't come back in? Are we going to live our lives behind the barrel of a gun? In our own home?"

"Olivia?" When I talked, my lips slid across the puddle of

mucus and drool I'd made on the tiles. It couldn't have been a convincing picture of sanity. "Why don't you ask me my side of the story?"

"Your side is clear enough, young woman." She spotted her phone on the counter and picked it up "Henry, let's call the police and have her sectioned again. Now."

She put the phone to her ear, and I felt his whole body jerk.

"Olivia, wait," he said.

She looked up. "Why?"

I twisted my head up and answered before he had a chance. "Because he's a con man. Because everything around you was stolen in one way or another. Your house, your cars, all the shit you have."

She stared down at me. I couldn't focus enough to see the emotion in her eyes.

"Isobel..." He inched my arms further behind me. Just a few more pounds of force, and my shoulder sockets would pop open, never to be the same again. It was too late for me, I knew that. But if Olivia ran for the car now, she could get away. She could take Dakota and Decker somewhere safe. I just needed to make her understand that.

"Your life, his business, it's all a lie," I told her. "He made me help him. He'll make you do the same if you stay."

She lowered the phone from her ear. "Henry, is this true?"

He didn't answer her. I just felt that breathing, a shifting weight on my back: a wild animal planning his strike.

"Henry?" Her voice was high and small.

He spoke at last. "Olivia, what I am about to tell you is highly secret information."

"Okay, Henry, you'd better tell me now."

"I really am an undercover FBI agent."

"Wait..." She slumped back against the wall. "You're saying that the crazy thing your crazy daughter said is not crazy after all?"

"I kept it from you for your own safety."

Olivia stood there, quiet, for several moments.

"I guess it does explain some things," she said at last. "Just give me a minute to get my head around this..."

"It's just another lie," I said. "Don't buy it, Olivia. He's clutching at straws. Why for God's sake would him being an FBI agent mean you can't section me? Go on, ask him that."

Dad answered before she could ask. "It's classified, Olivia. I'd tell you if I could."

"The truth is that I was never in a psychiatric hospital," I told her. "You hand me over to the authorities, they'll figure that out straight away. They'll investigate him. They'll find out he kidnapped Alicia. That's why he can't risk it."

"Henry? Is this true? Tell me, is she actually crazy, or is she not?"

"Please, Olivia," I begged, "get yourself and the twins out of here before it's too late. Call the police from somewhere safe."

But she didn't move. "I don't know. Maybe I should call, Henry. Your people can sort it out, right?"

"You call them, Olivia, and I'll be arrested for sure. I have many enemies in the Bureau who'd love to try and frame me for something I didn't do."

"Bullshit," I said. "Olivia, there's one thing that's true. Terrorists are planning to poison thousands of people at the State Fair." Damn. Was it going to be today? Tomorrow? I'd lost track of the days, but I knew it would be soon. "If you don't help me get free so I can warn people, they could all die."

Dad pulled my arms dangerously tight. "She's making that shit up. Don't fall for it." He leaned in close to my ear again. "After all that crying wolf? No one will believe you anyway, you stupid girl."

"You'd really let them all die," I asked him, "rather than turn yourself in?"

"It's not something I'll lose sleep over," he said, "because even I don't believe your crap."

"If you really don't know who Angrendir and StormShadow are," I said, "if Alicia and I were your only victims, then you really, really ought to reconsider that."

"She's crazy," Olivia said. "She's definitely crazy."

"Yes."

"So why can't we have her sectioned?"

"Like I told you, that's classified information," he said. "But I can tell you one thing. This girl beneath me, she's more dangerous than you could possibly imagine. She's an enemy of America."

I thought he couldn't hurt me more. I was wrong. All those years I gave to our country, and he called me that.

"Let me take care of her," he went on. "She'll be gone when you get back, and our life goes back to normal. Like it never happened."

"Did you kidnap Alicia?" she said. "Was she an enemy, too?"

"Goddamn it, woman," Hal said. "Call the police if you want. They'll find out that I had nothing to do with it. But you think about what that really means. There'll be flashing lights out front where everyone can see. It could be days before I can arrange bail. Are you going to be the one to tell Decker his dad can't take him to soccer this week because he's locked up in jail?"

"Shit," she said in a small voice. "I forgot about practice this week."

"Imagine the look on Decker's little face, Olivia, when he finds out you were the one who called the police. His own mom."

She placed the phone on the counter. "This is the week we were supposed to bring the snacks."

He paused. "Let me take care of her, and it will all just go back to how it was. You know it's the right thing."

Olivia nodded. She pulled herself straight. "What do I have to do?"

My neck was getting tired, so I laid my head back down on the tiles.

"Help me get her upstairs."

They half carried, half dragged me up the stairs and laid me on the bed. He got some chain and wrapped it around the long part of the bed frame several times and secured my ankles. He had another set of shackles for my wrists.

She stood at the door and watched him do this.

"The sheets," she said.

Dad snapped his head around. "What?"

She flinched. "It's just...there's these princess sheets in the linen closet. Dakota doesn't like them anymore. Maybe you could use those...I mean..." She swallowed. "...those ones on the bed are Egyptian cotton."

Dad sighed. "Sorry, sweetheart. You're right of course. You want to get them out for me?"

But she stood there, her hands clasped together. He walked over to her and gently cupped his hands around her shoulders. "Like I said, this is the right thing. It's the right thing for us. It's the right thing for our country."

"I know...it just feels wrong."

"Look, forget about the sheets. Why don't I come with you? I'll explain it all in the car on the way. We'll get you and the twins settled, and I'll stop by the hardware store for a plastic drop cloth on the way back."

She didn't even look at me. She just sort of nodded and left the room.

He came back to me and methodically tested the chains. They held.

"Hey, I have an offer for you," I said to him. "I won't go to the police. I'll even keep all the scams going. Just let me go to the State Fair now. Or tomorrow even. All I want to do is find the terrorists."

He leaned right in my face. I could see the pores on his nose again, the three long hairs under a mole that he hadn't manage to shave off cleanly, the web of fine veins under his eyes. His voice was low. "You know what? I am going to make you pay for this, you crazy, stupid bitch. The one good thing in my life was that woman, and you just made me shit where I eat."

He walked out and shut the door behind him.

PART IV

HUNTER

32

I lay there on the bed, not moving. I heard the garage door rumble open and shut again. There was enough slack in the chains for me to roll to the side of the bed and puke.

It had always been too good to be true anyway, the possibility that I would ever have a family.

I methodically tested the chains. They held.

I lay back. The drugs swirled through my veins, but if I didn't fight and instead lay perfectly still, the knowledge that I was trapped gave way to the illusion that I floated. I imagined the door opening and the light falling across the bed. It was Peter Angelopolos, come to release me from my shackles yet again. He gathered me up in his arms, and I nestled my head against the flat warm plane of his chest, and he carried me out of the house. Just before we got to the front door, I looked into his eyes, and he looked into mine, and we didn't even have to say we forgave each other because there never had been two souls who fit together so amazingly perfectly as ours.

And because I loved him so much, I said, "Put me down, Peter."

He kind of hefted me in his arms and pressed his lips to my forehead.

"Never, Rain. I've already explained our love to everyone. Even Carol Anne agrees that the FBI duty-of-care policies don't apply in our case."

I ran through this fantasy a couple of times. Tears slipped from my eyes and pooled, cold, in the cups of my ears—because some things in your head will only ever exist in your head.

Deep inside me, my metabolic processes rallied forces and counter-attacked. Gently, my body floated back down to Olivia's precious Egyptian cotton. I used all of the slack in the chain to reach my fingers deep into my pillowcase and pull out a thin wire that I had hidden there. Olivia might have found and thrown away my nunchaku before letting me have my bag, but she hadn't felt too carefully in the lining next to the zipper. Yesterday, I'd extracted a wire from this lining and hidden it in the bed, just like I'd hidden it in every bed I'd slept in since that night Roman had shackled me to the bed in Dmitri's basement. The thin wire was coated with sharp diamond dust and had two steel rings on the ends. Any self-respecting survivalist would recognize it immediately, a little saw that would take up almost no space in a bugout bag but could cut through firewood or a hardened steel deadbolt with equal ease. Carol Anne might have called it a coping mechanism, but you had to admit, it was more practical than your average coping mechanism. Knowing the little saw was there, slipping my fingers under the pillow and feeling its thin roughness, was the only way these days I could relax enough to fall asleep.

It wasn't easy at first; my chains made it hard to get a good angle. But finally, the wire bit in and the scores deepened to a groove. Tiny particles of steel gathered and glittered, star-like on my skin.

Call me crazy. Call me a bitch. Call me what you like. You could even call me stupid.

But that would be a big mistake.

DAD AND OLIVIA's neighborhood was not only uncharacteristically hilly for Fort Worth, it was also laid out in some sort of tortuous topological anti-grid. Meaning that, as the car drove, I could be a good mile and a half away just by hopping a fence.

As soon as I could stand up again, I packed my bag and staggered right out of that house. I hopped a couple of fences (okay, I fell over them once or twice) and spent the night in a culvert, counting on the dry weather to hold. The Texas autumn nights were beginning to chill, and the metal ridges sucked the warmth from my flesh without mercy. I dragged handfuls of leaves into the culvert, and they formed a surprisingly good if noisy insulator, although no matter how I adjusted myself, there always seemed to be a small twig or rock poking my spine.

I lay there in the dusty-smelling culvert and looked at the leaves in their various states of decomposition, noticed how the flat of the leaf crackled off in tiny squares to reveal the lace-like skeleton beneath. It was hard not to go back, because I still could. Olivia's parents lived in Amarillo, so I had several hours before Dad would get back and see me gone. I could still return to the house and wait for the son-of-a-bitch. Maybe garrote him with my wire saw, or bash in his skull with that baseball bat he'd used on me.

Or maybe start with his elbows and fingers. Force him to say he was sorry to Mom, wherever her spirit resided. Then I'd knock out his teeth and silence his lies forever. I'm sure Mom would have been up for that.

The thing was, I also had to get to the State Fair. As soon as I was functional again, I pretty much had one shot at that, too.

Maybe my whole life until now had been one sick joke. Maybe all my noble sacrifices for the greater good had not saved America from her enemies but instead fed the greed of one evil man. Maybe all that was true. But it made me who I am. So what the hell.

I stayed in that culvert and made other plans—not because

that was what Mom would have wanted, but because that is who she raised me to be.

33

I t was mid-morning and starting to get a little hot when I emerged at last, a little groggy and sick still, but finally walking straight. In the dappled shade of a suburban street, a black Jeep idled.

I opened the passenger door and got in.

"Thanks for answering my text," I said. Before I'd left the house, I'd found an old charger in a drawer and managed to get some charge into Leif's battery.

From the driver seat, Bailey grinned at me. "No prob, girl. I told you before to call if you needed help, and I meant it. Like the car?"

Paint flaked off the hood like a peeling sunburn. The rear view mirror swung from the ceiling by a tiny wire, having long ago fallen off the windshield glass. She put the car in gear. It didn't go the first time, so she jammed the shift stick hard. It stuck, and we drove off.

"Yeah," I said.

"Craigslist, two-hundred and fifty bucks cash," she said. "Where we headed?"

"South Fort Worth." I looked over at her. "How's Leif doing?"

She humphed. "More miserable than usual, if that's even possible." She shrugged. "But hey, it was obvious you two were never going to work out. The age difference, for starters." She pumped the brakes as we rolled towards a stop sign. "He'll get over it. How are you doing?"

I told her about the last few days, about Dad, and Olivia, and about how I had to get to the State Fair.

"Well, shit," she said. "The Fair's been running for a few weeks and no one's gotten sick yet. It would for sure be on the news if they had." She glanced over at me. "No offense but call the FBI for fuck's sake. Tell them what you told me about your dad and the terrorists. Let them handle it."

I sighed. On the one hand, she was right. On the other hand, today was Saturday; it was the original weekend planned for the dolphin attack. If I went to the FBI now, I'd probably end up in an interview room with a junior agent for five hours trying to remember how many ice machines the Sunrise Motel had while all of the real shit went down outside.

"I was hoping I could maybe leave that bit to you," I told her. I reached in my bag and pulled out about fifteen sheets from the Solar Sayings notepad, covered with handwriting. "All the details are here." I tucked them into the cracked ashtray on the dash. "It might take a little while to totally understand it. I was pretty drugged up when I wrote a lot of it. Plus I did it by flashlight."

We reached the highway. At about fifty-five, the steering wheel developed an alarming vibration. Bailey kept a death grip on it and stayed in the slow lane, just in case.

"What now?" she said. "Not to be negative or anything, but you're one girl against an unknown threat."

I kind of smiled. "Maybe, Bailey, but I'm a girl who's trained for this shit my whole life."

She glanced over at me. "You know that wasn't real, right? You did lots of training stuff, sure, but it wasn't real training."

I sighed. "Well, I guess I'll finally find out how good I really am. Drive me to south Fort Worth, near all the highway construction. There's an exit for Abilene."

"I think I know the exit. What's down there, exactly?"

"I'm not sure of the exact address, but I'll know it when I see it," I said. "You'll have to drop me off. I have to do this alone."

"You have another friend there?"

"I have an enemy. One with plenty of guns and men."

"Why would he help you?"

I looked at the baggie in my lap. It was filled with water. In it, one of Dad's bettas floated.

"Well, he hates me a lot. But I reckon he loves football more."

"AFTER ALL THE crap you pulled, you come around here? Do you have a death wish or something, Fish Girl?"

When his men brought me to him, Dmitri was still sitting on that nice couch, the widescreen TV muted but still playing something football related. Men hung around, drinking coffee. It was as if nothing had happened.

"Hang on a sec," I said, "you kidnapped me."

One of Decker's ways of annoying Dakota had been to point a finger at her head, just out of her direct line of sight. The barrel of the gun pointed at my temple irritated me in exactly the same way. I wanted to brush it away with my hand, but that was a sure way to get my brains splattered across the nice taupe upholstery. I had to concentrate on playing the game—on making the deal.

Dmitri was not swayed. "You have any idea what my life is like now? Ever since I made bail, business stands still. No one wants anything. The FBI are all over me. Every time I take a shit, ten agents listen to it plop."

"Thing is," I said, "they were doing that before I showed up. I kind of did you a favor, exposing it."

Dmitri grunted. "Not to mention it's gonna cost a lot to fix these kidnapping charges. Major problem when cash flow is not flowing."

"Just hear me out," I said. "I brought you a gift."

He looked at Dad's orange and green betta, flicking fins in its baggie on the coffee table.

"My man in St. Petersburg has explained how your little scam works, Fish Girl."

"Oh," I bit my lip. "I did try to tell you. But I can make it work out for you. Better than you had even planned."

"Ah well, thanks to you, those days are over for me. Here's how it goes. Boris with the gun here escorts you to front door." He raised his voice, and I realized he was speaking for the benefit of the FBI listening devices. "Then you take your talent for total destruction far, far away and bother someone else."

"No wait, please..."

He lifted his hand, gave a little finger flick: *unneeded*. One of his henchmen seized my arm and pulled me towards the exit.

I tripped on the small step to the hall. If I left this room, it really was over.

"Please," I said quickly. "I came because I need guns and men. You're the only real criminal I know."

He shrugged, lifted his hand again: *wait*. The grip on my arm eased and I staggered to my feet.

"There's only one thing one keeping you here right now," Dmitri said. "Mild curiosity about the guns. So get on with it."

"I have knowledge, pretty good knowledge, that there's going to be an attack at the State Fair. Today."

Dmitri leaned back against the couch. "What the hell is this?"

I explained about my game world, and about how Angrendir and StormShadow were still out there, still planning to poison thousands with the dolphins. I told him about Alicia, and the scams, and my dad. I summed up how the FBI would never believe me because I'd screwed it up so badly with them by running away to kill my dad and then accidentally getting brainwashed all over again.

At the end of it, he said, "To be honest, I'm kind of with FBI on this one. You sound like complete whack job."

"I know," I told him. "I probably am a little whacked. But the bit about the terrorists is true, and the Red River Showdown is happening at the State Fair today. It's the day with the highest number of people at the Fair. I think they'll attack during the football game, or right after, for sure."

He drummed his fingers on the coffee table. Then he turned to one of his men. "Has Magdalena left yet, or is she still in kitchen?"

"She's still here, boss."

"Get her for me." He turned back to me. "You wait outside please with Boris and Daniil, while I have word with my aunt."

Boris lowered his gun and the two of them led me to the front door. We stood outside in the heat.

Boris said, "You serious about the Muslims?"

"Yes," I said.

He shook his head. "We should round them all up like the Nazis did the Jews."

Danil said, "To hell with you, Boris. My granddad was Jewish."

"Not that I'm saying what Hitler did was good, I'm just using it as an analogy."

"Seriously? Even the little kids?"

Boris nodded. "Things are going to change in this country. One day, you'll agree with me."

The door behind us opened and a woman of about sixty walked out.

"Hello?" she said. "Hello? You need ride? You get in car?"

Her accent was much thicker than Dmitri's. She had dyed maroon hair and a fleece jacket printed with wolves. There were gold rings on her fingers, with gems the size of peanuts—real ones.

Not real peanuts, real gems.

"Fish Girl, do not just stand there." She handed me two grocery sacks. "Take these for me and get in car."

BORIS SHOOED me with his gun hand. "Do what Magdalena says, Fish Girl."

Oh, what the heck. I took the bags and put them in her car, a red Juke. Before I could sit down in the front seat, she had to move boxes and bags off of the seat. I peeked in the top of one: plastic forks and paper napkins. It took some arranging; the back was full of stuff too.

"My nephew," she said when we were finally on the road, "he says you need help."

"You mean Dmitri?"

"Yes," she said.

"I thought he was getting rid of me."

She shrugged. "Cut him some slack. He likes to ham it up when FBI listens. He's really happy as a clam."

"What?"

"If you hadn't come along, the FBI would have blown his big arms deal. He's in personal hot water, but the main business is intact."

"I need a particular kind of help," I told her.

"I am Magdalena, and I take care of you in particular way. But we need payment."

A glimmer of hope pierced through my chest.

"I can get you money." All that money earned from Finnegan's website should still be there, and at last it would be used for its original purpose: saving America. I looked in the back more carefully. "Do you have guns in those boxes?" Some of them appeared to be insulated coolers. Oh, please let them be guns. Big ones, with hollow tip ammo.

"He wants particular payment," she said. "You need to agree to particulars."

"What particulars?" I turned back to her.

"For my services, you drop your testimony against Dmitri."

It took me a moment to realize what she meant.

"Oh, shit," I said. "Forget about being kidnapped? That's a lot to ask."

"That's the price." She shrugged. "He likes you, Fish Girl, but business is business."

"Likes me? Your nephew threatened to kill me several times. And cut off my fingers."

She dismissed me with a wave of her hand. "Lighten up! He always says stuff like that—hardly ever does it." She reached over and turned the radio on. It was set to country. "You have until we get there to think about it."

"Where are we going?"

"State Fair," she answered. "Before you ask, the ride is gratis. I was going there anyway. You want more, you have to pay."

So I thought about it to the sound of twanging guitars and lyrics about love gone wrong. Never mind about love, my whole life was screwed up. Dmitri, that goddamn son-of-a-bitch, why couldn't we work something else out? The evil bastard was prepared to gamble with the lives of a hundred thousand people just to keep his sorry Russian ass out of jail—if he even thought it was a gamble.

If he was letting his aunt drive me into the heart of the attack, I was pretty sure he thought I was full of shit, too.

But my parents taught me to do the jobs that had to be done, no matter the price. No, scratch that. My dad had taught me they had to be done. My mom had shown me how to find the courage to do them. I'd already turned my back on making sure Dad was brought to justice. I was not prepared to let a hundred thousand people die just to make sure Dmitri went to jail. And if I died today, it wouldn't matter anyway.

Still, he was a son-of-a-bitch. He really was.

As we neared the fair, the traffic got worse. There were

people on the sidewalks, the ones who had parked far out to save money.

"Look at all of them," I said.

Families—harassed moms and goofy dads, toddling kids and strollers—draped with the masses of equipment young people apparently required for an afternoon's survival outdoors. None of which included biological attack survival gear, you could be sure of that.

"Crowded today," Magdalena said to me, "but you should see when the game ends."

As we drove past, she told me about how Fair Park was a permanent site, a mix of show barns, various-sized pavilions, carnival areas and pop-up food stands. The Cotton Bowl Stadium was right in the middle. The Oklahoma–Texas game, the Red River Rivalry, would be in full swing now. Even out here, even with the road traffic, you could hear the faint roar of a crowd rise and ebb with the drama on the field. In the sky, a camera blimp slowly circled, marking the spot like a vulture.

I looked over at her, at the soft fuzz on her chin powdered white, at her nails cut square and painted red.

"Here's the deal," I said. "I appreciate your offer to help and all, but I really just need a weapon. How much to buy one gun?"

Magdalena chuckled, low. "We're passing entrance now. Look carefully, Fish Girl. What do you see?"

I looked. "Not much. The entrance is mobbed."

"The crowd is being searched for weapons. With metal detectors. How you going to get in, girl?"

I gritted my teeth. I guess I should have expected it. Even here in the heart of open-carry country, the State Fair organizers at least still knew beer, football, and guns was a bad combination. The entrance was surrounded by high fences, placed there to stop people from getting in without tickets. They looked easy to scale, but exposed. There was no way I'd get over without being seen.

"What did you think you were going to do, walk in with a

dozen of Dmitri's men in black suits and sunglasses, all packing? Is that what you had in mind?"

Well, I would have gotten them to ditch the suits and put on t-shirts, but that would have been a pretty good plan. I bit a nail, looked down at the floor. We left the entrance behind and were now driving by vast parking lots. The sunlight glinted off wind-shields with Southern violence.

"My nephew does not give you what you want, but he knows what you need." She turned down a service road past more parking lots, but these ones were filled up with stock trailers and motorhomes. The fair perimeter fence was not as high as it had been right at the entrance, but it still looked exposed. "Will you give him what he needs? Will you pay the price?"

I let out an exasperated sigh. "So how were *you* planning on getting us in?"

Magdalena chuckled again. "I'm bringing these boxes to my daughter-in-law, who is already inside."

"They're full of what?"

"Food...and a few utensils. Nothing much."

"Oh."

"See those cards, on the dash?"

Squares of green card were wedged in the half-open ash-tray. I picked one up. "Participant Season Pass," it said. "Issued to: Ludmilla Mishutin. Department: Cooking."

"There's no photo on it," I said, turning it over.

"Exactly, Fish Girl. So you can borrow it."

"What does she do at the fair?"

"She and I are cooking contestants. We do it every year for five years. Last year we won third place."

"What, like you cook borscht or something?"

"Borscht? Why cook borscht in Texas? We cook chili...the real way. No beans."

I remembered the families, walking down the sidewalks on

the other side of the park. "Fine. I'll drop my testimony for your help."

We parked and unloaded the boxes, made our way towards a break in the fence with a sign: Participant Entrance.

"The guys back here couldn't shake shit off a shovel," Magdalena told me. "Watch this."

It was hard to lift her arms, loaded down as she was with five paper shopping bags that swung and clunked against each other. She walked past the guard, waving her card, just slightly out of his reach.

"Hallo! Lovely day today!"

He waved back.

I followed, carrying one overloaded box, the card inserted between my fingers and the box, like Magdalena had instructed.

"What have you got in that box?" He stopped me with a hand on my shoulder, peered in the top, and nudged a tin.

But before he could dig further, Magdalena stumbled. One of the bags tore open, spilling plastic bags of green chilies and kitchen utensils to the ground.

"Oh no," she cried, "now they get filthy!"

The guard rushed over and squatted down to help her put things back in the torn bag while I stood there, looking like a fool.

"Dude," he said, lifting up a twelve-inch knife that had fallen to the asphalt, "that is one nasty-looking weapon."

Magdalena actually giggled. "We have to cut up many chilies. They have to be fresh."

"And this cleaver?"

"We chop meat by hand too." She took it from him. "It's how you get the texture."

The guard nodded. "Man, I should learn how to cook that stuff. It sounds cool."

Magdalena stood, gathering up the torn sides of the bag like it was a blanket, the contents nestled inside. "Come by our station on your break. I give you good tips." She winked.

"I might just do that, ma'am."

"Oh, and Ludmilla! Ludmilla!"

Belatedly, I realized she meant me. "Yes?"

"Open that tin on top. Get something for this kind gentleman."

I set the box on the ground and opened the tin to find red iced cupcakes nestled in individual paper cups. I held the tin out to him.

He shook his head. "That is too nice. I can't take your cupcake."

"Sure you can," Magdalena assured him. "Is my specialty, Russian red velvet. With beets and sour cream."

"Okay, this one time." With a goofy smile, he carefully extracted one. He took a bite and had to catch falling crumbs with his other hand. "Wow, that is really, really good. Like a...red carrot cake."

But Magdalena was already heading into the crowd.

"See you later, I hope," she called over her shoulder.

I picked up the box and followed her. "See you."

"Yeah, definitely," he said through a mouthful of cupcake, "definitely."

I caught up with her in the crowd.

"Next time," she said, "don't actually take out the tin. Just open it and give him one."

"Okay," I said. "Why not?"

I looked into the box at the tin. A red checked tablecloth was folded underneath. It had shifted a bit, and in the corner I could see the bluish gleam of oiled gun black.

"Oh."

Magdalena shot me a look.

"Yes," she said. "That is where I pack the Glocks."

34

Magdalena stayed in the cooking pavilion with her boxes and the real Ludmilla, who was a statuesque blond with cheekbones like manta ray fins and breasts like halved grapefruit. Apparently, the chilies Magdalena had brought were just in the nick of time, and the two of them were going to be busy for a while. But I wasn't let loose to explore on my own. Ludmilla was married to Victor of all people. Still on sick leave (or whatever equivalent mafia guys got), he had been holding the fort with her while Magdalena was running errands. Yeah. Victor, who hadn't died with Finnegan in the car crash after all.

"Hell of a concussion though," he told me, "I was in the hospital for a couple of days. And my neck is still giving me shit."

"I'm sorry," I said.

"Why? You weren't the one driving."

I guess when you lead a life of crime, you have to either get over it or get another career. It seemed a bit weird to me, but I did need at least one gun-packing henchman for backup—I was damn well paying for it—so on balance, I guessed I was over it as well.

Harder to deal with was the fact that his hair glinted gold in the sun, like Peter.

"How is that little FBI shit, anyway?" Victor asked. "Did he get a promotion for ratting us out?"

"I don't know," I said. "We're not talking anymore."

"If I ever see him again, I won't have much to say either. But I will have a bullet with his name on it." He pulled sunglasses out of his polo-shirt pocket and put them on. "Let's get a corny dog. You have no idea how sick of chili I am."

"First off, we don't have time for that," I said. "Second, I don't eat that stuff."

"What's that supposed to mean? You some sorta health food nut or something?"

"Kinda."

"You're missing out, I mean, look at this shit."

We were in a narrow alleyway between the Fur and Feather Showroom (chickens and rabbits, Victor said) and the Creative Arts Pavilion. Food marquees ran along one side, each with a line of people snaking around the perimeter. Everything on offer was deep fried, from unlikely things like strawberries and meat-loaf to the outright bizarre, like deep-fried bubble gum.

"The acrylamides in that stuff must be off the charts," I said. "I feel sick just thinking about it. How do you deep fry Thanks-giving dinner anyway? Come on, we have to find the midway."

Victor shrugged. "Okay, boss girl."

The crowds were everywhere. College kids wearing same-colored t-shirts barreled past, loud, red-faced, and none-too-steady on their feet. Groups of girls with complicated hair piled high watched them pass with disdain. Sand-washed retired couples ambled through the midday heat: the men in custom cowboy hats, the lizard-skinned women flashing sharp white teeth under rhinestone glasses. One old boy in dungarees and checked shirt stood in the middle of the passage, mouth slack, a faded red gimme cap clutched in his hands.

"Lost his cow," Victor said around a mouthful of corny dog.

"There's cows here?" I bit through my corny dog, halfway down now. I know, but the line was short, and you need a full stomach to hunt terrorists. It turned out that antibiotic-laced intensely reared beef wasn't that bad if you ground it up fine with salt and battered it.

"In the old days it was all cows," Victor said. "Just a horse here and there for variety. So what are we doing next?"

"Listen," I said, "I don't know what Magdalena told you, but thousands of people are at risk. Today. Right here. There's going to be a terrorist attack."

"What?" Victor grabbed me by the shirt. "Where? Is it in the food pavilion? Is Ludmilla at risk?"

"I don't know! I'm still looking for it!" I said.

He let go of my shirt. "Looking for what, exactly?"

"Dolphins. Stuffed dolphins."

"Like that one there?"

I whirled around. A group of teenagers were walking past. The boys were carrying enormous stuffed animals, one of which was a dolphin. Its head was blue with white stars and its tail was striped red and white. I went up to him.

"You have to give me that dolphin," I told him.

"Uh, 'scuse me?"

"It has poison hidden in the blowhole. It will kill you."

The boy held the toy up and peered in the blowhole. The kids all laughed.

"Nice try. You want one? Go get your own." The smile dropped from his face. He turned to walk on.

I moved to grab his arm, but Victor grabbed my shoulders and pulled me back.

"What are you doing? You can't collect them all one by one. We need a different plan."

"There will be an activation device inside," I said. "If I get a hold of one, we can see what we're dealing with."

"Let's go get one."

If you're a person who isn't always sure where the line is

between reality and hallucination, the midway wasn't the greatest place to visit. Everything, the food stalls, haunted houses, smallest horse and crocodile lady peep show were all painted neon acid colors. Even the struts of the marquee over-head were lined with LEDs that strobed rainbows. The artwork looked as if it had melted over the Texas summer, lending even happy clown faces a sinister air. Rides for little kids where bizarre, giant teddy bears spun while toddlers sat in their body cavities; rides for big kids flashed with chrome and slammed passengers about with automated violence. Each body-bashing assembly-line contraption thumped out its own dance music at a 120-beats-per-minute war cadence. The crowd was screaming, laughing, shouting—or standing in lines with barely suppressed fury at the wait. Now that I was looking for them, the dolphins were everywhere.

"Hey," Victor said to me, "you okay? You're shaking."

"We have to stop it, Victor. All these people could die."

The carnival games were placed around the edge and people were busy playing them: throwing darts to burst balloons, fishing plastic ducks out of tubs of water, shooting stars out of paper targets with BB guns. The stalls were hung with rows of prizes: flashing plastic wands, giant inflatable footballs or palm trees, but mostly stuffed animals, teddy bears, pink kittens and blue puppies. And the dolphins.

"Okay," Victor said, "given my long experience on the wrong side of FBI operations, I'm gonna make a suggestion here."

"What?"

"We get one without making a fuss. We still don't know if they're dangerous."

"Speak for yourself," I said. "I know they are."

"Sparking off a panic is a bad idea. Plus, you don't want to alert the terrorists, do you?"

I ignored him and pushed my way to a game with a BB gun attached to the counter by security cables.

"I need a dolphin."

"Lucky you, I got plenty of those," the guy said. "All you have to do is shoot down that target."

I picked up the gun and examined the plastic stuff glued to the outside to make it look like an AK.

"Six tries for ten dollars." He held out his hand.

Oh, what the hell. Victor was right, it wasn't worth the argument. I reached into my pocket.

"I only need one try," I said. "Here's two dollars."

He looked at me. "Don't you want to bulk buy?"

I looked down the barrel. "Yeah, I probably need a shot to calibrate this piece of shit. How much for two?"

Victor let out an exasperated sigh.

"Just give him ten." He handed it over and leaned in close to me. "You're screwing it up, you know. You need to build rapport."

I laid my cheek against the needless appendages on the plastic barrel, squeezed one eye shut, and took my first shot.

"Rapport?" I lowered the weapon and frowned. Way off. I might even need two or three shots to calibrate.

"Don't you want to know where he got the dolphins from? Like it might be a clue?"

"Hey," I said to the guy, "where do you get your prizes from?"

"What the hell kind of question is that? You win the game, you can get one here."

"My niece," Victor broke in, "really likes the dolphins." He pressed a ten-dollar bill into the guy's hand. "Give me six shots as well. I don't want her to show me up."

The guy laughed. "I hear you, man."

I raised the barrel again. "Hope your aim is better than last time."

"What, you mean in Dmitri's car? Maybe it is." Victor raised his gun as well. "At least now I'm not shooting out the window of a speeding SUV." He missed and lowered the barrel. "Shit. Maybe not."

Two kids, about ten, came up and bought some shots as well.

I shot and got a bull's eye.

"Hey," the guy said when he'd finished setting the kids up, "looks like your niece got herself a dolphin."

"Ha," Victor took another shot, holding the fake AK at arm's length like a handgun. He missed again.

"What color you want?" the guy picked up a broomstick with a hook screwed into the end. "American flag, camo, or pink?"

Pfft. Pfft. Two more bull's eyes. "I'll take one of each."

"Hey, wait a second," the guy said. "One dolphin per customer."

"I paid you for six tries! I think you'll find that's a maximum of six dolphins per customer."

"No one ever gets all six."

"Fuck that." Pfft. Pfft. I emptied the chamber into the center of the target. "You owe me five now."

"Hey what are you trying to do to me? I have overheads!"

Victor broke in. "I'll give you another ten bucks. Give the shots to these kids. Will that cover your costs?"

The guy grumbled, but he got the dolphins down.

Victor took three under his arms and I took two. Feeling the furry surfaces that hid such horror underneath made my heart pound.

"Hey, mister," one of the kids said to Victor, "do you really need all of those dolphins?"

"Yes," I said. "These things are dangerous anyway. Stay away from them!"

The kid backed away, his eyes big.

"They'll kill you," I told him. "They spew poison out their blowholes."

The other kid set down his gun. They looked at me a moment, and then turned and walked away, quickly.

"Hey, what is this about? Now you scaring away my other customers?" the guy said. "What the hell is all this crap?"

"She thinks there might be something inside them, like a

biological weapon or something." Victor sighed. "I have to admit, now that I think about it, it sounds kind of unlikely."

"What?" I said. "I'm paying for your services, dammit. I expect some loyalty."

But the guy set his broomstick down and shook his head. "Oh man, you just should have said."

I looked at him for a long moment. "What do you mean?" I asked.

"Hand me a dolphin," he said.

I laid one on the table, and he took my hand, placing it on the dolphin.

"We get them from a wholesale warehouse, and these were really cheap. Suspiciously cheap. Feel here, in the stuffing." He moved my hand over a bit, and I felt it, a hard plastic cube under the furry cloth. "See, these days a stuffed animal isn't a good prize unless it does something too. There's all these electronics in them, and battery boxes."

"Yeah, but that's not unusual, is it?" Victor said

"That's the thing," the guy said. "The box, it just sits in there, no lights or anything. There's just this grill thing where the blowhole is. I can't figure out what it's supposed to do."

I snatched my hand back, dropped my other dolphins, and backed away. All of a sudden, taking them straight to the FBI seemed like a good idea. Victor frowned, but before I could stop him, he reached into his pocket, drew a flick knife, and gutted the porpoise. I flinched as polyester stuffing burst from the wound.

"Victor," I cried out, "be careful. You have no idea what you're dealing with. I could be sarin...or aerosolized anthrax..."

He pulled the black box out with a jerk, set it on the counter and began to unscrew the top with the knife tip.

"Please," I said, "you shouldn't..."

The lid popped off and he lifted it close to his face.

"Just looks like electronics," he said, peering in.

I pulled the cloth of my shirt up over my face and waited a

few minutes for his face to blister and melt, or his airways to swell up. Something, anything. What happened was he picked up a pink dolphin off of the ground and gave it a close look.

"Here," he said to the guy, "did you try this tiny switch?" He started to pick at it with the tip of his knife. "It's like there's some sort of glue over it or something."

I threw protective arms over my head. A tinny, whiny sound hit my ears. I lowered my arms to see the two men cocking their ears at the wailing that emerged from the blowhole.

"That's Chinese," said Victor, "isn't it?"

"Yep," said the guy. "Chinese folk music. Possibly even 'Jasmine Flower.'"

Victor looked at him.

"What? I wasn't always a carnival game guy."

"I'd better turn it off," Victor said. "No wonder they glued it shut."

"Yeah," the guy said. "Can't have Yankee Dolphin here spouting Chinese folk music."

"What," I said, "That's it?"

Victor raised one eyebrow. "Yeah. It's a factory fuckup, not a terrorist attack. Happens all the time. I should know, I've ordered plenty of stuffed animals from those jokers."

"Why on earth..."

"For smuggling weapons, drugs, that sort of thing. One of these dolphins would hold a key of cocaine inside easy."

I studied him for delayed onset of symptoms. Nothing, dammit.

"Come on," he said. "We all mess up sometimes. Don't take it so hard."

"I'm not taking it hard. I'm waiting for you to collapse from sarin poisoning."

"While you're doing that, you wanna have a look?"

So I did. He was right. We ripped apart all five to be sure. Sarin is unstable, so it would have to be contained in some sort of vial. There was nothing in the dolphins like that. Just cheap electronics that spouted Chinese music.

"Hey," Victor said. "Why are you crying?"

"I'm happy." I brushed some stuffing from my shirt. Angrendir and StormShadow must have screwed it up somehow. "I don't even care if this means I was crazy all along. Right now, I'm just happy. "

"Me too," said the carnival guy. He wiped his forehead. "Yay for America."

We stuffed the eviscerated dolphin carcasses in a trash can and walked away through the crowd.

"It doesn't mean they aren't still planning something," I said to Victor, drying my cheeks on my shirt. "I've got to find some way to contact them again. I have to know what they're up to now."

"I guess." Victor shrugged. "But why this obsession with terrorists, Fish Girl? Why does it have to be you that fights them?"

Through openings in the midway canopy, we could see the Top o' Texas Tower, rising 500 feet into the denim sky. Its glassed-in passenger cabin moved up and down at a snail's pace.

"No one else can die." I said. "I promised myself."

Victor looked closely at me. "Who was it that died, Fish Girl?"

I didn't answer.

"My parents were struck down by a speeding car in a Moscow suburb. You don't see me attacking black Mercedes twenty years later."

"But you wanted to," I said. "I bet you still want to."

He let out an amused huff. "What good would it do? I can't replace them, but I did something else," he said. "I found a new family."

We came to the base of the tower. Because the ride was the most expensive and comparatively boring, the line was pretty short. No large families here, just old men in pristine white cowboy hats and women in turquoise and silver and back-combed hair.

"Maybe you should do the same," he added.

"Where would I find a new family?" I asked him.

He put his hands in his pockets. "You should join us."

"Dmitri would never agree to that."

"You'd be surprised," he said. "You're pretty much a fuckup, but everyone is at your age. You should have seen me robbing people on the Moscow Metro back when I was just a wannabe *gopnik*. Usually, I ended up lending my victims three hundred rubles."

Despite myself, I smiled.

"I bet we could talk him around," he said. "Wanna go up in that tower before we head back to the girls?"

"Sure, why not?"

"Great. But I gotta take a piss before we go up. Can you stay right here?"

As I waited for him to get back from the toilets, I thought about it. Screw it. The FBI had treated me like shit, and the more I got to know the Russians, the more I liked them. But still. Join the mafia? In essence, join the bad guys?

"Rain."

I whirled at the sound of my name and saw the golden hair, saw the tip of his ear, red where the sun shone through it.

Peter.

35

N ow that Peter was here in front of me, breathing and warm just a few feet away, I hardly knew how to react. He was both bigger and smaller than in my dreams. "How did you find me?"

"Bailey gave us your report," he said. He took a step forward. "Come with me, Rain. Please."

"Why? So you can fuck up my life again?"

"We need you."

"That's what you said the last time. You don't need me. Not really." I started to back away.

"We do need you—as a witness, against Dmitri and against your dad." He took another step forward. "You owe that much to Alicia. She's not out of her coma. Even if she did wake up, she's in no condition to go to court." And another step. "We need help to understand your code...and Alicia's code. The computer guys are impressed with what you girls did, but a little confused by it as well."

"Did you even get my messages?"

"Yes, Rain, but you're..."

"What, I'm crazy? Delusional? Like my Dad said?"

"I was going to say wrong," he said. "We checked the

dolphins this morning. We check out every tip, no matter how unlikely." He held out his hand to me. "We don't think you're delusional, anyway. More like...obsessed. We know what happened to your mom, in Colorado. We know how Hal Wooten used it against you. But you can't make it better by saving someone else."

I took a step back. "You're just spouting crap that Carol Anne told you. She knows nothing about me."

"You can't do it because there's no here one to save."

"Angrendir and StormShadow are still on the loose. They could be planning something else."

"Rain, we've got people on it. You can let it go."

"This is what you don't know about me, Peter. If I let go, I have nothing else."

"That's not true," he said. "You have your freedom, your health, your whole life ahead—"

"But I don't have anyone. I don't even have you."

Peter winced.

Suddenly, I was shoved to the side, hard. It was Victor, returned from the toilet, shouting pure wordless rage. He landed a roundhouse punch square on Peter's jaw. Peter's head snapped to the side and he stumbled.

"You little shit!" Victor yelled at him. "After all we did for you! After all Dmitri did for you! Why?"

An empty space formed in the crowd around us. Peter spit blood. "It's my job, you worthless son-of-a-bitch." He slammed his head into Victor's middle and bowled him backward. Victor landed a few blows on his back, but Peter held on hard. They stumbled to the edge of the crowd. Victor changed strategies, reaching for his own Glock, the one Magdalena had given him. He brought the butt down hard on Peter's head, who fell down, stunned.

I could hear a few people moving through the crowd towards us. Other agents, of course. No way would they have sent Peter to get me by himself. But they weren't going to get to him in time.

"You know the really shitty thing about you, Peter?" Victor wiped his nose with the back of his hand. His eyes were red. "Even with all your fuckups, Dmitri liked you better anyway." He racked his gun and aimed the barrel at Peter's head.

Military shorts might not be much to look at fashion-wise, but I landed a perfect high kick on Victor's shoulder without ripping the crotch. The gun fired into the pavement next to Peter and Victor stumbled back, shouting in rage. I sensed him turning for me, pulling up the gun, and I didn't wait around. I'd never seen him hit his target yet, but I wasn't going to take that chance. I pushed my way through the crowd and ran like hell.

LIKE EVERYTHING TEXAN, the State Fair of Texas is big. So big, that once you circled the Cotton Bowl and passed the Texas Hall of State and the Truck Zone, you would hardly know there was a showdown between good and evil beneath the Top o' Texas Tower. I felt strangely light...as if my feet no longer touched the ground...as if the scene around me was projected onto tissue paper that I could rip away to reveal the black void behind. I came to a circular plaza with a giant statue of a cowboy in the middle—Big Tex—a ventriloquist puppet built for a giant, his grinning jaw hinged, and his shirt puffed up all funny. One hand was frozen in a wave, the other extended to welcome everyone. The statue looked vintage, but he was new, a replacement for the original Big Tex that had burned down.

I sat at his base, a raised circular flower bed about forty feet across. Pansies withered in the daylight. I knew how they felt; my cheeks and nose were feeling red. I'd come prepared for terrorists, but not the sun. Then again, I'd rarely seen the sun these past five years. Mom would have remembered sunscreen, at least for me. I looked at the faces of the people milling around. Laughing, eating, tired, amused. But none of them alone. Always in pairs or groups bound by genetics or football team loyalty. I didn't even have that.

Maybe it was time my mission was over. I had no one to report to. Mom was gone for good, and Dad—that son-of-a-bitch —would never give me another stupid True Patriot task to waste my time. Maybe I didn't even blame the FBI in the end. If there was no threat...if—like they said—it all checked out...I had to admit they had behaved pretty reasonably. I was the one who had pushed and pushed, obsessed by my need to save lives to make up for the one I had lost, as Victor had suggested. But terrorists hadn't even killed Mom in the first place. In the end, there was nothing and no one to fight.

"Howdy folks!"

The voice boomed over my head. I ducked reflexively and looked up. Big Tex's hideous jaw was working up and down. His anatomically improbable torso swung slowly back and forth to emphasize that he really meant everyone.

"Welcome to the State Fair of Texas!"

People laughed and pointed, aimed their phones at him. Maybe they liked it ironically. Cowboy hats weren't all that common in the city these days...no one wore them except the very rich and the poor who mowed their yards.

I stood. The adrenaline had run out of my system and I was tired of it all. I had to go back, to see if Peter was alive or hurt or dead. Then, when it seemed like a good moment, I'd hand myself into the FBI. Face the music about the deal I'd done with Dmitri, do what I could to make sure Dad was put away for life. If I got through that, then maybe, just maybe, I could try to live the rest of my life without maiming or killing anything else. Especially cats.

"Excuse me."

I turned to see a rail-thin brown-skinned guy in a white t-shirt.

"Is your dad an FBI agent?"

"What the hell..." I said. "Who told you that?"

"I recognize you. From YouTube."

"I have never, ever been on YouTube." I made to push past him, but he stepped in front of me. His shirt was soaked with impressive dark spots under his arms. He held up a phone.

It was hard to see in the daylight, but I could just make out the scene of a high school cafeteria full of kids. Someone, probably the camera holder, said, "This should be good."

Then a girl's hijab was torn from her head. Salmi. I stared at the screen as the expected fight unfolded.

"It is you, isn't it? You beat up the asshole who attacked my cousin Salmi."

I frowned. I vaguely remembered that the moment when someone pulled me off that football player, there had been a lot of smartphones aimed at us.

"These videos are all over the Internet, you know. Different viewpoints and stuff. You're definitely her."

I sighed. "Okay, it was me. Whatever." I gritted my teeth and turned so I could go the other way.

But he grabbed my arm with one hand and took off his baseball cap with the other. I would have dropped him to the ground and left him, but I was taken off-guard, and he spoke before I could get a foot behind his calf.

"You told Salmi and Niaz your dad worked for the FBI. Please, my name is Ib, I mean Ibrahim, and I need to speak to your dad. I need to speak to someone I can trust."

That was when I noticed that, despite the heat, despite the circles of sweat under his arms, he was shaking. He was looking for someone to trust so hard he was trembling. I grabbed his arm. It vibrated under my fingers. This was a kid who was so scared, he didn't care if I knew it. Or maybe he was just flat out of control. I took a chance.

"Angrendir?"

He flinched like I'd hit him. "How...how do you..."

I gritted my teeth. "It's Finnegan."

"Finnegan? You're a girl? You're...oh shit...you're a *spy*? For your dad?"

I stood there for a moment, at a complete lost for words. At last, I swallowed. "What happened to the dolphin thing? You guys didn't do the dolphin thing."

"You have any idea how hard little tiny aerosol things are to make? After Tabernakl went AWOL, we sorta couldn't figure it out." Ib closed his eyes. "God willed it not to be, I guess."

"But why are you here now?"

The sharp knot of his Adam's apple twitched under the thin skin of his neck.

"Look, I thought that stupid dolphin business would be the end of it, but my cousin...today he texted me."

"StormShadow? What did he text?"

He tried to speak, but it came out a gasping sob. Instead, he held up his phone so that I could see the screen.

Today is the day of dayz.

"That's what he texted?"

He nodded and tried to lower the phone but I grabbed it and held the screen up so I could read it again.

"What does it mean?"

He lacked the will to answer me or grab the phone back, so I started to scroll up through the messages.

Allah is the king of kingz. I know the Jabbar all around...stay strong bruv...

"He got a job here," Ib said at last. "Delivering oil."

"He told me he got a job here," I said. "I didn't know it was delivering oil."

StormShadow had also been forwarding him pictures by text. Inspirational sunset scenes mixed in with men in black posing with machine guns. Naked bodies in a tangle of arms and legs on a prison floor followed by figures kneeling in orange jumpsuits. I scrolled to a selfie of a pop star, her ass thrust to the camera.

They interpret peace as sex addict careless dump human being to stifle righteous altruistic feelings

I squinted at the words, confused.

turning human into less than animal

I'd seen this stuff, or stuff like this, a thousand times, but always from the sterile safety of my silent, air-conditioned basement. Here, in the sun and the heat, with hundreds of people milling about, laughing and shouting, I began to feel real funny between my shoulder blades.

Then I realized what the real question was.

"He got a job delivering oil? Delivering oil to what?"

"The deep fat fryers."

"He did something to the oil?"

"He did something to the fryers."

And then, on the phone, an image of a soldier, his head laid in rubble. Blood pooling. Teeth showing white in his black beard.

Masha Allah I will meet this mujahideen in heaven bruv.

"What the fuck?"

I scrolled back to the bottom.

Today is the day of dayz.

"Oh, fuck."

"Yeah."

Ib plucked the phone from my slack fingers. "Sometime today. The food fryers, they're all going to blow."

36

"Okay," I said. "Don't panic. We just have to think what to do next."

My stomach wasn't feeling too hot. And my need to find a toilet, which had been in the bottom third of my priorities, jumped to the top of the list. I clenched, resolving to ignore it. In a crowd like this, there would be a line for the ladies.

Ib pocketed his phone. "Will help me defuse them?"

"To hell with that," I said. "I know where there's lots of FBI. They can do it. They have like blast suits and stuff."

"Your dad is with them?"

"Not my dad, not him."

Ib shook his head. "I need someone I can trust. I don't want Rashid to get into trouble."

He started to walk away. I followed him.

"How can you say that? Your crazy homicidal maniac cousin has just set a fuckload of *bombs*, for fuck's sake. How can you not *want* him to get in trouble?"

"He's not a crazy homicidal maniac!" He stopped and looked at me, his eyes black and fiery. "He's trying to do the right thing. He just got a little fucked up in the head about it. We all did."

"A little fucked up in the head?" I asked him. "Just a little?"

"Yeah," he said. "Just a little. It's what happens when our brothers and sisters get murdered in the hundreds and thousands until it doesn't even make the news anymore. Twelve or thirteen white people in Europe get killed, and the world goes insane, but you can bomb twenty preschools in Syria, and no one cares. You know what? Four million Muslims have died fighting the West! Four million in the past thirty years!"

"That's not right," I said. "It can't be that many."

"Yes, sister, it can. And the crazy thing is," he said, "the really crazy fucked up thing is that you would have to be a fucking crazy sociopath serial killer not to get upset about it. But if you do, if you dare have a normal human response to this insane tragedy, then you are the crazy evil killer motherfucker. You are the radical threat for wanting children to grow up with moms and dads and baby goats and pomegranate trees and shit like that."

"Angrendir...Ibrahim..." I swallowed. For some reason there was no spit left in my mouth. "Ib, look around you at all the moms and dads and little preschool kids right here. You can't make it better by killing more people. It doesn't work like that."

"Then why do we keep on killing? If it doesn't work, *then why do we do it*?"

A little circle of space was forming around us. People stared. I glanced at the police podium. It was empty. The cop must have been called to deal with Victor and Peter. But someone would be making a 911 phone call very soon.

"I don't know," I said. "Honestly, I don't know."

Ib chewed his lip. "Fuck it. Even if it did work, I can't be the one that lets it happen."

If I walked away and got the FBI now, it might be too late.

"Look," I told him. "It's okay. I'll help."

WE RAN for the fried food vendors. When we got there, I could see StormShadow/Rashid's logic in placing the bombs there. The pedestrian way was tight, and with lines snaking around each vendor tent, it was hard to negotiate your way through quickly. Worse, the football game had just finished, and red-faced fans were pouring out of the Cotton Bowl entrances just behind the vendors. Hungry, red-faced fans with deep-fried chocolate chip burritos on their minds.

"Excuse me," I said, pushing my way through the lines with Ib. "Excuse me, we work here."

"Like hell you do," someone shouted.

I wished for Ludmilla's ID card, but Ludmilla had taken it back.

We made it to one of the tents on the edge. The deep fryers themselves, one or two per tent, were large industrial units of stainless steel. I pushed my way to the back of one just as a vendor lifted a basket of fried miscellany out. I was so close, little drops of hot oil misted onto my shoulders and burned like needle pricks.

"Do you have a screwdriver?" I asked Ib as I bent down to look at the back panel.

"No need," he said, pointing. He was right. Rashid had been careless. Some of the screw-holes were empty, others hung loose. "He would have had barely an hour to do all of the tents. This one was probably one of his last."

"How come no one saw him?" I asked Ib.

"The tent flaps are lowered when he delivers the oil in the early morning. He could have done anything under here."

"What are you two doing?" The vendor looked over the back of the fryer, shaking his basket. "Y'all gonna get burned, standing there."

"Something might be wrong with your fryer," I said.

"Bullshit," he said.

Ib plucked out a screw with his fingernails. The back panel bowed out. I pulled on the corner of the panel and it flapped loose, making a thundery metal sound. I stepped back so it wouldn't hit my bare calves and popped my fingers in my mouth. Damn, that thing was hot.

Ib kneeled down and so did I, looking in. Heated air made the view waver.

"Shit," he said. "I don't know what these things normally look like."

The underside of the oil vat was easy enough to identify, as was the red-hot heating element underneath it. The rest of the cavity was filled with black oil gunk...and bricks of something. Something that looked like Plasticine.

Ib pulled on the back panel of the fryer next to it. We peered in. Same thing: bricks of explosives, getting hotter by the second. When they blew, hot oil would fly into the crowd, thick and dangerous. Burning skin and hair flesh. You can't stop, drop, and roll with burning oil. It just keeps on burning, right down to the bone.

I stood. I felt calm. Like reality was through fucking around and was going to be real at last.

I said to the vendor, "Your fryers have bombs in them. We have to evacuate the area."

"Bullshit," he said again.

"Dude," Ib told him, "come around, have a look at it."

"No *dude*," he replied, "you put those panels back on my fryers and get the hell out of here before I call the police."

Ib looked up at me. Beads of moisture coated his nose and forehead. His dark brown eyes were shiny. "It's too hot. I can't reach in there and pull the explosives out."

"Yeah," I said. "We might even set it off doing that. Sorry Ib, but we have to get everyone out of here. Now."

He nodded and stood, waving his arms over his head. "Hey everybody, there's a bomb! You have to get out of here!"

"Nice try! Fuck off!"

"Hey man, back of the line is over here!"

Ib turned desperate eyes to me.

I shrugged and drew Magdalena's Glock. "Hey everybody, get the hell out of here before I blow your goddamn asses straight to Hell!"

Like the ripples of a pebble dropped in a pond, the crowd moved back. But not enough. Not nearly enough. I walked forward into the growing space and shot into the ground.

"I mean it! I'll shoot! Run!"

"Drop your weapon, you crazy bitch!"

The vendor had worked his way from behind the fryers and was pointing a gun at me. But his face was red, and his hands were shaking. I kicked my foot out and tapped the gun from his grip. It fell to the pavement and spun around a few times, but thankfully didn't fire. He'd probably forgotten to pop the safety.

"Pick it up, Ib!" I ordered. "Pick it up before someone else does!"

"*Allah Mustagath,*" Ib muttered, scrambling for it. And then, louder: "*Ya Allah el Mustagath.*" He picked the gun up with shaking hands and aimed it in long arcs around him. Where its blunt nose pointed, spaces opened up.

"That's the idea, aim it," I shouted at him, "but don't yell that terrorist crap. People will get the wrong idea."

"I'm not yelling terrorist crap," he said, his voice going high. "I'm yelling very scared prayers to God to help us out of this before the bomb goes off!"

"Holy shit," someone said. "Did he say bomb?"

"Yes!" Ib shouted, hopping up and down. "I said bomb! I said bomb, everybody!"

"He said he's gonna bomb everybody!"

Screams rose around us. People pushed away in a solid mass. It scared me worse than the thought of the explosives at my back. I shot into the ground again.

"You all, freaking will leave in an orderly fashion! I'll shoot the next asshole that stampedes!"

Some critical mass of terror communicated itself to the back of the crowds and the pressure around us eased. The street soon emptied.

"Shit, that cleared them," I said, looking around at the line of empty white tents with their hand-painted advertisements for fried foods swinging lonely in the wind. "I guess the prayers worked...in a way."

Ib said nothing, but I could feel him glaring at me. Instead of meeting his gaze, I stared at the ground. Then I saw a flat rubber strip, the kind that is supposed to be trip-proof.

"Look," I said, "electric wires. To the fryers."

"Of course," Ib said. He grabbed my arm. "Come on, let's shut off the supply!"

37

We followed the wires down the line of tents, until we came to a junction box on the outside of the Craft Hall. With a jerk, Ib pulled it free.

I turned to run, then something caught my eye—a sprout of black hairs near the entrance of the Craft Hall. Behind the wheelchair ramp, a little girl in a cotton flower sun dress scrunched up, her hands clutched to her chest.

"Hey!" I leaned down to grab her arm. "What are you doing? You need to get out of here!"

She shrank away from me. "I'm waiting for Mom and Dad."

The smell of deep-fried meat wafted past us, strong, but at the back of my throat, the air tasted of something scorched. There was no one left to pull the baskets out now, and all that bubblegum and Thanksgiving dinner was starting to burn.

"Look, let's go find your mom and dad together." My fingers closed easily around her little chubby arm. I considered lifting her over my shoulder and making a run for it, but she stood up and let me hurry her away from the steps.

Ib ran to the center of the empty through-way, looking south. "We have to find Rashid."

"To hell with Rashid," I said, catching up with him. "We have to get out of here."

"I can't abandon my cousin. He's family. You have no idea what I'm going through right now."

"Just so you know," I said, "my dad killed my mom. With a bomb."

He looked at me. The words were out there now. I couldn't take them back.

"You're Rain Wooten."

My mouth dropped open. "How do you know my name?"

"America knows your name. It's all over the news. Your dad was number one on the FBI's most wanted list."

There, standing on black asphalt in the middle of the hot September sun, with hot oil fryers about to burst into fireballs all around me, I felt as cold as ice. "What do you mean, my dad *was* wanted?" I grabbed Ib's arm. "You have to tell me!"

"All right...if I can even remember...I've kind of had other stuff on my mind," he said. "They got some guy...some salesman I think...on the highway from Amarillo. But his father-in-law was some super-hot defense lawyer and was all over the news about how he was illegally arrested and searched and stuff."

"Did they let him go?"

Ib shrugged. "I think they had a few more hours to find evidence."

"You think?" It was hard to breathe. Bailey must have had given my notes to the FBI, who had taken them seriously and caught Dad before he knew he was in trouble. But if they let Dad go now, he would GOOD. He'd done it before. Four times since I had been born, and they hadn't caught him yet. "I have to get out of here, Ib. I can't help you anymore."

"No," Ib said. A drip of sweat tracked down the side of his forehead and hit the corner of his eye. He blinked. "Please help me. I don't know everything Rashid was planning. We find him, get him to tell us, then we all get out of here."

Ib was right. Double bombs were a standard terrorist practice. You blow up one bomb, generate panic and chaos, and then let loose with another into the mix. I felt the girl, fidgeting under my grip. I had to get her to safety too. But that was going to be hard, if we did not know where it was safe. Oh, to hell with Dad. I had stuff to do here.

"Okay," I said. "Where do you think he is anyway?"

"We go back to Big Tex, it's where he said he would be. It's why I was there in the first place."

We walked quickly down the street, eerily empty. Past the Indoor Ostrich Races, past the Little Hands on the Farm. Sirens and helicopters echoed from far away. Crumpled food wrappers rolled past like tumbleweeds .

"It's like it's all over," Ib said, "and everyone went home."

"Not everyone," I said.

Police, in full body armor with guns, had quietly appeared on either side.

"Are they aiming at us?" Ib asked.

"Yeah, thanks to you yelling all that terrorist shit. At least they aren't shooting."

"Yeah, thanks to you taking a little kid hostage."

I looked down at the girl, white-faced and unsmiling. Crap. I stopped and knelt.

"Hey," I said to her, "we kind of got a lot of stuff to do right now. You think you could get one of those nice police officers to help you find your mom and dad?"

She shook her head.

"They're scaring her," Ib said. He looked around at the armed agents and raised his voice. "Hey, like maybe you guys could send over someone without body armor and guns? Maybe that would help the situation?"

We passed the Texas Wine Garden. We passed the Silverado Stage, now empty and silent.

Then, right between the Amazing House Carved from a Single Sequoia and the German Sausage Bonanza, a man. No body armor. Walking with a limp. Blond hair glinting in the sun, one ear red where the sun shone through. Fuck.

"Agent Angelopolos," I shouted, "shouldn't you be lying down or something?"

"You should see the other guy." Peter said, coming closer. Even here, in the midst of all these loaded guns, he managed a grin.

It broke my heart all over again. Double fuck.

I said, "How come you always show up?"

He said, "How come you always run away?"

Ib looked from him to me. "You know this man? Is he your dad?"

Both Peter and I winced.

"He was...a friend," I said. "Was. Go away, Peter, unless you're going to help. I got stuff to do."

Instead, Peter knelt down and spoke to the little girl. "Hey, kiddo, don't be scared. What's your name?"

"Grace," she whispered. Her chin crumpled like unwanted newspaper. "I got lost. I think I'm in trouble."

Peter gave her a half smile. "These big kids are the ones in trouble. Not you, Grace. Come with me and I'll help you find your mom and dad." He extended his hand.

I wished for a moment, hard, that he was extending it for me. Cause I would have fallen to my knees and pressed it to my face and cried tears into the skin of his palm.

Ib broke in. "What happens after you take her?"

Peter looked up. "What?"

"What happens to us?"

"Let me get Grace safe. Then we can talk about how I can help."

"No," Ib said. "Rain is right, we got things to do."

Just like that, Peter's face hardened. "Like what? You've already shut down the entire goddamn mother-fucking State Fair of Texas and caused a hundred thousand people to flee for their lives. What more could you want?"

"I had no choice, Peter," I said, "We had to clear the area before the bombs blew."

"Rain, for the thousandth time, we've checked the damn dolphins. There are no—'

Ib broke in. "Yes...yes there are bombs, sir. I can vouch for it. There are bombs in the bases of all the food fryers. There might be more, I don't know."

Peter went a shade paler. "Who the hell are you?"

Now that just pissed me off.

"What?" I said. "How come you all of a sudden listen to him?"

"It's not over," Ib went on, "the bomber is still here. We're going to Big Tex, looking for him now."

"Wait a sec," Peter said. He pressed his ear. Shit. He was wired, had been the whole time. He gave a slight laugh and shook his head. "No, it looks like Rain suckered you too. There's no one in the entire plaza. Just some Mexican gardener trapped at the base of the statue. Apparently, he's shitting his pants, thinking this is the biggest immigration bust ever."

"Rashid is out there somewhere," Ib said. "We have to find him."

"Come on, guys," Peter said. He held out his arms, palms up. For us, for all of us this time. "Let's put down the guns and end this."

And I wanted to put my gun down and run to those arms. And I knew then what I had suspected might happen all the way back that day we'd gotten a replacement Finnegan for Dmitri at the mall. That I was fucked over by this man. That I always had been. That I always would be.

I raised the Glock until it aimed at his face. He did not lower his arms or flinch, but his eyes followed it.

"Peter," I said, "why did they send you out here again?"

"Please listen to me. There are no bombers, Rain."

"Peter, why do they always send you to me?"

"You can stop this, Rain, before it goes too far."

I took a step closer to him. "I am trying to stop it." I touched the barrel of the gun to his forehead. "Was I just like Victor and the rest of them to you? Was I only ever your job?"

"You know I've always been on your side, Rain, even when it doesn't seem like it."

I felt the presence of dozens of armed agents around us, could hear helicopters beating above us, feel the thumps of the rotors faintly in my ribs. "So how are you helping me now?"

"I'm trying to get you out of this alive," he said. "You are a good kid. A very, very good kid. But sometimes—" He faltered. "—it's the firemen who want to be heroes the most...they're the ones who start the fires."

"What's that supposed to mean, Peter?"

"He's talking about that guy in California," Ib said, "the one who set two wildfires so he could fight them."

"You think I'm making this up, for fun?"

"I think you've had to be strong person to survive what your mom did to you. I think it's gonna be hard for you to adapt those strengths so you can live in the world the rest of us live in. But you have to do it before you destroy anything else. We're not just talking cats here, Rain. It's people now, they're in danger because of you."

"What do you mean, my mom?" I felt that cold again, grabbing hold of my soul. "You've been talking to Dad."

Peter nodded. "He's had a lot of things to say. About you, and about your mom."

"It's all bullshit," I said. "Whatever story he comes up with, he can't explain what Alicia was doing in our bomb shelter."

Peter shook his head. "Is it possible that somehow you recruited her to be Tabernakl? Like you recruited Leif, and this poor guy here?"

"I have no memory of that. I'd for sure remember that."

Peter pressed his lips together. "You might not. That might be a part of the delusions."

It couldn't be true. I tried hard to hold the gun steady, but my arm was getting tired. The sun was hot on my skin, and I'd definitely been out in it too long by now.

Drips of sweat dotted Peter's forehead. His fingers flexed. I could tell he wanted to wipe the sweat away but didn't dare lift his hands. "Think about what you did to Leif. He told us all about the bizarre tests you had for him, like the sewer and the egg-things. Now you've found someone to replace him, and you're following the same pattern. You're making him do the same things your mom made you do."

No. Leif had wanted to help me. Well, mostly, he'd wanted to help. I'd only had to convince him a little bit here and there. But Ib...he'd recruited me today, hadn't he? Or—I frowned—had Tabernakl and I been the ones who had recruited him and Storm-Shadow weeks before this? Could this really be my fault?

I blinked sweat out of the corners of my eyes. I said, "So basically, I have a choice. I lay my gun down, accept reality, and everybody goes home. I get a nice soft bed in New Transitions and art therapy once a week for the rest of my life."

"And no one gets hurt," Peter added. "There's that, too."

"But there's another option," I said. I pushed the gun right up against his forehead. I could see the soft little dent it made in his skin. "The one where I say fuck off to you and your reality, because I *want* to go kick some terrorist ass."

"Hang on," Ib said. "That's not exactly what we agreed to—'

"Shut up, Ib," I said. I bent close to Peter's face. "Guess what. Right now? I feel like kicking ass."

Peter swallowed. "Feelings can be wrong. They can mislead you."

I could smell him again. That clean scent of shower gel and deodorant working overtime. And underneath, a muskiness that promised me a whole new, unexplored world. Promised, but never delivered.

"They don't know, do they?" I asked him. "You never told your bosses exactly what happened between us at the hotel."

"They know," he said.

I remembered that one precious, fleeting moment when I'd pressed my lips to his and felt his body respond so strongly.

"I bet they don't," I said. "Not every last single detail."

Ever so slightly, he shook his head.

"But that's why they keep on sending you out to deal with me anyway. They think I'll do whatever you say because I like you...because I want you."

"Please, Rain—"

I frowned. "Thing is though, Peter, you're not here because you want me."

"Please, Rain. If we could just talk things through..."

But his voice trailed off. He had nothing more to say, and it was clear why. There was nothing to say because he really didn't want me back. But not because he didn't want me physically. He didn't want me because he knew I was broken.

The gun was starting to feel good in my hands—starting to feel like a good end to this conversation.

"Enough." Ib touched my arm with his fingers. Long, adolescent-boy fingers, just skin over bones and knuckles. It was a risk, because maybe I just intended to yell at Peter some more, maybe I was building up to something more. Had Ib pushed hard, I would have shot. But because he touched me gently, the barrel of the gun just moved away.

"We don't have time for all this," he reminded me. "I asked you to help me stop Rashid. You agreed. Please."

I looked up at him. Oh, hell. He was right. We had a job to do.

"Look," Peter said, "can you at least let me take Grace?"

It was Ib, this time, who raised his gun to Peter's head.

"No," he said, his voice cracking. "She stays with us a bit longer."

I looked from Peter to Ib and back. What the hell was this? Hostage negotiations? But then I looked around at the armed fighters surrounding us. As soon as we gave Grace to them, it really would be over for us and we'd never get to Rashid.

"Ib's right," I told Peter. "She stays with us a bit longer."

We began to walk away. Peter followed.

"What the hell are you doing?" Ib yelled at him.

"Keeping lines of communication open?"

"Ten feet, I want ten feet."

Peter dropped back. Little heat waves rose off of the pavement under our feet. Grace's soft damp hand gripped mine. Ahead of us, Big Tex came into view.

"There he is," Ib said. "There's Rashid."

38

A man in a uniform cowered at the base of the Big Tex
statue.

"That's just the Mexican gardener," I told Ib, "the one Peter
said was there."

Ib shook his head. "I know Rashid."

The gardener struggled to his feet. The weed-killer apparatus
strapped to his back made it awkward to move. "Ib, brother, you
came. Just like I prayed for you to come."

Oh hell, it was Rashid.

"I brought Finnegan," Ib called. We continued to walk
toward him.

Rashid looked at me, then he smiled. "Allah be praised, the
brother is a sister. Well, sister Finnegan, come join me. Isn't it a
good day for jihad?"

"No, it's a bad day," Ib yelled before I could answer. "We've
turned off the fryers and evacuated the area. You have to
surrender before this goes further."

A megaphone boomed across the plaza. "This is your first
warning: everyone in the plaza, lay down your weapons and put
your hands in the air."

"Ib, you coward. I had to give you a chance for glory but

thought you might do this." Rashid lifted his hand so everyone could see he held a phone. "I've been here two weeks, folks. I've laid many, many bombs, *inshallah*. And how the hell do you evacuate a hundred thousand people, Ib? They're choking up the parking lots and rail station, *just as planned*." He raised his voice to the police around us. "All I have to do is press call on this phone, and all the bombs will detonate. This is *your* first warning: don't fuck with me!"

"Is it true?" I asked Ib. "Did he set more bombs? Does he know how to detonate them with his phone?"

"I don't know," Ib said. "There's a good chance he does."

We were maybe eight feet away from Rashid. I bent to Grace.

"Run away," I told her. "Run away now."

When I stood up, Rashid was spraying weed killer on Big Tex. At least, I thought it was weed killer until the gasoline fumes hit the back of my nose. I looked behind me to see Grace sliding into Peter like he was home base. Peter scooped her up and limped as fast as he could for the ice cream tents. Ib stopping me was a good thing. I saw that now.

"How many helicopters, brother? How many cameras? All here to watch the final jihad begin!" Rashid pointed up at the several that hovered and banked around us now. There were probably cameras on the ground as well. He pulled a lighter from his pocket.

"YouTube this, Dogs of Satan!"

The fireball rose, orange, furious, hot...the lines of each flame fractally complex...strangely compelling...violent and beautiful. I covered my face as the heat rolled over us. When I dared lift away my arms, little filaments of ash curled stiff over pink skin. The smell of singed hair filled the back of my nose.

Small red flames licked dimly under the brim of Big Tex's hat, then faded away. The cowboy statue stood there, unscathed.

"Cousin," Ib shouted, "maybe that's a sign from Allah to stop the jihad."

Maybe it was a sign. Maybe it was a hell of a lot of fire retardant. Rashid stared up at Big Tex, his mouth open. For a moment, he had forgotten about the phone in his hand.

I looked around the plaza. The nearest police were maybe a hundred feet away from Rashid. None of them had a good shot that would take him out without possibly hitting the phone or the potentially explosive tank of gasoline on his back, which would explode the phone as well. If the phone went, the bombs might go off, and they couldn't risk it, not with so many lives at stake.

I, on the other hand, was eight feet away and damn good with a gun.

I raised my Glock and shot Rashid, getting him right in the wrist. The phone flew from his grasp and fell to the pansies several feet away.

Rashid clutched his arm, but he didn't fall. A shit-load of adrenaline must have been pumping through his system—making him impervious to pain—impervious to anything but the need to start the final war. He dove for the phone.

"No," Ib yelled, and ran toward Rashid.

Goddammit.

"Get back!" I yelled and lunged at him.

They shot us all.

39

B lack. Gray. Hospital.

Wow. wasn't that weird. There was a hospital room in heaven that looked just like the hospital rooms on earth. But I guessed it made sense. You come into life on earth in a hospital, don't you?

I turned my head. Carol Anne Cheung was sitting next to my bed, scanning her phone. She set it down.

"Welcome back, Rain."

It was unlikely we had both gone to heaven, so I re-evaluated my assumptions.

"I'm still alive? I was shot."

"You were shot with a Taser. But then you fell and hit your head pretty bad on the wall around Big Tex."

"Oh." I put my hand up to my head. Ouch, yes, there was a massive big knot, and the prickly feel of stitches. Holy fucking shit. They shot us with Tasers. But it made sense. They'd want to interrogate Rashid.

"The gas tank didn't explode?" I asked her. "That was lucky."

"It was lucky. Rashid used up all the gas on Big Tex," Carol Anne told me.

"Am I in trouble?"

"Look around the room."

I looked. Every horizontal surface of the room was filled with flowers, cards, and ridiculous stuffed teddy bears. Little Mylar balloons floated above the assemblage.

"A lot of FBI folks are deeply grateful to you, Rain, them and the public. See that enormous bouquet next to the window, with the orchids and the purple artichoke heads? That's from the president."

"Is Peter here?"

"I'm sure he sends his love, but it would be best if he didn't come to see you just now."

"Is that a euphemism?"

"Yes."

"Did I get him into trouble?"

Carol Anne softly snorted. "Honey, that man gets himself into trouble."

I turned my face away. Even now, even after all that had happened, the memory of our kiss—my first kiss—was diamond bright in my mind. It would never be the same with anyone else. A black mass of grief rose in my chest and I stowed it away deep inside, a lump of coal to gnash my teeth over at some point in the future.

Carol Anne sighed. "Sooner or later, all women get suckered by a man like that. If it helps, try to remember that in reality, he's kind of a dickhead."

I didn't look at her. But then, I remembered more about yesterday and tried to sit up. "Hal Wooten, Carol Anne. I need to talk to you about Hal Wooten."

She put a hand on my shoulder. "You need to focus on getting well right now."

"Bullshit. If he gets released, he'll be gone. Is it too late?" I brushed her hand away. A wave of dizziness made me sway, but I screwed my eyes up until it passed.

"Rain, lie back down."

I shook my head and swung my feet over the side of the bed. "I need a phone. Can I borrow yours?"

"Christ. If I tell you what happened, will you lie back down?"

Slowly, I eased myself back onto the bed.

"Olivia broke down and told them everything. He's been charged. Okay? I need you to understand that he's been charged."

I stared at her. "What are you not telling me?"

"A judge let him out on bail this morning. Shouldn't have, but we don't always get the good judges."

I kind of fell back against the pillows and stared at the ceiling tiles.

Carol Anne put her hand on my shoulder again. "We're building a damn good case against the bastard. We're gonna get him. And we're not dropping the ball with you again, Rain. Someone will protect you."

"He's not going to come after me. He'll run. I bet he's already gone."

"If he is, we'll get him back."

"Maybe." My eyes filled with hot unshed tears. It was exactly what I'd feared would happen. But then flashes of the State Fair filled my mind. Not the empty streets at the end, but the crazy full ones at the beginning, with kids in groups taking selfies and parents running after toddlers and football fans staggering past, happy and drunk singing out of tune. I remembered the moms, putting hats on protesting children, and even the dads, lifting their kids high on their shoulders so they could see over the heads of the crowd and laugh at the sky.

It wasn't over with Dad. It might never be. But yesterday, I'd done the right thing. That would have to be enough for now. When I was stronger, I'd hunt him down. If I could do it once, I could do it again. I'd get the bastard eventually.

On the table next to my bed, mixed in with the flowers and cards, a little betta floated in a bowl, Dad's orange and green one. A card was stuck under the bow. I could see Dmitri's name on it.

"Didn't see this coming, did you?" I asked Finnegan III.

He floated, oblivious. I sat back, unsatisfied.

"There's someone else who would like to see you," Carol Anne said. "With your permission, I'd like to—"

But I could already see the visitor through the glass of the door—a woman with a mass of brown curly hair.

"Mom," I said under my breath.

"Rainbow, you're awake!" Before Carol Anne could stop her, she came in the room and grabbed my hand. Her whole face lit up with joy. My heart leaped.

"Mom, I missed you so much."

But then her face fell. "Oh no, no, no. I'm so sorry, I'm not your mom, Rainbow." Her mouth trembled, open, moist, uncertain. "I'm your Aunt Rosemary."

I blinked.

She looked about the hospital room. "We're all here, Rainbow. We've been watching over you, waiting for you to wake up. Your Uncle Basil and Aunt Angelica and Mom...I mean, your Grandma...they just popped out to Sprouts to get some soy milk. That stuff they sell in the cafe is definitely GMO."

"Oh," I said, still confused. I never thought of Mom as anything but Mom. But of course, before she was my mom, she was a sister, a daughter, someone's cherished one. Because I'd always been told the missing-person posters were a trap, I never gave a second thought the people that must have put them out there. But here they were...her family. My family too.

"And there's some teenagers who keep on coming by," she went on. "Two boys and a girl with blue hair. One of them is called Lizard, I think? They can't come back here because they're not relatives, so they hang out in the break room making the senior citizens nervous."

That made me smile, even though my eyes were blurring up with unshed tears. "I thought I'd died and gone to heaven."

"We're really glad you didn't," she said. "I mean we have so many years to catch up on and we have so many questions about Saffron and...oh gosh...did I mess it up? I'm not supposed to go too fast. Not supposed to overwhelm you." She shot a guilty glance at Carol Anne. "Do you want me to go now?"

"No," I fought down nausea and squeezed her hand. It felt warm and springy, like happiness. "I don't mean to cry. It's just that you look so much like Mom."

She smiled, gently. "Yes, Rainbow, so do you."

EPILOGUE

We met under a lead gray sky. The stifling heat of the summer was just a fading memory now. Frost clung to the cars in the parking lot, and circles of barbed wire topped the high wall behind us—the wall of an anonymous federal facility, somewhere in East Texas.

"That's it?" I asked. "They just let you go?"

"Now that Rashid will never be free again, the jabbar have no more use for me," he said. "I have the paperwork to prove it."

"Well," I said, "the car's just over there."

He hefted the duffel bag higher on his shoulder, and I tried not to stare as we walked to the car. Skinny Ibrahim had filled out in prison. I guess there's not much to do in prison besides pump iron, but even so.

At the car, I popped the trunk open and he tossed the bag in. He stood there in his cheap hoodie, rubbing his hands, breathing white clouds of frost into the cold air, looking around.

I got in the driver's side and turned on the heat. He got in beside me. Along his right temple there was a fresh scar, an ugly pink lightning strike. Underneath it, his eyelashes were long, like a girl's. How had I never noticed his eyelashes?

"You want some food or something when we hit the next

town?" I said. "There's not a lot of places for a couple hundred miles after this."

"No thanks," he said. "Just drive away from this hellhole as fast as you can. I mean, as fast as you legally can. I'll be happy looking out the window."

He glanced at me and I swiftly looked straight ahead. I didn't want him to think I was looking at his eyelashes. I pulled out of the prison parking lot and onto the highway, heading north.

"Not much to see out here, it's pretty flat," I eventually said. "Just that gray sky."

"It beats looking at those cinder block walls and motivational posters," he said. I risked another glance. He'd spread his fingertips on the window glass.

"I thought maybe you'd want your family to get you instead."

"I couldn't face them straight away." He grunted. "I'm not the most beloved son right now. More beloved than Rashid, but that's not saying much. You're the only person in America that thinks I'm not some obscene waste of space."

"That's not true," I said.

"Don't lie. I've seen the videos on YouTube."

I didn't have an answer for that. The most famous video of Big Tex going up in a ball of flame had gone viral on the Internet, just like Rashid had wanted. Only it didn't portray the message he'd hoped. Someone somewhere had edited the soundtrack to play Johnny Cash's "Ring of Fire," and when Big Tex emerged unscathed from his fireball, the scene faded to an American flag and slogans would appear. Things like "Guess God is on OUR side after all." There were others too, plenty worse.

I said, "People would have died if it wasn't for you. Americans would have died, dammit. I keep on telling them. I keep on saying how you're one of us too."

He turned his face to the window, so I couldn't see it. "I was born here, but there's plenty of folks who think that doesn't count for much, at least not for people like me."

Eventually, I felt him turn back and sensed he was studying me. My ears went all warm. "Enough about my pathetic life," he said. "Sorry to hear about your dad going on the run."

I sighed. "It was always going to happen. But it doesn't matter. I'm trying something different this time. I'm building a new life without him."

"And how is that going?"

"Up and down."

Aunt Rosemary and Grandma and the rest of the Dunns had done their best, but it was never going to be easy. In the first flush of joy of having me back home in Albuquerque, they'd put me in Mom's old room with all her things and then bought me new things on top of that. It had taken some convincing to let me sleep in their basement, a room that I'd emptied of everything except my computer setup and a camp cot. But I was making progress. Two weeks ago, I'd hung up a picture of the Rocky Mountains on the wall. One week ago, I'd brought down one of Mom's old quilts for the cot. Progress.

"I'm getting my GED and going to apply for college, maybe MIT or Stanford. Turns out I'm 18, so I'm not too far behind at all." I said.

"That sounds cool," he said. "I wish I wasn't going home."

"After I drop you off, I'm heading home," I said. "Maybe you could come visit sometime. Hell, you could even stay a while."

Then my ears got even warmer and we drove a while in awkward silence. Baby steps. You have to take baby steps. I should know that more than most. But then I looked over and he was just staring out the window at the hills and the occasional trailer home, just kind of smiling.

It was a couple hundred miles to Dallas. A long time to talk. I told him about seeing a broken and abandoned Olivia in court, her hair gray at the roots, her pumpkin face fallen in on itself like it was six days after Halloween. She had inadvertently saved my life when she'd talked Hal out of killing me on her Egyptian cotton sheets, but I didn't think she would have if the sheets had been cheaper, so I'd turned away when she tried to speak to me.

The federal government had seized everything Hal had stolen. That included their house as well as the one in Fort Worth I'd lived in. The FBI had decided not to file criminal charges against me, but Hal's victims were coming out of the woodwork. Until they could get their hands on Hal (which might well be never), they were trying to take me to civil court left and right.

When I got to that bit, I looked over at Ib and his head was leaning up against the window and his jaw was slack. Asleep. Who could blame him? The intricacies of legal troubles are only fascinating if you're the one involved. So I shut up and drove until I heard him stir.

"Hey," he said, rubbing his eyes. "I wanted to ask, do you play online anymore?"

"Yeah, I do," I said. "I joined an Alliance guild, believe it or not. I'm a night elf now. It's kind of fun, doing the quests just for the hell of doing the quests..."

Then, even though we were alone, he lowered his voice. "Is that all? That's the only thing you do?"

I paused, wondering how much to tell him.

"I help out the FBI with hunting dad sometimes," I eventually said, "but it's strictly a team effort. How about you?"

"You can't access the Internet in prison," he said. "Not for games."

"That's not what I mean."

He was quiet for about five miles. "One thing about custody," he said at last, "they have to let you have a Quran and you get plenty of time to read it. Plus, I had a lot of time to think."

"Oh. Want to tell me about it?"

"Not really. It's complicated." He almost laughed. "Anyway, that jihad is over for me whether I want it to be or not. I'm on the terrorist watch list until I die."

"What do you mean, 'that jihad?' There's more than one?"

"There's the one inside me," he said. "I'll be fighting that one forever."

The fields and trailer homes we passed slowly gave way to car dealerships and strip malls. The trucks crowding the highway were joined by passenger cars. We had to slow for an overturned car on the median, surrounded by flashing emergency vehicles. Then we had to slow for highway construction. Texas highways: under construction for the next billion years.

Ib shifted in his seat. "Hey Rain, about your gaming guild...you think they'd be okay with another member?"

The question took me by surprise. "You want to play again? With me?"

"Yeah. I would. I'm done with being a blood elf too. Thought I'd try a worgen."

I had to think about it. Really, I had to think if it was okay with me. No one else needed to know who he really was online, but I would. By the time we passed the Mesquite exit, I decided I'd give it a try, at least. But...baby steps. You know how it goes.

"Izzard definitely would agree," I said. "We can ask the others. I'm pretty sure they'd be okay too."

We sat in slow traffic for a couple of miles.

When we got into Dallas, he directed me to his house. But he didn't need to. We could see the circus from a block away. Media vans, and one or two cop cars. But, also a crowd, despite the freezing rain, all wearing jeans and camo jackets, gimme caps of all colors on their heads, all waving flags. We passed two hairy guys sporting beer bellies on their fronts and semi-automatic rifles on their backs, ambling toward the house.

Ib sank in the seat until only his hair poked above the edge of the window.

"They know it's today I get out," Ib said. "They didn't know the time or place, but they knew the day."

When we passed it, his house was just another suburban house just like a million others, brick facing on the bottom half, arched windows trying to imitate Spanish architecture on a budget. I could see it was a security risk in about a thousand different ways. And you could bet he didn't have a bomb shelter in his backyard for emergencies.

Ib peeked over the window sill. "You passed it."

"I can't drop you off there," I said. "It's too dangerous."

"You have to. About ten different government agencies are expecting me to show up."

A couple of blocks down, I pulled up to a four-way stop. I turned to him. "Here's the thing. If you really don't want to go back, you don't have to. You can disappear instead. I'll help you do it."

He laughed. "Turn around and drop me off. There's no way you could do that. " Then he looked at me closely when I didn't start the car. "You're serious."

"My dad and I called it Get Out Of Dodge," I told him. "I've done it four times since I've been alive. He's just done his fifth, and he taught me just about everything he knew when he thought I was on his side. So you happen to be in a car with one of the few people in America who could."

"What about you? Won't they know it was you?"

I chewed my lip. He was right. I might have to go with him. I'd love to leave the lawsuits behind, but I'd also have to leave Aunt Rosemary and the Dunns and forget about my college applications.

He sat up straight again and put his hand on mine where it rested on the steering wheel. "Rain," he said, but then he just looked at me, the muscles of his jaw working.

A knock on the driver's window startled us both. I turned around and saw the watery profile of a cop through the slush-streaked window. I rolled it down.

"Ms. Wooten," he said, "I'm here to escort your passenger back to his house, ma'am." He peered in the car at Ib. "Your mom asked me to do it. She recognized the top of your head when you drove past."

"He's a free man," I said. "He doesn't have to go anywhere."

Ib squeezed my hand once, then took his away. "It's okay. I'm going back. I was anyway." He opened the door and got out. When he shut the door, I saw a penny on the seat—maybe it had dropped out of his pocket or something—those darn things get everywhere. I ought to sit down over a day with a pencil and paper and do a hundred flips or so. I ought to, just to be sure, but I never seem to get around to it. I'm not sure I want to know the answer.

He got his bag from the trunk and came around to peer in the driver's side window. His eyebrows were lifted and kind of scrunched up together.

"Just don't drive away thinking I never want to see you again. I'd be sad if that happened."

That meant he wanted to see me again, despite everything. Okay, Rain, play it cool. Keep your dignity.

"It won't."

"Good." He took a deep breath. "By the way, I forgot to say about the dress you're wearing and the new haircut. They look really nice on you."

I'm not sure what I did next. Probably simpered. Or giggled. Whatever it was, it was pretty damn undignified. It made him smile for the first time. A sweet, goofy smile that slowly went all sad in the corners. He sighed.

"Goodbye for now," he said. "I'll see you in Azeroth."

"Okay," I said. "Definitely see you there."

He and the cop walked back down the frosty road behind me.

Well, that was that. I'd lost my chance to tell Ib what I was really doing on the computer, late at night when no one was looking.

I'd only spent an hour with Alicia's code in that bomb shelter. Despite Peter telling me otherwise, the FBI would never let me near it again, and I didn't feel like asking Alicia about it either, but I remembered the main ideas.

And every now and then, I would have a play. Turns out it

wasn't just illegal online betting you could predict using Twitter. There were other things—bigger and more important stochastic series that you could predict.

Like the whole freaking stock market for instance.

Yeah, I know, but it was probably for the best if I didn't say anything. Really it was just me playing around. If I was making a shit-load of money again, it was nobody's business but my own. And don't even bother to ask—what I plan to do with the money is my own damn business as well.

I flicked the penny onto the floor out of sight and put the car into drive, heading home.

AUTHOR'S NOTE

A way to predict future events has been sought by many. By the 2000s, however, it was well understood that randomness (or stochasticity) made it unlikely that events such as the outcomes of sports games or the stock market would ever be predicted with any certainty. Even throwing all possible computer resources at stock market data yielded nonsensical predictors, such as the production of butter in Bangladesh [1]. Then, in 2010, three computer scientists analyzed all the tweets from Twitter over one day to determine whether they were mostly positive or mostly negative tweets. This, to everyone's immense surprise, predicted the stock market fairly accurately [2].

Since then, analyzing tweets (and other social media posts) has become a popular research topic called "sentiment analysis." Unfortunately for Alicia and Rain, the method does not work quite as well now, because too many people are using it. However, immense quantities of social media data on all sorts of topics are now available online, and new tools are quickly being developed to help design commercial products, formulate government policy, and respond to large-scale disasters.

Hal's mail order scam is a variant of the Brooklyn stock-broker scam. Although it has appeared in several popular math books as entertainment, it doesn't seem to have been a con that was ever used (for instance, David Maurer did not mention it in his research into American cons in the 1930s [3]). However, Jordan Ellenberg, in his book *How Not to be Wrong*, argued that investment companies utilize a similar concept [4]. These companies launch many mutual funds before they go public. Most funds will yield average performance, some will perform badly, and a few will perform very well. Somehow, only the few superperformers are ever offered to the public. However, there is no guarantee they will perform as well in the future.

Rain's plan to test reality using coin flips was inspired by the discussion on this topic in *Here's Looking at Euclid* by Alex Bellos [5]. Hal told Saffron to avoid men with red ties because he had seen it in the movie *A Beautiful Mind* [6].

Like all mathematical systems (from the natural numbers to obscure analysis) geometry has an underlying structure that consists of a set of elements, operations, relations, and assumptions (or axioms). Euclidean geometry has five axioms. The fifth one states, in essence that lines that aren't parallel meet in a point.[1]

But, as Alicia argues on the dream road in Tennessee, they do. Our own eyes tell us this.

In the 1800s, mathematicians developed a new type of geometry in which distances were not unique and there was a single point at infinity where all lines met no matter which direction you faced. Just as for the non-Euclidean geometries, which were discovered by messing about with the fifth axiom in other ways, mathematicians cared less about the geometry itself than fact that the underlying structure of the geometry could be messed about with and still work. It was the subject of a few books at the turn of the century, and then largely ignored. Then, in the 1990s, computer scientists realized this forgotten geometry was actually quite useful [7]. Projective geometry now lies at the heart of all three-dimensional computer graphics systems, bringing us virtual reality, computer vision, and special effects.

Another curiosity in Euclidean geometry is the fact that it is easy to divide an angle in half, but dividing it into thirds is much harder. There is, in fact, a proof saying it is not possible. However, in the 1970s, Japanese mathematician Hisashi Abe showed how to use origami to trisect the angle without any additional tools [8]. On the one hand, Euclid never said you could fold the paper. On the other hand, he never said you couldn't.

Although there is no public evidence that terrorists have used online games as a platform for planning attacks [9], among Edward Snowden's leaked 2012 documents, there is evidence that the CIA thought they might [10]. The online game assignment was sought after by agents, so much so that enthusiastic gaming agents posing as terrorists had to create a "deconfliction group" to avoid recruiting each other.

Finally, in this book, Ibrahim states that the number of Muslims killed by Westerners over the last 40 years to be four million [11]. This number is believed to be true in the Muslim world, but in practice, this number is hard to determine because people are killed in war zones and remains are decomposed, already buried, or lie in places where no one can get to without risking their own life. Still, the numbers are likely to be substantial [12]. Obviously, it is not just a numbers game, but for a sense of scale, the Nazis are believed to have killed six million Jews and an additional eleven million other Europeans [13].

In contrast, as of this author's note,[2] a total of 3,694 civilian Americans and Europeans have been killed on US/European soil by Muslim extremist terrorists since 2000 [14–16]. Not including 9/11, this number is 717. Further removing attacks in Europe, this number is 98. This does not necessarily indicate that the extremist threat is small; it could be that the security services are just extremely good at their job. Without access to classified information, we cannot draw conclusions. Even more importantly, we cannot predict the future.

Author's Note

1. i) Two points define a unique line. ii) A straight line can be extended infinitely. iii) A point and a radius define a unique circle. iv) All right angles are equal. v) If a straight line falling on two straight lines make interior angles on the same side that are less than two right angles, the two straight lines, if produced indefinitely, meet on that side where the angles sum to less than the two right angles.
2. April 8, 2019

REFERENCES

[1] Leinweber, David J. "Stupid data miner tricks: Overfitting the S&P 500." *Journal of Investing* 16, no. 1 (2007): 15.

[2] Bollen, Johan, Huina Mao, and Xiaojun Zeng. "Twitter mood predicts the stock market." *Journal of Computational Science* 2, no. 1 (2011): 1-8.

[3] Maurer, David. *The Big Con.* Random House, 2011.

[4] Ellenberg, Jordan. *How Not to Be Wrong: The Power of Mathematical Thinking.* Penguin, 2015.

[5] Bellos, Alex. *Here's Looking at Euclid: A Surprising Excursion Through the Astonishing World of Math.* Free Press, 2010.

[6] Internet Movie Database. "A Beautiful Mind." http://us.imdb.com/Title?0268978, 2001.

[7] Mundy, Joseph L., and Andrew Zisserman. "Projective geometry for machine vision." In *Geometric Invariance in Computer Vision*, pp. 463-519. MIT Press, 1992.

[8] Hull, Thomas. "A note on 'impossible' paper folding." *American Mathematical Monthly* 103, no. 3 (1996): 240-241.

[9] Justin Elliott. "World of Spycraft: NSA and CIA Spied in Online Games." ProPublica, Dec. 9, 2013. https://www.propublica.org/article/world-of-spycraft-intelligence-agencies-spied-in-online-games (accessed April 8, 2019).

[10] National Security Agency. "Exploiting Terrorist Use of Games & Virtual Environments." *New York Times*, Dec. 10, 2013. http://www.nytimes.com/interactive/2013/12/10/us/politics/games-docs.html (accessed April 8, 2019).

[11] Nafeez Mosaddeq Ahmed. "Western wars have killed four million Muslims since 1990." *Voltairenet.org*, April 11, 2015. https://www.voltairenet.org/article187299.html (accessed April 8, 2019).

[12] Andrew Buncombe. "America has no idea how many innocent people it's killing in the Middle East." *Independent*, Nov. 20, 2017. https://www.independent.co.uk/voices/us-isis-air-strikes-civilian-deaths-syria-iraq-america-no-idea-how-many-dead-the-uncounted-a8066266.html (accessed April 8, 2019).

[13] United States Holocaust Memorial Museum. "Documenting numbers of victims of the Holocaust and Nazi persecution." https://encyclopedia.ushmm.org/content/en/article/documenting-numbers-of-victims-of-the-holocaust-and-nazi-persecution (accessed April 8, 2019).

[14] Wikipedia. "September 11 attacks." https://en.wikipedia.org/wiki/September_11_attacks (accessed April 8, 2019).

[15] Wikipedia. "Terrorism in the United States." https://en.wikipedia.org/wiki/Terrorism_in_the_United_States (accessed April 8, 2019).

[16] Wikipedia. "Islamic terrorism in Europe." https://en.wikipedia.org/wiki/Islamic_terrorism_in_Europe (accessed April 8, 2019).

ACKNOWLEDGMENTS

Thanks to Tex Thompson, Daniel Benson, the members of DFW Writers' Workshop, JB Sanders, John Arundel, and many others for their insight and advice. Many thanks also to Mary-Theresa Hussey for editing. Finally, thanks to Fawkes Press for their strong vision and invaluable support.

You have excellent taste in books! If you want to read more fantastic stories:

- Leave a review on your favorite book review site
- Tell a friend about the book and author
- Ask your local library to put Trilby Black's work on the shelf
- Recommend Fawkes Press books to your local bookstore

You make great books possible.

VISIT US AT:
WWW.FAWKESPRESS.COM/NEWSLETTER
WWW.TRILBYBLACK.COM

FAWKES PRESS

CPSIA information can be obtained
at www.ICGtesting.com
Printed in the USA
BVHW081041120421
604723BV00004B/434